T0277973

16 LATINX REMIXES
OF CLASSIC STORIES

RELIT

EDITED BY SANDRA PROUDMAN

OLIVIA ABTAHI • DAVID BOWLES • ZORAIDA CÓRDOVA
SARACIEA J. FENNELL • RAQUEL VASQUEZ GILLILAND
TORREY MALDONADO • JASMINNE MENDEZ • ANNA MERIANO
AMPARO ORTIZ • LAURA POHL • SANDRA PROUDMAN • NONIEQA RAMOS
MONICA SANZ • ERIC SMITH • ARI TISON • ALEXANDRA VILLASANTE

ISBN-13: 978-1-335-01001-8

Relit

Copyright © 2024 by Sandra Proudman

Shame and Social Media
Copyright © 2024 by Anna Meriano

Break in Case of Persephone
Copyright © 2024 by Olivia Abtahi

Thornfield
Copyright © 2024 by Monica Sanz

La Cotorra y el Flamboyán
Copyright © 2024 by Amparo Ortiz

Goldi and the Three Bodies
Copyright © 2024 by Saraciea J. Fennell

This Mortal Coil
Copyright © 2024 by David Bowles

Juna and the Fox Boy
Copyright © 2024 by Raquel Vasquez Gilliland

Prefiero No
Copyright © 2024 by Alexandra Villasante

Trespassers Will Be…
Copyright © 2024 by Torrey Maldonado

Isla Bella
Copyright © 2024 by Ari Tison

Evermore
Copyright © 2024 by NoNieqa Ramos

Celia's Song
Copyright © 2024 by Jasminne Mendez

Esmeralda
Copyright © 2024 by Laura Pohl

Twenty Thousand Leagues Away from Me
Copyright © 2024 by Eric Smith

Heart of the Sea
Copyright © 2024 by Zoraida Córdova

Tesoro
Copyright © 2024 by Sandra Proudman

All rights reserved. No part of this book may be used or reproduced in any manner whatsoever without written permission except in the case of brief quotations embodied in critical articles and reviews.

This is a work of fiction. Names, characters, places and incidents are either the product of the author's imagination or are used fictitiously. Any resemblance to actual persons, living or dead, businesses, companies, events or locales is entirely coincidental.

For questions and comments about the quality of this book, please contact us at CustomerService@Harlequin.com.

TM is a trademark of Harlequin Enterprises ULC.

Inkyard Press
22 Adelaide St. West, 41st Floor
Toronto, Ontario M5H 4E3, Canada
www.InkyardPress.com

Printed in U.S.A.

CONTENTS

For Rio, and every Latinx reader like him

A FOREWORD FROM THE EDITOR

Thanks so much for picking up *Relit*! This anthology began with a hope, a dream, a spark of an idea that the contributing authors and I felt passionately about: to take some of the most popular classics out there (the novels, myths, and plays we've all read in class or seen adaptations of on TV and in movies)...and reimagine, reignite, remix them into some epic science fiction and fantasy tales, with Latinx characters at the center of all the action.

We've added in a little magic, a bit of outer space, visions of the future, lessons from the past, and above all, mucho, mucho amor (all the love that we have for our community of readers and writers).

We hope all readers love the stories that make up *Relit*—and don't worry, you don't need to have read the original classics or be familiar with them to join our characters in their adventures.

But if you do know the original tales, we hope you'll enjoy the way we've shaken them up a little.

And, for our Latinx readers, while this book is for everyone, it's here because of you! To the readers we see ourselves in, we've given the representation in stories we wish we'd once had.

SHAME AND SOCIAL MEDIA

a remix of *Pride and Prejudice*
Anna Meriano

"...it is the hardest thing in the world, that your estate should be entailed away from your own children; and I am sure, if I had been you, I should have tried long ago to do something or other about it."

—Jane Austen, *Pride and Prejudice*

- ❖ Drive: Starship Video Archives
  - ➤ Category: Recreational Video
    - ▪ Folder: Earth Accessible Livestream
      - • Passenger: Bernal, Isabel
        - ♦ Title: "Well, That Happened"

Audio transcript:
Isabel Bernal: Hiiiii, new followers! Well, hi, loyal star chasers too, but I've gotten a truly astronomical number of new followers since my last video, so I'm doing a quick reintro in case the only thing you know about me is how I rejected Douche-face Darcy's stars-awful proposal of a date. If you missed it, click heeeeeere!

[embed video: "Please Share the Joy I Got from REJECTING This Kid XD"]

Anyhoo! I'm Izzy, and if you couldn't tell by the dire industrial background, I'm broadcasting live from the *ISS Hertford*, where I've lived for most of my sixteen years. We'll hit our future home planet eventually, and maybe someday the trip will be faster, but for now we keep in touch with you Earthlings through the magic of FTZ streaming and communications technology.

A lot of people follow me for my space-walk content, which I stream about once a week, and you can find all of the old videos on my profile page.

[embed link: ISSH://shiplogs.gov/passengerprofiles/Bernal.Isabel]

We're a small community here on the spaceship, and we're facing some attempted bullshit that I've been documenting in my streams. Short version: the rich folks who bought their tickets for a lifetime luxury cruise are trying to argue that people like my dad, who works on the spaceship to earn his bit of planet, can't pass his quarters onto his kids when he retires, since the rooms are technically part of his work contract and not his property. Leaving me and my sisters shit out of luck unless we learn to manage everyone's shit. Oh, yeah, that's my claim to fame on this ship. My dad keeps the plumbing running.

I know, I know, Earth is still working on *Housing is a human right*, but up here the issue is a little more life-and-death! I mean, we won't actually get sent out of an air lock if we don't have rooms, but what exactly are we going to do? Pee in the cargo hold? No, we'll be forced to take on jobs we don't want to "earn" our housing.

So, yeah, if you came here because you loved to see me dunk on a rich jerk, you'll be extremely happy to hear that you can help us supposedly lower-class star voyagers out by raising awareness about the problem and putting public pressure on our council before they make their official ruling on the cabin-inheritance issue next week. Use the hashtag #HomeAwayFromEarth to show support.

And if you *really* disliked that rich jerk from my last video, you can get personal by supporting #JusticeForWick. You might have seen Wick on my channel; he's great and works for ship security because *someone* whose name rhymes with Farcy the Fouchebag didn't think he belonged on the fancy decks and got him expelled. So please, keep liking the rejection video, and subscribe to my channel for more interstellar—Lety! Get out of here!

Sorry, my little sister is being The Worst. I've told her a hundred times that my channel is not for soliciting donations, it's for raising awareness. Plus, monetization would open a whole can of worms, so we're extremely not allowed to do that.

[off-screen speech inaudible]

You are not a content creator, Lety! You're not even allowed to stream to Earth until you're thirteen!

[off-screen speech inaudible]

It's not my rule, it's Mom's rule! Would you—?

[door slam]

Okay. Anyway. Sisters.

So that's me! Please keep the good vibes coming, talk to your friends about #HomeAwayFromEarth, and I'll see you all in a few light-days! (Get it? Because we're always moving?) Muah! Bye!

[livestream ended]

- ❖ Drive: Starship Video Archives
  - ➢ Category: Recreational Video
    - ▪ Folder: Earth Accessible Livestream
      - • Passenger: Bernal, Isabel
        - ♦ Title: "Day in the Life <3"

Audio transcript:
Isabel Bernal: Hi, star chasers! Today's video is going to be a little different! Mission Control has put a hold on all space walks this week except mandatory or emergency repairs. Something about radiation from a passing… I don't know. *But* I thought I could use this as an opportunity to show you a Day in the Life here on the spaceship.

So let me flip the camera… There we go! My cabin! This is my bunk, and below me is Joana, my sister, who you might understandably mistake for a lump of covers. Today Joana is feeling…?

[inaudible]

Yep, she's still feeling eternal despair! This is because of a terrible boy who—

[inaudible]

All right, all right! I'm leaving! You know one of us should really take time to clean the bunk so there's somewhere to walk…

You probably couldn't tell from that angry grunting, but Joana has a beautiful voice. She also plays about five instruments. She's wildly talented, but lately she's been so heartbroken about Brantley that she's just been hanging around the bunk. Which is good motivation for me to show you…the rest of our family's cabin!

Outside of our bunk we have my family's hub, or common space. You might notice that we avoid the Earth concept of *rooms* on the ship, and that, star chasers, is because we don't have enough room! *Bah-dum-tss!* But we have seating for my family—Mom and Dad, Joana, me, and Lety—and between that and the cooking space, we can play epic games of The Floor is a Black Hole. Things are slightly less industrial here, but don't worry! Just underneath that wallpaper is plenty of steel!

[off-screen speech inaudible]

No, Mom! I'm not messing with the wallpaper! Come say hi to my audience!

This is my mom, and there's my dad. They're great.

Mira Bernal: Izzy, what are you doing? Is Joana awake yet? Take her some tea. And don't bother your father.

Morris Bernal: I'm not bothered. Hello there, Earthlings. Welcome to my humble estate. It's not much, but it's home.

Mira Bernal: It won't be home when you retire. It will belong to Carla Rios if Izzy doesn't put her stubbornness aside...

Isabel Bernal: Allll right, that's enough of that! Bye!

Mira Bernal: Izzy! Your sister's tea!

[hydraulic door release, footsteps]

Isabel Bernal: Uh, ha, I did say we were going to see everyday drama. It's... Yeah. My mom really wants me to do a waste-management internship and then ideally be a protégée at waste management and take over Dad's job ASAP so that he can retire. Then the cabin would transfer to me, no matter what the council decides. Poor Dad is getting up there in years—and climbing around the access tunnels hauling heavy pipework is not a sixtysomething's game. But does it have to be mine?

It's understandable, because it's not like I really have a *passion*, like Joana. I mean, obviously I love entertaining all of you with these videos... *Ouch*, hair flip gone wrong. Joana's music is so cool, and she works so hard on it! She deserves to follow her dreams. So…yeah. That means I'm the sucker stuck with doodie duty. Say that five times fast!

Mom doesn't get that I *want* to help with our housing problem—I just have a different way of doing it. I'm thinking bigger picture here. If the council ruling next week goes in our favor… Speaking of which, please support #HomeAwayFromEarth.

[sigh]

Anyway, my so-called friend Carla already took the internship. So there's that. Oh, and that reminds me, another thing that I'm a teeny bit uncomfortable with, even though I know y'all mean well and are trying to support me, and I really appreciate you: I've been seeing some comments like "Save Izzy from being a janitor," and that kind of implies that the unfair part of this is the waste-management part? Sure, I don't want to go into waste management, but that is definitely not because it's a *bad* job. Like, first, All Labor Has Dignity, and second, my dad, in addition to crawling around the access tunnels, is a rocket scientist who designed the sanitary movement of hazardous materials through a nightmare-complicated system of pipes jammed into a city-sized machine hurtling through the universe at inconceivable speeds. So please never take my campaign to mean that I don't respect what he does. I just want to make sure that we maintain our amazing community where everyone is a respected member of a functioning whole. I want to have the space to learn different things and figure out what my passion really is, besides talking to you Earthlings. I want to keep my home.

Oh! Another fun fact about life on the ship! We don't really have school. Definitely not like you have on Earth, the weird factories of kids the same age sitting in rows. Mom dedicates herself to our education—the ship usually tries to hire one parent and leave one free for that kind of thing—and we have a lot of free time to like, use the media and music room, visit the greenhouse, read, learn crafts, or just do whatever interests us. There are social events to keep everyone entertained, holidays and dances and things like that where the whole ship shows up and mingles. I mean, we're *supposed* to all mingle. There's still a lot of cliques and in-grouping, and I've still never met half of the folks from the passengers' quarters because, you know, rich snobs.

That's how Joana and Brantley had their meet-cute, at one of the ship-wide dances where he wasn't being a rich snob. And that's also how—apparently—I first caught the eye of Darcy the Douche. He picked me out as one of the "few decent options" onboard who could "probably" be trusted not to take advantage of his generosity or money or something? Meanwhile, I clocked him as a rich snob to rival all the other rich snobs, who refused to have any fun and looked pained at every interaction with someone outside his snobby rich circle. Ugh. I wouldn't date him if he was the last human left for a thousand light-years, no matter how rich and handsome he is.

Carla Rios [off-screen]: Izzy?

Isabel Bernal: Oh! Carla! Hi!

Carla Rios: Hi. Uh…yeah.

Isabel Bernal: Are you…?

Carla Rios: Off to work, yeah.

Isabel Bernal: Cool. How, uh, how is it?

Carla Rios: You know! I'm managing! The waste, that is. Ha.

Isabel Bernal: Ha.

Carla Rios: Oh, are you filming right now?

Isabel Bernal: Yeah, yeah, just doing a day-in-the-life thing.

Carla Rios: Well, I'll let you...

Isabel Bernal: Totally. See you.

[footsteps, long sigh]

So, yeah. That's Carla. She's one of my oldest friends, but obviously things are, uh, a little awkward right now. It got...complicated last month.

First Carla and I tried dating—oh, don't act like you couldn't guess from that painful conversation—which I think we both thought would be a lot, I don't know, easier? But we just... didn't click like that. Which is fine! But then...right after that, she took the internship with my dad, and maybe I didn't react super maturely, even though the truth is that I was kind of relieved when she took it because it meant that I didn't have to. But it felt like she was doing it *to me*, you know? She obviously knows about the housing issue—I mean, her mom already retired, so if the council ruling goes poorly, *they're* actually facing eviction, so she's feeling the urgency even more, which is probably why she... It's all just a mess.

She...never really got it, my videos or the hashtag. Anyway. I'm happy for her, but...it's complicated.

Oh! *Shhhh*, don't look now—I mean, you can't until I flip the camera, there you go—but there's Darcy the Douchebag! He's best bros with Brantley, and if you look carefully, you can observe the two of them being jerks, not at all repentant about their behavior toward the Bernal sisters. Whoa! Wait, is Brantley...crying?

[footsteps, heavy breathing]

Phew! Pretty sure they didn't see me! All right, I think that's about enough—maybe too much—of a Day in the Life! Don't forget to keep #HomeAwayFromEarth trending, and check out other ways you can support. Love you all, see you in a few light-days! Muah! Bye!

[livestream ended]

- ❖ Drive: Starship Video Archives
  - ➢ Category: Recreational Video
    - ▪ Folder: Earth Accessible Livestream
      - • Passenger: Bernal, Isabel
        - ♦ Title: "Space Walk pt. ??? ... Cool Star Systems"

Audio transcript:
[21 minutes, 43 seconds of silence with soft breathing]

Isabel Bernal: Wow. It really is beautiful out here.

[15 minutes, 6 seconds of silence with soft breathing]

[livestream ended]

- ❖ Drive: Starship Video Archives
  - ➢ Category: Recreational Video
    - ▪ Folder: Earth Accessible Livestream
      - • Passenger: Bernal, Isabel
        - ♦ Title: "Tour the Ship pt. 7 Takes...a Turn"

Audio transcript:
Isabel Bernal: Hi, star chasers!

I'm resurrecting this tour series to bring you one part of the ship we've never seen: the luxury cabins! My uncles—they're lawyers—live there, so today we'll visit them and see how the other half lives!

I'm joking, mostly. Their cabin is pretty much the same as ours, except they get to keep it forever. Also, the hallways are nicer here. They even put irrigation and sky-grade lights so plants can grow right in front of your doorway.

Here's my uncles' cabin. The wreath is cute, right? It's recycled from replaced insulation foil.

[knocking]

Umm…

[knocking]

Oh, no… I told them I'd be here… Hang on, incoming text. They got stuck meeting with a client onboard the ship… They told me they had work, but I assumed that meant video chatting with someone on Earth—people up here don't usually need lawyers—but they're saying I can join them at the client's cabin instead, and nobody will mind.

Is that weird? A little. But will it get us a chance to see a probably even fancier cabin? Yes! Let's go!

[footsteps]

Let's see… It's in row P—that's not far from here, but we're moving deeper into the fancy rows. There are twenty rows in all, and the final row T is for the council, a whole hallway that houses only three cabins—as y'all know, most hallways, like the one my family lives in, house twelve cabins each. I heard the cabins in row T are like, a thousand square feet each. Can you *imagine*?

P-MB, unit Y. This is it. Okay, I'm going to put y'all in my chest pocket, just in case…

Here goes nothing.

[knocking, soft humming, hydraulic door release]

Oh!

Darcy Fitz: Izzy. Hello. Uh, hi. Hey.

Isabel Bernal: Hello, hi, and hey to you.

Darcy Fitz: What…

Isabel Bernal: Am I doing here? Yes, well, apparently you're working with my uncles? They said that I could come over. Gardener and Gerardo Greenburg-Garcia?

Darcy Fitz: …Please come in.

Isabel Bernal: Thanks. Oh, but do you mind… I do these livestreams…

Darcy Fitz: Of course. Is that your phone there? You can take it out. #HomeAwayFromEarth.

Isabel Bernal: Yeah! Wait… You've watched?

Darcy Fitz: What kind of self-important asshole would I be if I didn't watch my own viral video?

Isabel Bernal: Oh. Oh, wow. Was that a joke?

Darcy Fitz: Partially.

Isabel Bernal: Oh, no… Does it sound really fake to say that I never considered that you would watch the video? I was kind of over-the-top, I guess. I hope nobody really bothered you about it…

Darcy Fitz: Even if any of your followers puzzled out my full name, I am not easy to find online. And your video was a fair description of my behavior. I am sorry for implying that I pursued you on the basis of a shallow dating pool.

Isabel Bernal: You also implied that you would date me on a trial basis until I could prove that I was trustworthy and not a gold digger.

Darcy Fitz: That... Yes. I had a past experience that... It doesn't matter. It didn't have anything to do with you. That was not my best moment, and I apologize. I would...be happy if we could move forward without a grudge between us.

Isabel Bernal: No hard feelings? I can get on board.

Darcy Fitz: Thank you. Did you still want to come in?

Isabel Bernal: Yes! Thanks.

[footsteps]

Isabel Bernal: I was going to show my audience how cabins look on this side of the shiiiiiii—holy waste management!

Darcy Fitz: I would offer to get your uncles while you wait in the sitting room, but I imagine your audience wants a complete tour.

Isabel Bernal: Sitting...room? Right. And my uncles are...?

Darcy Fitz: Probably in my father's study. We can stop by the kitchen and the dining room on our way.

Isabel Bernal: The...dining room. The room for dining. Totally. Yes. Let's show that.

Darcy Fitz: Am I doing something wrong?

Isabel Bernal: No! Not at all. It's... Is this furniture *wood*?

Darcy Fitz: I am aware that most cabins are smaller and come with built-in furniture of plastic, steel, and foam. I believe my father made some modifications to the basic design.

Isabel Bernal: Made some... Darcy, this is an International Space Ship! You don't just make modifications! Who is your father?

Darcy Fitz: I... Didn't realize you didn't know... Is this the reason you always call me Darcy Douchebag? You don't know my last name? I thought you were gallantly maintaining my privacy.

Isabel Bernal: *Who* is your dad??

Darcy Fitz: ...William Fitz.

[heavy breathing]

Isabel Bernal: ...I'm sorry. Excuse me one second.

Darcy Fitz: ...Should I leave? Would you like to leave?

Isabel Bernal: No, no. Please. I just need to take an aside to the camera.

[heavy breathing]

Uh, star chasers, I assume you're either equally shocked or laughing at me. All this time, I've been feuding—one-sidedly—with the son of the actual inventor of FTZ streaming tech! *The* reason we can stay in contact with Earth! The single piece of technology that let this voyage take place!

Darcy Fitz: Arguably.

Isabel Bernal: Arguably!

Darcy Fitz: We couldn't have made the voyage without the proper waste-management systems, either. Or without the workers in offices and factories across the Earth who made my father's theories into material products.

Isabel Bernal: I… You…

[off-screen speech inaudible]

Darcy Fitz: Georgie! Come here! Uh, Isabel—

Isabel Bernal: Izzy. Izzy is fine.

Darcy Fitz: Izzy, do you mind if my little sister is in your video?

Isabel Bernal: I…really don't. Does she mind?

Georgiana Fitz: I don't mind! Hi! What are you filming? Oh, you're Lety's sister. My brother talks about you all the time.

Darcy Fitz: I do not. I talk about many people. I talk about the housing problems on the ship. Your name may come up, occasionally. It's not— My father is an accomplished businessman, but he is not naturally tuned into many social conversations. Georgiana, don't you have piano to practice?

Georgiana Fitz: You told me to come over here. Do you want to hear me play?

Isabel Bernal: Please don't tell me you have a piano in your bunk.

Georgiana Fitz: Just a keyboard. Our baby grand is in cargo.

Isabel Bernal: Wow. Okay, yeah. I'm calling it. See you in a couple light-days everyone. Thanks for coming with me on this...whatever this was. Muah.

Darcy Fitz: #HomeAwayFromEarth!

Isabel Bernal: Mm-hmm. What he said. Bye.

[livestream ended]

- Drive: Starship Video Archives
  - Category: Recreational Video
    - Folder: Earth Accessible Livestream
      - Passenger: Bernal, Isabel
        - Title: "Yes, I'm SORRY!"

Audio transcript:
Isabel Bernal: Hi, star chasers! Uh, following up on the abrupt ending of today's earlier livestream. Yes, the dining room was huge. No, I didn't meet William Fitz. I did hang out with Darcy and his sister until Darcy had to meet with his private Earthside tutor. It was...fun.

I'm still mortified about how I treated Darcy before. He's... well, he's even richer than I imagined, but he's not a jerk or full of himself. Maybe he used to be those things—unlimited wealth and privilege can probably have that effect—but he's working on it. He's…nice. And I'm *not* just saying that because he likes my videos.

Also thanks for not harassing him on my behalf even though I totally encouraged you to. I shouldn't have done that. I always knew my followers were good eggs.

Darcy *Fitz*… I don't know how much y'all know about FTZ data streaming. It lets us broadcast data back to Earth, thanks to our breadcrumb trail of simple transmitters and an incredibly sophisticated system of data compression that lets us send huge—nearly unlimited—amounts of data via simple transmitters. It's so good that my dad and Uncle Gerardo can watch soccer matches live while online with their brother on Earth, with zero lag.

It's a great system. It's also privately owned and regulated by William Fitz and his veritable army of lawyers, who have crafted pretty strict terms of service. Like, if you've heard me talk about why I don't make money off these streams, it's because FTZ's terms of service are absolutely draconian about monetization. Because, of course, William Fitz didn't become rich just because of his brilliant invention. He also knows how to cut himself in to everyone else's profit.

I hope my videos are opening some eyes and hearts to the inequalities here on the *Hertford*. Maybe I'm being idealistic, but I really feel like this housing decision, the council meeting at the end of the week, will set the tone of the whole interplanetary venture. Do we want to keep reinforcing patterns where the rich get richer and everyone else has to fall in line? I don't. Please, keep #HomeAwayFromEarth trending, and help us build a more just world somewhere out here in the universe.

Oh, and all of you suddenly saying Darcy is handsome—you're *incredibly fickle* and you should be embarrassed. That is all.

See you in a couple of light-days. Muah! Bye!

[livestream ended]

★ ★ ★

- Drive: Starship Video Archives
  - Category: Recreational Video
    - Folder: Earth Accessible Livestream
      - Passenger: Bernal, Isabel
        - Title: [Untitled stream]

Audio transcript:

Isabel Bernal: Okay, okay, hi, star chasers! I have an update!

So I was minding my own business and walking around the greenhouse, when who should I see but Brantley Bingley III, crying again, in the hydroponic hanging-crop corner. And *who* was he crying to? My beautiful and talented older sister, Joana.

Well, I marched over there and death-glared until Brantley left, and thank goodness I did! Joana would've totally fallen for his *boo-hoo I made a mistake* shtick.

He didn't ask her to get back together, thanks to my interruption, but he was clearly heading there. Nope, I'm sorry, you don't get to ghost my sister and then come crawling back. *Maybe* if he showed any real growth or change, or could at least tell her *why* he went radio silent in the first place, but no! Just more mysterious apologies! Anyway, I saved Joana for now. But I have to be vigilant! There's no telling what pretty lies Brantley may be concocting. That boy is a menace, mark my word—Lety? Is that you? Hey, what's wrong? Are you oka—?

[livestream ended]

- Drive: Starship Video Archives
  - Category: Recreational Video
    - Folder: Earth Accessible Livestream
      - Passenger: Bernal, Isabel
        - Title: "I'm Alive and I'm Pissed"

Audio transcript:
Isabel Bernal: Hi, everyone. Uh, star chasers. Sorry. I didn't realize I had you all worried. I mean, I'm worried and furious, but no one's dying or anything. Except maybe Wick when I get my hands on him.

[long sigh]

Okay, so, y'all know my little sister, Lety? Twelve, annoying, wants to be a viral streaming star with all her prepubescent heart? A totally sincere person that only a monster would manipulate for his own gain?

Y'all have heard me talk about monetization on Earthside communication content, right? Anyway, Lety should know all about those rules, but she's also twelve. So it turns out she's sneakily started her own streaming, and she was...*approached* for a collaboration. She's literally seen *me* collab with Wick before, so why would she refuse? And he told her his long, practiced sob story—you know, how he was treated unfairly by Darcy and the council—and she wanted to do the right thing. So she followed Wick's advice (even though he's *never* risked doing this on his channel) and asked her tiny audience to donate to his cause.

And she got caught and slapped with—I'm not exaggerating—a lifetime ban on Earthside communication!

I'm just so pissed.

She's...heartbroken, of course, and I don't even think she realizes the long-term effects... You know how important FTZ streaming is...

[long sigh, off-screen speech inaudible]

Uh-oh, my mom's calling me. I'll...try to think of a hashtag, some concrete steps to support Lety, but right now I'm just...

Thanks for listening.

[livestream ended]

★ ★ ★

- Drive: Starship Video Archives
  - Category: Recreational Video
    - Folder: Earth Accessible Livestream
      - Passenger: Bernal, Isabel
        - Title: "I'm on an Emotional Roller Coaster and You're All Trapped with Me"

Audio Transcript:
Isabel Bernal: Hi, star chasers! I *may* have overreacted. Customer Support reached out just a few hours after I filmed my last video and took back Lety's punishment. I'm fuzzy on the details, but it seems like she'll have normal streaming rights in six weeks. Wow. Maybe I have you all to thank for this?

Thanks for all your supportive comments, for caring about my little sister, my home, and my life. It's really cool. I don't take it for granted.

See you all in a few light-days. Muah! Bye!

[livestream ended]

- Drive: Starship Video Archives
  - Category: Recreational Video
    - Folder: Earth Accessible Livestream
      - Passenger: Bernal, Isabel
        - Title: "Are Your Legs Sore from Jumping to Conclusions?"

Audio Transcript:
Isabel Bernal: Hi, star chasers! Or should I say super star sleuths? Y'all, we have no proof that Darcy had anything to do with Lety's case! It might be a totally automated process. It probably is. Please stop commenting about it. You know he checks out my videos sometimes, and I don't want him to feel awk-

ward or pressured to do anything about FTZ stuff. My family isn't his problem.

Um, and if by some totally wild coincidence, you are on the right track…then I'm sure he already knows how much this means to Lety and to my family. And to me. So we can just… drop it. Okay. Thanks y'all. See you in a few light-days. Muah! Bye.

[livestream ended]

- ❖ Drive: Starship Video Archives
  - ➢ Category: Recreational Video
    - ▪ Folder: Earth Accessible Livestream
      - • Passenger: Bernal, Isabel
        - ♦ Title: "Things Keep Happening"

Audio Transcript:
Isabel Bernal: Hi! Yes, I heard the announcement. No, I'm not totally sure what it means. Trying to figure things out now. I—

[off-screen speech inaudible]

Hey. What's up?

Carla Rios: Can you put the communicator away for a second?

Isabel Bernal: What? Why?

Carla Rios: Because I want to talk to *you* about the council's decision. Not your audience.

Isabel Bernal: My audience might be our only chance to change the ruling.

Carla Rios: That's not— Your little publicity stunt isn't working. You can tell by reading the report.

Isabel Bernal: The report is contradictory. They're saying that ship employees whose jobs came with cabin assignments have no *legal* right to their cabins once their employment ends, but then at the same time they're saying they could change the rules if they decide it's best for ship life, but they won't officially rule on this yet because there are too many factors to consider—including public opinion. That means it is working. And, look, I've been distracted recently with Lety and Joana, I know, and I should have done a much bigger push with #HomeAwayFromEarth as we got closer to the ruling, but we can still do it now. We can capitalize on this bullshit announcement, we can show the council that—

Carla Rios: The council doesn't care about—and *you* shouldn't rely on—a bunch of teenagers light-years away! You need to be a little bit practical! Maybe consider providing an actual service to the actual place where we live!

[footsteps, sniffles]

Isabel Bernal: Sorry, everyone. Uh, obviously the decision—the lack of a real decision—is making emotions run high… I really should have stayed focused…because we *can* make a difference. We could have. I'll… I don't know. I don't know what happens next.

[livestream ended]

- Drive: Starship Video Archives
  - Category: Recreational Video
    - Folder: Local Broadcasts
      - Passenger: Bernal, Isabel
        - Title: "This is about Us"

Audio transcript:

Isabel Bernal: Hi, *Hertford* passengers. It's me, Izzy Bernal. You probably know me, or someone in my family—it's a small spaceship. I make a lot of videos, but I'm not livestreaming this one, and it won't be accessible to people on Earth. This is about us.

You've heard the council's decision about cabin inheritance. Maybe you know a lot about this issue, or maybe it hasn't been on your radar. I invite you to watch my old videos if you need more background, but I also want to apologize for the way I went about it. Because I was always talking *about* the ship, about the people, but not *to* you. And that's not right.

We're way out in space together, y'all. There aren't that many of us, and we live close together, and we're all affected by what happens to everyone else.

You've heard my sister Joana perform at social events. You've applauded her, and complimented her, and asked for more. We're all very proud of Caroline Bingley and how her visual art made Earth take notice of the next generation of *Hertford* passengers. But she can do what she did, dedicate herself to her art, because she doesn't have to worry about not having a place to live in the future. If this ruling doesn't go our way, Joana won't have that option.

I know, some of you think artistic careers are a frivolous thing to fight for. We didn't choose artists for the original mission crew. We needed engineers, botanists, waste-management experts. But this ship holds more passengers than essential workers—some among us have always been granted the right to be frivolous. The rest of us are asking for the same choice.

I think we can do better than generational labor classes. If you agree, I invite you to join me tomorrow to continue this conversation. I'll be standing outside the council's cabins, trusting that they'll listen to their community. Hope to see you there.

[broadcast ended]

★ ★ ★

- Drive: Starship Video Archives
  - Category: Recreational Video
    - Folder: Earth Accessible Livestream
      - Passenger: Bernal, Isabel
        - Title: "Wow..."

Audio Transcript:
Isabel Bernal: Hi, star chasers! Sorry it's been a while since I've given a real update. *A lot* has been happening. I barely know where to begin.

Darcy Fitz: Begin where you left off.

Isabel Bernal: Well, we're a week out from the council's initial ruling, and while we've started some really important dialogues between the actual council members and the people of the ship—

Darcy Fitz: You. You started the direct dialogue. You're also leading a council-appointed committee to research and present findings about citizen quality of life.

Isabel Bernal: Yeah, that's what I said. Dialogue's happening. But honestly, the council is trying their hardest to kick this problem down the star field. They've already asked me to take—what was it? Six months?—to form my preliminary draft of my poll questions. Just absurd. So I turned that in yesterday.

Darcy Fitz: It's very good.

Isabel Bernal: It doesn't have to be good. It's preliminary. The council will probably make me go through twenty drafts before they even consider it.

Darcy Fitz: True. But it is good.

Isabel Bernal: Heh. I wish I had more exciting news to share. Truth is, instead of a clear ruling and celebration, it's probably going to be a slow and boring push for change. I'll try to keep you updated, but I'm also about to start an internship with the mechanical systems and emergency repair department, so…less time for streaming and spacewalking, unfortunately. It's not a huge passion, but I should be able to move up to full-time employee within a year, and all the jobs in the department come with some kind of cabin situation, and, you know…my dad can't wait on the council's timeline to retire. Also, Joana had an Earth university approach her about their degree in music performance, so she'll be taking classes with professors soon. So I needed to look into some kind of practical backup plan.

But that's not to say the fight is over! I'll be sharing resources, asking for y'all to take action at home. And because I appreciate you so much, I'll keep posting fun space content, too. Including the update that Brantley and Joana are officially back on again!

Darcy Fitz: Is that fun space content?

Isabel Bernal: You have *no idea* how many Joana stans are out there! And they'll be happy to hear that she has my full approval. Brantley finally shared the whole story, how *someone* told him Joana was going to break his heart and steal his bank codes.

Darcy Fitz: He shouldn't have protected me for so long. I was absolutely in the wrong. I…I've explained this to you, but perhaps it is time for me to share it with your audience as well. Wick, as we are all aware, is a devoted manipulator, and Lety was not the only one to be caught in his web. He pursued a relationship with me to leech off my father's wealth, and I unfairly carried that experience into my own and my friends' later romantic exploits.

Isabel Bernal: [sigh] We all really fell for him, didn't we?... And now he's employed as *security*?

Darcy Fitz: Add it to the list of issues we plan to take up with the council. Along with FTZ privatization, housing, my idea for smaller social gatherings, and at least a handful of other injustices.

Isabel Bernal: Okay, don't bore the viewers. Now, I believe I promised y'all fun space content, which brings us to today's collaboration! It turns out that the famous Darcy Fitz happens to be, and I quote, *not particularly fond of* space walks—

Darcy Fitz: Actually. Before we do that...

Isabel Bernal: Huh?

Darcy Fitz: I may have misled you about my idea for this video. Georgiana has been helping me research what types of content draws high viewership. I believe that this fits into several popular categories, such as *Surprise*, *Wholesome*, and *Outrageous Gift-giving*. So I believe it is appropriate to do this on a livestream, since high viewership will ultimately drive more engagement with the #HomeAwayFromEarth initiative.

Isabel Bernal: What? Uh, sure, that's all fine but...gift-giving?

Darcy Fitz: Follow me, please.

Isabel Bernal: Literally what is happening right now?

[footsteps, nervous laughter]

Isabel Bernal: What row are we in? Are we going to your cabin?

Darcy Fitz: Most decidedly not. Here.

[hydraulic door release]

Isabel Bernal: Hello? What is this? Why does this cabin look abandoned?

Darcy Fitz: This ship was designed for efficiency. Families are expected to live multigenerationally, siblings are expected to share rooms. A common level of…inconvenience, resulting from an understood scarcity of space.

Isabel Bernal: Right. Housing is a problem specifically *because* we don't have empty cabins lying around.

Darcy Fitz: That's mostly true.

Isabel Bernal: *Mostly?*

Darcy Fitz: You know my father sees these shared inconveniences as optional for himself and his family. So you are looking at a cabin that used to be reserved for when I turn eighteen.

Isabel Bernal: A cabin…to yourself…just sitting here?

Darcy Fitz: Wick almost convinced me to move the two of us in together, but…

Isabel Bernal: …I'm sorry. I'm really sorry he did that to you. But… Wow, there never was any hope of equality on the ship, was there?

Darcy Fitz: Maybe not originally. But there could be, now.

Isabel Bernal: Darcy...

Darcy Fitz: I have an absurd amount of wealth and absolutely no talent for interacting with people. I am very nervous to be on your videos. I have trouble explaining important issues to my own father, much less to the council. So by process of elimination, I have discovered that the best thing I can do to advance the cause I feel passionately about...is to support others. To support *you.* This cabin is yours, whenever you need it. The paperwork is already complete. You can devote yourself fully to your work with the council and your online activism.

[vocal noises indecipherable, heavy breathing]

Isabel Bernal: I...can't accept this.

Darcy Fitz: Then, you're welcome to let it sit empty. But that won't fix the problem. Only you can do that.

Isabel Bernal: You can't just swoop in and save me!

Darcy Fitz: I see it differently. You swooped in with your viral video and saved me from a life of ignorant privilege and prejudice. I don't want to be the person who owns an empty cabin on a ship with a housing crisis, and that's because of you.

Isabel Bernal: This is...

Darcy Fitz: Another popular category of viral content is *Happy Crying.* I think this video will be a hit.

Isabel Bernal: I am never going to live this down. I will forever be the jerk who virally mocked the guy who *gave her a home.*

Darcy Fitz: Well, I deserved it, then. I felt entitled to your attention without making any attempt to earn it, and I tried to set boundaries on a relationship we didn't have yet. I assumed that you would behave like Wick if I didn't stop you. It was a terrible way to ask someone out.

Isabel Bernal: Yeah. It was. You should try again some time. You're bound to do better.

[vocal noises indecipherable]

Darcy Fitz: I, uh, hardly think that would be appropriate, especially now. It would make my gift seem as if it had strings attached. It would put undue pressure on you to—

Isabel Bernal: Darcy. I'm not pressured. I'm *asking you* to ask me again. If you want.

Darcy Fitz: Do you want to—

Isabel Bernal: Wait! Wait, one second. Let me sign off real quick.

Sorry, star chasers! Please don't scream at me too much in the comments! I just want to keep some things off-camera. For myself. You get it! Update soon! See you, light-days, etc.!

Darcy Fitz: You forgot something.

Isabel Bernal: I did? Wh—

[kissing sound]

Darcy Fitz: Muah.

Isabel Bernal: Ummmm, yeah. Yep. Bye!

[livestream ended]

★ ★ ★ ★ ★

BREAK IN CASE OF PERSEPHONE

a remix of the myth of Hades and Persephone
Olivia Abtahi

"I was joyfully gathering the flowers, and then the earth beneath me gave way..."

—Translated by Gregory Nagy, *Homeric Hymn to Demeter*

Everyone in the quiet, sleepy town of Rancho Verde knew that Demetria Griega wasn't just an incredible gardener and horticulturist, she was *magic.* Wherever she went, vines stretched toward her, flowers bloomed, and trees swayed in her direction. Her daughter, Persefonía, inherited the same green thumb, and wildflowers filled in her footsteps. They were like small-town doctors, with Rancho Verde townsfolk stopping the pair at the grocery store to talk about a spider plant that was giving them trouble or flagging them down to ask about fiddle-leaf fig woes.

Demetria thanked Dios every day that she'd found a haven where nobody asked too many unwelcome questions, where she could raise her daughter by herself and still provide for her. Demetria couldn't believe how lucky they were, considering the legacy they'd had to run from. How grateful Demetria was, how truly thankful for every good thing!

Persefonía, however, hated it.

She hated this small town with its small people. She hated

how she knew the difference between a Chevy Silverado and a Ford F-150, how the boys in town only cared about her body and not her brain—not the things that grew inside of her, itching to break free and find their sunlight.

In her last home, there had been cinemas and museums, beaches and festivals. But Mamá said that their cover had been blown, so they had to move somewhere tiny where there was no way they'd ever be found. And so Persefonía smiled and waved and acted the part of the perfect daughter, while her roots struggled to find cracks in the flowerpot of her life.

That day, Persefonía walked home from her shift at the nursery exhausted, glad she at least had dinner at her friend's house to look forward to. Graduation loomed, and school had become painful as classmates announced the far-off places they'd get to explore while she would stay behind.

She stopped midstride. Behind her was a sprinkling of cornflower and lupine pushing through the sidewalk. She turned around to make sure nobody was watching, then ground the tiny petals down with her sandals. Satisfied, she walked on.

These tiny acts of rebellion were the only things keeping her afloat most days. Persefonía knew her mother could sense her growing unhappiness springing up like a weed. But they were safe and had full bellies and a place to rest their heads. What could Persefonía possibly complain about? Except…

There was one thing that could choke their safety. A small, twisted blight on her mother's dream. A curse, a whisper, a tale from the old country: a prophecy of granadas. Pomegranates.

Family legend said the lush fruit could destroy everything the two had ever loved. One seed had the power to destroy a legacy going far back to when there wasn't just one god but many. Never had the Griegas eaten one, much less a kernel. The risk was too great.

And so, mother and daughter knew to never even look at the

plump red orbs at the grocery store. Persefonía had a deathly allergy, she told the school nurse, as per the note her mother had sent with her on her first day at school. Even Nasreen, her best friend, knew to never offer the fruit that was so prevalent in her Persian household.

Chaos, the word whispered in Persefonía's ear. She craved it after her endlessly predictable days spent at school and the flower nursery. *Chaos*: her fingers itched to get out her phone and buy a ticket to somewhere, anywhere but here. *Chaos*: the thing that could break her mother's heart, that could tear her family in two.

Her mouth drooled, wondering what one kernel would taste like. She turned around and stomped on some more wildflowers.

"You can take over the nursery one day!" Demetria had told her daughter, and Persefonía had nodded, trying hard not to cry.

At least she could celebrate graduation at Nasreen's house tonight. They had been the only kids in their grade with foreign parents, and she couldn't wait to eat all the delicious, wondrous food Nasreen's family had been preparing all week. But after that, there was nothing more to look forward to.

Persefonía would enjoy her time with Nasreen while it lasted.

"Welcome, welcome!" Nasreen's family shouted later that night, welcoming her and her mother inside their home. Nasreen led them to a table sparkling with crystal glassware and real silver. Persefonía's eyes went wide. Usually when she was at her friend's house, they ate at the kitchen counter. Nasreen's mom, Fatemeh, always insisted on cooking for them. She never let Nasreen or Persefonía fend for themselves in the fridge: that was her domain.

Tonight, Fatemeh had pulled out all the stops. Persefonía felt underdressed next to the family's sleek black outfits and multiple forks for every place setting. She dared not look at her mother. Demetria had worn her one outfit that wasn't overalls, and her gingham dress looked frayed and ratty next to all the silver.

"Wow," Demetria said. "This sure looks like a fancy meal!"

"I'm so sorry," Persefonía whispered to Nasreen. "My mom does not clean up well. Or, like, ever."

Nasreen laughed. "My parents just wanted an excuse to bust out the nice china. Come on." She led them to the table, and the family toasted with sparkling cider. Persefonía had coached her mom not to ask about the wine, and yet—

"Got anything stronger?" Demetria asked, winking at Nasreen's dad. The immediate downturn of his huge, forbidding mustache made it clear that no, they did not.

"Mamá," Persefonía groaned. "They're Muslim, remember?"

Demetria shrugged, her dangly earrings flapping, her curly hair bouncing. "Figured I'd ask."

Then, horror of horrors, Persefonía watched as her mom clutched her sparkling cider flute just a second too long. The color of the cider went from crisp yellow to deep gold. She hated how her mother was so cavalier with their magic, all while insisting Persefonía stay locked away in Rancho Verde.

She cleared her throat, trying to draw attention away from her mamá. "I can't believe you're leaving," she said to Nasreen. "I'll miss you."

Nasreen gave her a sad smile, her copper-colored eyes dimming. "I know. Who's going to binge travel shows with me?"

Persefonía grinned. "That's what video chat's for."

"My daughter!" Nasreen's mother wailed. "Why must you go to college so far away?"

"Oh, boy," Nasreen said, rolling her eyes. "Here comes the guilt trip again."

Nasreen's mother sniffed and adjusted her headscarf before ladling dinner onto her guests' plates. "Here the community college is good. Why you are wanting to leave?"

"Nasreen, what kind of classes will you be taking?" Demetria interrupted, her flute of hard cider already half-gone.

"They've got me in all the beginner sciences classes, plus some core classes I have to take for my degree," Nasreen replied.

Persefonía could feel her friend trying hard not to sound excited, as if the happier she was, the worse Persefonía would feel. Nasreen was right, of course: Persefonía felt awful, but this pitying was a new low. She tried to smile and nod as her mom and best friend prattled on about agricultural sciences, something Demetria knew way too much about.

"Try," Nasreen's mom ordered, spooning some stew onto Persefonía's plate.

Persefonía's stomach growled. She smelled walnuts and saffron, the brownish stew bleeding into the rice. "What is it?" she asked, drooling.

"Fesenjoon," the woman replied. "It's chicken. Very good, very tender." All around them were dishes piled with herbs, lavash, and tureens of different stews. Mounds of steamed rice sat like big, fluffy clouds.

"Umm… I don't eat meat," Persefonía said, looking to Nasreen for help. Alas, her friend was deep in a conversation on plant biology with Demetria, their food untouched.

"Yes," Fatemeh said, like Persefonía was a bit dim. "That's why I made you chicken."

Persefonía balked. She knew how important hospitality was in Nasreen's culture, and she didn't want to upset Mrs. Shoja. She lifted her fork, deciding to nibble the tiniest bit possible just to please her hostess.

"Mmm," Persefonía said, chewing exaggeratedly on the stew. But then her discomfort turned to genuine pleasure. "Wow, it's so sweet! But a bit tart, too. What is this again?"

"Chicken, saffron, walnuts, and anar," Nasreen's mom replied evenly.

"Maman!" Nasreen whipped her around as if a gun had gone off. She looked horrified. "I told you she's allergic to pomegranates!"

Nasreen's mother looked between her daughter and Persefonía like they had gone mad. "What is this pomegranate? I didn't use! I used anar."

"That's what anar means in English! Pomegranate!"

At the word *pomegranate*, Persefonía's dinner fork clattered onto her plate.

"No!" Demetria moaned, her voice unnaturally low, the sound tearing through her chest.

Persefonía's heart raced. Her lips tingled, as if she'd eaten something ice-cold. She felt her pupils dilate, the low candles of the room getting brighter and brighter, a high-pitched sound ringing in her ears.

"Perse? Estás bien?" Demetria cried. She was already out of her chair, running to her daughter on the other side of the ornate dining table.

"Mamá?" she asked. "What's happen—"

And then everything went white.

Persefonía blinked. Instead of a warm, candlelit home, she was suddenly in what looked like the sterile waiting room of a doctor's office. A man behind a white desk typed away at his computer, either unbothered by her sudden appearance or not yet aware. She clutched her chest, still recovering from the pomegranate betrayal. What had just happened?

"Hello?" Persefonía called out, her voice frantic. "What's going on? Where am I?" She hated how much her voice echoed, the cavernous room making her feel exposed.

The typing stopped. A pale face peeked out from behind the computer, one with dark black eyes and obsidian-colored hair. He looked young, about Persefonía's age, and the surprise on his face was enough to make her feel like she wasn't hallucinating.

"Oh, my gods!" the guy shouted. "It's happening. Okay, don't panic, Hectór. Don't panic!"

"*What's* happening?" Persefonía choked out, but Hectór ignored her as he riffled through the folders on his desk. She watched, stunned, as he wrenched drawers open and slammed them shut, clearly looking for something. This was not like her normal dreams of traveling and leaving home. This fantasy was much too clerical.

Suddenly, Hectór spun around, staring at a glass case in the wall that held a fire alarm. No wait: not a fire alarm, a sheet of paper. Dimly, Persefonía read the words *Break in Case of Persephone* above.

"Aha!" he cried, breaking the glass with the tiny ax right next to it. He shook the shards off his hand and held up a laminated piece of paper.

"Dearest Persephone," Hectór began.

"Persefonía," she corrected, her teeth chattering with adrenaline. *This isn't real,* she reminded herself. *In a second, I'll wake up.*

Hectór faltered, his chalk-white hands trembling. "Sorry," he said. "I've never had to break the glass. *Dearest Persefonía, welcome to the underworld. It seems you are in breach of contract and have consumed...* One sec."

He typed something into his computer and read from the screen, "*approximately six seeds of pomegranate. Per the previous arrangement of our ancestors, that means you must spend the next six months in the underworld.* Here. With me," he added, trying to sound important. He puffed up his chest, then quickly deflated.

"What?" Persefonía cried. "*This* is the underworld? Am I dead?"

Hectór laughed. "Oh, gods, no. You're in the waiting room. Still alive, just like me."

"Okay?" Persefonía replied, looking around for an exit. It was no use: the room was a white box. She couldn't find a window, much less a door. "All because I ate some pomegranate?"

"Six kernels, yes," Hectór corrected. "Don't you know the legend?" he asked, seemingly trying to be helpful. "I'm surprised your mom didn't tell you. She's a Demeter, right?"

Persefonía rolled her eyes. "*Demetria.* That old curse again."

"Listen, it's not all bad. We have Wi-Fi, unlimited simulations, and all the food and drink you could want. It's only six months."

"I'm supposed to stay in this bucket of bleach for half a year?" Persefonía was hysterical now, her voice bouncing off the blank walls. "Please tell me this is a joke. Is there anyone else I can talk to?"

Hectór's face went dark. "You don't want to talk to my grandpa," he said quietly. "He'll make you stay here forever."

Persefonía gulped, noting how what little color was in Hectór's face drained at the mere mention of his grandpa. She'd clearly gotten the good cop in this nightmare. She found a stretch of wall and slid to the floor in disbelief. "But…I was going to go to community college. And help my mom run the nursery."

Hectór winced. He pressed a button and a fancy kettle slid out of the blank wall. He poured tea for Persefonía, who was now quietly crying.

"Here," he said, handing it to her. "It's herbal. It'll calm you down."

"Matricaria chamomilla," Persefonía hiccuped. "Thanks."

Hectór looked around the waiting room, as if seeing it through her eyes. Then he snapped his fingers, transforming the space into one of those quaint English gardens she'd seen in movies, complete with rosebushes, moss-covered statues, and small brick footpaths. Persefonía practically fell out of the wrought iron chair she was now sitting in.

"Gah!" she flinched, spilling her tea. "What just happened?"

Hectór grimaced at the blue sky, the budding flowers, the perfume in the air. "In the legends, you like flowers, right? I thought you'd be more comfortable here."

He, however, seemed anything but.

Persefonía clutched a hand to her chest. "I could've used some warning, you know."

He bit his lip. "Right. Sorry."

She looked around, drinking in their surroundings. "Where are we? Are we out of the underworld now?"

Hectór shook his head. "This is just a sim."

"A what?"

"A simulation," he clarified. "None of this is real, even if it feels real."

Persefonía gawked. She held her hand out to a rosebush and plucked a pink damask petal. "This is incredible," she breathed. "I can even smell it."

"Thanks," Hectór said, smiling for the first time since the strange encounter began. "I built this one a long time ago. It's based off a garden in the UK."

Persefonía looked back at him, eyes wide. "*You* made this?" she asked. "Just you?"

Hectór shrugged. "I helped digitize this part of the underworld for my grandpa. Elysium was a lot more crowded before. Just a bunch of fields."

Persefonía squinted at the person in front of her, recalculating. He *did* look like the computer superstars at her high school, the ones who'd gotten in trouble for using school property to mine crypto. *Elysium*. Her mind tickled at the word. It pulled up memories of meadows and golden hills. A kind of limbo for worthy souls before they moved on. *This* was Elysium?

"So we can go anywhere?" Persefonía asked. "As long as it's a simulation?"

Hectór nodded. "Exactly. I've made thousands of simulations, all based on real places in the above world. And a couple random ones, for other planets and stuff that I made up."

"Wow." Persefonía leaned back, recalculating. "Okay. Take me to another one." Her heartbeat had finally slowed down, and it hummed with pleasure from being in a completely new garden, one she'd had no hand in growing. Just being in this space, away from the flora of Rancho Verde, felt like taking one step closer to the life she wanted to lead.

"Where do you want to go?" Hectór asked, as if this was the simplest request in the world.

"The ocean," Persefonía said simply, closing her eyes. It was almost as if she could feel the salty breeze on her face already. "Take me back to the ocean."

HECTÓR

Hectór snapped his fingers again, and Persefonía opened her eyes to crystal-blue waters and whitewashed buildings. A beach crashed below them, islands smudging the horizon.

She shook her head in wonder, amazed by the abrupt transition. "That will never get old."

He watched as she leaned against a tree and gazed out at the horizon. He'd never seen someone so taken with a sim before. Usually, they kicked and screamed and demanded to see a loved one, then Hectór would have to calm them with a different sim that was basically a loop of their old life. In fact, he rarely did personal showings anymore. He'd programmed the system to feed new souls into whichever sim he thought they'd like best and kept himself out of it.

He didn't like meeting new people, and face-to-face interactions with souls always left him feeling drained and anxious. Persefonía was the first living human he'd interacted with here in a long time.

It was a strange sensation, to stand beside a person again. They were two living beings, two prophesied stewards of the underworld. The first time he'd shepherded someone to their afterlife, he'd had a panic attack, which was why he rarely met them in person anymore, letting the software do its job. Now he could feel his heartbeat race as he struggled to stay calm.

He'd never had a coworker before.

"You get to do this all day?" Persefonía waved at the water. "Just think of an amazing place to go to and, poof, you go?"

"I mean... I have to build it first, but...yeah?"

"Can you leave, though? Go to the real world?" she demanded.

Hectór shrugged. "Yeah, but why would I want to?"

The real world was terrible. He couldn't control anything up there, and that felt like its own punishment. Anyway, his parents handled the above world, his grandfather handled the underworld, and Hectór got the job nobody else seemed to want: Elysium. His family complained it was boring here, but Hectór knew he had the better part of the bargain.

"Dang," Persefonía said, looking wistfully at the skyline. Hectór detected notes of jealousy in her voice. *Why would she be jealous of me, though?* he wondered. He felt like a loser with a computer. Above world, he would have fainted at the thought of having to talk to someone as gorgeous as Persefonía. The comfort of his sims and the shock of his surprise were the only things keeping him afloat through this conversation.

"You're taking this a lot better than I expected," Hectór admitted. "The last Persephone ran away, then her mom had to get involved, then Zeus came in, and it was a whole thing." He shivered. He was paraphrasing what happened, leaving out the grisly bits.

"This is *amazing*!" Persefonía suddenly shouted, fist pumping in the air. "Where else can we go? Ooh, I've never been to the top of a mountain before! Or maybe we could go skiing? Wait, are we in a different country right now? Can we go to different countries?"

Hectór laughed, a light and airy sound that surprised him. The novelty of his sims had worn off so long ago. Gods, he must have looked like such a serial killer in his all-white office. When was the last time he'd spoken to someone who wasn't dead?

"Hectór?" Persefonía poked him. He jumped back at the

touch. The last time he'd had physical contact was a couple months ago when his grandfather had patted his shoulder in a threatening way, as if to say, *Good dog. Stay.*

"We can go to different places, right?" she repeated.

"You know none of this is real, right? Just ones and zeros."

Persefonía sighed happily. "I don't care. Now let's climb a mountain."

Hectór snapped his fingers, and they were on a sim of Pike's Peak, the highest mountain in Colorado.

"More!" shouted Persefonía.

He snapped again and brought them to a night market in Singapore, handing her a bowl of laksa. "Yum," Persefonía moaned. "This tastes so good."

"Not real," Hectór reminded her.

"Don't care," Persefonía sang back.

He showed her a glacier in Patagonia, a castle in France, an asteroid belt in the Andromeda Galaxy. And the tiny playground his parents took him to when he was little, back when he hadn't minded leaving the house and risking going somewhere with too many unknown variables.

"Again, again, again!" Persefonía cried, the tears from the waiting room long gone. And bit by bit, Hectór's heart began to soar. After so many neat and predictable days, it was nice to embrace the chaos of breaking his routine, even if it did ratchet up his anxiety.

Instead of getting tired, Persefonía seemed to become more and more energized with every new place. And Hectór, for the first time in a long time, started to enjoy himself.

Hours later, at a vintage sim of the Chicago World's Fair, Persefonía finally took a break.

"Okay," she said, taking a deep breath. "I'm officially tired."

"Finally!" Hectór gasped, collapsing next to her on the bench. "It's 2:00 a.m. Earthside, and I'm still circadian, you know."

"Two o'clock?" Persefonía shot up. "My mamá must be so worried! I've never been away from her this long. Oh, my God! Or wait—gods? Can I tell her where I am?"

"I'm sorry," Hectór said, shaking his head. For a second, he was almost jealous of Persefonía. What was it like to love someone so much it was devastating to be away from them, even if only for a few hours? He had no idea. *Man*, Hectór thought to himself, *I forgot how weird other people are.*

"My mamá… I was so mean. So ungrateful. She's *everything* to me."

He watched as she lectured herself on what a bad daughter she was and then went on some rant about how Iranian food was delicious but sneaky. He shifted uncomfortably, and that's when Persefonía noticed him again.

"I'm sorry," she hiccuped. He handed her a handkerchief. "I know this isn't your fault."

"It's okay," Hectór whispered. It was his turn to feel wretched. Is this what his ancestors had felt like, all those centuries ago? How could they have delighted in taking someone away from their home?

"I always wanted to move out. But not like this."

"Tell me about her," Hectór said. The words were out of his mouth before he could catch them. Feelings seemed so messy and complicated, but he wanted to know what it felt like to love someone that much.

Persefonía gave him a shaky smile, and something in Hectór's chest thawed. Souls never looked at him that way, never smiled at him that way: with hope. Today was a day of firsts.

Persefonía took a deep breath. And then she told him: told him how her mamá had always made sure she was safe; how she had worked odd jobs until she could afford a nursery of their own; how a competitor had discovered her magic with plants in their last town and they'd had to run away; and how, through it all, she had always supported her, always loved her, even if she couldn't give Persefonía all the freedom she wanted.

Persefonía sighed, spent. "It's silly. I've dreamed about leaving her so many times. Now all I want is one of her hugs."

Hectór sat stock-still, the lights and laughter of the World's Fair suddenly far away. Slowly, he turned his head to look at the beautiful girl beside him, at her swollen lips and tearstained cheeks. Despite his trapping her here, she still gave him that watery, hopeful smile.

Something broke inside Hectór, and instead of rushing to fix it, to reprogram the bug, he sat with this new feeling. Slowly, tenderness and affection crept into his heart. Just hearing her talk about her mom had made even more parts of Hectór's chest unfreeze. Yet, here he was, keeping her from that love.

He cleared his throat. If he couldn't fix the bug, then he could be the good programmer he was and find a work-around. "There *is* a loophole," he said quietly. If only GitHub could see him now.

Persefonía froze. "A loophole?"

"Yes," Hectór continued, voice shaky. "You don't have to necessarily stay in the underworld for six months. You just have to stay with *me*."

"Wait," Persefonía said, slowly turning to him. "So I could see my mamá? If you came with me?"

"Technically, yes." Hectór coughed. What was he doing? It wasn't any skin off his nose to keep her here. He didn't have to stay with her. He could drop her into a lovely sim and collect her when her period was up. Easy.

But then he looked at her, watched the rise and fall of her thick lashes, her lovely, brown-gold hair, her hazel eyes, and he knew he couldn't do that. He found himself bending toward her, like a flower to the sun, and he knew his life was forever changed.

Would his grandpa be thrilled? No. But would Hectór still be Persefonía's keeper for the required amount of time? Yes.

"Would you do that, Hectór?" Persefonía breathed, her tears drying on her cheeks.

Hectór looked away. Here came the embarrassing part. "I... um...I haven't been Earthside in a long time. I'm not good with new...environments." *Not good* was an understatement.

"You're afraid," she voiced the realization out loud. "No. It's more. You're terrified."

He turned away from her, ashamed. "It's safer here."

He hated how pathetic he sounded, but after everything Persefonía had just shared with him, he felt like he could do the same. It was horrifying being somewhere with new people and new things that were out of his grasp.

The last time he'd had to meet with his grandfather, he'd been forced to go to the above world and interact with all his staff. He hated touching their sweaty palms in greeting. He hated being somewhere he didn't know the language. Every new sight and smell seemed to assault his senses. It had taken weeks to recuperate from his trip.

What if something happened? What if he wasn't prepared? That was why his family was happy to let Hectór run Elysium, because the truth was, Hectór had volunteered for the job. Being down here in a domain he could control made him, if not happy, then at least feel a bit less overwhelmed.

What if he wanted to do something different, though? He couldn't stay in Elysium forever. He just hadn't felt like there *was* anything else for him until he had met Persefonía. It had only been a few hours, but she had planted a seedling of hope inside of him. Shouldn't he see if it could grow more?

"Hey," she said, interrupting Hectór's thoughts. "Take a deep breath, okay?"

He hadn't realized he had been hyperventilating. He inhaled deeply, releasing his brain from his anxiety spiral.

"It'll be okay," she reassured him, clasping her hand in his.

"Yeah?" he asked.

His jet-black eyes poured into her sunflower ones, and suddenly he didn't feel embarrassed for telling her the truth, why he never saw his parents aboveground. Why he never left this in-between space. He could feel his own eyes shining now, but instead of feeling embarrassed, he felt relieved. Here he was, baring his soul. Here he was, putting himself out there.

She gripped his hand tighter. "We can do this. You and me. I won't leave your side, and you won't leave mine, okay? We can go to all these places the sims are based on, travel the world, and it'll still be okay."

"Are you sure?" Hectór could feel the panic threatening to claw its way back in. "How do you know?"

"I don't, Hectór. You just have to have faith. I haven't seen much of the world, either. But we can do it together."

He gulped. The World's Fair had dissolved away, and the two were back in the waiting room. Suddenly, it didn't feel as comforting as it once did. Now it felt hollow and cold, the opposite of what being with Persefonía felt like.

"Okay." He gulped. "I can try."

Persefonía gripped his hand. "Thank you," she said, looking into his stricken face. "Thank you."

Hectór squeezed his eyes shut. He was so, so scared. But for once, staying here felt even scarier. The compass of his soul had shifted, with true north now pointing up. The thought of going somewhere new, he realized, could also be *exciting.* Unknowns could be fun, not just uncomfortable and draining. Being in the same place reliving the same day indefinitely now felt much worse than the unknown.

He opened his eyes up again, only to find Persefonía looking at him, and something about her gaze gave him the last bit of courage he needed.

"Here we go," he said. The white walls melted around them.

Hectór felt wind on his skin, and it was a shock to feel something he hadn't coded.

PERSEFONÍA

She blinked, her eyes adjusting to the warm glow of a real sun. There was the lone stoplight, swinging in the wind as the sun crested the horizon. Her phone beeped in her pocket, magically turning back on after being a dead brick all night; it was already 5:00 a.m.

Hectór gasped, removing his sweaty hand from hers. Persefonía could see the terror in his eyes, the way he shivered from fear and not from cold.

"Come on, our nursery's this way." She gently led the trembling boy to the corner of Main Street (its only corner, really) to their little plant store. Persefonía unlocked the door and turned on the light, praying her mamá wasn't too worried.

"Ah!" Hectór screamed, pointing to a figure in the corner. There, in the gloom, was Demetria, who appeared to have fallen asleep in the chair behind the register. With a start, Persefonía realized she had waited there the whole night, knowing that being surrounded by her plants gave her comfort when her daughter couldn't. Demetria startled at the noise.

"Mija?" Demetria asked. "Is that you?" Her voice was croaky and rough. There were bags under her eyes, the kind Persefonía hadn't seen since they'd first moved here and she'd had to work day and night to establish the store.

"Mamá!" Persefonía cried. She hugged Demetria close, inhaling her earthy patchouli smell. For the first time ever, Persefonía was glad to be here, in this small town, with her.

Hectór cleared his throat. Demetria looked up from her daughter's embrace and gasped at the pale boy who seemed to suck the color out of the jade greens and warm browns of the shop.

"Is he... Is that...?" Demetria's voice faded, as if unwilling to believe who she was looking at.

"Mamá, this is Hectór," Persefonía began in a calm, even voice. "He's a *friend*."

"Friend," Mamá spat, her relieved face turning to rage. "How could he be a *friend*?"

"It's nice to meet you, Ms.…uh…Demetria," Hectór stuttered.

Persefonía looked between her furious mother and scared new friend.

"I don't understand," Demetria spluttered. She looked up at her daughter, and the helpless expression on her face reminded Persefonía that her mother was getting older, that she wasn't as tough as she appeared to be.

"Hectór said that instead of staying in the underworld, I just have to stay with *him*. There's a loophole."

Demetria gasped a second time, looking between her daughter and the boy whose family was everything she had ever feared.

"So…you can stay? Here, with me?"

Persefonía nodded. "But Hectór has to stay, too."

Demetria pursed her lips. A thorny vine began to sprout from a pot next to the register, mirroring her displeasure with the idea.

"Mamá," Persefonía said, sitting down next to her. The day's events had shown Persefonía what she really wanted. What she *needed*. She girded herself for what she was about to say. For the words that would break her mother's heart even more than it had already shattered. "The worst happened. We've been found. That means we don't need to hide anymore. That means that *I* don't need to hide anymore."

Persefonía watched the understanding bleed across her mother's face like soil growing damp. "Oh" was all she said.

"I wouldn't mind staying here," Hectór said, finally breaking his silence. Persefonía shot him a glare that read *shut up shut up shut up!* "For like, a day?" he added, trying to save the situation.

She turned back to her mamá, waiting for her response.

Demetria swallowed hard. She stared at her daughter, as if trying to remember every line of her face. Persefonía sat calmly under her searching gaze.

"Every seed must find its sun," Demetria said sadly. "I suppose it's time to grow."

"Segura?" Persefonía asked, eyes brimming over with happy tears. Before, when she had been in a simulation, it felt both wonderful and wrong to travel the world without her mother knowing where she was. But now? To get her mother's blessing? That meant everything to her.

"Sí." Demetria hugged her daughter close, her tears smelling more like petrichor than salt. "You must grow your own roots where *you* choose to grow them. I can't keep you here forever."

Persefonía's heart practically burst, she was so happy in that moment. "Te quiero, Mami."

Hectór coughed. "Before we travel the world or whatever, I wouldn't mind seeing more of this place," he said, eyes looking hopefully at the shelves of succulents and monsteras. It was probably the most greenery he'd seen in years.

Persefonía smiled. "First stop on our grand tour," she said. "Welcome to Rancho Verde."

★ ★ ★ ★ ★

THORNFIELD

a remix of *Jane Eyre*
Monica Sanz

"I remembered that the real world was wide, and that a varied field of hopes and fears, of sensations and excitements, awaited those who had the courage to go forth into its expanse, to seek real knowledge of life amidst its perils."

—Charlotte Brontë, *Jane Eyre*

I should have let him burn.

I was asleep when a tightness in my throat woke me. I found my room filled with smoke pirouetting in the dark like phantoms. I hurried to the door, half-dressed and frantic, with one thought in mind: Adelina, my charge. Was she responsible for the fire that caused the smoke? Reason told me she was. Her magic was unstable, and she was always afraid. Who wouldn't be, knowing they were accused of being a bruja and were sentenced to die?

I pulled open the door. My feet, thoughts, and breaths stopped; a bluish-green hue glowed from down the hall, confirming my suspicion: witch fire. To make matters worse, it didn't come from the direction of Adelina's room, but of her brother, Ezra's.

I'm ashamed to admit it, but I hesitated. So many of my problems would have been solved had I simply raced the other way, to Adelina's room, collected her, and carried her away from this heinous place before anyone was the wiser. I should have. Adelina was the reason I had come here, after all.

"Her father, Eduardo Calderon, has requested an evaluation," my sister superior said the day I left the Convent for the first time, handing me the dossier—my first-ever assignment. I was eighteen now, which meant it was time for me to do my part. I was being sent to search for brujas in the Convent's realm.

My hands trembled, but pressing them onto my lap, I forced myself to listen as Sister Superior went on.

"Señor Calderon claims that some days before his daughter Adelina's thirteenth birthday, the flowers in their courtyard rotted, then the trees surrounding their estate. The morning she turned thirteen, the ponds on their land turned to blood. She is the only one of manifesting age on the premises. Her nineteen-year-old brother, Ezra, already passed his evaluation."

I nodded. When a witch came of age, unchecked power rushed through their veins and often caused disturbances. I had witnessed this often. I had been sent to the Convent's orphanage at the age of nine after my aunt no longer cared to keep me. I didn't remember much about my life before then except for loss, first my parents, then my uncle. With him gone, my aunt sent me away, and I lost the last of my family and my home. I was no better than a bruja: unwanted, unloved, never to belong. Given my luck, it was a wonder I wasn't discovered to possess witch malady at thirteen, when all orphans at the Convent are tested, lest the nuns inadvertently bestow their kindness on a bruja. But fate had something harsher in store for me.

"You are to go to her in her father's estate of Maldición and conduct her trials. When she is undoubtedly found to possess witch malady, she will be purged."

Purged.

The word rattled the bars where I kept my memories safely

tucked away. To the Convent, brujas had no place in the world, and as the ruling power in the realm, they would see to it that all brujas burned...as they had with Helen, my best friend and my heart.

"I will do it." I took the folder and started for the door, lest she see how my eyes watered and hands trembled, the memory of Helen's screams crowding my thoughts.

"Best of luck, Paloma," Sister Superior said behind me. "I'm told Maldición is not the great estancia it once was. There is nothing left now... Nothing good, anyway."

As I sat in the carriage en route to Maldición, I read through the folder. It said that at one time, the hinterland boasted profitable coffee plantations, grazing fields crowded with workers and animals, and a lush cloud forest cut by a generous stream that ran from the mountaintop to the southern coast. But when we arrived, all that greeted me were acres of barren wasteland, gnarled brambles covered in oozing, crimson thorns, and the pungent scent of sulfur. What trees stood resembled the charred remains of burned brujas; their split trunks seeped blood, and their branches rose like arms, shielding them from the pain of a pyre death.

But worse than the view and smell was the silence. There was merely the sound of my own breathing, the groaning carriage, and the tap of hoofbeats on the gravel as the driver entered the gates of Maldición, a scripted *M* wrought into the rusted iron.

Eduardo Calderon was a notorious inventor of torture devices, commissioned by the Convent to build contraptions meant to peel away a bruja's evil flesh in order to free the spirit. He'd named his hacienda Maldición, as he considered himself a curse to all brujas.

He was.

But I would make sure Adelina, his own daughter, did not join the ranks of the many brujas who had died at the hands of his contraptions.

★★★

I sprinted down to Ezra's room and pushed the door open. Flames crawled up the curtains, illuminating his room in shifting shades of green and blue, and he lay unaware.

The brujas and their sympathizers who had secretly recruited and mentored me after Helen's death said I was to focus on the goal: save the bruja and ignore all else. I didn't question it at the time. I was angry at the Convent…at the world, just as all sympathizers were. They, too, had lost loved ones to the trials and the Convent's cruelty. They channeled that rage into forming their network of rogue nuns and evaluators, part of a larger movement seeking to undermine and destroy the Convent. They welcomed me into their ranks, taught me to focus my pain and rage into something useful.

But though they taught me all I know, from conducting false trials to smuggling brujas to the many safe houses across the realm, they never once spoke about the conundrum of morality. Should I let an innocent person die, if it meant a bruja would live? Was I to play God and decide? Did that not make me the same as the Convent we all so wished to destroy?

Standing there in the smoky dark, I thought of the many brujas who had fallen to Señor Calderon's inventions, a man whose footsteps Ezra was expected to follow. Could I—should I—let the potential for such hatred and evil remain in this world, or let it burn as so many brujas had burned? As Helen had burned?

In those moments, debating my integrity amid the gathering smoke, my first meeting with Ezra came to me in a burst of paralyzing memory.

The maid ushered me into the drawing room where portraits of Señor Calderon hung on the walls, including one where he stood proudly, one booted foot elevated upon a pile of corpses. Brujas. The sisters at the Convent spoke of his greatness, heroism, and beauty, none of which I saw. Rather, he was tall and reedy, with a tight, venomous set to his mouth. I was sure if his mouth were open, I would find it crowded with fangs stained with blood and witch flesh.

"The Convent sent *you*?" a voice asked, startling me. I spun to find a young man with tousled curly hair standing by the terraced window, staring out onto the rotting woods. He looked like a younger version of Señor Calderon and shared the same grave expression. "What qualifies you to evaluate my sister? You look practically her age."

I hated that I'd wondered the same on the drive here. At only eighteen, I was the youngest of the Convent's evaluators. Had I been too ambitious in my desire to prevent Helen's fate from befalling any more innocent girls? What if I didn't have what it took to fool the Convent and the likes of Eduardo Calderon? Had the sympathizers—so ardent in their mission—taught me all I needed to know, or had they sent me out half-trained, hoping for luck to make up for whatever training I lacked?

Perhaps, but a bruja needed me, and I wouldn't fail this time.

"I'm a trained evaluator, sir. My age is irrelevant," I said. "And, no offense, but you are not much older than I."

A slight smile passed his lips, as if he held a secret between himself and the woods outside. "Indeed, I'm not, but I'm not the one who might sentence my sister to die, am I?"

I would never sentence a bruja to die. His sister and I would be long gone before that ever happened.

"You're not," I said. "And to that end, I was told I was meeting Señor Calderon."

"My father is a busy man. There are many brujas in this world, after all. My name is Ezra Calderon, and I will be overseeing your testing of my sister. You will meet her in the morning."

Cold skittered down my spine. "Forgive me, but evaluators typically conduct these evaluations alone. We find when family is present, manifestations take longer, as brujas feel ashamed of their power and strive to suppress it in front of their loved ones—"

"If there is a problem, you may go, and Father will find another evaluator."

His stare was wrath and fire, and all at once I was afraid. Was I truly up for this challenge? Could I conduct my false tests, earn Adelina's trust, and take her from this place right under Ezra's and Señor Calderon's noses?

I would have to.

"That won't be necessary," I said. "I will interview her tomorrow, and then we will begin testing. I assure you, you can trust me."

He chuckled, humorless and bitter. "I know all about the Convent's bloodlust. You probably *hope* my sister is a bruja, a broken thing you can rip apart. I will not let you put this blame on her without proper proof."

"Despite what you may think, I am not a machine without feelings," I ventured. "With all my heart, I hope I find no magic in your sister. But you must be ready to accept that my test will only support what the Convent already believes." I motioned to the black woods. "Someone is to blame for this."

"The woods began to rot *before* her birthday. Yes, the river turned to blood on her birthday, but that must be a coincidence. It is no secret there are many who hate my father for the inventions he supplies to the Convent. Someone else has cursed these lands, and *they* deserve to die."

Anger coiled in my belly. Of course he thought of brujas as broken things and didn't care if *another* witch did this and died for their actions, so long as it wasn't *his* sister.

Still, I tamed my rage and explained, "Perhaps, but often with brujas of great power, their magic begins leaching out before it formally manifests on their thirteenth birthday, hence us testing your sister now."

"Then, conduct your tests, but I will be watching you, closely."

I opted not to protest lest I draw his suspicion, and I nodded. "Very well."

"My father expects an answer in a week's time," he said. "He is having a demonstration to test his latest contraption. If you do not prove that Adelina is not a bruja by week's end, the machine will have its first victim."

"Understood," I said, with no intention of letting that happen.

I ran to Ezra's bedside and shook him. "Ezra, wake up!" I shook him again. "Ezra!"

He didn't rouse. Was I too late? Would I now have to live with this added guilt on my conscience?

As I shook him again and again, I cursed myself for having been so foolish as to leave Adelina alone when she was in such a state of anxiety and worry.

I'd seen what happened when she got upset before...

Adelina sat before me on a small stool. She was thin and pale, dark circles cradling brown eyes that focused on her hands, which she wrung on her lap.

"Will you not look at me, Adelina?" I poured her a glass of water and slid it over to her, but she flinched and recoiled into Ezra.

"I promise, I only want to talk to you and get to know you a little better and perhaps learn why you're so scared or mad... or sad."

If I could find the source of her sorrow and anger, I could show her she was not alone. More, that with me, she was safe. I had to establish trust. If we were going to escape successfully, I couldn't have her magic rotting our every surrounding and giving away our location. In finding out what upset her, I could help calm her down and, in turn, help her control her powers.

"I am not sad," she said, her voice just above a whisper. "Or mad."

"You're frightened, then," I ventured.

She shut her eyes tightly, her grip tightening on Ezra's hand.

"Can you tell me what frightens you?" I already had a sense of what scared her. I knew whether she failed or passed, the outcome was the same. She would face either her father's contraption at the end of the week or a horde of angry villagers ready to purge her themselves, and I decided: I had to take her away, regardless of whether she proved to be a bruja or not.

"What is the point of this inquiry?" Ezra asked. "Aren't you supposed to be here conducting your *tests*?"

"Yes, but there is more to the trials than simple *yes* or *no* answers. We also aim to gain knowledge with the tests we run, so that the Convent might gain better insight into what triggers a bruja's magic in the first place…and the test will go much smoother if she is not scared of me." I also had to do everything in my power to gain her trust quickly before our imminent escape.

He chuckled bitterly. "Or maybe you revel in her fear of you." Beside him, Adelina curled into herself. "In the power you hold over her life."

Ezra couldn't have been more wrong, but movement at the window caught my attention before I could conjure a response. Vines slithered along the panes, sprouting bloody thorns that scraped against the glass. Surely this was Adelina's fear manifesting. I hadn't even conducted the first test.

"Maybe we can discuss this later," I said, forcing a lightness to my tone. "You're scaring her."

"Scaring her? She's long been scared, hearing the many brujas begging for their lives during Father's house parties."

"Ezra, please stop," Adelina begged, shaking her head from side to side as if to rid her mind of his words and whatever memories they prompted. At the table, the water within her glass rippled, and the vines along the window continued to grow as if desperate to claw their way inside. Furious, Ezra went on.

"Do you know, he and the guests hunt them for sport, chasing them through the forest?" he said. "Other times, they make them tell their fortunes, and whoever gets the worse fate gets to kill them. Wouldn't you be scared—"

Adelina clapped her hands over her ears. "Stop it!"

The glass of water shattered, and my breath caught.

There was no more water, only blood smearing across the table like spilled wine.

Ezra yanked Adelina from her chair and moved her behind him. "It wasn't her. She didn't cause this. I—"

"I know," I lied, cutting him off, and knelt before Adelina. I had to calm her down and help her rein in her power—because yes, she had caused this. And if I didn't calm her down, it would only grow worse, and taking her from here would become all the more impossible. "Everything is fine, Adelina. This is all my fault. I should have known everything in Maldición is contaminated, including the water. Good thing you didn't drink any of it," I said, forcing a smile.

"So you will not report it?" Ezra asked. "You will not sentence her to die immediately?"

"I must include it in my reports, but I will not sentence her to die. Yet. This was only the interview portion. Tomorrow is the real test."

At the window, the tangled mass of vines stopped growing, and the fang-like thorns receded.

Ezra nodded, though he watched me warily as he walked his sister out of the room. "Thank you," he said. "And I am sorry for what I said."

I saw that the agony of potentially losing his sister was a mirror image of my own, a deep, dark, monstrous ache with teeth and claws. He was swift to turn his attention back to his sister, though I still felt seen by him, as if our souls recognized one another's pain and called out for communion.

All at once, whatever offense I felt before waned. He had the markings of an ally: he did not want me here, evaluating his sister or sentencing her to die. I could use this to my favor; it wouldn't hurt to have someone willing to help should my plans of escape go awry.

"It's been forgotten. All of it," I said, hoping they both understood I could be trusted.

Adelina glanced at me, but the moment I met her stare, she dropped her gaze as if afraid I would see the bruja malady within her.

I didn't need to see it. The blood spilled on the table was all the proof I needed.

I promptly wiped it up, set the napkin in the fireplace, and burned it.

Finally, Ezra startled awake and, quickly assessing the situation, lunged out of bed. Together, we tore down and stomped on the curtains, until the fire was doused. He pushed open the windows and pressed his hands on the sill, his head hung low between his slumped shoulders.

"Ezra..."

He turned to me, eyes pooled with distress, and he nodded, knowing what had to be done. We both knew, since that morning in the pond...

There was a pond in Maldición that hadn't yet turned to blood. Adelina said it was her favorite place, which further convinced me that the girl was wholly unaware of the havoc her emotions were causing. It was the one place that held meaning for her, she had subconsciously spared, while the rest of the grounds quickly succumbed to her growing fear. But it wasn't her fault; she simply needed to learn to control it.

I let Adelina play at the pond's edge to relax before the test, and Ezra approached and sat beside me.

"Adelina doesn't know how to swim," he said, his gaze locked on the grand statue of Señor Calderon looming over the pond.

"I will be with her the entire time. Once I take her to a comfortable depth, I will submerge her and hold her under until she's out of air. The natural will to live will cause her to fight, and if she is a bruja, this is when magic will come to her aid. Given the state of Maldición, I suspect we will see a change in the water. If so, she will be detained until your father's demonstration. But while she is with me, she is safe."

He nodded, paling, and looked to the pond. "So you've done this before, you've seen this test draw out a bruja's power?"

"I haven't personally conducted this test, no, but I have seen it done. When I was younger, and..." Memories pressed down on my chest, and I gulped back the words.

"And..." he prompted.

"Nothing." I rose and dusted off the back of my skirt. "Yes, I can vouch for its accuracy."

I started to move away, but Ezra touched my arm, saying, "That wasn't what you were going to say."

I hugged myself, hating how our mutual sorrow linked us like an invisible string. When one of us drifted too far into pain, it tugged on the other. I wasn't certain that I could trust him, but I needed an ally. It would be better for me to have a partner in this than continue to pretend to work against him.

And so I said, "When I was Adelina's age, a friend of mine failed her test."

Emotions knotted my tongue and I paused, but Ezra's warm hand touched mine when I finally let him really see me. I should have drawn it away, but I didn't. It felt good not to be so alone in my pain.

Remembering my aim, I drew my hand away.

"It's time, Adelina," I said and plucked out my pocket watch, the Convent's emblem—an all-seeing eye—engraved on the metal lid. "Perhaps you can help, Ezra? Once the arrow reaches the eye, the trial is over." He did not know this watch was altered and would mark time more quickly than it was supposed to, allowing me to pull up a bruja before the time her powers manifested. Escaping would be easier when she passed the test: no one would expect a bruja to flee after a test proved their innocence.

"I want no part of this. I will not condemn my sister—"

"Ezra, please. There can be no doubt about the test's validity. Given what happened yesterday, it is best if you hold the watch."

Ezra took the watch, and I met Adelina at the riverbank, took her hand, and led her into the water.

Submerged to our thighs, I turned to Adelina, pressed my hand to her back and chest, and tipped her backward into the pond. She was calm, if somewhat stiff, but when her air ran out and the instinct to live kicked in, she fought to get up. I braced and held her down, hollowly reciting my Convent vows to keep time and ignore the pull of my memories.

Adelina thrashed and clutched my wrist, but the water didn't allow for a firm grip.

"Time," Ezra yelled from the riverbank. "It's time, Paloma!"

It was. I had reached half of my vows, and the stopwatch would have marked the all-seeing eye by now. I began to bring her out of the water but stopped myself just in time—because I glanced up and saw that Señor Calderon watched the test from across the pond. He held a pocket watch and was keeping his own time, verifying my test.

"Paloma!" Ezra yelled, but I fought against the desire to pull Adelina out of the water, not with Señor Calderon watching.

I finished my vows as Adelina's body grew limp in my arms. Ezra rushed into the water and helped me yank her out and drag her to shore, where she collapsed against her brother's arms, water bubbling out of her mouth with each racking cough.

"You're fine, Addy. You didn't manifest any powers. You're not a bruja," he said, his voice a mix of relief and unveiled rage. "Why didn't you pull her out sooner?"

I couldn't answer or look at him but rather only at Señor Calderon approaching the pond. Kneeling, he dipped his fingers into the water and drew them out, grimacing as he pulled out a handkerchief and wiped his hands, his fingertips stained red with water that had turned to blood.

Adelina *had* failed her test, and I had failed her.

★ ★ ★

After the events at the pond, I knew Ezra would not want to speak to me, but I had to apologize...and convince him to let me take Adelina away to one of the safe houses where the Convent wouldn't find her. Moreover, to distract Señor Calderon as I smuggled her out of the house.

Closing my fingers into a fist, I knocked on Ezra's door. It groaned open, and he appeared.

"I have nothing to say to you," he said, deadened, his lashes wet and eyes bloodshot.

"Please, Ezra. It's important."

He walked back inside but didn't close the door behind him.

I followed him into the crowded room and pressed the door shut. On every flat surface that could support them, there were stacks of books on brujas and the manifestation of their power. Between them were dead things: moths and butterflies held pinned behind frames, rats and frogs contained in jars. The floor was littered with papers crumpled into balls and torn pages with discarded thoughts and equations.

I explored, considering the best way to broach the subject of taking his sister away, and whether what I was seeing made that still the best course of action. He stood at the window, his frame illuminated in the flickers of lightning from an approaching storm.

"Do you practice your father's methods?" I asked, needing to know my trust would not be misplaced.

"No. I study brujas, hoping to find out how to fix them without having to hurt them. If they weren't broken, then they wouldn't have to die...like my sister." His moss-green eyes met mine, glinting with fresh tears. "Why didn't you pull her up?"

"I'm sorry, Ezra. It wanted to, but when I saw your father... I couldn't pull her up or else he'd know."

"Know what?"

"That the watch you had was altered. It marks time faster,

allowing for me to pull up a bruja before their powers usually manifest."

His brow furrowed, then rose as awareness dawned on him. "You're…a sympathizer?" he asked, and I saw the war between fear and hope raging within him.

"Yes, and I would no sooner sentence Adelina to die than I would Helen…my friend who failed her trials. She failed them because of me."

He sat still, stunned, doubting, and so I filled the silence, recalling, "It was during my own trials. One of the sisters at the orphanage held me down in the water until my lungs were wrung out of all breath. Her name was Sister Gloria, and she hated me from the moment I questioned how someone so cruel could claim to honor God. She was certain I was evil, and so even though I manifested no power, she kept me submerged…"

Memories threatened to drag me back and paralyze me, but Ezra let out a shuddering breath and brought me back to the present.

"The waters parted then, and Sister Gloria let me collapse onto the muddy ground. I was certain I was responsible for parting the lake and would die a bruja's death, but then I realized Sister Gloria did not look at me. Instead, she stared at the riverbank where Helen held a hand before her, creating a path in the water with her magic. Whether she knew of her power or not, I don't know, but she used her magic to save my life. As I watched her burn, I promised her that I would never let a bruja suffer her fate, that one day I would be worthy of her sacrifice. And here I am."

He blinked once and again, and I waited on bated breath, hoping that putting my trust in him hadn't been a mistake. All was lost if it had.

Tears filled his eyes, and he moved to me, reached his fingertips to my face but dithered, as if scared. Scared that I was lying. Scared that none of this was real. I leaned into his touch, and then we were embracing. I had never been held in such a way. It felt like forgiveness.

"So you will take her to safety?" he asked.

I nodded. "There is a large network across the Convent's realm. We offer brujas sanctuary and train them to grow and control their magic, then reintroduce them into society with different names and lives."

"And I will never see her again..."

"It is the only way to save her, Ezra. Will you help me?"

Ezra pushed back off the window. His sorrow in that moment felt so raw and potent, I reached for him instinctively, certain it was going to tear him apart. But then he looked at me, and once again, I saw myself in him. Saw resoluteness wash over his gaze, the same I felt when I'd watched Helen burn and decided the monstrous pain I'd felt would not be for nothing.

"Very well. Take Adelina. I will handle my father."

"Thank you, Ezra."

"I suppose this is goodbye," he said. I nodded, yet neither of us moved. "Thank you, Paloma. Not just for saving Adelina, but... I should have been brave enough to stop my father long ago. Now I can be brave while you take Adelina away."

Taking my hands, he gave them a gentle squeeze and departed, and the invisible string between us tugged. I didn't expect it to hurt so much.

Back at my room, I moved to the window, a lamp in hand, and held it toward the black woods, turning it on and off to alert the sympathizer who would drive us away. The same pattern flickered back in the distance, and my knees weakened at what now had to be done.

I fetched Adelina, and thankfully, she did not fight me at first, but when we dashed out of her room, she dug her heels into the floor and stopped.

"Adelina, we must go—"

She looked at me, fully, eyes wide and panicked. "You have to help Ezra!"

"Ezra is helping us so I can take you away to safety."

"You don't understand! Helen says I will be fine, but Father will kill Ezra unless you help."

Cold tore through me at the sound of my dead best friend's name. "What did you say?"

She glanced beside me, and though I sensed her terror, she set her jaw. "I see brujas, the dead ones. I see and hear them, especially when I get upset. There is one that's always standing beside you, though she is much fainter now than when you arrived. Her name is Helen, and she says she is happy, and you must be, too… And for you to remember what she said, about the world of spirits all around us…"

"Are you scared you will be found to be a bruja?" Helen asked as we waited on the riverbank at our turn for testing.

"Sister Gloria already thinks I am one, so I suppose I wouldn't be surprised. Are you afraid?"

Helen shrugged a shoulder, her red curls like a mass of fire atop her head. "Not really. I have this sense that there is…more than this life. I like to think there is a world full of spirits, protecting us."

"Hush, Helen. Someone might hear."

"I'm not frightened, Paloma. Fear is poison. Look at the Convent. They fear brujas because they do not understand their power and therefore seek to destroy them. But if I am a bruja, will that change who I am? Will you feel differently about me?"

"Never."

She smiled, tugged a daisy from the ground, and threaded it in my hair. "And neither will I think differently of you. Bruja or not, I will love you forever, and the Convent may burn my flesh, but they can't ever take that love away."

There was no way Adelina could have known about Helen's words to me so long ago, words that set my life's course. And so I ran. I hid Adelina in my room and raced to Ezra in Señor Calderon's workroom in the attic. I had to trust Helen—I did. She'd loved me in life and in death, and she wouldn't fail me now.

"You can't kill her. I won't let you," Ezra said as I entered the room. Neither of them turned my way, they were so consumed by each other. "She's your daughter—"

"She is a bruja, Ezra," Señor Calderon said. "Look at what she's done to the lands. She is no daughter of mine."

Ezra shook his head, and a bloody tear spilled onto his cheek. When the droplet fell to the ground, it bloomed into a black flower.

For the first time since I watched Helen die, my world stopped turning. "Ezra?"

"It can't be," Señor Calderon said, eyes wide. "Your sister has bewitched you."

"No, Father. This magic, it's all mine." Ezra sighed and soon, vines slithered, and flowers bloomed from every crevice in the room. "I learned to hide it, but as I grew older, my powers got stronger...as did my hatred of you, of what you do to my kind, of how scared and powerless I felt around you. Then Adelina's birthday approached, and I feared she was like me and would not be able to hide it. My fear and loathing are what rotted your precious woods."

"Those are lies," Eduardo hissed. "No son of mine would ever—"

"Would ever what?" He held his open hands up at his sides; roses bloomed in his bloodied palms. "Would ever like flowers?"

The next moments were a blur of petals, thorns, and blood. Señor Calderon lunged for Ezra, his roar feral. I raced to stop him, but Ezra raised a hand, and vines burst through the walls and the floor and the window and wrapped around the older man's arms and feet like shackles.

Ezra moved closer to his father. Slowly, thorns grew from the reedy trunks, piercing Señor Calderon's skin. "How does it feel, to be tortured simply for existing?"

"Ezra, don't." I grabbed his arm, hoping that this invisible string between us hadn't yet severed. That I could pull him back before he did something he would regret. "I can help you, but if you kill him, you will be the same as him."

"Aren't I already? While he was murdering my kind, I stood by, studying and tinkering, trying to find ways to fix us, but I failed, and it won't ever stop. And when we are all dead, they will turn on their next idea of who is different."

"But you didn't fail, Ezra. How could you? There is no fixing witches, because witches are not broken."

At this, a sob poured from Ezra. His knees buckled, and he collapsed into my arms, the vines loosening from around his father. I'd known the witch responsible for the blight had been festering with rage and sorrow, so much it leached from them and poisoned the land. I hadn't observed such a rage in Adelina, but it stained Ezra. Connected us. Now, as he wept, roses pooled around me, the vines along the room grew flowers, and bees emerged from within like windswept pollen.

Yet, this beauty and Señor Calderon's hate could not coexist. Dragging himself up, Señor Calderon ran for his son, tripped on a vine, and tumbled out the broken window.

It pains me that Ezra will live with the memory of what happened to his father, and every time I think about that night, I wish I had asked Ezra to come with Adelina and me and let Señor Calderon burn. But what's done is done, and Adelina and Ezra are free. And with my report turned in to Sister Superior, the case is closed.

"The fire raged into the early morning," I said. "When it was finally tamed, the wreckage was searched, and no bodies were found other than Señor Calderon's, strewn about a bed of black roses."

"And what happened next?" Sister Superior asked, her brow troubled.

"I concluded my testing of Adelina Calderon and found her to possess not one ounce of magic. She is as small and plain and little as me."

"Well done, Paloma. To think that all this time it was Señor Calderon repressing his powers and poisoning his own land. Such a champion of our cause. What a waste."

"Indeed." I rose and walked to the door, my next assignment dossier in hand.

"Do you know if his son plans to continue his work in Maldición? His malady aside, Eduardo Calderon was a tremendous inventor. Surely the same could be expected of his son."

"Ezra has decided to devote his time to studying witch powers and their manifestations."

My superior smiled. "So the legacy of Maldición lives on."

"Not quite," I said, adjusting the black rose in my hair. "It is not called Maldición anymore, but Thornfield."

★ ★ ★ ★ ★

LA COTORRA Y EL FLAMBOYÁN

a remix of "The Nightingale and the Rose"
Amparo Ortiz

"Night after night have I sung of him, though I knew him not: night after night have I told his story to the stars, and now I see him."

—Oscar Wilde, "The Nightingale and the Rose"

Only fools believe that death is a promise.

To me, promises imply agreement. They suggest we have a choice or say in the matter. But we don't consent to death once we're born. We never ask to be born in the first place.

Neither do the beauties found in each garden on Isla Esmeralda. Whether it's the amapolas on the eastern coast, the Flor de Magas in the north and west, or the sprawling flamboyán garden in the south, our flowers don't bloom knowing they'll die. These gardens weren't even barren during winter—Isla Esmeralda remained a lush haven through the seasons.

Then came la bruja.

We don't know where she once called home. But one night, three years ago, she appeared in the flamboyán garden, her red dress flowing in the wind, and walked up to the couple stargazing near a fountain. Then she dragged them behind a hedge and fed on their souls.

She loved it so much that she never left.

None of the islanders agreed to have their heads cut off, their burned carcasses tossed into the sea, never mind deserved it.

The more la bruja consumed souls, the faster a chill spread across Isla Esmeralda, freezing everything from root to tip. *Killing* everything. She brought the cold and doomed us all. But la bruja spared shape-shifters, those who could turn into birds. She needed a magical army to fetch her more souls from beyond the island.

I'm one of her soldiers. My station is the flamboyán garden.

Where I also watch over the boy I love.

A boy cursed to slumber inside a glass coffin.

"Mind your manners, Cotorra. It's rude to stare."

La bruja runs her crimson nails through her waist-long hair. Even when I'm in human form, she refers to me as the bird I shift into. So what if my winter coat and leather clothes are as emerald as my feathers? I'm still a *girl* right now. My real name is Angélica Mercedes, but there's no one left that remembers it.

"I'm sorry." I only bow to aim my glare at the snow. Making me apologize for looking at Arnaldo Santiago is more salt in the wound. His beauty is undeniable. I've never seen brown skin that glistens like his when moonlight falls upon it. It's midnight, and the full moon casts a glow on Arnaldo that would make the sea jealous. I don't have the privilege of knowing what it feels like to touch his curls, but they look so, so soft. I once held silk that had warmed under an afternoon sun: Mamá had left her scarf on the rocking chair in our porch. I imagine Arnaldo's curls under the sun, too, and I suspect they would feel the same way.

Well, they would've before la bruja cast this wretched winter. Now his hair must be as cold as her heart. His curse doesn't let him grow old. He's been trapped for three years, but centuries will pass and he'll still look seventeen. He'll still be the same boy who stole my heart, my very breath, when I was fourteen years old, and I'll be long dead.

"No te culpo," la bruja says. "He *is* lovely."

Is it supposed to make me feel better that she doesn't blame me for staring? All it does is make me want to dig a hole in the snow, shove her inside, and bury her forever.

"You wanted to see me," I say instead. The faster I get my orders for the day, the faster I can leave her side.

"I'm changing your route this week. The bodies you've brought me have been too old." La bruja grimaces. "Why do you bring such decayed creatures?"

"Their souls don't age."

"But they're not as tasty." La bruja licks her lips, still shuddering. "I want more like him." She taps the frosted glass twice. "Beautiful boys."

Arnaldo is seventeen. Boys like him have their whole lives ahead of them. It's best to choose someone whose days are almost up, even though it's still murder. Even though I'm still participating in taking someone's life. Not only am I going against everything I stand for, I'm staining my family's name with the blood of innocents. I'm shaming their memory, their sacrifice, to please a tyrant. And I'm corrupting my own soul.

But I can't challenge la bruja. *Anything* I say or do will be considered a slight. If I want her to spare the young, I must appeal to what she loves more than eating souls: her power.

"Beauty is subjective," I say, "but age is undisputed. I may bring you someone I deem attractive and you could easily think they're foul. An older soul also means more life experience. They've felt more passion, hope, regret, fear...all the things that nourish your magic. Without a broader range of emotions in your diet, you can still be strong, but you'll never be invincible."

La bruja nods. "You make a fair point. However, youth doesn't always mean less life experience. Their range of emotions could be broader and far more complex than that of an older soul."

Damn it.

"Besides, beautiful things grant me pleasure that age never could. Take Arnaldo, for instance." La bruja laughs cruelly. "I've seen you staring at him. Clearly, you're quite familiar with the pleasure that comes with gazing upon a beautiful face, even if he'll never be with you."

Don't fall for it. She's baiting you.

"What's this new route I'm taking?" I try changing the subject.

But la bruja laughs again. "Why is it that every time I find a beautiful boy, there's a long line of silly girls thinking they're the one he'll fall for? It's like a *disease.* So many broken hearts in the making, and no one seems to see it coming. Or perhaps they do, but they're too delusional to accept their inevitable fates."

This witch knows nothing about me. She doesn't know why I care about Arnaldo. I don't just see him as a beautiful face, and I never will.

"He thought he was invincible," la bruja continues. "He swore he could charm me into letting him out of the island unscathed. That he could buy time for his mother to sail away and for him to meet her after he'd killed me. But that's what beauty and money do to a weak mind. They feed lies in the shape of truths, and he gobbled them up."

She's lucky I can't hit her. I'm not looking to end up chained to a cliff or burned at the stake like my parents. They died so I could fly out of Isla Esmeralda, a distraction that turned into their dooms. They died so I could repay them by failing to escape. La bruja caught me before I could leave the amapola garden. All because of the boy she says has a weak mind.

What he *really* has is a good heart. This is the boy who offered me his seat on the first day of seventh grade. I was late, as usual. Our instructor didn't think I'd show up. But I did…to a full classroom. Arnaldo hadn't uttered a word—just stood up and waved at the empty chair in the middle of the room—while everyone else stared at him. He then interrupted another class and brought back a chair for himself. I was so flustered that I couldn't even thank him.

That was the beginning of Arnaldo taking root in my heart. He set himself apart the first day of seventh grade, and gradually did more and more until I couldn't see any other boy the same way ever again. It didn't matter that we never spoke and ran in different circles. That he was so popular and coveted. Kindness always leaves an unforgettable mark on anyone's soul.

It's not Arnaldo's fault that I failed my parents. He never asked me to help him, watch over him, care for him at all... *I'm* the only one to blame.

I still remember shifting into my cotorra body, ready to take flight in the middle of la bruja's snowstorm, when he tripped on a rock. Arnaldo landed at my tiny feet. He was crying, bleeding profusely from one ear, with sweat and dirt mixed all over his reddened face. His silk clothes were torn, as if claws had scratched up the fabric.

"My island is lost," he whispered. "Everything I love is lost. My life...is worth nothing."

"No. Get up. You need to get up!" I whispered back. I couldn't let this kind heart—this familiar stranger always out of reach yet so, so close—quit. I couldn't let him *die*. It was the only way I knew to repay him.

But my words were only squawks to Arnaldo. Shape-shifters in animal form can't communicate with humans. I was too deep in the moment—the unrelenting chaos—that I forgot.

By the time I heard their screams, my parents were burning.

They weren't shape-shifters; magic had skipped a generation on both sides of the family. I grew up listening to them recall how they celebrated my birth for three months straight. At long last, there was another magic-bearer in their bloodlines. I would leave feathers all around our house. Mamá had to sweep multiple times a day, but she never complained. She said I was a gift to Isla Esmeralda and that I shouldn't forget it.

And I let them die.

"Oh, you're not listening to me anymore, are you?" La bruja clucks her tongue. "Serves me right for treating such a lowly creature as someone worthy of my time and effort."

I put my hands behind my back. If I keep them at my sides, they're likely to find her neck and attempt a swift twist.

"This is just what I look like when I'm concentrating."

"Sure it is." La bruja runs a hand across the glass. "You know what I haven't done in a long, long time?"

"What would that be?"

She draws a circle in the glass above Arnaldo's lips. "Play a game."

I can't retaliate or refuse her. The rage nestles deeper and deeper in my heart, shaping it into a hollow cavity. One day I'm going to wake up as a shell of myself; I won't recognize the girl staring back in the mirror. La bruja is determined to shove me toward that fate, but she's also the reason I haven't embraced it yet. I never want my soul and hers to be the same. To let hatred consume me until I'm nothing more than poison and decay. Everything inside of her is rotten, and I refuse to waste away.

"Which?" I ask against my will.

"I ask for something, and you find it. Kind of like your soul hunts." La bruja looks from Arnaldo to me, smirking. "Do you wish to save this beautiful boy?"

My heart leaps into my throat.

She's asking me about the *one* thing I've secretly begged for. I can't bring back my parents. I can't defrost the island I've always called home. Arnaldo Santiago still lives, though. His glass coffin can only be opened with la bruja's magic, but she's never been willing to do so. I've already asked her to—right after she captured him. When I turned to watch my parents burn, she swept in and snatched Arnaldo. He'd tried to kill her, she said, and she wanted him to pay. Death was too kind, she said, a mercy.

She chose eternal slumber instead. A lifetime of nightmares

forcing him to relive her invasion, the islanders' heads being cut off, their bodies burning and being thrown into the sea afterward. Sometimes I see him wincing as if he's right there again. I see him hurting for everyone. I hurt knowing that I can't change the past. At least Arnaldo is only being haunted behind closed eyes. But I'm breathing inside a waking nightmare. I have to end both his pain and mine. I have to avenge my parents…redeem myself for failing them…and it starts with freeing the boy in the glass coffin.

"¿Cotorra?"

"Sí. I wish to save him."

La bruja nods. "If you win the game, I'll wake him up and set him free, unharmed. My word is my promise to you. But if you lose, he remains locked in here forever."

So I truly *am* fighting to save him: there's no obvious trickery in her conditions. Unless I'm not being careful enough? La bruja is smart; she could still be laying out a trap for me despite how sincere she seems about the terms of this game. But it's a risk I'll have to take.

"I understand. What must I retrieve?"

"Bring me a flamboyán, Cotorra. The brightest one you can find. You have until dawn."

My brow furrows. "A…flamboyán?"

"That's what I said."

"But everything is covered in snow. The trees are barren. There aren't any flowers blooming on Isla Esmeralda."

La bruja shrugs. "My instructions are clear. Bring me a flamboyán before dawn, and this beautiful boy will be set free."

"Do I have to find the flower on this island?"

"Yes."

"How?"

"That's for you to discover, Cotorra. Now, go. You only have a few hours left."

In human form, I dash deeper into the garden.

★ ★ ★

Before la bruja's arrival, red and green lined the grassy paths ahead.

My sandals would crunch underneath the many fallen leaves and a few strewn petals. I would gaze at the flamboyán tree branches overhead, which seemed to reach for the sun. They were loyal friends who had all the time in the world to listen to ramblings. They provided shade to those seeking a respite from the scorching rays, held islanders up high whenever we wanted to see beyond our cliffs and shores, kept our crimson flowers safe from the harshest winds.

I don't remember what it's like to wear sandals.

But I can't forget how *alive* I felt when my fingers brushed against a flamboyán's petals. It was like being summoned into the truest version of myself—a call to feel deep gratitude for everything I am. Mami used to say that nature heals, and she was right. It could heal a little girl who didn't even have wounds yet—only a desire to never part ways with her simple joys.

There's nothing joyful about the cold. *Nothing.* I touch every inch of the white wood overhead, all of which is weighed down with snow, in the foolish hopes of finding the slightest hint of a flower. Even without la bruja's terrible magic, it's not flamboyán season, anyway. It's currently February. The bitter, biting cold makes the shortest month of the year feel eternal.

I feel the rough bark, pushing away as much snow as I can.

There are no flowers on this tree.

I move to the next one, just a few feet behind the first.

It's also barren.

So I continue my search, going from one tree to another and another.

But there are no flowers in this garden.

I press my forehead against a trunk. "How am I supposed to get the flamboyán I need like this?" I say breathlessly. Running around has depleted me of more energy than I anticipated. Not even the freezing temperatures can stop me from pouring sweat onto the wood.

"Did you say you need a flamboyán?"

A woman's voice falls from the snowy copse.

I can't see her, though. She must be in animal form. Even when a shape-shifter is in their human body, our magic lets us understand one another. I can hear words instead of whatever noise the creature I'm speaking with is making.

There aren't other shape-shifters allowed in this area. La bruja has always reserved the largest amount of guards to the Flor de Maga gardens in the north and west. This has to be a scout—someone who's also searching for whatever la bruja desires. But if she's waiting for further instructions in the same garden I'm stationed in, why haven't I heard her voice before?

"Yes!" I crane my neck toward the topmost branches. I can't see anything, though. "Do you know where I can find one?"

"I do. Can you reach me up here?" the woman says. "I don't want anyone overhearing us."

I take a step back, still searching for her in the snow-covered wood, but she's completely hidden. Soon the stars will vanish. I'll stare up at a pale pink and blue sky, the colors of sunrise. I might not know this mysterious woman, but if she has what I'm searching for, I have no choice but to give her a chance. I've already failed my parents. I can never bring them back.

But I can free a boy with his whole life ahead of him. And I *will*.

"Fine," I tell her. "I'll fly."

Through the years, many have asked me if shape-shifting hurts. I don't think I'll ever have the proper words to describe it. But no, it's not painful, it's liberating.

It starts with closing my eyes. I breathe slowly, letting the chilly air enter my lungs, then exhale as if blowing out smoke. The longer I suck in deep breaths, the faster my bones shrink. Nothing bruises or cracks while I grow smaller. During my descent, slight pinpricks break out across my arms, legs, and back. One by one, emerald feathers cover most of my tiny body. Beady black eyes replace my larger hazel ones. Having such an extended range of vision did take some getting used to; it's disorienting to notice even the smallest things from miles away. Thankfully, it doesn't make me nauseous anymore. A long thin tail extends behind me, helping me keep my balance and better feel a change in the wind's direction.

The last part is always the beak. My lips pucker and fold into the rest of my face. When I push them out again, hardened bone replaces flesh. I cluck my dark tongue and squawk for the whole island to hear. I flap, flap, flap my wings, standing on top of the messy pile of clothes I wore as a human. Clothes that will undoubtedly get colder lying in the snow.

But that's a concern for later.

I have a stranger to meet.

People have also asked me what it's like to fly.

Flying in freezing temperatures—ones I'm not even supposed to be able to live in, under normal circumstances—is the worst. I can spread my wings and jump off the frigid ground well enough. It's the steering that bothers me. I barely have mobility during flight in this dreadful cold. Everything stiffens and contracts; I have to exert so much more energy than usual just to fly a few miles. After la bruja arrived, I knocked my head into several trunks and branches. I couldn't get the hang of flying at all.

Now I pump harder, faster, and I don't stop for anything in the world. I alert the stranger of my imminent arrival with louder squawks. A sudden, swift chill threatens to push me off my trajectory. I press onward, setting my sights on the topmost branch, from where the stranger's voice first came. As I approach, I still can't see whoever promised me a flamboyán. It would be helpful to know what I'm looking for—species, size, colors—but all I get is more snow.

I land on the fluffiest pile of white powder. "Hello?"

"Over here," comes the woman's voice behind me.

She's much smaller than me. Her head is flat; her feathers are so, so thin, alternating between gray, brown, and black. They remind me of leaves that have long dropped from their host trees and have been stepped on many times. I suspect they help her stay hidden during flight—they don't look like they make much noise. The only thing we have in common is the color of our eyes. We drink each other in with matching dark orbs, but hers are bigger, rounder.

"What are you?" I ask. "I've never seen your kind around here."

"You're not supposed to. This is very much not where I belong," she says. "I'm a nightjar. My home is farther north of yours. Isla Rubí."

I gasp. "That's where the most beautiful roses grow! I mean, I haven't seen those roses, but my parents used to tell me about them. And is it true the sun never rises there? Like, *at all*?"

"Never. Everyone on Isla Rubí is used to the dark. I believe you call us…nocturnal."

"If you know you don't belong here," I say, "why are you in Isla Esmeralda?"

"The winds changed when la bruja came to your island. She never visited Isla Rubí, but her proximity affected our weather, too. These winds are too strong for my small body, and I'm much weaker in the cold. I was swept away as I traveled with my family across gardens. We've been warned to keep out of Isla Esmeralda ever since…"

She doesn't have to finish her sentence. I don't want her to.

"I understand," is all I say.

The nightjar nods. "I was plucking up the courage to face the winds again and finally go home, but I overheard you asking for a flamboyán. You're looking in the wrong places."

"This is the only location that has flamboyán trees."

"It is. But in my desperation to find a hideout, I wandered around for hours and walked past a flamboyán on the way to this garden. It's with the amapolas."

"With...the amapolas?"

"Sí. A different garden full of them."

Her words are a shower of sunlight in this unnatural chill. She's lucky I'm not in human form. That I don't know her well enough. I would've tackled her into a hug otherwise.

But the longer I let her message of hope fill my waking, despairing thoughts, the less sense it makes. Unless the flower has been ripped from its tree and dropped off elsewhere, the chances of it growing outside of its natural garden are nonexistent. The people of Isla Esmeralda would *never* tear flowers out. Our normal weather conditions aren't as windy or dark as now, either. This island was known for constant humidity and sweltering temperatures.

The nightjar can see much better in the dark, though. Right now, the stars and a full moon hang overhead, and even though their shine is slowly dimming, I wouldn't be able to spot anything in the snow this effortlessly. Dawn will be here in three or four hours—do I really want to waste such precious time doubting my only ally? Or do I take a leap of faith?

"How can there be a flamboyán outside of its natural habitat?" I ask.

"I asked myself the same question, but I swear it on my mother's life. I know what I saw. This is a real flower." The nightjar lowers its head. "It's just...frozen. The petals aren't red anymore. They're a little shriveled, too."

My heart shatters. Will la bruja accept the coveted flower in such a poor state? Or is she expecting a normal flamboyán despite this punishing weather? She knows I can't find anything in perfect condition on Isla Esmeralda. Maybe that's why she set me up for this retrieval game in the first place: she *wants* me to lose. She's desperate to make me regret ever choosing to help Arnaldo. It's not enough to send me on soul hunts targeting younger victims. Not enough to have murdered my parents. She has to humiliate me, too.

She won't. A frozen flamboyán is still a flamboyán. La bruja never specified anything else.

I lift the nightjar's beak with my foot until our gazes meet. "Show me the flower."

The little bird aims its body to the east. "Very well. Follow me, Cotorra."

She flies away.

"My name is Angélica," I mutter.

Then I'm flying right behind her.

The flight to the amapola garden lasts twenty minutes.

Even after we arrive, the nightjar doesn't halt. She peers down as she slowly circles the area. I mirror all of her movements, wondering if we're close but too worried to ask. What if speaking makes her lose focus? Or she suddenly forgets where she has to go? All I can hope for is a quick end to this torturous journey—the last time I visited the east, my parents were killed.

The last thing I want is to step foot where I failed them.

And the more I keep up with the nightjar's pace, the quicker I realize where she's headed.

"Just over this mound!" she says. "The flamboyán is poking out of the snow. But you have to be very careful. There is also a lot of—"

"Wood," I finish on her behalf.

What's left of the wooden stakes is still here. Splintered. Scorched. Scattered.

This isn't just the same garden where la bruja killed my parents. This is the *exact spot*.

After they burned, their bodies were tossed into the sea, lost forever.

But their dying screams still echo in my head.

I tap my tail against the snow they were dragged across. The snow that once felt the heat of their blood, which spilled from multiple cuts as they shielded me from la bruja's wrath. Blood that stained me, too, with every second I spent clinging to them, begging them to come with me.

"¡Vuela, mi vida! ¡Olvídate de nosotros!" my mother had said.

"I'm not leaving you!"

"No!" I'd never been shaken that hard in my life, but my father's grip was deathly tight. His eyes were wider than usual and filled to the brim with tears. They reflected my panicked expression back at me. "Listen to me, Angélica! You have to escape! Forget about us! We're not letting this bruja touch you. Now, *get out of here!*"

Those were their last words to me.

That's what I heard seconds before I sprinted away. Before I left them here.

"Can you see it?" the nightjar says.

I squint, but my vision isn't as powerful as hers. "No."

She points between two thick slabs of wood buried in the shape of a cross. "There."

I notice the stem first, then the five shriveled petals. Even covered in snow, the flamboyán looks like a heart that's been ripped open and laid bare for all to see—one of the reasons why I love this beautiful gift from nature so much. It's not supposed to look like it's hanging its head in defeat or like it carries the weight of the world on its back. A flamboyán is fire itself, burning bright with energy that seeps into its beholder's veins. This one is but a remnant of flames that will never be fanned again.

It's still a flamboyán, though, and now it's mine.

I hurry toward it, trying not to step on the splintered wood. I don't have time or patience for cuts and bruises. Once I'm about two feet away, a loud hiss sweeps across the sky.

"Cotorra," comes la bruja's voice, which has been magnified for the entire island to hear. "You have three hours left until dawn. Find the flamboyán before then and claim your prize. But don't forget—the flower must be as crimson as your heart's blood."

Another hiss signals the end of her message.

"Wait. Was that la bruja?" the nightjar asks.

I don't have it in me to speak anymore. I can only nod. This flower is useless; its petals are nowhere near the color la bruja demands.

"You need that flower for *her*?" The nightjar shakes her head as she backs away. "Have I been helping that witch this entire time?"

"No! You've been helping Arnaldo Santiago. He's a young boy under her sleeping spell. But she's given me a mission in order to wake him up. I need to return with this flower. Only it's...not what the witch is asking for."

The nightjar and I turn to the flower. I sigh heavily.

"Do you think she'll use it to enhance her magic somehow?" she asks.

"I have no idea. And honestly, all I thought about was saving Arnaldo."

"So...you're in *love* with this boy?"

I wish I could say no. After that first day in seventh grade, Arnaldo sank deeper into my heart by writing affirmations on the board during oral reports to encourage us, swiftly opening doors for anyone in his path, and even comforting a male classmate who cried after failing a history exam. His humility, his unflinching desire to save his mother, his selflessness, and his plan to stop la bruja... How could I not love him?

"He doesn't deserve to be kept in a glass coffin. He deserves to be free," I reply.

"What makes him so great, though? I understand no one deserves what's happened to him, but you're risking your life for this boy. *Why?*"

"Arnaldo Santiago's heart is greater than anything I've ever known. I first noticed him when he gave up his seat in class for me." I swallow hard as the nightjar cocks her head. "But it's so much more than that. He is *good*. We've actually *never* spoken, but I haven't forgotten what he did for me. What he's done for others at my school, too. And la bruja confessed that he'd tried to kill her while his mother fled."

"So the coffin is his punishment for trying to kill la bruja, and he was kind to you once."

"To sum it up, yes."

"And these are good enough reasons to potentially die for him?"

She makes me sound delusional for wanting to free Arnaldo. The nightjar doesn't need my justifications. We can discuss them after I've taken Arnaldo out of that coffin.

"I won't die for him," I say. "Because I won't fail."

The nightjar nods. "Since you can't use this flower, how can we find another one in time for her deadline?"

"We can't," I whisper. "There's nothing I can do to change those petals. There's no way it will ever be crimson again and—"

La bruja's new orders cut into my thoughts like a dagger. *The flower must be as crimson as your heart's blood.* Isla Esmeralda doesn't have the exact flower she's requested.

But I do have heart's blood.

What if this is how I save Arnaldo? Not by finding the perfect flower—by creating it. I could spill some of my blood onto the petals and stain them crimson. I wouldn't have to use much; a few drops will go a long way, especially since the flamboyán isn't too big.

"I need to shift back into human form. Once I have flesh

again, I'll cut just enough to bleed on the petals. They'll be as red as la bruja wants them."

The nightjar holds up a wing. "You're using your *blood*?"

"It's all I can use!"

I shut my eyes tight and imagine myself shedding feathers, tail, and wings for flesh and limbs. For the most part, transforming back into my real body takes less time than becoming a cotorra, but it also depends on how tired I am. Right now, there's so much adrenaline coursing through me that I don't even allow for the idea of being exhausted anymore.

A few minutes pass.

I don't feel any different.

When I open my eyes, I still have feathers, wings, and a beak. I'm still a bird standing in front of a dead flamboyán, wondering why my magic isn't working.

"This hasn't happened before," I say breathlessly. The adrenaline ramps up with my panic, and it feels like I've been running for weeks without end. "Why am I not shifting?!"

"Try harder?" the nightjar offers unhelpfully.

And I keep trying, in vain.

An hour later, I'm still a bird.

My magic is no longer working.

"You're too stressed," says the nightjar. "Relax and try—"

"I'm done trying! I have to do this *now*!"

I make sure I'm standing over the flamboyán, then cradle a small piece of sliced wood between my wings. Digging it into anywhere but my chest—my very heart—while I'm in this form would be a waste of time. I won't pour out enough blood to stain all five petals. It *has* to come from the bloodiest part of me. The part that's beating, feeling, hoping it didn't have to come to this.

I do have to die to save Arnaldo.

Right where my parents were killed.

Their deaths were my fault. Protecting someone who didn't

cherish their sacrifice cost them their lives. All they did was save a pawn whose fate is forever tied to the witch they defied.

If I leave this garden, my life remains the same. I'll still go on soul hunts. My parents would hate that I'm on Isla Esmeralda, but they'd hate what I do for la bruja more. I've become what they never wanted me to. I don't control my waking moments. I don't think I ever will again, if I leave this garden alive, but my death…

I can control *that.*

I can pay back my parents' sacrifice with my own: I can give Arnaldo the chance to reclaim the future that was stolen from him. His heart is bigger than mine, anyway.

My island is lost. Everything I love is lost. My life…is worth nothing.

Those were the last words I heard him speak.

But those won't be his last words.

"¿Cotorra? Are you well?"

Only fools believe that death is a promise.

But sometimes we choose to greet death willingly. We agree to the light in our eyes fading forever, our hearts stopping, our veins running dry and going cold.

Sometimes there are promises worth keeping.

"Make sure every drop of my blood falls on these petals," I tell the nightjar. "Don't stop until they're completely covered. Once the flower is crimson, leave it by the glass coffin in the flamboyán garden. La bruja will know I've won the game. Can you do this for me?"

"But you'll…you'll *die.*"

"Can you do this for me?" I speak louder, more irritated.

The nightjar watches me in silence.

Then she says, "I can. But this is *wrong,* Cotorra. You shouldn't—"

"My name," I say, "is Angélica."

I stab the wood through my chest.

Everything I am bursts into incalculable pain. It's like I'm burning from within and heat is also spilling out of me. The blood comes slow, biding its sweet time, but I don't pull the wood away. The nightjar is speaking hurriedly, shaking her head, shedding tears, but I motion to the petals with my beak and urge her to place them right below the hole in my chest. She obeys.

I don't know how long we spend facing each other.

All I know is that the world keeps growing darker, darker...

Los amo, Mami y Papi. Los veo pronto. Y lo siento mucho.

I close my eyes...and the promise is kept.

THE NIGHTJAR

The glass coffin is right where the cotorra said it would be.

La bruja is leaning against Arnaldo's coffin. She grins at me as I descend at her feet. The red flamboyán touches the snow first, then I land a few inches behind the cotorra's gift.

"Where is the one who made this?" la bruja asks.

"Dead. She pierced her heart with the same wood her parents were tied to." I bow. "Just as you requested, mistress."

La bruja laughs. "And you kept her in bird form?"

"My psychic magic prevented her from shifting. It was quite difficult not to laugh in her face." I glance up at the witch. "May I return to Isla Rubí with my soul?"

"You've kept your end of the bargain, Nightjar. You helped me get rid of a treacherous creature that tried to defy orders. It's more fun to have your enemies dive off the deep end all by themselves." La bruja blows me a kiss. "Go home. Tell everyone I have no business entering Isla Rubí. Your people will never know my wrath."

"Muchísimas gracias, bruja."

It's only for a moment...a finite stretch of time...

But I look at the boy in the coffin.

A gasp escapes me. No wonder the cotorra died for him—Arnaldo's beauty surpasses anything I've ever seen in a human.

Before today, I didn't know boys could also be soft. That they could have high cheekbones, glistening skin, or lips without cracks. Before today, I didn't know boys were poetry—hope and healing sprinkled in each verse, compelling you to read them again and again.

"Nightjar? Is something wrong?"

"No, bruja. Adiós."

I fly out of the snowy island. I don't look back at the woman who promised to leave my country alone. At the slumbering poem inside that cursed coffin. I fly, fly, fly...

And conjure a plan to rescue Arnaldo Santiago.

★★★★★

GOLDI AND THE THREE BODIES

a remix of "Goldilocks and the Three Bears"
Saraciea J. Fennell

"She ran here and she ran there, and went so far, at last, that she found herself in a lonely place..."

—Robert Southey, "Goldilocks and the Three Bears"

I've always been good at keeping secrets. So this should be no different, I think to myself as my train pulls into the Prospect Avenue station. I'm meeting my prima Marí so we can hit up this party uptown. It's been a long time since I've twerked—hell, even *moved*—my body. For the past few months I've kept away from crowds, ignoring the fire licking at my throat, the gnash of teeth against my tongue. Marí says I need to stop living under a rock. So here I am, just trying to live wild, young, and free, before my world comes crashing down on me.

"Yerrrr," Marí yells from the platform as the iron horse slows to a stop in the station. Her hands are cupped around her tiny heart-shaped lips as she lets loose the guttural Bronx greeting. I shake my head, cracking a smile from my side of the scuffed, foggy glass and graffiti-stained metal doors.

I swear if you bottled up Marí's energy it would be like lighting a pack of firecrackers: you can't contain her. Marí beams at me, flashing her custom *bo$$ gurl* wire braces. (They were the only way Titi could convince my cousin to get braces in the middle of her junior year of high school.) I didn't think you could make custom braces, but if there's a way, Marí was going to make sure it happened. She was just that damned determined.

We practically look like twins tonight, minus my gold faux locs and her long thick curly hair. We're both rocking large gold hoop earrings and the brightest red lipstick we could afford from the local beauty-supply store. Damn, I've missed my primita. I love Marí so much. She's my ride or die, and I can't really say that about anyone else these days.

Pero how do I tell—no, no—there's no telling Marí nada! *Dejalo, Goldi*, I think to myself. Things are bad enough already. Am I really out here trying to make them worse? Don't get me wrong, I hate what's happening to me, but I'm going to keep these lips of mine shut. This is a secreto I might just have to take with me to la tumba because there ain't no way. I did everything I could today not to mess up tonight. Everything's under control, I haven't had a messy relapse in over a month. And my cravings have become manageable. I do the cross over mi cuepro. Yep, things will be fine, if I just—I lick my lips—remember to keep my cool. When I'm too nerviosa, Mami always reminds me to *breathe*.

Yeah, just remember to breathe, Goldi. Bueno, I got this. Then, why do I feel so anxious?

The train doors open, and my heart pinches between my ribs at the thought of keeping a secret from Marí. Would she even believe me if I told her?

Nah, she wouldn't. Just like Mami ain't believe me when I tried to tell her I was craving sangre. At first, she swore it was just a random symptom of my period: her solution was comer carne, knowing that I didn't even like red meat, but anything to increase my iron, she said. That's why locking myself away in the apartment for the past ninety days was the best and only option. Thankfully, Mami works long shifts at the hospital. Her grueling schedule keeps her away so much, we barely even see each other these days. When we do, it's for a couple of hours a day at most, and she's so deliriously sleep-deprived that me saying I've been craving sangre doesn't even get more than a blink out of her these days.

Marí rushes onto the train faster than you can say Usain Bolt, pumping the breaks on my thoughts before I spiral further. I hear the blood sloshing in her veins. The thump, thump, thump, of her heart as she wraps her bony arms around me excitedly.

"Y tu, Goldi!" Marí plucks my arm and leans back to look at me. "Mírate, thanks for *finally* coming out with me." She shuffles her feet, closing the gap between us again, and squeezes me tight. Her curls invade my face like unwieldy weeds in a garden as we embrace. At first, I get a whiff of honey and lavender—*mmm, so soothing*—I inhale deeper. The sharp smell of garlic oil that comes from her scalp stings my nose and makes my eyes water. My cheeks burn, turning my ochre brown skin the color of a summer sunset.

I tense up.

Marí doesn't notice. She finishes her greeting, kisses me on both cheeks. I force a smile. Her skin is warm against my stony face. *Stand clear of the closing doors, please.* The train doors shut behind her. Instead of my reflection in the windowpane, I'm left with a monster staring back at me. Hallowed eyes, pointy cheekbones, and razor-sharp teeth from a smile spread so wide my lips almost touch my ears.

"I feel like we haven't seen each other in forever," I say, breaking free from her grip, turning away from the window. I dab under my eyes, making sure I don't smudge my mascara.

"Yo, my bad!" Marí giggles, guiding us deeper into the train. "I got lipstick on you."

"Where at?" I point around my face.

"I gotchu, right here." She licks her thumb and smushes it into my cheek, rubbing the red stain away. There's a Band-Aid wrapped around her pinky. It grazes my lips. The proximity of fresh blood makes my mouth water.

My incisors break free from their tomb.

I panic.

This is the moment I've feared.

This is it.

The thing I will regret the most.

Forever.

I'm going to kill my favorite cousin.

"It's all good, Marí." I bat her hand away. The train lurches forward, and my face collides with her neck.

Shit. *Shit.* I turn my head and bite my tongue instead of her.

"You good?" Marí asks, her warm amber eyes locking onto mine. Her voice is filled with more concern than I like.

I'm too rattled to respond as my own blood pools in my mouth.

I squeeze her other hand instead, and twirl around her, putting some much-needed space between us. She's just about to lean in closer, but I manage to pull myself down into the empty seat behind us.

"Whose party is this, again?" I grind my teeth and look down at her feet. It's best we don't see eye to eye right now, while my brain tries to convince my body not to pounce as she towers above me. I hear a rustle and then the smack of gum, before a silver wrapper flutters to the floor. Marí dangles the packet in front of my face.

"Hello, Earth to Goldi." She waves her hand, and I follow her pinky. She nods her head silently, gesturing for me to take one. "Do you want some gum?"

I pull out a stick and shove it into my mouth before she can catch a glimpse of my teeth.

"It's my friend Nelson's party. You don't know him, but yo, no te preocupes." She plops down beside me. "Like we legit won't have to worry about any old heads trying to regulate us during the party, either."

I know Marí is trying to get me hype, but the thought of being around horny teenagers makes the hair on my arms stand up. Not because it doesn't sound fun, but because the last boy I trusted turned out to be a bloodsucking asshole, literally. "Mmm, yay for no viejitos," I say, waving my hands in the air with as much enthusiasm as I can fake at the moment.

Marí doesn't miss a beat. "¿Que te pasa?"

"Nothing," I say with a shrug. "I'm ready to have a good time tonight."

My palms are slimy. I wipe them on my jeans and smile.

"We used to have fun, all. the. time. Remember? Tonight will be no different, Goldi!" Marí bumps shoulders with me and dances in her seat. "Just you wait. We turnin' up tonight! It's gonna be an adventure."

I crack a smile and shake my head.

Before I know it, we're off the train and walking to Nelson's crib. My head's pounding. I spit out the stale gum and rub my temple. What happened on the train with Marí cannot happen at this party! I need to eat something before we hit this place, especially if I'm gonna be on my best behavior tonight. We turn down a dirt road. All of the streetlights have been knocked out so it's hard to see. I move in closer to Marí and put my hand on her elbow. "Hey, Marí, you sure you know where we going? How do you even know where Nelson's house is?" I whisper.

"Chill. We good, we good, I promise. We almost there." Marí continues leading the way.

There are a couple of parked cars lined up a few feet ahead of us. They have their lights on, shining, and music blasts from speakers. Reggae bounces off the wooden frame of an abandoned house. Marí tells me she'll be right back and runs off to hug some boy leaning on one of the parked cars.

I recognize Nelson from school.

"'Sup, I'm Nelson." He strokes his barely there goatee with one hand and extends the other when I approach.

"What's good," I reply with a head nod. "Yeah, I recognize you from school," I say, feeling awkward, as the rest of his friends stare at us.

"Feel free to grab a drink. Get your dance on." Nelson pushes off the car completely and spreads his arms wide. "You know, enjoy the vibes."

He grins, and I notice he has a single gold-capped tooth.

"Word, thanks. But yo, before I do that, can I hit the bathroom?" I ask him.

"Yep, in the house, upstairs on the left." He points to a small window on the second floor.

"Aight, thanks! Marí, I'll be right back."

"Cool, sounds good. I'll be here, Goldi," Marí says, taking a beer from the cooler on the ground beside Nelson.

I head inside the house. There's reggaeton playing on the first floor. Packed as hell inside the living room. No furniture, just a couple of speakers in one corner, and a makeshift bar in the other. I make a mental note to visit the bar after I use the bathroom. Couples grind on each other in the middle of the dance floor bathed in disco lights as I creep past others making out on the steps. There's more music coming from one of the rooms upstairs. Once I reach the top, I see a group in the room playing a game, but I can't make out the console from this angle. I turn left and knock on the bathroom door. Someone from the gaming room shouts, "Victory!" and throws their hands up in the air. I smile at them and jiggle the bathroom handle. It's unlocked, so I push the door open and slide in, quickly shutting it behind me. Tonight might not be so bad after all.

I grab the faucet's metal knob and twist it on. The water cools my hands. I splash some on my face and let loose a long exhale. Even though I don't need air to survive anymore, centering my breath really helps me to focus. I flip my T-shirt up to pat my face dry.

"My bad. I know you just walked in here. But I just got hit in the nose," a girl says behind me. "Do you mind?"

I turn around and see Tasha Lee standing in the doorway. The girl I was dared to kiss in the playground barrel in fifth grade but I chickened out, and she made sure to make my life shit anytime I ran into her. It's been a minute since I've seen her, but she's about my height, with deep brown skin, rocking boxed braids, and currently pinching her nose.

"Nosebleed," she says, congested, and points to her nose. "Gotta love gettin' hit in the face at a party as a souvenir."

My entire body is stiff—I'm too afraid to move a hair. Does she recognize me with these faux locs? We look at each other awkwardly, and it's times like this that I wish I *could* hold my breath. She turns her head over too quickly, and droplets of blood dance in the air. She tilts her head back and bends her knees to grab some toilet paper. The predator in me takes over, and I'm behind her in an instant, unable to control myself because the sangre calls to me.

Her eyes bulge with fear when she sees me towering over her, and she falls back right into my arms, knocking us into the corner. I run my tongue over her nose lapping up some of the blood like a puppy. She slaps me in the face, pushing herself forward. I yank her by the braids, pulling her back into my embrace. She creates tension, using her arms to grip against the door and the wall, but she does me a favor by forcing the door shut.

"Get off me," she says and shoves into me.

I snarl, baring my teeth, slamming back into her.

Everything happens so fast after that. My teeth sink into her flesh. She tastes like cake batter and sweat. *Far too sweet*, I think to myself. I really would've enjoyed draining a bully, but I can't stomach any more of her.

Her pupils are dilated. I look her straight in the eye and say,

"You won't remember any of this. I didn't attack you. I just helped you stop your nosebleed." She still looks dazed, so I repeat myself for good measure. She nods her head a few times. I help her get cleaned up, and even prick my finger and put a few drops over the bite marks on her neck. They seal up instantly, and I sigh in relief as the girl walks out of the bathroom, only slightly confused.

Something skitters behind the curtain in the bathtub. At first, I think my eyes are playing tricks on me as a silhouette appears. Still filled with adrenaline, I tear the ratty shower curtain away. There's a girl lying in the tub squeezing a bottle of Henny to her chest.

She moans.

"Ugh." I roll my eyes. I thought I was safe in an empty bathroom, but I guess there's always a stray when it comes to a party. Thankfully, it looks like this girl wasn't fully awake for what just happened.

"Hey." I hunch over and slap the girl's hand. "You good?"

"Mmmmm," she moans again. Her eyes flutter like she's fighting passing out.

"Come on, mama. Can you get up?" I ask, ready to help pull the girl to her feet.

"I...I think so," she says, pushing herself upright. "I'm good. Don't need your help." She waves me off.

"Aight, aight," I say with raised arms, backing away to give her some room.

She leans forward, one hand gripping the bottle, the other the tub. I watch her try to climb out, but she never makes it over. I crouch forward again, ready to brace her fall. She gives me the leave-me-the-hell alone look, so I take the hint. Let her ass fall, what do I care?

It takes her a minute, but she finally grabs hold of the curtain and pulls. It snaps from her weight.

Bam!

Before I have a chance to catch her, her mouth slams onto the side of the tub, and her teeth go flying.

Damn.

Some clatter and circle the drain in the tub, others skid across the bathroom floor. The girl hollers in pain, just as the bottle of Henny flies in the air and hits the floor, breaking at the neck of the bottle, splashing on both of us. Blood drips from her nose and mouth, she catches some of it in her hand.

"Ohmygod, ohmygod. I can't believe this," she cries.

In an instant I'm on my knees, sliding toward the girl.

My teeth break flesh—blood and tears—and—

Salty warmth floods into my mouth.

I hug the girl closer to me, my fingers wrapped around her neck, squeezing tightly. Blood shoots into my throat, and I immediately start to choke. It's so bitter from the taste of alcohol it burns. I spit it out, angry, and my grip tightens on the girl's neck until I almost crush her windpipe.

Someone fidgets with the door handle. "Anybody in there?" a male's muffled voice booms from the other side.

Time for me to wipe yet another memory and hide the evidence. I frown; there's nothing I can do about the drunk girl's teeth, but I hope I can dull her pain. I convince her that none of this just happened, and that she needs to sleep it off. Before I can heal the bite marks around her neck, though, the person from the other side of the door walks in, and I let the girl's sleepy body slump to the tiled floor.

"Ayo, I thought nobo—wait, what the hell you doing to Angie?" He rushes to the girl's side, leaving the door ajar.

Shit—it's Jorge Reyes aka the high-school basketball team's Dominican "Black Mamba" whom I've had a crush on since forever. I take in my surroundings and start to freak out. It totally looks like a murder scene straight out of a movie. "No se que paso—listen, I'm so sorry. Pero I found her like this."

Jorge looks up at me. "Whatchu mean you don't know what

happened? Why is she covered in blood?" He stuffs two fingers under her cheek to check for a pulse. "She's okay. She's breathing," he says as he repositions her head gently, exposing the puncture wounds I couldn't seal before he walked into the bathroom. "What the hell. What did you *do to her?*"

"Listen. I can explain," I say with my hands up. "You don't need to do nothin' crazy." Not sure what's about to go down between us. When I hear more footsteps approach, I immediately kick the door closed and push the lock in. "I swear I only came in here to wash my face. Shorty scared the shit out of me in the bathtub." I point over to the tub nervously, my shoulders hugging my ears. "She was drunk. I was just tryna help her out, but she fell before I could catch her."

"But I saw you—when I walked in here..." His fingers run across her neck, leaving a bloody trail, and his eyes suddenly narrow before he lunges forward.

There's only one way this story is positioned to end: one of us is dying tonight, and I'll be damned if it's going to be me—to hell with this crush of mine. Our bodies collide like two football players tackling each other. He's almost got me pinned until his left foot slips on Angie's blood. His chin digs into my shoulder as he loses his balance. I take the advantage, shifting my weight to lift him off his feet and push. We collapse into the tub, momentarily tangled by our limbs. Jorge wastes no time and punches me in the chest as I try to reposition myself on top of him. He throws blow after blow; I laugh and claw him in return. When his fist aims for my face, I block it with my hand and tighten my grip around his knuckles. I stretch out my leg, smashing my foot into his throat, and twist over while keeping his arm extended. He cries out in pain and uses his free hand to retaliate, but I catch him by the wrist midswing and bite down fast and hard.

There's a pop sound as my teeth penetrate into the bone. My stomach flip-flops as I sit on his belly. Jorge tastes better than both of the girls combined, exactly to my liking. The venom starts to set in, and Black Mamba begins to relax. I lose myself in the euphoria.

I don't stop until I hear his heart peter out.

Even then, I'm slow to let go, the taste of him too good to pass up. Everything I feared that might happen tonight is happening.

Now I need to figure out how to hide the body. I close his eyes and think about how I'm going to cover this one up.

I shove the dead boy's body out of the way and climb out of the bathtub. It's best I distance myself, cutting off my emotions to cover my tracks. His hand slaps the porcelain with a thwack.

There's fresh blood all over my face and a smattering of it soaking through my shirt and jeans. Thank God I decided to wear a black shirt tonight. I stand and look at myself in the mirror. I no longer see a monster staring back at me but the most beautiful creature I've ever seen. I wipe the blood from my chin with the back of my hand and lick it, closing my eyes to replay what just happened. Damn it, I've got to get out of here. I search for a towel, a rag, anything to clean myself up. There's nothing in sight. Just a few sheets of toilet tissue left. *Shit, shit, shit*, I think to myself, and slap my hand on my thighs.

I pull off Jorge's shirt (he won't need it anymore). I have nothing else to use to wipe Angie's face or mine, plus the blood on the floor. I leave the pendejo in the tub, refastening the shower curtain to its tiny metal loops to block him from view. When things look somewhat normal again, I get back to what I was trying to do before: healing Angie. I'm annoyed by the pressure at first, but I force my incisors to appear. I prick my index finger and dab the puncture wounds on her neck with my blood. Even after all of these months, I still can't believe this is my life now. I watch as the two holes disappear, then wipe away the evidence of the blood. I shake Angie awake. "Welcome back to the party, muñeca!" I say, eager to get out of here before someone else comes barging in. Trying to act like everything is normal,

I wonder for a moment if I should explain her mouth situation but decide against it.

"Why am I on the floor?" she asks, speaking with a lisp.

"Umm, you had a lil bit of an accidente," I say, tapping my lips.

I help her to her feet and escort her out of the bathroom. Before we enter the hallway, the tub groans—one of its ancient legs has collapsed. Angie turns to look over her shoulder, and I quickly shut the bathroom door.

"Let's find someone who can help you, yeah?" I say, leading her past the linen closet and into the gaming room. There are fewer folks in the room than before as I creep in with Angie by my side, unnoticed at first.

I clear my throat and ask, "Does anyone here know Angie?"

Nobody answers me, so I speak up louder over the music. "So umm, Angie had an accident in the bathroom. I think she needs stitches."

All eyes are on us now. I guide her forward while someone else switches on a lamp. I keep focused on the bathroom door to make sure nobody enters. I need to figure out what to do with the boy's body, but first things first—getting Angie some help.

Marí, where are you? I wonder where the hell she could be and if she's noticed that I'm not back yet. A few people mumble and comment on Angie's face. I feel the middle of her back tense up.

"What are you staring at?" Angie says with a lisp to nobody in particular.

She reminds me of that meme with the girl jutting out her head and lips with her hand cocked to the side.

The room starts to clear out. Two people take Angie off my hands and a third starts to shut down the gaming console, leaving me alone. I race back to the bathroom; there's nobody in the stairway at the moment, so I take the opportunity to grab the dead boy and move him to the linen closet. I enter the bathroom. The tub is definitely broken. The boy is caught in the cracked shoulder of the tub. It's gotta be vintage; there's no way a tub could have broken this easily. I drag him out and make my way to the closet.

The hallway is still empty, but the music has been lowered. I try shoving the body in the closet, but the door just doesn't stay closed, even when I push with my hands and my feet.

"Goldi, you up here?" Marí calls from the stairs.

Of course, Marí *would* come looking for me right now. I wish the universe would be on my side tonight. This is exactly why I preferred hibernation. "Yep, I'm here. Be right down. Dame un segundo."

"Mirame! Déjame entrar, Goldi. I gotta pee," Marí says, slurring her words a little.

"Loca, I'm not in the bathroom anymore," I say a little out of breath as I finally get the closet door to stay shut.

Marí appears in my line of sight and then shoots past me into the bathroom, hissing, "Muevete, I gotta pee."

The closet door splinters behind me. *Shit.* I need to find another place to hide this body. Marí comes out of the bathroom. "Okay, let's go. I want to introduce you to some of my other friends." She grabs my arm to pull me from the door.

But I don't budge, too scared that the shirtless boy will come tumbling out. "I'll be right down. I just need to reapply some lipstick." I slide the red tube out from my front pocket. "Can you maybe get them to play my favorite song, though?"

"Yes! And it's *our* favorite song. Hurry up and do your thing. I'm going to talk to the DJ now." Once Marí's out of view, I step away from the door, and it pops open. I drag the boy into the bedroom and drop him on the bed just as another couple walks over.

"Oooh, hell yeah, I guess we aren't the only ones looking for some alone time, babe," he says to the girl standing next to him. "I don't know who the lucky guy is, but I'll give you two some privacy." He cheeses at me and closes the room door.

Thank God. I toss my locs out of my way, wrapping the front half into a bun. I'm slicked with sweat from carrying this dude, and I haven't even begun to figure out what to do with him next. I walk over to the window for some air and see the dumpster again. The window has guards, but they're the slide-out kind, and I've never been happier. I remove them, wrap up Mr. Shirtless in a sheet, and pray that nobody will notice a body flying out the window. I toss him out Superman-style (head and arms first). His body dives straight into the giant metal container, and the lid flaps close loudly behind him. My heart skips a beat, and I jump out of view just in case.

I open the bedroom door and hear Bad Bunny's "Tití Me Preguntó" start to play. My feet pound the stairs, and I don't stop until I find Marí at the bar. She hands me a drink, and I guzzle it down. I feel more relaxed than I have in months. I take a few shots with Marí and even mingle with some of her friends. After an hour I convince myself that it's too good to be true—I better get home before someone discovers the dead body in the dumpster or, worse, what I did to it.

Just as Marí and I are leaving and making our way down the dirt road, I hear the screams. I pull my prima in closer. This night was just what I needed.

★ ★ ★ ★ ★

THIS MORTAL COIL

a remix of *Hamlet*
David Bowles

"To sleep, perchance to dream. Ay, there's the rub.
For in that sleep of death what dreams may come,
when we have shuffled off this mortal coil,
must give us pause. There's the respect
that makes calamity of so long life."

—William Shakespeare, *Hamlet*

It's almost time for combat. I climb into my mech suit, heart pounding.

I'm still not sure if my backup will work. Will the most important parts of me continue to exist if I happen to die?

My opponent wants to kill me. But it's too late to turn back now.

Death is better than surrender.

I

Three months ago, I was sitting in my suite at the Haebyeon, the boarding school I attend on the outskirts of Ellisium Siti. I stared at the hologram of my mother. My mouth opened, but all that emerged was a sob.

My father had never been perfect, but I loved him.

Mother's face scrunched up again at the sight of my tears.

"I'm so sorry, Lacho. We're all devastated. He was still so young."

An aneurysm at forty-seven seemed unlikely. But in truth… *life* is the unlikely outcome. Death? Chaos? Entropy? Much more common.

"When's the funeral?" I rasped.

"Tomorrow." Mother dabbed at her eyes. "You know how observant he was. Rabbi says we should get him into the earth soon."

I nodded. "I'll head out on the skytube in a few hours."

"Te kyero, miho."

Terminating the call, I muttered in return, "Yo tammen te kyero."

My impulse was to sit and stew in my rising grief. But the entrance cycled, and three voices filled our little foyer. One I was expecting. The other two surprised me.

Wiping my face, I walked out into the communal space of the suite.

My roommate, An Ba-rae, son of the governor of Ellisium, was grinning at two men who towered over him.

The sandy-skinned bald one was Bernardo Gomes. His darker companion with the braid was Marselo Sainz.

My father's most trusted bodyguards.

"What are you doing here," I snapped, "instead of at my father's side?"

Bernardo lifted his hands. "Lacho, peldõ. But your apá told us that if anything bad happened to him, we should come protect you."

"From what?"

Marselo gestured broadly. "Maybe l'Ermandá? They may attempt to expand Brotherhood black markets into Sefarad. Eliminating the heir could be their next step."

"Also," Bernardo added, "your apá's been suspicious for a while."

I stepped closer. "Of?"

"Your uncle, Claudyo," Bernardo said after a pause. "Don Horasyo thought that his brother might try to take control of Serfaty Automation."

My brow beetled. "But Claudyo's already the CFO and chairman of the board. My father couldn't make a move without his consent."

Marcelo put a meaty hand on my shoulder. "Lacho, some men need more than might. They need to be acknowledged as el mero chingõ, to have others bow and scrape and call them king. And they can't stomach sharing power, even with family. That's why I…ah, kid, I think your uncle killed your father."

An Ba-rae sucked in air, his smile gone. He hadn't known till that moment.

Bernardo scratched his head. "It's shocking but makes sense. You know those men been rivals since your abuelo died. A decade of rivalry. And Claudyo wants to use the connections Polonyo Bos has with l'Ermandá to expand operations and establish AutoSerf as the biggest corporation on Mars."

I began pacing, thinking.

"They're not wrong," my roommate put in. "Even in Ellisium, elites have been talking. When my father met with prefects about AutoSerf building factories in our region, some objected because of the Brotherhood's possible involvement. Dude, your COO is the uncle of a mafia counselor. Looks bad."

"It's complicated," I said, lifting a hand. "Yes, Don Polonyo suggested selling mekabok to the Brotherhood's paper companies, but my father made it clear that we would *not* contract with criminals. So he backed off."

Marselo reached into a pocket of his coat, pulling out a rectangle of plastic. “We stand outside many doors, Lacho. Believe me, Claudyo kept pressuring him. A week ago, your father gave me this coded message for you.”

I took the rectangle. It was my father’s handwriting. Three syllable blocks in Hangul, then a string of numbers.

베레싯 5523B2K140Y721.

“What does it mean?” I asked, turning the card over and over.

“No idea,” Marcelo said. “But he said you’d figure it out.”

An hour later, just three of us boarded the skytube at the rim of Lockyer Crater. Ba-rae couldn’t come but promised to help.

“Anything you need, Lacho. My family’s plugged into law enforcement outside Cimmeria.”

Strapped into gel-cushioned pods, we shot our way across the Martian sky, crossing from Ellisium to Cimmeria and hissing to a stop on the shore of Lake Gusev. A company transport awaited us, and soon I was back in the ancestral compound, carved into the eastern cliffs at the mouth of Ma’adim Valley.

We’ve built buffers against despair. Grieving families must host friends and relatives, diplomats and rivals, descending to pay their respects. You’re never alone. Perhaps that’s why my mother smiled more than she frowned as people paid their respects.

Condolences, Doña Gertrudis.

My sympathies, Senator.

Kõdolensyas, Doktora Werta-Serfaty.

The men of the family prepared father’s body, washing and wrapping it, setting it in a simple wooden coffin. My uncle Claudyo led these rites, eyes red, dripping silent tears. Giving me sidelong glances.

I was not moved. This weeping was a charade, the sort of deft manipulation he often used to the corporation’s advantage. Now I could see the truth. His every emotion was a mask.

I helped carry the bier to the Sephardic cemetery in the eastern highlands overlooking both river and lake. A crowd had gathered, and a flash of auburn hair drew my gaze. Ofelya Bos, my girlfriend. She had sent me two brief messages, but I hadn't responded.

It wasn't grief that kept me silent. It was suspicion. Of her father Polonyo. Of his possible role in my father's death.

Still, as psalms were chanted, eulogies given, the coffin lowered into stony soil, I couldn't stop myself from glancing her way, yearning for comfort. When I let a spadeful of dirt tumble into my father's grave, her green eyes caught mine, and my lip began to tremble.

Ofelya pulled away from her brother and father to console me as the final psalms tore mournful cries from the lips of many.

"Syento muncho tu példida," she muttered into my neck as she hugged me. "You must be heartbroken."

The warmth of her slender body made cold grief fade. An urge overwhelmed me to burn away my pain with her flesh, to fuse with the girl I loved and escape my lonesome void.

"Will you come with me to the villa?" I whispered.

Her lips on mine were her answer.

The following morning, Ofelya kissed me awake. The smell of coffee and pan dulce wreathed her robed form.

"Can't we just stay in bed all day?" I muttered. "Father bought me this place so we could meet without interference."

Her smile dazzled. "And I love him for it. But my parents don't know about our lakeside hideaway. Your mom, either. Won't be secret for long if they hunt us down."

Just then, shouts came from outside. Ofelya's brother, Riko, arguing with the bodyguards.

"I'll take care of him," she said, leaving the bedroom.

Pulling on some pants, I hurried to the entrance. Riko was spitting insults in Kaló.

"Puta de myelda. You think that fardi loves you? The minute he uses you up, he'll toss you out."

Marcelo had a hand against Riko's chest, keeping him at bay as I emerged.

"You're the one getting tossed out, Ósriko Bos. Take your gangster strut elsewhere before I have these two lose your ass deep in the highlands."

He left, but not before shooting me a look of utter hate.

II

In retrospect, I can't believe I didn't seek revenge for the next two months, though I did decide to finish my junior year remotely. Ba-rae was disappointed, but he understood, reiterating his readiness to aid me.

Ah, but love has a way of scabbing over every wound. And I was head over heels.

Ofelya and I spent more time together than we had since first kissing two years ago. I would pick her up from the corporate prep school nearly every afternoon, and we whiled the hours away in our little villa, a universe of two, guarded by Bernardo and Marcelo.

I could tell they were impatient for justice. To placate them, I asked Uncle Claudyo to let me intern in the R & D department. The roboticists gladly accepted me. I'm considered a prodigy, both at AutoSerf and the Haebyeon. Father taught me the basics of machine learning and motion perception when I was a kid. I designed my first rudimentary AI when I was eleven.

As part of my duties, I appointed myself general liaison with management. When Uncle Claudyo was appointed CEO—his cousin Reynaldo moving up to CFO—I made a point of congratulating him while dropping off a report.

"Grasyas, sobrín," he said, a grin spreading across his bearded cheeks. "I hope I can count on your support."

He meant *loyalty*, of course. I lowered my head in respect.

"Pol supwesto, tiyo. I'm keeping an eye on department heads. Everyone seems solid, except for Dr. Lusyano Robles. He takes a lot of calls on his personal com. Keeps the walls of his office polarized."

Cold ire glinted in Claudyo's eyes. "Interesting. Let me know of further developments."

The weeks went by. School, work, sex. Humans fall so easily into routine, which blots out emotional spikes and mysteries. Occasionally, I would make a half-hearted attempt at understanding the strange rectangle of plastic my father had left me, but my time was occupied by love, final exams, the need to fool those I mistrusted.

Until, on a single day, everything was upended, and my facade shattered.

A message from Ofelya pinged my percom not long after lunch.

`At the villa. Come when you can.`

Wondering whether something had happened to her at school, I told my supervisors that I needed the rest of the afternoon off. Bernardo and Marcelo flew me to the lakeshore, where I found my girlfriend sitting in the living room, flushed from crying.

I kissed her forehead and knelt before her. "What's wrong? Ke t'isyeron, nena?"

She shook her head. "Nobody did anything. It's what we *didn't* do, Lacho. That first time, after the funeral."

Understanding rocked me back on my heels.

"You can't be."

"I am. Now we've got to make a decision."

I stood, running fingers through the curls of my pompadour. "It's yours to make. Your body. But, damn. Terrible timing."

"Not just my fault." Her voice trembled with indignation and sorrow.

A vise of regret and hope squeezed my chest. I loved her, dreamed of forming a family with her someday, prayed for a son I could dote on. But I still had years of schooling left before I earned my doctorate.

And if I delayed my revenge much longer, how would my enemies react? If we gave Polonyo a grandchild, would I even dare?

"I don't mean that." I pulled Ofelya to her feet. "Just—tell me what you need, nena. Whatever your choice, I'll make it work."

Then I held her until the new sobs subsided.

No sooner had I dropped Ofelya off at her family's estate on the island of Arsila than I got a call from my mother.

"I need to tell you something." Her eyes were nervous. "Can you come to my office?"

Mother was one of the senators from the Sefarad Prefecture in the regional diet. Many laws benefiting Serfaty Automation had been proposed and passed through her wily politicking. She was vital to the ascendency of the corporation on Mars.

Her secretary and chief of staff waved me through. Soon I had plopped down on the plush sofa in the meeting alcove of her ample office. She took a seat in a high-backed chair to my left.

"Let me preface this by reminding you how hard your father and I have worked to get AutoSerf where it is today, a thriving and essential part of Martian economic prosperity, ready for you to inherit."

I could sense that something about Claudyo was coming next. But I was not prepared for her proposition.

"I want you to have a controlling interest, Lacho. Right now, no one does. But if I consolidate my, your father's, and your uncle's shares—"

I interrupted, "The other shareholders won't allow it. The

exchange in Ellisium Siti won't, either. Even if you could pull it off, the tax burden would be nuts."

"Unless," Mother countered, leaning forward, curls perfectly framing impassive features that might have been carved in mahogany, "your uncle and I get married. Then we have joint control of what your father left me and what we separately own."

My stomach flipped. "Marry? Claudyo? Are you out of your damn mind?"

"Miho, kalma…"

"Fuck calm, Mother. It's a stupid plan. And it's immoral. Sinful. We're Sephardim. You can't get married to your dead husband's brother if you already have a child. Yibbum doesn't apply."

She tapped her fingernails against the wooden armrest. "As long as there's no sexual intercourse, it's not a transgression. Rabbi Noé has agreed."

I leaped to my feet, all the pent-up suspicions and frustrations pouring out.

"And how much did you pay him? Chingau, amá—you can't be serious about this shit. It looks bad. It looks like you and Claudyo have been lovers all along. Just waiting for my father to die."

She struggled to maintain her composure, jaw tight, eyes widening.

"Horasyo Eliyas Serfaty, apologize at once!"

I leaned close, rage pounding in my temples, spraying words in a thoughtless snarl. "Or maybe you two nudged him toward death. Did you plot his murder after rutting in his bed? Was it poison? Nanobots? What will I find if I dig up his body?"

She slapped me, then shoved me back as she stood.

I had gone too far. But her eyes suggested I might be right.

"Get out of my office! And don't come home. Go back to school."

I didn't obey her. I went to my villa, slammed things around for a bit, then sat down and stared at the plastic rectangle.

The Hangul read *be-re-sis*. But tumblers turned in my brain, fueled by fury.

That *sis* block was pronounced *shit*. Bereshit. A Hebrew word. *Genesis*.

My heart racing, I pulled up the Torah on the house terminal. Could the first numbers be chapter and verse? No. Chapter five didn't have a verse fifty-two, and there was no chapter fifty-five.

Then it hit me. The alphanumeric string was meant to be read right-to-left, like Hebrew!

127Y041K2B3255

Genesis 1:27. "And God created humanity in His own image: in the image of God He created him; male and female He created them."

The rest of the code was now so recognizable, I wanted to slap myself.

The serial number of an automaton.

III

Robot Y041K-2B3255 was still in the warehouse, part of an order made by Kozancorp that wouldn't be filled and delivered for another three months. Once I'd bypassed the security protocols, I stood before the two-meter-tall glossy blue automaton and spoke its activation code.

Its eyes lit up yellow, and my father's voice whispered forth.

"Lacho? Miho, ez tu?"

Such intense relief and joy flooded me that I almost sobbed.

"Sí, apá. It's me. What… How did you make this happen?"

"A year ago, I implanted a new device into myself. It reads the firing of neurons in a human brain and broadcasts them into an artificial one. With time and much work remembering the past, most of a person's identity can be mirrored. So I'm your father, but he has also died."

I took the automaton's metal-and-rubber hand, so different from the leathery warmth I'd loved as a child. I stifled a sob of loss.

"What made you take this step? Something your brother did?"

Father's ghost in the machine placed its other hand on my head. "Oh, son. I discovered…an affair."

My heart had already been wrenched from its mooring. "Between Mother and Claudyo, right? They're getting married. So I can inherit a controlling interest."

Father leaned his insectoid face closer. "You'll never inherit anything if Claudyo gets his way. Nor will any children you might one day sire."

I sucked in air. "About that, Father."

"If Ofelya is pregnant with your child, she's in danger. You need to get her out of Cimmeria altogether."

"Okay, I will. But first—what is Claudyo's plan?"

"The kasike of the Brotherhood has agreed to let AutoSerf operate in the four prefectures it controls if that crime syndicate can buy a thousand units of Mekabok 3 to facilitate their expansion throughout the solar system."

"Tempting, sure," I said. "We've never gotten a foothold in the rest of Cimmeria."

The automaton curled its hands into fists. "The old rivalry. Outsiders see us as all one ethnicity, but the Simeryanes of the midregion and south—with their Catholicism and Terran Latine roots—have never accepted northerner Sephardim under that umbrella. Since those prefectures are Anka l'Ermandá, homeland of the Seys Familyas, a relationship with the Brotherhood would change the dynamic, give Sephardim access to Catholic markets."

"But screw that, right?"

"Sí. I was putting together proof for the authorities when—" a whining of gears "—when…"

"They killed you."

"Correct. But my memories are incomplete. Your mother lured me into a building. Claudyo and Polonyo were inside. As the door shut behind me, the connection was severed. My organic memories end."

I spat. "A Faraday cage. In case you were wearing a wire. But they probably never suspected…*this*."

My hand presses against the warm ovoid of his dark blue torso, emblazoned with the corporate logo.

"I worried they might. I've been immobile, but aware. For two months."

Tears prick my eyes. "I'm so sorry, apá. I should've figured out your clue faster."

He lifts my chin up with a metal fist. "Don't worry. You'll have a chance to pay me back very soon."

"How?"

"I need your help to dig up my corpse."

Father needed to physically upload the remaining memories from the device in his rotting human brain. So I snuck the automaton out of the warehouse in the dead of night. Then—with me clinging with happy dread to his back—he climbed up the sheer cliff face to the cemetery.

"I've got this, miho," he said, ripping through the stony soil with his powerful new hands. Gone forever were the smaller human hands that helped me build sandcastles beside Hellas Sea.

Father stopped and hefted a bundle out of the grave.

I took several steps back, retching. Dead bodies do not smell sweet, especially those buried the Sephardic way.

"This next part will be unpleasant," he warned. Ripping the shroud from the back of his former head, he thrust his fingers into squelching flesh.

After rummaging around, Father pulled a glittering net of black and silver from the skull.

"Bingo. Now, give me a hand. Let's see if the final broadcast is still in the buffer."

Grimacing at the putrid slime on the device, I wired it into the automaton's processor.

His yellow eyes glowed brighter.

"I've retrieved it, son."

"And?"

He cocked his insectoid head. "I was right. They killed me."

It was dawn by the time Marcelo and Bernardo—both overcome with shock and relief at their boss's digital survival—helped me hide my dad-ex-machina at the villa.

Before I could drop into bed for a few hours of rest, my terminal started dinging. It was Uncle Claudyo. While I considered how to keep him from killing me before I could reveal his crimes, Ofelya arrived, insisting we talk.

"I've decided to keep it. I'll turn seventeen next month, a legal adult. My dad and brother won't like it. You know those assholes treat me like property to be bartered for the good of the family. But they can't stop me. And if you recognize the baby as yours, they'll back off."

The adrenaline had worn off. Drowsiness pulled at my mind. I could hardly process her implied hopes.

"Nena, I support you. I want to play my part, be a good father..."

Her eyes smoldered. "Your next word had better not be *but*, Lacho."

"You don't know what's going on. I've got to do things that you won't like, that could hurt you."

She stepped closer, concern crinkling her brow. "Then, tell me. It's love, right? This thing we have? Your problems are mine, kerido."

I sighed. "It's too much for you, believe me. Let me...send you on a cruise of the Ahandae Sea or something."

"Now? Have you lost your mind?"

Seizing my curls, I groaned. "Almost. The pregnant daughter of my enemy might push me over the edge."

Ofelya balled her thin fingers into fists. "Your enemy? Since when? Why haven't you said anything to me?"

I opened my mouth but couldn't form the words.

Tears of frustration and fear rolled down her cheeks. "What the fuck are you hiding, Lacho? I have a right to know!"

I'd been lying to the most important person in my life for months. My knees buckled with the sudden weight of shame. I took her hands in mine as I crumpled, weeping at last.

"Are you on my side, nena? Can I trust you?"

She knelt beside me, her voice softening. "Of course you can. Don't you know how much I love you?"

Though fear gripped my heart, I decided to believe her. Raising my voice, I called out.

"Apá? Can you come out for a second?"

An hour later, Ofelya left the villa, shaken and somewhat depressed. Her world had been upended, so I had Bernardo follow to watch over her as she played her part. The next few days were going to be chaotic. I didn't want anything happening to her or the baby.

Also, I'd put my existence in her hands. If she betrayed me, all would be lost.

"The problem with handing the recordings over to law enforcement," my father stressed that afternoon, "is that they could claim you've doctored or generated them."

"Even if we get around all the compromised officials and cops. Between Mother and the Brotherhood, that's most of Cimmeria."

"Then, get a confession to the Martian Office of Intelligence."

"How do I get them to confess?"

"The hardest thing you'll have to do is apologize to your mother. Then, the fun begins."

Just before nightfall, I stood before my uncle's massive stone desk and lowered my head.

"I'm ashamed by my behavior, tiyo. I've just been holding back my grief, and it sort of exploded. But I've begged amá for her forgiveness. Your plan *does* make sense. It's just that it's only been two months since I lost him, sabes?"

Claudyo came around to hug me. I wanted to shudder, but I let myself melt into his embrace.

"Of course, Lacho. I wish your mother had better prepared you. Our only desire is to preserve the Serfaty patrimony, keep our hard work out of the hands of others."

"I know. And I want to help." I pulled away to look up at his grizzled mug. "My roommate at school is the son of Ellisium's governor. Father wasn't able to make inroads into that region, but I've arranged a dinner for tomorrow evening: the An family and us. I know that Mother and you can charm the governor, easily."

I couldn't tell whether his smile augured good or ill. But I hoped he was deceived.

It was a lovely dinner at an exquisite restaurant, multiple courses ending with korbina freshly pulled from Lake Gusev. My mother and uncle are gregarious, great conversationalists, and An Him-jul seemed entranced by their patter and proposals.

An Ba-rae and I, meanwhile, made quite a show of getting caught up in sharing fond memories. Eventually, our talk turned to that winter's skiing trip to Hyperborea.

"Oh, wow, you three just *have* to see the faux recordings we took of the slope toward the Chasm," Ba-rae exclaimed. "Incredible. Here! Everyone connect to my percom."

The adults humored us begrudgingly as the pink light of faux connection danced over our foreheads, pulling us into a virtual environment.

But not the snowy vistas Ba -rae had promised.

A muddy field on the island of Arsila. The back of Mother's head as she walked toward a concrete bunker of some sort.

"It's just inside," she turned to shout.

The door opening. Feigned looks of surprise on the faces of Claudyo and Polonyo.

The door shutting. Father's voice: "What is this?"

Claudyo, lifting a syringe. "The end. Cardiac arrest via nanobots that will then exit through your pores, leaving no trace. Hold him down."

A struggle. The faces of Polonyo and Mother, twisted with effort.

Then darkness.

Mother threw up all over the table. Claudyo stood, fumbling for his phone, pulling her after him.

"I d-don't know why you decided to pull such a bizarre prank, boy," he stuttered at me. "But just wait until..."

I pulled up the live news feed on my percom, projected it holographically.

Scenes of MOI agents pulling Polonyo from his home. Ofelya weeping beside her mother.

"Today the Martian Office of Intelligence arrested AutoSerf COO Polonyo Bos for the alleged crime of credit-laundering for the Brotherhood crime syndicate. Viewers may not know that Don Polonyo's nephew Baldemar Bos is the konsehero to mafia boss Pablo Samarripa, who rose to control of l'Ermandá five years ago when—"

I muted the feed. "Admit what you've done. You killed my father. I've got proof, pero tu se omme i dímelo en kara, kabrõ."

For a second, I thought I had him with the *Be a man* bullshit. But Mother slapped her palm across his opening mouth.

"Say nothing. Let's go."

IV

The worst was yet to come.

After thanking the Ans and apologizing profusely, I hurried to the villa, where I'd left Marcelo guarding my father.

The entrance was cycled open. The wood and steel were pitted by small-arms fire.

Inside, Marcelo lay dead in a pool of blood.

"No!" I howled with sinking premonition.

Rushing to the guest room, I found the automaton partially dismantled. Someone had pulled its cerebral core from the casing.

"Please, not a wipe." My hands trembled as I reconnected the core. "Let him still be there, God."

A hum of initialization, then those yellow eyes. Then a hollow, generic voice.

"Greetings. This is service bot Y041K-2B3255, ready for owner imprint and instructions."

The definitive loss of my father destroyed me. It took me days to climb out of that despair. A silent Bernardo took care of Marcelo's body and continued the duties I'd assigned him. Only once did he speak.

"Mourn, and then act. We give our lives to you Serfatys. Don't let it be for nothing."

But it was the return of Ofelya's brother Riko that stirred me at last. He pounded at the entrance for fifteen minutes before I used the intercom.

"What, Ósriko?"

"Let me in."

"No way in hell."

"Then, listen, bastard. You know why I go to Riyo Negro Kolehyo in Morelya and not some prestigious university in the north? For AutoSerf. So that this fardi-ass company can be accepted by real Simeryanes, most of whom see l'Ermandá as their rulers. But you've blown that to shit, huh? And destroyed my sister, too. So much for being in love. Your betrayal *broke* her, pendeho. She's almost suicidal."

It's an act, I reminded myself. *I can trust her.*

"Is that all?"

Riko sucked his teeth in anger. "You've got to come out someday. You'll be alone at some point. Then you'll be dead."

The threat was real. I started reaching out to other shareholders, trying to create a coalition against Claudyo and the Brotherhood. But my uncle had already gotten to most of them. For a few days I thought representative Canuto Kranz might throw in with me, but he flaked out once my mother got his latest bill filibustered.

Finally, my father's childhood friend Federico Rosen returned my call.

"Lachito, sorry. I don't own enough shares to make Claudyo even blink. And I don't need that heat. But I'll give you some inside information you might use. Riko has helped your uncle set up a demo of the Mekabok 3 to Baldemar Bos at a remote location in Tayshas. Let me forward you the coordinates, date, time. Maybe you can go secretly record them or something. Gather evidence for the authorities."

Dangerous.

Probably a trap.

But I had to try. Standing in the doorway to the guest bedroom, I stared at the shell of my father and the device on the nightstand that had given him back to me for such a short time.

Then a crazy idea occurred to me.

A week later, I helped Bernardo get the automaton into his transport.

"You sure about this, Lacho? It could really go sideways."

"I'm sure. We've tested it. There should be enough evidence, no matter the outcome. Just keep them safe. Ofelya, the baby, the automaton. At all costs."

He gave me a hug. "You got balls of steel, kid. Excuse the pun."

I took public transport down the Ma'adim River, through the Ariadne Hills, and to the outskirts of Syudá Krul. We'd paid good money to get me a caterer's uniform, and I slipped among the company employees entering the Brotherhood compound.

No matter how criminal, big gatherings always need food. But I had barely laid my first plate on a table when my uncle's voice boomed out.

"I'm so pleased to demonstrate to our partners just how remarkable the Mekabok 3 is. Pero, kerido karnal Baldemar, the best way to demonstrate military hardware is by combat. And AutoSerf has a rivalry it needs to settle. So let me introduce our two jockeys—your cousin Ósriko 'Riko' Bos and my nephew, Horasyo 'Lacho' Serfaty!"

Applause went up all around as Brotherhood foot soldiers seized me by the arms.

V

That's how I got here, inside this mech suit.

The bell sounds. I take bounding, augmented steps into the arena as criminals and corporate employees cheer.

Riko flies through the air. The ground shudders when he lands a few meters away, encased in a magenta mekabok.

I let him punch me a few times, trying to time the surprise I have planned for these assholes. I block a blow or two, swing a fist uselessly at his head.

Then I toggle a channel open.

"Engineering override, authorization alpha omega 13 X. Enter stasis."

Riko stops midkick and topples over, his suit deactivated by my backdoor code.

I turn and look up. Claudyo and Baldemar have risen from their seats.

I crouch and leap toward them.

Brotherhood lieutenants and foot soldiers draw their weapons and shoot. The mekabok deflects much of it. But not all. Something shreds my leg as I send projectiles whistling into my enemies.

The return fire rips through my arms, bursts in my stomach. Despite the pain, I slam into the far wall, killing a half-dozen men.

As the smoke clears, my uncle stands over me, laughing.

Then the black transports descend, and his smile is gone.

Armored agents of MOI spill out, weapons drawn, acting on the tip I fed them through Governor An Him-jul about battling mafia factions.

Claudyo raises both hands and drops to his knees, his grin gone.

Knowing I've avenged my father, I let darkness swirl me away.

coda

My eyes open.

No, that's not it.

My visual sensors *activate.*

"Lacho? Can you hear me?"

I'm taller than I once was. Tilting my head, I look down at Ofelya.

Her belly is bigger.

"You're huge!" I say.

Shaking her head, she gives me a tinny tap with her fist. "Those are your first words after being reborn? Really?"

I reach out and take her hands. It's not the same as human feeling, but I sense pressure, warmth, texture.

"Did it work?"

"Yes. They arrested Claudyo and Riko along with whatever yakuza survived."

"And Mother?"

"Just this morning."

I pull her into a hug.

"You were so brave. Such a great actress." Looking down at myself, I add, "And you found me the best mechanical body ever."

"Cute. But after seeing that recording, I had no choice. I love you, Lacho. I'll stand by you forever."

"I love you, too."

After a moment, she sighs.

"But the shareholders are freaking out. What's left of the board of directors is meeting tomorrow."

"Will they listen? We're the heirs, but we're also a pregnant teen and her robot boyfriend."

Ofelya's laughter is bright and fills my mechanical heart to the brim.

"Baby, our plan just took down dozens of criminal conspirators, including our closest relatives." She touches her belly. "Together? The three of us can do *anything*."

★ ★ ★ ★ ★

JUNA AND THE FOX BOY

a remix of "Beauty and the Beast"
Raquel Vasquez Gilliland

> "To see you was instantly to love you. Entering your apartment, tremblingly, my joy was excessive to find that you could behold me with greater intrepidity than I could behold myself."
>
> —Gabrielle-Suzanne Barbot de Villeneuve, "Beauty and the Beast"

When my grandmother would tell a fairy tale, she'd start it differently every time. It was never *Once upon a time.* She would say, "Before the earth had trees, and after the sun had burst, there once lived a boy."

She'd switch it up each time, but it was always that formula. *Before the earth had seas, and after the sun had laughed, there lived an old man who cried tears of diamonds.* Or a woman who had leaves for hands, or a leaf who had woman hands—whatever the story required.

I used to skip around the avocado tree behind our apartment, singing all kinds of versions of that fairy-tale beginning, imagining *I* was the main character. At any moment, the apple tree would open its mouth and speak. Or maybe a boy with a tail would take my hand and lead me somewhere unspeakably beautiful.

Unfortunately, being the star of your very own fairy tale *seems* magical, all up until you're locked in the mayor's dungeon, banging your fists against the stainless-steel door.

"Come on!" My hands were well on their way to bruised. "This isn't cute anymore!"

After another minute of silence, I let my sore legs go and sat on the floor. "Stupid small town and their stupid superstitions."

After my grandmother died, the day after my eighteenth birthday, and I had no one in the world, I took a walk to the library. I grabbed a book filled with maps detailing historic towns. I closed my eyes, flipped the book open, and slapped my pointer finger on a page.

Neck of the Woods, Maine. Population: 800. Best known for their superstitious town festivals. These folks gathered glasses of mulled wine every fall, pouring the blood-bright drink along the fallen-leaf earth, to keep away the worst of winter frosts. They marched through the main road every spring to lure away the dark, each townsperson holding a flickering candle—all looking like a thousand hovering stars.

The creepiest festival was called Beast of the Woods. An old town legend said that there was a beast who feasted on human necks who lived in—surprise!—*the woods* (insert spooky music here). Every year they offered the Beast a girl, and in return, he spared his bloodshed the rest of the year.

Of course, she wouldn't legit get her neck eaten. They'd put a flower crown on the girl's head, parade her around, and give her a medal before she went back home to her regular life.

Neck of the Woods sounded charming, sweet, and yes, just like a fairy tale—a little bit strange and dangerous. The *perfect* setup to a happy ending.

And after all I'd gone through, I wanted my happy ending really, really bad. I spent the little money Welita had hidden all over our apartment on a bus ticket there. (I could hear my grandmother's voice as I raced out the door: *Before the earth had clay, and after the sun had sneezed, there lived a girl who ran away after her grandmother died.)* As soon as I got to town, I got a job mixing teas at Señora Moonlight's Tea House.

Sighing, I stood and turned back to the basement door and tried a different tactic. "I really, really have to pee! And I'm sure you don't want me to do it all over..." I glanced around. The walls were made of bare cement blocks, with no furniture, and there was only one narrow window near the ceiling covered in duct tape. "...this really weird black tile. Am I right?"

The door opened so fast, I had to jump back. And there stood Mayor Johannessen. His normally blue eyes had this weirdly red glow.

"Uh... Mr. Mayor? You don't look so good." I took a step back. "Maybe you should get to the doctor? I could, uh—"

Before I could finish my sentence, the mayor grabbed my arms with one hand and blindfolded me with the other. There was no time to fight, unless you counted me flailing my legs as though on an invisible bicycle a fight. Which I certainly did not. Just like I could no longer consider Neck of the Woods anything close to resembling a place where *anyone*—least of all me—would get their happily-ever-after.

The mayor pushed me through another layer of thick brush. There must've been blackberries around, because for the hundredth time, thorns tore into my skirt and slashed my legs.

When he first dragged me up from the dungeon, I'd called the mayor a lot of names. Red-eyed creep, pink-eye McPink-Face. Because I guess after all this—being plucked out of the crowd at the Beast of the Woods festival and crowned with sunset-pink cosmos before being shoved into the basement—well, I just imagined that this was all still part of the celebration. I truly had believed that at any point, the mayor would laugh, tell me what a great sport I'd been, and send me back to the Tea House.

Now, though, I was pretty sure a Very Bad Thing was about to happen.

It took me a long time to gather the courage to say it aloud. “You’re going to kill me, aren’t you?”

The mayor *laughed*. “I don’t have to. The Beast will do all the work for me.”

My blindfold was ripped off. I turned around, looking for a pair of red glowing eyes, but the mayor had vanished.

Like in a freaking stupid fairy tale.

The only thing I could make out, besides woods, was a little log cabin that looked as though it were going to collapse at any moment. Woodsmoke slithered out of its tiny pipe chimney. My heart lifted. *Someone* was in that ramshackle house, and chances were they had a cell phone. I could get unlost from these woods. Maybe I’d also get the mayor arrested. So I marched right onto its rickety porch.

This time, the door I was trying to break down was made of carved cedar. I recognized the smell because my grandmother used to rub the oil in my hair at night. *Cedar is a protector,* she’d tell me.

I felt like I might’ve reached protection in that moment. Until the door opened.

A boy stood there, glowering at me. My jaw dropped.

This guy was beautiful. He had dark eyes framed by thick lashes, a full, pouty mouth, and brown hair that turned red in the day’s last sunlight. His skin was as brown as his cedar door, and glowing, too. Not in the weird-vampiric-mayor way. More like a fifteen-step-skincare-ritual way.

He was so beautiful I could ignore his strange clothes. The starched button-down, the pressed trousers. The suspenders.

He wasn’t beautiful enough for me to ignore the foxtail.

Or the pointed red-furred ears.

“Is that—” I pointed before I realized his glowering had now turned into a full-on murder glare. “I mean—” I pulled my hand behind my back. “He—the mayor—*trapped* me. He put me in a dungeon basement, with really odd, dark tile, and then his eyes turned into freaking headlights, and then he just left me *here*, you *need* to help me, I *need* to get—"

And you know what the fox-tailed boy did?

He rolled his eyes. "Jesus. Not again."

And then he slammed the door in my face.

Threatening to pee all over the Fox Boy's porch did not inspire him to open the door, unfortunately. "I need your help!" I kicked the cedar. The sun was low in the sky, and I was not used to this much nature. I'd about passed out at the sound of a distant owl's hoot ten minutes prior.

I sat by the door as the woods filled with the sound of shrieking crickets. Something tickled my hand. When I lifted it up, a big, harmless black ant was there, as curious as a squirrel. "So what are the chances those ears on that boy are actually a costume?" I whispered to the bug. No response, fortunately.

So maybe the boy's foxtail wasn't exactly fake. Regardless, he was the only chance I had to get back to my little one-room rental behind the Tea House with its amazing vintage lamps. I sighed and let the ant walk off my finger back onto the porch.

If Fox Boy wouldn't help me, I was looking at one heck of a bleak fairy-tale ending.

I had one more angle to try. Guilt.

I made my voice as trembly as I could. "Fine. I'm leaving now. But if I die of exposure, that's on you, buddy."

The door swung open, and there he stood.

"Get in," Fox Boy snarled. And then he disappeared from view, leaving the door open.

I walked in slowly. "Very rustic," I said. Which was my nice way of describing a kitchen with a small woodstove, a living area with two blankets, and a fireplace that looked as though it had been constructed out of river rocks.

Fox Boy reappeared so suddenly, I yelped and jumped back. "Sit," he growled.

I was too exhausted to argue. As soon as I sat, he dropped a bucket of soapy water and a rag next to me. "Clean your wounds."

I looked down and saw drips of dried blood all over my legs. I ran the rag over my skin, washing away the blood. "Ouch." I scratched at a thorn, buried in my knee cap.

"What is it?" he barked.

"Nothing."

After a long moment, he sighed and turned toward me. He pounced my way, pushed away my hands, and used legit *claws* to pull the thorn out.

"Ow." I winced. "Thanks."

He rolled his eyes and pulled out a jar of what looked like green putty. He went to work, gently covering each scratch and scrape with the balm. He glanced up at me when he finished.

I about jumped out of my skin when I met his eyes this close. There were these gold rings around the irises that spun and spun like planets. I swallowed. "You're not human." I'd known it when he answered the door, but it felt very vulnerable, and raw, confronting the fact aloud. He smiled and flicked his tongue over an extra-long canine. "You learned a lot slower than the last girl he dropped off."

The last girl he— I froze. "You don't mean—"

"I do."

"You mean to say—"

"I do."

"Let me finish a sentence, will you!" I took in a frantic breath. "*You're* the Beast of the Woods."

As in, not just a random shape-shifter, or halfling, or changeling you'd find in a fairy tale.

He was the actual creature this town warded away to save their literal necks. Because he was the actual creature who *ate necks.*

He widened his smile as he stood, his tail curled behind him. "I am."

"So let me get this straight," I said over a bowl of fideo soup. "The mayor is a brujo. And he enchanted you however many years ago—"

"Five," Fox Boy said. "Five years ago."

"Because the town wasn't scared about the Beast of the Woods anymore?"

"Brujos eat fear, and the mayor was starving. He specifically eats the girls' fear. The townspeople still think it's just a charming old tale."

"A charming old tale? Even though girls disappear every year?"

He shrugs. "They find their way back. Everyone thinks they're nuts when they say they met *the Beast*." He makes scary fingers—*claws*—at me.

This doesn't surprise me. People barely believe teenage girls with plenty of evidence of the horrible things that have happened to them. "So he eats the girls' fear. *One* girl's fear."

"Terrorizing one girl a year is enough to sustain him, I guess." Fox Boy popped a piece of tortilla in his mouth. "I don't know why he can't just scare a girl. Why he's got this whole setup." He lifts his arms, then drops them again.

"He's theatrical."

Fox Boy shrugs.

"So the story went from just a story to literal. And he drops off a girl so you can eat her neck—"

Fox Boy growled. "I don't eat necks."

"So what happened to the last girl?"

Fox Boy shrugged. "I dunno. She ran off after she saw the tail."

I raised an eyebrow.

"I'm telling the truth. I *don't eat necks*."

"But you're cursed to never leave the town *unless* you eat a neck."

At this, Fox Boy bit at his lip.

"What?" I asked. "What aren't you telling me?"

"I *can* leave town. I just...won't exactly be the same, after."

"What the hell is that supposed to mean?"

He sighed and, I could tell, barely refrained from rolling his eyes. Eyes that were a little sad, to be honest. "If I leave Neck of the Woods, I sort of...dissolve. And become a part of the woods."

I threw my spoon down. "You mean you die."

"It's not exactly that—"

"Dissolving and becoming part of the woods is what dead bodies do, Fox Boy."

He looked down. "*My name is* Lago." He stood. "Not that it will matter for much longer."

His words were way too heavy. "You're going to do it, aren't you? You're going to die on purpose."

His back was toward me, his tail flitting—with nerves, maybe. "You don't know what *this* is like."

"To be fair, very few people know what that's like."

He turned and took my bowl and spoon. "I will show you back to town tomorrow. You can sleep in the living room. There's bedding stuff in the bathroom cupboard." His cheeks reddened. "Sorry, I don't have any beds. At all."

I shrugged. "It's okay. I'm used to the floor." My welita made sure we always had enough to eat. But we were poor enough that saving up for sleeping bags felt like the biggest luxury of all time.

This made him blink. "Okay, well. One house rule. You can't look at me from sunset to sunrise."

I furrowed my brow. "What is that code for? You don't want to make out or something?"

Now his cheeks were scarlet. "*Looking.* I was talking about *looking.* As in *don't.*"

I raised my hands. "Fine. No looking." I turned my head and shut my eyes to illustrate my point. "By the way, in case you were wondering, I have a name too!" I called as he turned away. "It's Juna."

But just as the horizon line pulled in the sun, and he closed his bedroom door, I glanced toward it really fast. I breathed a sigh of relief when all I saw was a shadow in the sliver of door before it clicked shut. I didn't *want* to be that kind of person. Someone who couldn't stop themselves from crossing a boundary. And yet… I didn't know why, but I felt like I was only getting about one-quarter of the story.

And if I had to break his rule to figure the rest out, I would.

"So," I said.

"So." Fox Boy—er, Lago—was walking me back to town. He'd jostled his dark hair to hide the points of his ears and tucked his tail along the side of his pant leg. He couldn't do anything about his claws, or those spinning-planet eyes, but he grunted that he wouldn't be going into town, anyway, when I'd pointed out someone might notice.

"So there's no way to break the spell? Other than eating a neck."

Lago said nothing. But his cheeks grew pink.

"Ha!" I said, pointing as I stepped over a giant river rock. "There *is* a way."

"It's nothing."

"It's something. Otherwise you wouldn't be turning as red as a pepper."

"It's impossible."

"Is it that you have to make out with someone?"

Lago tripped, but bounded up so fast, for a moment he was just a blur. *"What?"*

"You're about as embarrassed now as when I mentioned making out last night. Which means maybe there's a connection." I tried and failed to hide a smile.

"Making out with anyone isn't going to stop the curse," he grumbled.

"You sure? You ever tried it?"

His cheeks were even pinker, but he didn't answer the question. Instead, he gestured for me to follow him on a log serving as a bridge over a wild, rambling river.

"We have to go on that *thing*?" I gasped. "Why can't we go *around* the river?"

"Around the river." He raised an eyebrow. "You realize it goes about thirty miles in each direction? And one of those directions is right into the sea?"

I groaned. "Fine."

Halfway across, I was the one who tripped. My reflexes weren't as refined as Lago's, but he more than made up for it, appearing instantly in front of me, grabbing ahold of my waist to keep me steady. I wrapped my hands around his forearms, which flexed underneath my grip.

We were close. Closer than we'd ever been. Each of us breathed probably harder than necessary, and I was certain there was pink in my cheeks to match his this time.

"No," he grunted, shaking me from this strangely charged moment.

I dropped my arms, and then so did he. My skin tingled where his hands had been. "No, what?"

"No. I've never…made out with anyone."

"Like, ever?" I side-grinned, despite my recent brush with death.

He grunted something that sounded like a *no*.

"But it's so much fun!"

He grunted again.

"Maybe you should try it before you go on and dissolve into the woods. You know? Live a little before dusting yourself."

This time, his grunt was this super-annoyed groan, and once we were on the other side of the river, he walked at a breakneck speed so I had to jog to keep up.

"Here." He stopped at the edge of the woods. "The Tea House is to the left. The museum is to the right. You know your way from here, I take it?"

I nodded, but then he started back off into the woods before I could say anything. As in, he was going to just leave without saying goodbye!

And maybe I hit my head last night, getting dragged through the woods by Mr. Headlight Eyes, because...I didn't *want* this to be the last time I'd see Lago.

I didn't want him to turn to dust on the edge of town.

My mother chose to turn to dust herself after we lost my dad in an accident. She wasn't cursed to turn to literal dust for leaving town, but her overdose had pretty much the same result.

"Lago!"

He turned just enough to angle one of those furred ears my way.

The words came without any forethought. "Could you point me to the mayor's house?"

Now he turned all the way. "What did you just say?"

"The mayor's house. Where does he live, again?"

"Everyone knows where the mayor lives."

"All the houses on Mansion Avenue look identical." The street isn't called Mansion Avenue, but it may as well be.

He walked slowly toward me. "Why do you want to know?"

"I—" I looked around, at the bright sun through the thick leaves of the woods. What could I say? *I'm trying to figure out a way to keep you near me, and I'll say anything to do so.* "Well, I left something in his dungeon."

He narrowed his eyes. "You're lying."

"I'm not." I was. I totally was.

He began walking away again.

"Fine!" I shouted. "I'm going to go tell the mayor to reverse your curse, you ungrateful jerk! And if you won't tell me where he lives, I'll find out myself."

I stomped toward Main Street, but an arm held me back suddenly. I turned and saw nothing but the gold, undulating planets of his eyes.

"He'll kill you. You don't get how easy it would be for him. He can conjure *extra hands* to do whatever he wants."

Well, I guess that explained how the mayor was able to put a blindfold on me while holding me down at the same time. I put my hands on my hips. "You know what? I'm tired of people I care about dying." First my dad, then my mom. And lastly, my welita's heart attack earlier this year. I'm not only tired of everyone I care about dying, I'm also tired of having *no one*. "So I've got to try, okay? Before you go and disperse into weeds or whatever."

Lago blinked. "You…care. About…me?"

I thought of how he made sure I cleaned my wounds. How he carefully pressed balm into them so they wouldn't get infected. How he made me extra fideo. How he saved me from falling without hesitation.

How pink he turned when I first mentioned the idea of making out.

Lago was like me. Wildly lonely, for one. We'd each gone through many impossibly cruel things. We were stars, hurtling toward each other, and I didn't mind at all that there was not exactly a small chance of a white-hot explosion once we got together. Why couldn't we go through everything awaiting us together?

For the first time in a long time, I could imagine someone else in my fairy-tale-wish of a life.

I shrugged. "Yeah. I do."

He swallowed and then turned toward town. "This way."

"This is it." Lago sounded exasperated.

"Okay." I wasn't sure what to do now. Which made sense,

considering the reason I thought up this plan was to figure out how to get Lago to stay—not to actually face the mayor again.

The mayor doesn't scare me, I told myself. And then I realized something—it wasn't just a little pep talk. It was *true*. The mayor *didn't* scare me. Being alone had. But now I was trying to keep that from happening again. And besides, what could he do in broad daylight, anyway?

I marched up the brick path to the ugly, colonial-style home, until Lago pulled me around one of the tall hedges.

"Juna," he hissed. "You can't just walk up to the front door."

"Why not? It's polite."

We were, like, really close again. Enough that I noticed a single freckle over the line of his bottom lip, and the planets of his eyes started looking more like electrons orbiting atoms.

Maybe that's why we didn't notice the mayor until it was too late.

"Well," Mayor Johannessen said, clapping his hands so that Lago and I both jumped. "If it isn't the girl and the Beast."

"Mr. Mayor," I said. "Looks like you got your pink eye cleared up. Good for you."

He blinked and scowled. "You're not afraid, are you? That's why..." He paused.

"What? You didn't get your evil fear feast?" I asked.

"Juna," Lago said in a warning.

"That's fine," the mayor said, smiling. "There are many ways to make you afraid."

And just like that, I was blindfolded. Again.

Unfortunately, being the star of your very own fairy tale *seems* magical, all up until you're locked in the mayor's dungeon for the *second* time, banging your fists against the stainless-steel door.

But this time, I wasn't alone.

Lago was currently pacing the room, grumbling about what an idiot I was.

"It's not a big deal." I gestured to the room. "I've totally been locked here before."

"That's not the point, Juna." Why did I get a shiver every time he said my name? "You don't know what he's capable of."

"I know he has like twelve brujoish hands. I know he's capable of turning a human boy into half a fox." I gestured to Lago's claws but…he didn't *have* any claws.

I bounded to him and grabbed his hand. "What's going on here?" I glared at him. "You're—"

He groaned. "It's sundown, isn't it?"

"What—" And I glanced at his ears—normal, shell-shaped. I didn't want to invade his space by feeling for a tail, but I was certain that was gone, too.

"What do you mean, sundown?"

"I turn…you know. Back to normal. At night."

I cupped his face, forcing it to angle down toward me. "Oh, thank God."

"What?"

"You still have your planet eyes."

His cheeks pinkened. "You…like them?"

"I like everything about you, Lago."

The air was so charged between us, the hairs on the back of my neck stood up. It felt just like the moment before a lightning strike. Or a kiss.

"Want to make out?"

The answer must've been yes, because then Lago bent down and pressed his lips to mine.

He was warm, and soft, and…all the things I thought a fairy tale should be. Entirely *magical*.

He pulled back. "Is this okay?"

I responded by getting up on my tiptoes and connecting our mouths again. I put my hands on his waist and pulled, until my back hit the door. He groaned in a way that made my knees weaken, and he did it again when I slid my tongue against his.

When he leaned more, to press his lips over my neck, I trembled. "This is the best make-out session of my life."

"Agreed."

Just as I was about to point out that it was the *first* make-out session of *his* life, the door swung open. I tumbled right on top of Lago, and he steadied me with his hands on my hips, and even though I knew that dumb mayor was probably going to mangle us with his three hundred hands, I kissed Lago once more. Why not, right?

"Enough!" Lago and I pulled back as the mayor shouted. He reached toward us, pulling Lago by the neck. With eyes aglow like a couple of bottles of fridge-lit Pepto Bismol, he grunted, "You won't want anything to do with him after this."

And then Lago contorted his spine in anguish. He groaned as his tail returned, as his ears narrowed and reddened with fur.

It didn't stop there. His nose pulled and pulled until it was a snout. His hands rounded until they were large paws. He let out a whimper that made my heart drop.

"He's hurting! Stop it! Just let us go, you creep!"

But the mayor did not stop. He kept working his brujo magic, until Lago was no longer a boy. Instead, he was a fox—*all* fox, from the fur along his body to the whiskers on his face.

"Turn him back." My heart thudded as my hands shook.

"Ah." The mayor closed his eyes and took a long, deep inhale. "There it is."

He meant the fear emanating from me like fog over the mountains. Because, fact was, what I told Lago was true. I may not care about myself much, but I was sick and tired of losing the people I cared about.

So I took my own deep breath and pushed that fear down and away.

The mayor's eyes flickered open. "Oh, so you're going to be fearless again?" He reached one series of seemingly endless hands toward Lago, and one toward me. Both of us tried to fight back, but it was pretty futile. My hands and legs were bound within moments. Lago managed to snap his jaw around one of the hands but didn't hold on long.

Then we were both bound, with one of his hands around each of our necks. "Your choice, Juna," the mayor said as he squeezed. "You are free to go. You can return to the Tea House and live your life as you like."

"What's the catch?" I sputtered out.

"Lago will stay as he is. A fox."

I closed my eyes briefly. "What's my other choice?"

"Well, I crush my hand around your neck until it snaps your spine. But Lago will be able to become as he was. Half fox, half man."

When my grandmother passed, I had no one and nothing. Neck of the Woods was supposed to be *my* choice. *My* happily-ever-after.

And the mayor thought he could take that from me?

Absolutely not.

So I said to the mayor, very slowly and carefully, "Once upon a time, before the sun had set and after the earth had flowered, there lived a girl who kicked a brujo's ass."

I guess that rendered him speechless for a moment, but it was long enough. I dug my nails into his hand, and when all his other hands loosened, I jumped on the man like he was a runaway train I needed to catch.

I stomped. I slapped. I kneed him right where it hurts the most, and that's when he let Lago go. And then it was two against one.

"You've just ensured both of your deaths," the mayor said, snapping his fingers, and all those invisible hands came around us. We were trapped once again, me trying to get hands off my face, Lago baring his teeth and snapping and growling. Mayor Johannessen shook his head. "You could've gone free, Juna. I don't understand this insolence."

"If you knew what it was to love anyone, you'd understand."

The mayor blinked. "What did you say?" He sounded weird, his voice catching in a way I'd never heard before.

He sounded *afraid*.

So I yelled it this time. "I said, if you knew what it was to love anyone, you'd freaking understand!"

And out of nowhere, the invisible hands just…dissolved. They became the texture of sand, prickly at my skin, before disappearing altogether. The mayor's eyes widened, but their pink dimmed until they were regular, old, creepy-man eyes. "No," he gasped.

"What's going on?" I whispered.

"It's the curse." I turned in a rush, because—oh, my gosh—Lago. He was *back*! Everything looked human. Everything except for his beautiful planet eyes. He grinned at me and my heart stuttered. "You broke the curse, Juna."

"Because of love?" I asked.

But he didn't need to answer. In the fairy tales, love always broke curses. And maybe I actually was in one, after all.

"No!" the mayor screamed. "I put my *blood* in that curse. It couldn't be broken or else—"

"Or else you'd be just a regular old guy again. No more brujo," Lago finished.

Lago wasn't kidding about *old*. The mayor looked as though he'd aged a decade. He also appeared terrified out of his mind. I might've felt bad for him if it weren't for the fact that he had been about to kill us with a thousand sightless hands.

"I suppose you'll want to off me and be done with it now." The mayor's voice was shaky.

"Is that a joke?" I said. "You seriously think you'd be worth the effort?"

The mayor sneered in response.

But that was all he could do. He couldn't hurt us anymore.

So Lago took my hand. He said to the mayor, "You living

the way you hate to live—your idea of weakness—is revenge enough for me."

And then he led me out the door.

"So," Lago said, once we'd reached my little room in the back of the tea shop.

"So," I said.

"I'm not part-fox anymore."

"I noticed."

He bit his lips. "Is that okay?"

I shrugged. "Why wouldn't it be?"

He took a breath and sat at my desk chair. "Well…before, I didn't want you to see me as a whole human, after the sun set, because I was afraid you'd prefer that. But now I guess, I'm a little…"

"You're afraid I prefer Fox Boy?"

He shrugged, and then gave me a reluctant nod.

I stood and walked closer to him. When I placed my hands on his shoulders, his breath hitched. I couldn't help but smile at his reaction to my touch. "I prefer Lago, okay?"

His eyes welled just a little, and he said, "Thanks for saving me."

I smiled. "Thank you, too."

He scoffed. "I didn't do anything, though."

"You cleaned my wounds. You protected me. You made out with me. You were my friend when I desperately needed one. You made me feel loved, and so I loved you back."

His eyes dropped to my lips. "I'm not sure if we've made out enough to warrant a thank-you."

I nodded my head, making my expression serious. "I think you're right. I definitely need to experience a great deal more of it."

I sat in his lap and kissed him, soft. He pulled back and said, "Juna?"

"Yeah?"

"I love you, too."

And then he lowered his lips to mine.

And I realized then that I *had* gotten my fairy-tale ending. And the thing was, it wasn't just about getting together with the cute (former) Fox Boy. It was about the fact that I had wrangled my way to Neck of the Woods. It was also the fact that I had fought for who I loved and let myself be loved, too.

Welita would have been proud. In fact, she might've said something like: *Once before the earth had set and after the sun had whispered, there was a girl who fought a brujo with a thousand hands and won.*

And she earned *her happily-ever-after.*

★ ★ ★ ★ ★

PREFIERO NO

a remix of "Bartleby, the Scrivener"
Alexandra Villasante

> "'I prefer not to,' he respectfully and slowly said, and mildly disappeared."
>
> —Herman Melville, "Bartleby, the Scrivener"

No.

They were going to say *no.* Grace held on to the grubby old shoebox like it was floating debris from the *Titanic*, like she was frozen to it, like it could save her.

But the contents of that shoebox had probably sunk her. Three faculty members had sat in front of her, stone-faced, watching as she set up her work on the folding table, fumbled with the delicate acetate cuttings, and nervously stammered a speech that she'd memorized.

They hadn't said the word *no.*

They'd said, *Thank you.*

They'd said, *You'll hear from us.*

Then they'd turned to the next person in the admission queue.

Her face burned as she stood on the sidewalk outside the School of Visual Arts, as people—artists, real honest-to-Diosa artists—weaved in and out of the building on Twenty-Third Street, making art, talking about art. Being artists.

A text from Mamá popped up on her phone. It was a single letter, *¿Y?*

It meant *And?* And, what did they say? And, was I right?

Graciela Capris Ramos was not gonna answer that text. Her mother *had* been right, and Grace was too stubborn, too caprichosa (like her middle name), to admit it.

That left the problem of what to do with the rest of her day. She didn't know anyone in Midtown; her nearest friend, Emilio Chen, lived in Chinatown and was more of her brother's friend than hers. The thought of getting on the downtown train, walking through the overheated subway to then climb into a frigid train car that invariably had the AC jacked all the way up, even in mid-May, actually repelled Grace. She wished she could blink her eyes and appear in her room, in the apartment where she lived with Mamá and her brother, Bambi, six blocks from Van Cortlandt Place in the Bronx. Going home would take a subway ride and would solidify the defeat she felt starting to suffocate her. She couldn't.

A white girl, with bright red locks, carrying a huge portfolio and looking like she'd won the lottery, pushed past Grace without a glance. She was probably gonna get accepted into the school that Grace had been dreaming about since she'd stolen Bambi's copy of *Maus* out of his room and found out that Art Spiegelman had taught at this school. She didn't want to be an illustrator like him, though. She wanted to make treasures.

She started walking west and turned right at Madison Park, seeking the cool of the shadows in the scant trees. As she passed a garbage can, she had an urge to ditch her shoebox and give up. Her high-school art teacher, who, yes, was a nun and also the math teacher at the tiny all-girls Catholic school she attended, had told her not to show her new work at the admissions review.

"It's a bit morbid, don't you think?" Sister Anne had asked, frowning at the little displays.

"It's not. They're beautiful scenes. Look, this one is a flower,"

Grace had said, holding up the wood-and-acetate box. The precise, laser cutouts in the shapes of flowers and tiny insects created large flower shadows against Sister Anne's office wall.

"It's not the shapes, Grace, that are the problem. It's what they're made of."

Grace was lost in remembering the encounter, how determined she had been to show her new work, the works she was finally, seriously passionate about, instead of the technically good, soulless portrait paintings that had gotten her awards at school. When she looked up to see where she was, she was already at Thirty-Second Street.

She had to decide what to do: head home to explanations, *I told you so*s, and sympathy, or somehow escape her failure.

An M4 bus was idling right next to a sign that said *No Idling*. The bus driver, a stout man with a mustache and black hair clinging to his sweaty forehead, stood outside his vehicle, shaking a finger at a girl who was inside.

As Grace approached, she could hear the driver's tense words.

"You can't stay on the bus!"

The girl said nothing.

"You've ridden the route three times already! Don't you have other things to do?"

The girl shrugged and responded, so low that Grace could only hear her when she'd stepped closer. "Prefiero no."

"Hijo de la Virgen," the driver muttered. "Look, you have to get off. You can't keep riding around like this is a freaking tour bus. I'm off shift in two minutes, and I need you off!"

The driver held his hand out to the girl, maybe to help her down the two steep steps or to implore her to become someone else's problem. Grace moved closer still, with a feeling that she needed to witness whatever this was.

"Prefiero no," the girl repeated as she shuffled her feet farther from the exit.

The driver took a menacing step closer to the bus. Before

she knew what she was doing, Grace put herself between the driver and the girl.

"Hey."

"What?" the driver said to Grace, shifting his view down to where she stood, all five foot nothing of her.

"Can I get on?"

She held out her MetroCard to the driver like it was a flag of truce.

"I need to get this kid off the bus first," he said, gesturing to the girl on the bus.

Grace didn't turn toward the girl, keeping her eyes on the driver.

"Why?"

"What do you mean, *why*?"

"Didn't she pay the fare?"

"She's been on the bus since I came on shift at 6:20 a.m.! She says she lost her MetroCard."

Again, Grace experienced the feeling of doing without thinking.

"I've got an extra card. She can have it. So no problem, right?"

He looked from the girl on the bus to Grace and back again. Sighed. "I guess," he said. But still didn't move. Grace was aware of the glances from passersby, gauging if this was an ordinary chaotic moment that they could ignore, something to watch to break the tedium, or one of those times in New York City where people would ask, *Where were you when this cataclysmic thing happened?*

Grace put on her best, nothing-to-see-here face and repeated, "So no problem, right?"

She didn't know why she did it—probably something to do with her lizard brain, if Bambi, who was studying psychology at Baruch, were to be believed—but she sat down right next to the girl who refused to get off the bus.

"Hi," she said, sliding her shoebox and backpack under her seat.

The girl said nothing.

"That guy, right?" Grace said, gesturing to the driver who was gathering his bag, his newspaper, and getting off the bus—all while telling the other driver, a Black woman with long magenta braids, about how terrible it was that he had to deal with Crazy Ass Customers. The woman nodded sympathetically but looked through the window at where Grace and the No Girl sat. She was probably thinking what Grace was thinking. *How could that girl make so much trouble?*

The No Girl—that's what Grace called her in her mind—was pretty, with deep brown eyes, lashes that looked false but weren't, and light-brown skin a full two shades lighter than Grace's on the cafecito scale. Grace and her best friend Lainey had created the cafecito scale in middle school (Grace was like a cortado, especially now that she'd bleached her short curly hair nearly platinum; Lainey was a milky Thai tea with boba for the freckles—yes, tea was also on the cafecito scale.)

The No Girl had straight black hair twisted into a claw clip and bangs. She wore a spaghetti-strap peach tank top and a denim skirt. Her toenails were painted to match her tank top, which also matched the chunky bangle on her wrist. She kept her gaze steadily out the window. On Madison Avenue, a man leaned against his *Repent! End of the World* sign, and a young girl skated in place, handing out flyers. A few steps behind her, people discarded the pink flyers—for watch repairs? Sandwiches? Comedy nights?—into a garbage can; most of the ads flitted out of the bin to skip along the sidewalk with the south-blowing breeze. The girl in the skates didn't notice.

Grace raised her phone to take a picture of the mundane and iconic street scene when the girl next to her flinched and put her arm up, as if to protect herself.

"Whoa! I'm not gonna hurt you."

The girl's mouth opened slightly. Grace could see very straight white teeth behind her full lips and peachy gloss.

"I'm Grace."

The girl said nothing.

"What's your name? I promise it won't cost you anything to tell me."

The new bus driver slotted herself into the seat and shut the folding doors, cutting off the previous driver complaining about a passenger who wouldn't get off the *damn* bus. Grace caught the bus driver's eyes in the rearview mirror. The bus driver raised an eyebrow.

"All good?" she asked.

"We're great," Grace said, in her chirpiest voice and even waved idiotically.

When she turned back to the girl next to her, she heard a breathy whisper say, "Davina. That's my name."

The M4 bus moved like it didn't know what time, traffic, or other vehicles were.

Davina was no longer looking out the window; she kept her eyes trained in front of her. Unlike Grace, who balanced her sketchbook on her knees, examining every person who got on or off the bus, looking for interesting colors or shapes, using her color pencils like a seismographic needle, recording the flux and shifts of gente moving through the city.

One old woman with a wheeled shopping buggy sat in the accessible seats near the front, presenting Grace with a profile like a Mesoamerican queen. She made a boxy outline in gray for the woman's shabby coat, then used every color she had to form the deep shadows and highlights of the woman's face.

"Es como un jarrón de flores," Davina whispered. She'd been so quiet, Grace had forgotten she was there, which often happened when she was sketching. But it also happened when she was relaxed. Something about Davina's silence was a balm against the riot of emotions Grace had boarded the bus with. Now she'd been distracted by the work of drawing, and it took her a minute to process the girl's voice, then translate the Spanish.

"It's not a vase of flowers," she said, hesitating.

Davina rolled her eyes. "I didn't say that."

"Oh. What did you say?"

"*Como* a vase of flowers," Davina said.

Like a vase of flowers. Grace looked down at the sketch again. She'd been lost in making the tonal whorls of pinks, oranges, and browns of the old woman's skin, like van Gogh's starry night, but in firework colors. That face above the column of the black-and-gray raincoat *did* sort of look like a vase of flowers.

"Yeah. I can see that," Grace said, slightly squinting.

Davina looked out the window, a flush on her cheeks like she'd said something embarrassing.

"You have a really good eye," Grace said, then nearly smacked herself for saying something so boring. That's the kind of thing her art teacher said to her when she didn't know what else to say. What did *having a good*—or bad—*eye* matter when making art?

Davina lifted one shoulder in a shrug, then curled herself farther away from Grace. Outside the window, Madison passed by in fits and starts and sluggish runs. Grace was getting hungry. Luckily, she was never without food, stashed in various pockets inside and outside her backpack. First tier of snacks was always the bulkiest, and that meant the plátano chips con limón.

She opened the bag with a little pop, and the sound got Davina's attention, as Grace had hoped.

"Want some?"

Davina's headshake didn't seem all that definitive to Grace.

"You sure?" Grace waved the open bag comically in front of Davina.

"Prefiero..."

Here it comes, Grace thought. She was a *no* magnet.

"Prefiero...chicharrones. Do you have any?"

★ ★ ★

The M4 stopped at Fort Washington and Cabrini Boulevard. Grace and Davina were the last people on the bus. The driver eyed them from her seat.

"I'm getting coffee. Are you getting off?"

"Prefiero no," Davina muttered. She sounded weary.

"No, thank you!" Grace said.

"Don't do anything weird," the driver said and closed the doors from the outside so new passengers couldn't get on without paying.

The engine idled, one of the last remaining buses that were not part of the clean-energy electric fleet. The more heat exhaust the bus poured into the summer air, the icier the air-conditioning inside became. Davina shivered.

"I have an extra sweatshirt," Grace said, digging into her backpack.

Davina giggled, holding her hand over her mouth as if to hide her amusement.

"What?"

"It's like a magic bag," Davina whispered. All of Davina's words were faint. Grace liked it. It meant that she had an excuse to lean in a little closer to the girl to hear. Her breath smelled like artificial peaches—the lip gloss. Grace wished she could lean even closer.

"Gracias," Davina said, once she'd popped the borrowed hoodie over her head. Grace already had her black velvet-and-lace cardigan on, over her madras plaid-shirt dress and fishnet stockings.

"If you're still cold, we could get off the bus. There's Fort Tryon Park and the Cloisters. I have more snacks, we could—"

"No."

This *no* was hard and absolute. It had been going so well: she'd made Davina smile, shared plátanos and mint M&Ms, and best of all, Grace had been able to firmly ignore her disastrous morning. What had happened?

Davina's face closed down. In Grace's black hoodie she looked incongruous and lost. Now she turned away from Grace, back to the window that was her refuge.

Grace felt the urge to stuff all her snacks back into her bag and find another place to sit. Or just get off the bus. She could easily walk to the A train and be home in no time. Her failure at SVA seemed to be a lifetime ago, though it still stung.

"I'm sorry," Davina murmured. "I want to go with you. But I can't."

"You mean, *you prefer not to*," Grace said, grudging and hurt.

"Sí. That is what I prefer. But not because of you. Only because..." Davina turned in her seat.

"What?"

Davina's solemn eyes met Grace's. "On the bus is safer than off the bus."

"What's in your box?" Davina pointed to the shoebox Grace had placed at her feet.

"Would you believe me if I told you they were just shoes?"

"No."

"Why not?"

"Because no one guards shoes like they are their whole life."

"You haven't met my brother, Bambi. He's a total sneakerhead."

"Bambi?"

"His real name is Gonzalo—we're *the* Gs, Gonzalo y Graciela. But I call him Bambi because he's got these huge brown eyes like liquid chocolate and gold—like the deer in the Disney movie." Grace shrugged. Bambi had texted before his classes that morning—*Buena suerte, nena, not that you need it, you art genius*—and it hurt to think of having to tell him that the School of Visual Arts didn't share his opinion.

"So what *is* in the box?"

Grace lifted the box from the floor and settled it on her lap. She'd allowed herself to believe she had some talent: that's what hurt so much. If she was talented, then it wasn't just the fact that she could sketch realistic-looking faces or knew how to combine colors in ways that made each color brighter, deeper; her ideas had to be good, too. And if they were ordinary, if they didn't move people or make them think, what was the point? She might as well go into advertising or architecture like her mamá wanted. Something *practical.*

Davina waited patiently next to her, as if she had all the time in the world.

The lid came off almost as if by magic, Grace's hands moving before her mind could clamp down and say, *No. No more making our heart vulnerable today.*

She took out the slivers of plastic, one of the wooden box frames, the electric votive candle, the wooden base with the slots, and took a deep breath.

"I'm an artist," she said, and it was hard to say, as it always was. "I make things like this. Wait, it will take me a minute to set it up, okay?"

"I'll wait."

Grace put the lid back on the box to act as a table, then assembled her piece. She was aware of the bus moving through the city, the swings and turns, the shudder of the engine, and yet her hands were steady. She settled on the piece she called Al Pastor, named after her abuelo's favorite kind of taco and for the way it made her think of him and his summer garden.

When she was finished, there was an eight-inch wooden cube in her hand. Davina leaned in to look at the diorama and gasped.

"It's so beautiful!"

Grace waited.

"The light makes the shadows, and it's a picture—is it a garden?"

"It's supposed to be my abuelo's garden in Punta Gorda."

"The little flowers and the trees, and the figuritas! And... the little pieces are cut out..." Davina looked up at her. "Are those—como se dice?—radiografías?"

Grace nodded. "They're X-rays. Most of the ones I use, I found in a dumpster outside St. Luke's Roosevelt Hospital. These are the last set of X-rays Abuelo had. I cut them into shapes to build an image on the little wall inside the cube, and the light makes the shadows, see?" She pointed to the battery-operated votive candle. When she'd showed the admission board the candle, one of a pack of six she'd gotten from Jack's 99 Cent shops, she'd been so proud of her ingenuity, the neatness of the piece, and the way it contained so much of her heart, her sorrow over Abuelo's death, and her effort to keep a part of the beauty she remembered of him. And they'd looked at her art like it was tacky, like it belonged on the shelf of Jack's 99 Cents and nowhere else.

Davina grabbed Grace's hand, surprising her back to where she was, on the M4 bus, on a sunny afternoon in May.

"It's beautiful," Davina said with finality.

The M4 traveled down Broadway, passing Riverside Church on the right. Davina was asleep against Grace's shoulder, somehow still holding her hand.

Grace glanced at her watch—the ancient one that her grandfather had given her for her communion—an analog heirloom that needed to be wound periodically to keep going because it kept time through the intricacies of gears, not batteries. It read 12:34 p.m.

It had been twelve o'clock when Grace had utterly failed in front of the SVA admissions panel. It had been nearly twelve thirty when she'd walked up to Thirty-Second Street; she'd seen the clock in Herald Square.

Davina opened her eyes, looking up at Grace with a wide smile that warmed the air between them. It surprised Grace, like a shocking pink flyer fluttering in a trash can. When words came out of her mouth, they weren't the ones on her mind.

"Do you know what time it is?"

Davina's face folded into blankness, like it had with the suggestion that they leave the bus. She pulled her hand out of Grace's and gazed back out the window. "It's twelve thirty-four."

"That can't be right."

"That is the time," Davina said. "It's always the time."

The despair in her voice moved Grace beyond her own confusion.

"Hey." She touched Davina's hand lightly enough that the girl could withdraw, say *no* even to that small touch.

Davina turned her face back to Grace. There were tears on her face, and Grace wanted to hold her more than anything.

"Hey, hey. It's okay," Grace said and lifted her arm so Davina could settle against her side, like she belonged there.

The bus stopped, air brakes giving a short squeal. The doors opened, and people stepped on, swiping their cards; people stepped off, finding their equilibrium between the icy atmosphere on the bus and the stifling steam of an unseasonably hot May noon.

Noon.

Grace took out her phone, which she'd ignored except to take pictures because the service once she'd gotten on the bus had been so bad. The phone read 12:34 p.m. in large, friendly numbers. Her battery was at 3 percent. They'd ridden this bus uptown and down. She'd drawn different faces, moods, and gestures and had felt soothed by the ride, the time away from her humiliation making it bearable. She might be able to go home soon, maybe face Mamá and Bambi. But no matter what it felt like, her watch, her phone, said it was still 12:34 p.m.

"Will you stay with me?" Davina asked.

Grace was afraid and did not answer.

"What happened to you?" Grace asked.

"I was on my way to meet a friend. I don't remember her name. I liked her, and I think she liked me. I couldn't show up at her apartment, so I used to call from the pay phone in front of the hot dog place on Thirty-Fourth Street to tell her I was a block away. Her mamá didn't like me."

Grace tried to imagine Davina outside a Gray's Papaya using a pay phone. She'd never used one herself, but she knew what it looked like.

"Then a boy came up to me and asked for change. I said I needed it to call my boyfriend. I said *boyfriend* because of the way he looked at me. I stayed on the phone while it rang and rang and rang and no one answered. I don't know why she didn't answer."

At Thirty-Second Street, more idling as the bus drivers changed again. The new driver, a wiry white guy, nodded at them as he put on a navy-blue MTA uniform sweater, then sat to work the bus up and down the island until it was someone else's turn.

Grace wondered what the new driver saw when he looked at them: two brown girls—friends or lovers—but definitely not strangers. Did he wonder what they were doing here? Did he wonder if they would ever get off?

The bus turned left onto Madison Avenue. Inside the air-conditioned bubble of transportation, for the two of them, it was still 12:34 p.m.

"The phone rang and another boy came, then another boy with him. They circled me, and I didn't know what to do. Finally, I pretended that someone answered. I laughed and said into the ringing phone that I'd be right there, then hung up. I wasn't very convincing. I turned quickly and started walking toward my friend's house. I thought she'd come out. I thought I'd be lucky."

Grace could see it all in her mind, from Davina's sandals to her peach lip gloss, the excitement of meeting someone you like, someone you hope likes you. Then the excitement grown sour, poisoned by—what? Bored boys? Dangerous boys? Wolves in human clothing.

"It was overcast and warm, and it looked like it was about to rain any minute. I had a little umbrella with me. When the first boy put his hand on my shoulder and the second boy laughed, I hit him with the umbrella. Then the second boy, or maybe a third one, grabbed my umbrella. I ran."

Grace squeezed Davina's hand and felt her squeeze back.

"I run fast. I run barefoot at home all the time, so running with sandals is nothing. I ran to the bus—this bus—and jumped on. I had one token left in my pocket. I'd used all my change on the pay phone."

Tokens. Grace didn't know when the MTA had stopped using tokens, but it was probably before she was born. Heat from her panic fought with the cold of the bus, resulting in a shiver that traveled from her to Davina through their joined hands.

"I'm sorry. I said *no* to you to protect you. I didn't want you to be stuck like me."

"But we can get off the bus. Can't we?"

"You can. I think. Whenever you want. But it's too late for me."

Not all the bus loops that Grace and Davina had been riding went into the lushness of Fort Tryon Park, but this one did. It continued past Fort Washington and Cabrini on to Margaret Corbin Drive, the last stop before the inexorable loop began again.

Grace walked to the front of the bus. In a hushed voice, she asked the driver for the time.

He looked at her with skepticism, anticipating a joke or an insult. With a sigh, he turned his wrist toward her so his watch lit up: 4:49 p.m. it read. Then the driver said, "If you're going to the Cloisters, this is your last chance. Closes at six, and next loop around doesn't stop near the entrance."

Grace sat back down next to Davina.

"I thought you'd left me," she said.

"I do want to leave. But I want you to leave with me."

"It's impossible."

"Are you sure?"

"I've tried before. When I get near the doors, there's a buzzing in my head like angry bees, and I feel like I've swallowed espinas. Then I'm ashamed of my weakness, and I sit back down. Besides, I don't have any more tokens. If I get off the bus, I won't ever be able to get back on. What if I need to escape again?"

Grace handed her one of the spare MetroCards she always carried.

"This can be your way back on the bus. It's even better than a token because it's got lots of rides on it."

Davina's expression grew thoughtful. The driver stood and stretched.

"Last stop, ladies. If you're heading back to Midtown, I'm leaving in thirty minutes," he said, before turning off the engine and leaving the bus doors open.

"I want to show you something. This is the place where I learned about making things," Grace said.

"What if there isn't any place out there for me?" Davina whispered.

"Will you trust me? This place is magic." Grace gathered her things, then pulled Davina gently by the hand. At the door, Davina stopped sharply. A wide cobblestoned drive led to an incongruous building situated on the highest point on Manhattan Island.

"Es un castillo?" Davina asked.

Grace descended a step with a tug on Davina's hand, but Davina didn't move.

"I used to think it was a castle when I was little. It's called the Cloisters. It's part of the Met Museum, and it's built from like four or five old monasteries from Europe. I want to show it to you." She turned to face Davina. The girl had taken off the borrowed hoodie and was looking with awe at the imposing building that rose against the blue of the sky and the glitter of the Hudson River. Grace's heart was a hummingbird thrum. Would Davina get off the bus that had become her whole existence?

Davina's face was filled with anxiety and longing as her gaze took in the grandeur of the bell tower, the red banners streaming from the parapets. Behind the bus, a Mister Softee truck dispensed impossibly tall swirls of ice cream. Grace was aware that they looked a mirror image of the first bus driver she'd seen hours or minutes ago, the one she'd snapped a mental picture of as one figure entreated the other figure. She took another step down to stand on the cobblestone, her arm stretching to keep hold of Davina's hand.

"Will you let me show you?"

Davina looked into Grace's face, as if she could determine how safe the world was by the look on a young girl's face. She took the last step, feet on solid ground for the first time in decades, and somehow, she was still whole.

"Sí."

Davina's grip on her hand was growing painful, but Grace didn't care. They'd made it up to the ticket desk and she'd shown her ID, purchased two student tickets. Grace wanted to show Davina so much: the unicorn tapestries, the intricately painted home altars, the tiny, precious treasures. But she didn't know how much time she had before Davina either bolted back to the nearest bus or just disappeared entirely.

"It's just a bit farther. I hope you like it," Grace babbled. As she led the way past treasures in cool galleries lit by stained glass windows, Davina's head turned, tracking each beautiful object. They descended spiral stone steps that surely must have been part of some lost monastery hundreds of years in the past and arrived in a gallery on the lower level that was surprisingly modern with blank museum walls and modern carpeting. A scattering of glass display boxes populated the gallery, spotlights picking out glittering objects from the dimness.

Next to an illuminated prayer book no bigger than a woman's palm and a set of Flemish playing cards was the object that had inspired Grace's recent work.

The size of a large walnut, an intricately carved rosary bead opened on tiny hinges to reveal dense scenes from the life of Christ. There was Bethlehem, Los Reyes Magos, camels, the temple in Jerusalem. The bottom half of the bead depicted the crucifixion. In the foreground, Mary wept over her son's death; in the middle ground, Roman soldiers and disciples were extras in an extraordinary play; in the background, houses, trees, all of creation grinding on. Each figure was no bigger than the tip of a finger, each carved with infinite care and detail. Gazing at it, Grace felt like she could fall into it and find an entire universe, that if she were small enough, she could see the tiniest pebbles at the base of a wheelbarrow.

She felt Davina next to her as she leaned closer to the glass that separated them from the minuscule miracle. She was afraid that Davina wouldn't understand; that she would be bored, or angry, or, worst of all, think that Grace was some kind of Jesus freak. It wasn't that: she was an agnostic at most and believed in the maxim Be Ye Not Un Pendejo.

She tried to explain, "I love the way the whole world is there, like—"

"Like even the smallest parts matter," Davina finished. They grinned at each other.

"It is like your box, the one of your abuelo. It contains his heart and yours. Is that right?" Davina asked.

"It is so right."

★ ★ ★

They sat on the warmed paving stones of one of the gardens, hidden from the view of the patrolling museum guards by tall, waving stems of lavender.

"Does your magic bag have any more snacks?" Davina asked.

"We ate almost everything, even the Flamin' Hot Cheetos you didn't like." Davina made a face. "I do have some candy. Strawberry or mint?"

"Como yo soy muy fresa, I'll leave you the mint," Davina said with a laugh. "I can't believe I'm so happy," Davina said as Grace snapped off a stem of romero and stroked its spindly leaves.

"I can believe it. I'm pretty awesome."

Davina giggled. "You are awesome. And I've been so fearful. I forgot how much beauty there is in the world."

"You won't forget anymore. I won't let you." Grace stretched like a cat along the path. She knew her watch had started ticking again; she could feel it, hear it, tiny and insistent. She closed her eyes, willing herself to exist only in this moment.

A shadow passed, replacing the heat of the late afternoon with coolness. She opened her eyes to see Davina hovering over her.

"Is it okay if I kiss you?" Davina asked.

Grace wanted to leap up, not let this chance pass her by, but she made herself move slowly, raising herself up on her elbows, keeping her eyes on Davina's.

"Sí. Prefiero que me beses," she whispered, as Davina's lips closed on hers, peach gloss on her lips and strawberry candy on her breath like every summer promise made and kept. Time stopped. It always does for kisses.

Outside the bus, the driver had rolled up his sleeves and was attacking a mountainous chocolate-and-vanilla-twist cone like his life depended on it. The girls walked up to the bus; the driver nodded and went to sit on the grass in the shade.

Davina hesitated at the door. "Now that I've made it off the bus, I don't want to go back on."

"You don't have to. We can take the A train at 190th Street. You can come home with me, meet Bambi y Mami and—"

Stay, Grace wanted to say. But didn't.

"And then what?"

Davina said it kindly, like she could see and understand things that Grace couldn't. But Grace was familiar with partings that were inevitable, bitter and still sweet with the time spent together.

"It will be okay," Davina said as she pulled Grace onto the bus. Grace knew this was the kind of *okay* that would hurt.

They sat on the seats that faced each other near the driver. The driver wiped his hands carefully on a napkin, removing all traces of summer from his fingers, put his MTA sweater back on, and started the bus.

They held hands, watching Fort Tryon Park recede and pockets of the city reassert itself around them. Grace tried to think of things to say, but all her words caught in her mouth. She knew there was no tomorrow for them, no next time, no someday. Yet her brain tried to get around the inevitable.

"How will you know when to get off?" she asked.

"I'll know when I'm home," Davina replied.

At Broadway and 110th Street, the bus turned onto Cathedral Parkway, and soon they were looking at the imposing facade of St. John the Divine. Grace thought about the treasures at the Cloisters, the treasures in all the churches, synagogues, museums, temples, and mosques. Art made by people for millennia for the sole purpose of reminding time that human hands can make sacred things.

At Central Park North and Malcom X Boulevard, the bus

stopped, though no one was getting on and no one was getting off. The bus windows gave onto the view of a cloudless May evening, but when the bus driver opened the doors, a rectangle of torrential rain, a humid midday, waited.

"I wish I had my umbrella now," Davina said, trying to smile.

"Use my hoodie. It'll help a little." Grace placed the hoodie over Davina's head and hugged her. "Suerte," she whispered.

"It's going to be okay, Graciela," Davina said. She pulled up the hood of the Salem Witch Academy sweatshirt and ran down the steps, into the rain and out of time.

At Thirty-Second Street, the bus driver looked back at Grace, as if he wondered if this girl would haunt the M4 loop like the other one. He'd heard stories. But Grace got off the bus and confronted the change of day as the sun dipped in the west. The heat had lessened slightly, and a breeze was blowing. Bambi was waiting for her where she'd texted him to meet her.

"Mamá te va matar," he said, obligatory big brother words about vengeful mothers who spend hours worrying about daughters who don't come home or answer their phone.

"She is definitely going to kill me. And she's going to say I told you so while doing it."

"That bad?" Bambi asked, falling into step next to her as they walked toward the 1 train.

If he'd asked her hours ago, she would have cried, fallen apart, sure she was a failure.

"Not that bad. I probably didn't get in. But there are other schools."

Bambi stopped dead in his tracks, annoying a commuter behind him, who was probably going to miss his train home to New Jersey, anyway.

"Other schools? You've been dreaming about SVA since you were eleven!"

"There are other schools, other possibilities." Grace shrugged.

She looked up at the twilight sky, quilted with new stars. Somewhere, she hoped, Davina was happy under similar stars.

"I'm not giving up. My art is good, and someone will give me a chance. Someone will say sí."

★ ★ ★ ★ ★

TRESPASSERS WILL BE...

a remix of the myth of the Theseus and the Minotaur
Torrey Maldonado

"Two different natures, man and [beast], were joined in him."
—Plutarch, *Parallel Lives*

Here's the thing. I hate talkin' in front of my class. I'll *only* do it if I *have* to, or *really* wanna. I'm fifteen in the tenth grade and my mom'll tell you since kindergarten (when I was short-short with a lollipop Afro) to me today (at six feet) I basically stay allergic to talkin' to crowds. But right now? I *wanna* speak after Mr. Ray, my history teacher, just said the wildness—describin' a giant half animal, half man livin' in a maze eatin' people.

Lately, he's taught about monsters in Greek myths, and this unit is lit since I feel some monsters be real, but I wanna talk more about this one monster he just said cuz Mr. Ray said people it ate went "missing" and that's similar to what happens here. Six years back, a fourth grader in our school went missin'. Then the next year, Mr. Pete vanished in the stadium with his dog. Each year since, someone from our projects disappears. Fourth grade was when I first realized. Then I learned it's been happenin' since before I was born. And now my best friend is missin'?

Mr. Ray said the giant half animal, half man livin' in a maze sounds too similar to what Uncle Henry told me in fourth grade and the rumor made people know about where we live. Uncle Henry is not blood-related: he just treats me better than some family do.

I eye our class's digital clock above the SMART Board and hype myself up in my head to talk. *Only a few minutes left in the whole school day. Just ask Mr. Ray. Then we out. How bad could it go?* I slow-raise my hand.

Whisperin' starts here-and-there.

Tracy giggles with Jasmine, mentionin' me. "Watch Corey mention something weird."

Jasmine says, "Right? He's even wearing his bummy *Stranger Things* T-shirt."

"Like the one his little friend wears."

I wanna tell them: *You know I hear you, right? I'm* one *table from you. And how you giggin' on me and Eddie? Especially with Eddie missin'? Don't you see he's missin'?!*

Eddie is in another tenth-grade class, and yeah, we rock sci-fi and fantasy shirts how other kids rock Jordans or Converse kicks. We stick out in our Brooklyn projects when we shouldn't cuz our projects is basically Black and Latino and we got Black in us cuz we mixed. I'm Black and Puerto Rican; he's Black and white. But we stick out there and in school since heads rock name brands and we don't own any. I'm not sayin' name brands is wack (it's just our moms are broke and can't afford that). So we into *Ancient Aliens*, monster shows, and ideas like Antarctica bein' an ice wall surroundin' Earth and keeps us from more advanced continents, giants, and aliens. With the little our moms can afford, we rep what we into with our clothes. Anyway, we stick out cuz of who we are and how we dress and can't dress, and when haters knock us bein' different, we just stick together, tighter.

So Jasmine says we bums because we usually rock *Vox Machina* or *Guardians of the Galaxy* or some other not-mainstream T-shirt. I wanna dis back, but I don't. Prolly cuz my mind is on Eddie missin'. Plus Eric interrupts me, "Tell me what you want to ask

Mr. Ray. Is it like when you said the mayor was lying for saying they found a gator in the Gowanus Canal but you believed it was the humanoid Lizard in Spider-Man?" He points at his cell phone. "If yeah, I'll record you." Dude's a class clown who loves when kids embarrass themselves. His TikTok account is all videos of that.

I raise my hand higher.

And every kid who believes everythin' adults, the government, or internet says eyes me. I wonder if they expect what Tracy, Jasmine, and Eric expects—me to connect supernatural stuff to reality cuz I'm the only one who does. Ugh.

Nah, I'm not keepin' quiet because my boy went missin' yesterday, didn't answer my texts, and isn't in school today, and what Mr. Ray just said has me makin' connections.

I raise my hand even higher.

"Yes, Corey?"

Did his voice just sound—? Does he think I'm a joke too?

"So the Greeks did nothin' when their family and friends went missin'?"

Mr. Ray shrugs. "One person did something about it. He—"

Kids interrupt him and get chatty in different spots, then Fiona grunts at me. "Corey, you're not bringing up *missing people* from here, right? Because police said they disappeared," she says it how parents tell toddlers who don't know how to speak yet: *dis-a-pear-ed* with extra oomph on the *D* and makes it sounds like *Duh.*

It's like the whole class nods, agreeing with her. Yeah, their reactions remind me why I don't talk in front of class.

But a monster in a maze who eats people? This is somethin' I wanna talk more about.

"Can you describe that Mino monster more?"

"The Minotaur," Mr. Ray explains, "has a bull's head and a man's body. Here, I'll show you." He types on his laptop, then an image flashes on the projector's screen.

Sean—two tables from me—blurts out, "He's the Hulk's size!" He's into-*into* comics but only for fun. I quizzed him once durin' lunch about people havin' powers, but he said, "That's fake."

Antonio points at the Minotaur's fangy teeth. "His teeth are *crazeee*."

Mr. Ray nods. "Guess he needs those to digest the number of people he eats each year. Girls, boys, adults."

Mr. Ray connects the Hulk to this monster again. "The Minotaur has Hulk-like strength."

Sean starts more back-and-forth with Mr. Ray. "Like lift-a-car strong?"

"He'd pitch a truck across the gym."

Sean cocks his head. "Super strength means super speed?"

Mr. Ray smiles wide. "Imagine a motorcycle racing down the street outside. The Minotaur could keep up with it."

Chloe—hair dyed different colors, who always rips looseleaf from her binder to make shapes—says, "I'd build a super prison for him."

"He *was* in a super prison." Mr. Ray pauses, then asks everyone, "Can someone name the prison he was jailed in?"

No one knows.

Mr. Ray draws a huge *L* on the dry-erase board, then eight dashes after it. (He plays hangman with us sometimes to help us guess words. I bet he plays them games endin' in *RDLE* on his phone that teachers talk to each other about—Wordle and whatevs.)

Quick, kids shout-laugh different letters.

"A!"

"Q!"

They keep yellin' right and wrong answers until a word I never saw is written.

Labyrinth.

Mr. Ray tells us its meaning. "It's a *maze*."

A maze?! My mind starts connectin' things how when I play

Tetris. (Word games are Mr. Ray's thing, and *Tetris* is one of mine.)

I usually do this to figure out stuff. Instead of seein' *Tetris* pieces, I see people and thoughts. I fit them together to form a big picture.

Here's the first piece I see: Uncle Henry telling fourth-grade me about the abandoned factory called the Gray House on the edge of our projects and that its insides is all mazes.

The next piece: Eddie carrying this plastic toy maze the size of his palm that has the tiniest metal ball. Blue bottom, see-through top. He stays tiltin' it side to side to see the ball roll toward its center. He carried it so much I once asked, "Why you keep that on you?"

He smiled and said, "Mazes are dope."

I think, *Maybe that's why he stays tryna go in the Gray House.*

Then I picture times this year he's dared me: "Let's see inside." And each time I said *no*. Why? Cuz I was scared, that's why. I'm *still* scared to go in that building. It's the scariest haunted house–type abandoned factory. All burned twentysomethin' floors towerin', makin' our whole neighborhood pip-squeak-small—and that's wild, seein' that our tall projects has sixteen flights.

Another memory flashes from two days ago: us at the Gray House's No Trespassing sign with him clutchin' the fence, hawkin' through its holes, fiendin' to go in, and I remember Eddie said with a seriousness I never saw in his face before, "I'm sneaking into here with or without you."

The fifth piece: that was the last time we spoke, and now he's missin'.

I *know* he's in there.

My eyes go to our classroom window and my mind starts doin' that *Tetris* thingy and seein' stuff that might fit. I stare at the edge of Red Hook projects and beyond, to the Gray House. And just like when I play *Tetris* and I'm about to set the high score, I get this feelin': *This is it. I'm right. Eddie's there.*

Nah. I shake my head, tryna shake the image of him in that abandoned factory away. *He doesn't have the heart.* I'm buggin' cuz if anyone has the heart to go in there, it's him. He has more heart than kids three, four grades older than us. Most kids' brains seem to have a computer chip to tell them to be scared of some stuff and stop, but his chip must tell him to challenge the biggest dudes and do the craziest dares.

For example, when this ninth grader my height dissed me as we walked into school at the start of eighth grade. "Bruh, you can hang glide with your ears."

I got tight cuz if I'd change anythin' about me, it'd be my ears. I wanted to dis him back, but he had four other ninth graders with him.

Just as I was gonna ignore him, who jumps in? Eddie—the shortest kid in our crowd. "You dissing his ears? Your front teeth are so far apart, I could kick a soccer ball through them."

And that ninth grader couldn't even dis back cuz the whole crowd exploded so loud laughin' at Eddie's dis.

"Ohhhhh! Shorty roasted you."

"Son said your teeth are a goal post."

Eddie always defends me and other kids—older, younger—and he's so good at dissin' and does it so loud for everyone to hear that heads stay too shook to dis back. He reminds me of Kevin Hart—a shorty with the loudest, biggest personality. Standin' side by side, I'm six feet and Eddie's up to my stomach. Kids not from our school be shocked when they hear he's fifteen too.

He might look young, but heart? Bruh has it. And it's not just his heart steppin' to people. Mad heads in our projects are down to do anythin' and go anywhere, but everyone knows to stay out of one place—the one place Eddie always *tries* goin' in. Only one other person might be crazy enough to go in there: my cousin Wayne, named after Lil Wayne. I'm usually not glad to see my cousin Wayne cuz he got *no* fear. He's in the eleventh grade, and he does wild-wild stuff. Trespasses into the docks and climbs onto the ships and up to the top of those big metal storage containers how rock-climbers go up mountains. He's always alone. His clothes stay dirty and ripped cuz he climbs everything. Wayne and Eddie got a similar personality, except Wayne hurts animals. It's why I don't visit him. Once I did, and he pointed at his German shepherd's tail and told me, "Watch," then he yanked it mad hard, making his dog yelp and cry. He's told me he wants to sneak into the Gray House too, which is why I kept him from bein' friends with Eddie.

Back to Eddie. Once I tried talkin' sense into Eddie. "Why you always jumpin' to fight bigger kids?"

He shrugged. "Who says cuz they big I gotta be scared?"

I wanted to tell him, *You good, bruh. It's fine how tall you are, and it's fine just where we be.* But I didn't cuz he wants to prove he's big too, and I didn't want to mention his height since he's sensitive about that. Instead, I told him, "You know, it's cool to be you. Like you don't always need to be extra and do the mo—"

He interrupted me, "That's easy for you to say. Look at you. In two years, you shot up nearly two feet. In two years, I stayed the same height."

That deaded the conversation.

Right now, I turn from lookin' at the Gray House to block out the image of him in there.

Uncle, I think. Gotta talk to Uncle.

He's the only grown-up who listens when I talk paranormal stuff. It was him who slipped and told fourth-grade me, "I think missing people from our neighborhood got caught by a monster in the Gray House."

I told him, "Tell me more," but he shook his head.

"Corey, if I got specific, you'd call me crazy." I told him I wouldn't, but he didn't change his mind. I get not wantin' to be called *bugged* for what you believe. Heads call me names for what I feel.

Right now, Chloe speaks again. "Maybe if the Minotaur is in a maze, he can't figure how to get out."

Mr. Ray asks her, "And guess who else couldn't figure how to get out? The kids and adults thrown into the maze for the Minotaur monster to eat."

I *gotta* talk to Uncle Henry.

Walkin' to Uncle Henry's apartment, my mind plays *Tetris*, and I see a clear picture again: Eddie's in the Gray House.

He didn't come to school yesterday. After dismissal I went to his apartment, and his mom wasn't worried cuz they'd just argued and Ed threatened to run away to his dad's house. His moms and pops are separated. She figured that's where he was.

But my Miles Morales spidey-sense said dude's not with his pops in Park Slope.

Yeah, his mom didn't react to him vanishin', just like how ancient Greeks didn't react to their missing cases.

Soon, I'm a block from someone who won't think I'm buggin'. Someone who believes in monsters. Someone who described the Gray House's inside as all mazes.

As I walk to Uncle Henry's stoop, one guy says, "Corey, where's your mini-me?" He means Eddie.

I ignore him and try walkin' through him and his homeboys. One steps in front of me, blockin' my way. I try steppin' around him, but he blocks that way too. He snarls, makin' fun that I'm into sci-fi by saying, "Can't you teleport? Zap yourself into the building?"

His friends chuckle and smirk.

He steps aside. "Go in. Guess your superpower is to be weird."

I go in and up to the second floor and knock on Uncle Henry's door and shout, "It's Corey," so he knows to answer.

My mom never believed in superpowers, monsters, and magic, so I don't talk to her about those things. Uncle Henry doesn't just believe in that, he usually brings it up in different ways. Like now, as he opens his door, he nods at me and says, "Whattup, Black Adam?"

Very cool. Dwayne "The Rock" Johnson killed it in *Black Adam*, and Shazam powers are fire. I sorta look like the Rock when he was my age.

Uncle Henry checks the hall. "You alone?"

"Yeah."

"No Eddie?"

"That's why I'm here."

He jerks his head for me to come in. His apartment is the same as always, books and newspapers scattered nearly anywhere I step. His place is a hood library. Messy, not dirty. I call Uncle Henry our project's historian cuz he knows our history to way back to before it was built and the wife of President FDR showed up for our projects' openin' ceremony. But back then the projects was built for white people.

I go sit on his couch and get right to it, reminding him of when I was in the fourth grade and built a maze for a science project and he pointed out the window and told me that the Gray House is all mazes inside. "Then you said somethin' about a monster takin' people missin' from here. Then you stopped, sayin' I was too young to know any more. I need to know now."

"Nope. Sometimes, let sleeping giants sleep."

I have no clue what he means, but I heard the word *giants*, so I say, "You mean the giant livin' in there eatin' people."

Uncle Henry's face turns as serious as a heart attack. "What you say?"

I was half jokin' about a giant in there. I'm not right, right? "No disrespect, but...you heard me."

He comes and sits right next to me. "You not a fourth grader no more. What you, an eleventh grader?"

"Tenth."

"I ain't sure what's in there. Something in there can't be explained. Boy, why you bringing this up?"

"My friend Eddie is missin'. He's in the Gray House."

Uncle looks like I threw a cup of ice water in his face. "For real?"

I tell him what happened. "He always said he wanted to go in, but I didn't think he'd do it."

Uncle Henry nods. "When I was your age, that factory had a pull on me too. The Gray House is as old as our neighborhood. The 1930s. And you need to know our projects' and that factory's histories to know why it's best to stay out of there."

"Tell me."

"This projects used to be paradise. No shootings. Clean everywhere. And the stadium? Hundreds of people came from faraway to relax, party, and play sports there."

"For real, for real?" I don't believe him. "Then, why's it fenced up now?"

"You mean, what's it hiding?"

"Hidin'?"

"It hides what used to be there, all the death that happened there. Did you know the newspaper did an article on our stadium, calling it the *Killing Fields*?"

I shake my head again.

"Try to rewind your mind to the 1930s. Whites ran everything. Us Blacks and Puerto Ricans had no rights."

"I learned about that in school. Segregation."

"Worse than segregation. So the Gray House gets built—so white it almost shines compared to all the brown and concrete here. The Gray House advertised it would hire as many of us as possible, so we felt brand-new too. We thought management was friendly because they wanted to hire us, but that was a trick to get us to work there. We didn't know that a racist man from down south who came from slave money built the Gray House for his son to run. That management saw us almost as slaves. That that son had something to prove. And oooh, he was cruel. One time, I burned my hand—not bad-bad enough to stop working, just enough where I needed to see a nurse in the building. Turns out he never put a nurse or first-aid supplies in the building and ordered me to keep working, no break. It became the worst managed company here. But us Blacks and Puerto Ricans needed money so we worked there."

I'm scared to ask the question—not cuz I was worried he'd think it's a dumb question but cuz I'm scared to hear the answer. I ask, "How did the stadium get the nickname the *Killing Fields*?"

"Well, we called it that because it used deadly chemicals that got into the stadium's fields, on purpose and by accident. It practiced *no* safety—the chemicals got into *us*. Our skin soaked up the steam and smoke. They polluted and poisoned everything. I feel they knew what they was doing. Why else was the insides all mazes? All of us who worked there didn't know how to walk from A to B without a white manager holding his floor plan and leading us. That's how we moved in there. Like chain gangs in prison under constant white supervision."

I stop Uncle Henry's memory cuz my mind tetrises together what he said about chemicals killin' us. I speak without meanin' to. "Grandma worked there and died at fiftysomethin'. Aunt Maggie too, and she died before sixty. They coughed all the time, sounded like barkin' nonstop. Phlegm all colors mixed with blood."

Uncle puts a hand on my forearm, real carin', and it takes away some of the hurt of rememberin' that. "That white boy running the Gray House went *too* far. He started leveling up harsh work conditions. Harassing workers, verbal abuse, locking us in sealed rooms with no masks so we inhaled those fumes. Sexual harassment. He started bringing in white managers who were real plantation-like. I know how bad it was because I worked there a month but friends stayed. You wouldn't know nothing about this because it was before you was born. In the 1960s.

Around the time Dr. Martin Luther King, Jr. was killed. Anyway, workers complained to him and other bosses that their kids were being born...different. Seven fingers on both hands. Some had vampire-sharp teeth and wouldn't eat regular food. Kids had—" Uncle Henry looks at me like he doesn't want me to judge him "—abilities. Some even say them chemicals turned workers and their kids into monsters. Some of these people still live out there, but their families keep them inside because for whatever reasons."

I interrupt, "Why didn't everyone just quit?"

"And work where?"

"The government didn't help?"

"The mayor made a big statement but must've been friends with them rich family because some companies changed, but the Gray House's boss became meaner."

"So what happened?"

"Rumor is that white-boy boss sexually assaulted a woman, and her teen son did it as revenge."

"Did what?"

"One person said a Black guy did it."

"Did *what*?!"

"But that's as good as saying a Puerto Rican guy did it, because out here you can't tell differences between Blacks and Puerto Ricans."

"*Uncle!* Did what?!"

He's so in his head down memory lane that he's talkin' and not hearin' me. He continues, "Another rumor says a few Black and Puerto Rican workers secretly agreed to do it. *Whoever* did it—they set a fire that burned the whole Gray House. But it didn't burn down. It stood there, just like the white-boy boss. Folks said he refused to leave the burning building. Everyone escaped the fire except him, yelling something like, 'My father put me here, and this is where I'll stay!' Him staying isn't the craziest part. Folks said they saw him through the chemically steamy smoke and flames and he was *changing*."

"Changin'?"

Uncle hums. "Mmm-hmm. Maybe them chemicals combined did something extra to him? That white boy was maybe two feet shorter than me, but everyone said the same thing—in the clouds his fingers stretched, and he grew three feet taller than me."

"You sayin' he transformed into some Hulk?" I tell him about the Minotaur.

"I'm not saying anything. I'm *telling* you what people I trust told *me*. They say as the property fell and closed him in, he had stretched into this huge monster-shaped, half-animal, half-man figure and let out a howl that wasn't human anymore. I ain't saying that white boy became a Mino—what you call him. But people disappear every year since that fire. Only people who go in the Gray House, not near it. He don't come out where people see him."

"I tell kids and teachers that people missin' here is more to them disappearin'!"

Uncle remembers his drinking buddy who was last seen years ago near the Gray House. "I went to that hellhole looking for him. It was right after sunset where there's just a little light out, and I won't lie, a gigantic figure stood there in the shadows, in a doorway of the Gray House, waiting for me to trespass past that fence. I swear, it didn't want to come out and be seen. I'm ashamed to admit it, but I nearly peed my pants and turned and ran until I got home."

"That's scary. And messed up. Your friend, now mine." More thoughts come to me, and I don't know which to say first. I let the first one come out. "All over Brooklyn, land's needed cuz so many expensive apartments are bein' built. So a gigantic, burned, abandoned buildin' almost skyscraper-tall that takes up ten city blocks is just left alone for over fifty years? No one tried to tear it down and use that wasted space?"

"Not one company. It makes no sense why a company won't knock down the Gray House and use the land."

It goes quiet between us for a few seconds. "Uncle, maybe companies did offer money, but they can't buy it. Because someone is not sellin' it?"

"Agreed. I think it's the monster's family. They know he's in there, and they leaving that as his home. They rich and keeping that land and keeping him there and don't want to him hurt." Uncle shakes his head. "You know, I've seen people go in and come out safe. You know *who* goes in and comes out safe?"

I shake my head no, then wonder, He doesn't mean whi—?

"All white people."

He eyes me serious-serious. "But everyone else don't make it in and out alive."

My mind does that *Tetris* thingy and clicks together everythin' Uncle just said, and the words come out. "That's because that white-boy boss was a racist and he has a forever hatred against us. Maybe he keeps grabbin' us to get revenge for us burnin' his factory."

Uncle nods. "But your friend, if he went in, he'll be all right because he's white, right?"

"No. He's mixed. White and Black."

Uncle's face says he's sorry.

I stand. "I gotta go."

His hand snatches my forearm. "Say you not going into the Gray House."

I tell the truth. "I'm not gonna go in." And that's the truth cuz I'm goin' *near* the Gray House to find someone crazy enough to go in with me first.

When I get to the stadium, it's almost sunset. The Gray House fence's No Trespassing sign makes me swallow hard. I peek through its holes at the other side of the junkyard and spot another fence. I have to get past this fence, a junkyard, then another fence just to get in the Gray House. I look up. *This fence is too high to climb. And that barbed wire on top'll slice right through my skin.* I get on my knees. *I can't believe I'm tryna sneak in here. Let me try somethin' out.* I lift the fence until I yank enough up for me to wiggle under. I do.

On the other side, all these things I planned on bee swarm in my head. Questions I wondered so I'm ready. If this monster is real, it prolly can sense I'm on its turf. Does it move as fast as the Minotaur? If yes, I gotta be strategic about how I move and where I be because the Minotaur can keep up with a speedin' motorcycle.

I inhale real deep and exhale. *Calm. Down. Uncle says it won't come out the buildin'. Just get to the pier. You're not goin' in the Gray House, yet. If a monster is in there, it doesn't want to be seen. It won't shoot out of the buildin', and if it does, it has to hop that fence and cross this junkyard. By then, you'll jet and wiggle under the fence into the stadium.*

Walkin' in the junkyard, broken glass and pebbles crunch under my kicks. My heart beats with so much force that I feel my ears pulse red-hot. My brain is sayin' *Leave.* It takes my whole everythin' to keep walkin', and I walk until I hear it… Splashes.

There's an uneven rhythm to them.

One, two, three: *SPLASH!*

One, two, three, four, five: *SPLASH!*

One, two: *SPLASH!*

I climb the hill of garbage and look down to the shore of the pier, and there he is.

My cousin Wayne.

He grabs horseshoe crabs by their tails and flings them far out into the water. About seven just lie there on their backs. I guess keepin' them on their backs stops them from crawlin' into the water.

"Hey." I get his attention.

He spins around. "Hold up? Corey? When you grow a pair

and get the heart to come this close to there?" He points at the Gray House. It's maybe eight burned, broken-down cars away.

I know a lot about my cousin Wayne, but one thing matters most right now: his rep for trespassin' into places everyone has sense to stay outta. Right now, I remember how his mom said he comes here almost every day, and I remember him sayin' he wants to sneak into the Gray House, which is why I'm here.

He eyes me. "My moms and pops told you to come here for me?"

I try to make conversation with him. "Nah. How you get all them horseshoe crabs?"

He picks one up. "You mean this?"

Eww! Underneath a horseshoe crab looks like Predator's face from the movie *Predator* when their masks are off. *Scary!* I pretend to not be shook. "Yeah. How you get so many?"

He flings it Frisbee-style far out into the water. *Splash!* Then he points at his bare feet and sweatpants rolled up above his knees. "I go in the water and pull them out. You wanna go in?"

I turn and point at the Gray House. "How about we go in *there*? You been yet?"

Wayne's eyes almost pop to the size of hard-boiled eggs, then he gets the hugest smile. "No. That's something I told you a few times I want to do, but you always said, 'Never.' Now I'm s'posed to believe you'll really go in there?"

I give him a long for-real look. "That's because I never had a good-good reason to go in. But Eddie already went in, I think."

Wayne leaves the upside-down horseshoe crabs there, struggl-lin' to turn themselves over, and puts on his socks and jacked-up Air Force 1s. Then he walks up to me. "Let's catch up to Eddie."

He's movin' so fast ahead of me that it's hard to keep up, and it's hard for me to figure out what to say. I wanna tell him about the monster that's maybe inside and about everythin', but Wayne's so freakin' fast. Before I know it, we're at a busted window with the least amount of glass stickin' out of its frame.

Wayne climbs up and hops into the pitch-black Gray House darkness.

All of a sudden, a hand pops up out of nowhere. He's holdin' his hand for me to grab. "You want me to hold your hand for you to come in?"

I breathe deep. Then I taste it. Sweat drips from my forehead and runs into my mouth. I'm too scared. I put both my hands on the window and just as I'm about to lift a leg up to climb in, my body starts shakin'. I pause, squeeze my hands into fists, and tell myself, *Think, Corey. Remember why you doin' this.*

My mind starts doin' that *Tetris* thingy again—seein' pieces, faces, reasons that fit that makes it clear that Eddie might be in here and I need to get him. Then I picture Eddie hidin'. I picture the monster has him alive but left him stuffed in a locker or oven waitin' to come back and...

"For Eddie," I say under my breath, and I climb into the window frame and practically fall off and stumble in the pitch-blackness.

I didn't expect it to be this dark, and I squint. Shadows of machines are here and there. "Can you see?"

"Not really," Wayne whispers back.

Somethin' on the floor slowly bops side to side, and I strain my eyes fast-hard but it's a plastic shoppin' bag, just swirlin' how tumbleweed does in those cowboy movies. Soon, my eyes adjust, and a slice of his face is seeable in this darkness. He nods, and our eyes lock.

"You see better too now, huh?"

"Yeah."

"Now, c'mon."

He turns, and the more we walk, the more the light from the busted windows appears until we walk in a room of dark and shadows. Only enough light for me to— I kick somethin' on the floor. I squint. *Is that...?* I crouch and grab it. Eddie's toy maze. Then right near where I found it, I see footprints outlined in the dirt. That's Eddie's size sneaker, for sure! But is that another footprint? I turn on my cell's flashlight, expecting to get a clearer look of more sneaker tracks, but right next to Eddie's footprint is the shape of a foot so huge that it reminds me of those Bigfoot footprints they show on monster-hunter shows. Except the toes on these stretch long and thick and sharp as if the toes are claws. I wonder if this is what the foot of the Minotaur from Mr. Ray's class was like.

I turn my head and see Wayne's scared eyes starin' straight at those monstrous footprints.

He stutters, "Wh-what are those?"

"I don't know," I say as I lift up the toy maze. "But this is Eddie's." I shine my cell's flashlight on his sneakers' footprints. "And those are his kicks." I lift my cell up and see a trail of Eddie's footprints runnin' away in the dirt, and the monster's feet follow.

Right then we hear a howl-growl so loud that it has surround sound and makes this whole dark room quake.

"What the—?" Wayne's face flips from scared to straight terrified. "That's not human."

"We gotta go toward that sound. That's where Eddie is."

Wayne slow-shakes his head. "No, *you* gotta go toward that. I'm out." And he jets to a window exit.

Every muscle in my body says, *Go. Go catch up to Wayne.*

But another voice inside says, *Stop. Think.* And I do.

I think of everyone in my neighborhood who vanished. Prolly in here.

I think of everything Uncle Henry told me about the bad that's happened in this factory.

I think of all the bad that might happen if no one does anything about it.

I think of Eddie and his heart—how he's always had my back.

I hear his words in my head. *Who says cuz they big I gotta be scared?*

I hold my cell's camera up and do a three-sixty of the room. A crowbar leans on a machine, and I go grab it.

I breathe in real deep, then exhale. *For Eddie. Imma find you.*

I slow-lift my foot that's cemented into the floor from fear, and I start walkin' in the direction of the howl-growl.

★ ★ ★ ★ ★

ISLA BELLA

a remix of *The Great Gatsby*
Ari Tison

> "A new world, material without being real, where poor ghosts, breathing dreams like air, drifted fortuitously about…like that ashen, fantastic figure gliding toward him through the amorphous trees."
>
> —F. Scott Fitzgerald, *The Great Gatsby*

My aunties have always said the island of Uvita was cursed. When I first told them of my internship, they counseled me to be careful. We sat by the fire in the evening in our hammocks, and they whispered reminders. *Niece, you already know the Ocean is a woman. She herself allows nothing but the plant and the animal beings to survive.* Only one of my aunties had snuck away to the island when she was young, but she didn't stay long: she had seen a figure on the shore. She had heard weeping.

The island was just off the Caribbean coast of Costa Rica. The same island Columbus docked on his last trip to the Americas. When he came inland, he encountered my tribe and sister tribes. It was the start of genocide. Then the island was otherwise abandoned until a monastery was built in 1886. But that eventually fell into disrepair. Then there was a short season where the sick—people with yellow fever, leprosy, tuberculosis, and ailments with no cures—were sent to the ruins to spend their last days until that horrendous practice dissolved as well.

It seemed that nothing was meant to stay on the island. It had lain dormant until recently when it was purchased by Isabella Santiago—a woman appearing out of nowhere with money beyond money. I'd watch my father turn his lips down when any intrigued tourist asked about her at the Cahuita National Park front desk. "No sé," he'd reply with his hands up. But even I knew that our park had been given sizable donations from Isabella. It wasn't enough to convert my father, though. He'd change the subject with tourists to tell of the island's wildlife. He'd share how he wanted to study there, but no one had been allowed onto the island for decades until she came along. Not even our people, he'd say, frustrated.

Of course, how the island was even up for purchase was a mystery, and everyone had their ideas. Some said Isabella was connected to the cartel, that she was a rich descendant with ties to the Costa Rican government. Some thought that as she had attended Harvard Business School, perhaps she had rich investors from the States. Some said that she'd stolen the hearts of people in power and had blackmailed them. Whatever it was, she had purchased the island a few years ago and since had built up various high-end living spaces and made her entire island available to all sorts of people who could afford it. Football stars, the Kardashian grandchildren, attendees of galas and private elite parties. Still, Isabella herself stayed away from the media outlets. Her island was indeed private, despite everyone knowing about it.

Locals couldn't resist the wordplay and had dubbed it with a new name: Isla Bella. I rolled my eyes at this because its ancient name was more poetic.

Quiribrí, or the place of birdsong.

And it was the birds I was going for. I'd been accepted into an internship program at Harvard's Museum of Comparative Zoology. My time in Costa Rica gave me a competitive advantage, the summers when I stayed with my father on the coast, just an hour's drive and a few minutes' boat ride south of the island. Shadowing him in his work at the Cahuita National Park, I grew up counting turtle eggs, spotting sloths for tourists, and photographing pythons and the crab spawning season. The Harvard internship program had made a deal with Isabella, an alum, to set up hands-on research on the island.

From my dad's passionate speeches, I knew it was home to an extensive amount of untouched biodiversity, including *Sula leucogaster*, or brown booby, a type of seabird that did not nest inland due to predators. Neither of us had ever seen one in person, but based on our research, if you looked beyond their overall black color, the males had a blue ring around their eyes, almost like glasses, while the females had a yellow orbital ring around theirs. It was said to be quite striking, and I was excited to see this flair that natural selection had sorted for them. The birds seemed to keep their eye on the island, continuing their existence through every dark part of its history. I imagined them keeping the Ocean company there, the animal and water kingdoms colliding.

Isabella was to send over a boat to the port to pick me and the two other interns up. The two were already slathered in sunscreen, had large stuffed backpacks, and seemed decent but anxious in that academic-and-alone sort of way. Meanwhile, I carried a small backpack and kept my long hair braided in our traditional Bribri two braids. I wore my Tevas, navy shorts, a loose floral tank, earrings my auntie made me, and a decent sports bra. Just a few changes of clothes in my bag. Minimal. The way we do it.

"How long is the ride?" Jordan, the brunette boy from Seattle, asked, looking up at the sky. It was four o'clock and not usually this dark.

"Only a few minutes," I said. I hadn't been nervous before, but the Ocean grayed the way she does before a storm. I was hoping she'd want me to come to the island since our people hadn't been allowed for generations. But maybe not. I told her I didn't intend to make friends with anyone but the birds during this internship and hoped that the Ocean—my aunties' voices sounded in my head—would approve.

"Gotcha." Jordan shook off some of his nervousness. "Is that all you're bringing, Lana? I thought I packed light."

"Yeah, just this." I put down my sunglasses.

"Have either of you been to Costa Rica before?" he asked, looking at me and then April, the other intern. April folded her book and looked up from beneath the shade of her blue cap. "I've only been on the Pacific side."

"Most people have been to that side if they've come to Costa Rica," I said. "All the resorts are over there."

"My family and I stayed at an ecolodge," April responded with a little edge.

I already had her pinned as the do-good tourist, so this didn't surprise me. Most of those ecolodges could probably afford to pay folks who worked there a bit more, or even give back the land if they cared about it so much, but I kept my thoughts to myself.

"So have you been here, Lana?" Jordan asked. He kept saying my name with each question. It was kind of nice. But I crossed my arms.

"Not to the island, no."

I prepared my mind for this short boat ride. It was heavy to know I'd be spending time at the starting place of my people's genocide. Columbus called the island his orchard. Some seed, I thought. But it wasn't the island's fault. Though, perhaps the Ocean didn't want anyone here. My people don't traditionally touch the Ocean unless it's for ceremony. She is not someone you mess with, a powerhouse. In our legends, she's married to Thunder. And if it takes Thunder himself to put up with you, well, that's saying something. But I was just here for the birds, for my father. Living our small dream.

"I wonder what it's like. You know, I heard that Isabella treated the interns last year to really good food and boat rides. She likes talking with potential Harvard students because it reminds her of when she went," Jordan said.

"Ugh." April sighed. "I hope she just leaves us alone. I hope she doesn't try to get us to join some sorority."

Maybe April had some good sense.

"Agreed," I said. "I don't want to think about what the ecosystem had to go through when she built all of that."

"Gosh, right? It's nice of her to welcome us, but it's totally weird having their business department, the most capitalist part of the university, partner with zoology." April shook her head.

"Absolutely," Jordan added genuinely, though I wondered if he could have come up with anything of the sort himself. He wore expensive clothes and looked like the kind of legacy guy who golfed with his dad on the weekends but secretly liked frogs and animals a lot. Probably surprised his folks by choosing zoology. But who was I to say?

"I don't know how long she'll last here to be honest," I said. "No one has been able to make it on this island."

They both got quiet.

Large waves came in wider and heavy. Then I saw *her.*

A shadowed, glittery-brown figure turned in a distant cresting wave.

My father said he had seen her before when he had to swim after a tourist who had neared the riptide. This was my second time seeing her. I had once glimpsed her in the moonlight during a night shift at the national park when I'd stayed up late shielding a hundred baby sea turtles to the water. She had lifted her head and given me the slimmest smile as the turtles fluttered through her cyan and green locks before sinking back and disappearing in the night.

But our people just don't go around telling people we can see the Ocean: people wouldn't believe us. Call us a bunch of crazy Indians. Jordan and April definitely didn't see. Though, I'm sure they'd be beyond scared if they could. She was beautiful. But terrifying to the wrong sort. In another moment I saw her fingers lace the water under the dock. I told her that the two interns seemed kind, that I'd make sure they didn't harm our relatives. And after a bit, she listened, fingers disappearing back into water. That must have been what she'd wanted from me. The waves lightened just so, and then we all saw a bright white double-decker pontoon headed right toward us.

A man in a green hat shouted, "Hello, you three! I'm Sergio." He docked the pontoon. "I'm your humble guide. You are minutes away from Isla Bella! Isabella has been known to love and hope for change and beauty. She is a dreamer and funds this internship opportunity for dreamers like you. We are honored you are here."

I tightened the straps on my backpack and stepped over the gate before he could open it. I took a spot in the midback of the boat, swung my bag to my left, and looked out at the island now that the waves subsided. No sign of her. I want to dislike Isabella and maybe these interns too, but I remembered what my aunties taught me: sikua, our word for *outsider.* It meant *friend until proven otherwise*. I needed to try a little, at least with these two I'd just advocated for.

"Thank you for the ride, Sergio," I said.

"You bet, Miss—?" He lifted his hat in my direction.

"Miss Dominguez."

"Oh, wonderful, yes! We've heard good things about you, Miss Dominguez! A local! Our first."

April and Jordan raised their eyebrows at me. They must not have picked that up. Most people don't think I'm from here with my Midwestern English.

"I live in Minnesota most of the year," I said looking back out at the water.

"Right, right. But a Costa Rican getting a national internship? Big deal," Sergio said.

I shrugged. "I have dual citizenship, so it's not that big of a surprise. They got the internship too." I nodded at April and Jordan, who were getting onto the boat. I wanted to add that it wasn't like they were letting those of us *without* American citizenship come to the island whenever they wanted, but I bit my tongue.

"That's so cool you live here sometimes, though." Jordan smiled at me as he gently put down his things. I guess he was kind of cute. Brown hair, green eyes. But even if I was being nice, I didn't want some fling on an island. Like, how absolutely basic.

I shrugged. "It is what it is."

"You two must be Jordan and April. Pleased to meet you." Sergio dazzled another smile at us. "Now, let's go see those boobies."

Jordan was the only one who laughed a short hiccup. April rolled her eyes. I smiled for a second. The birds, they were worth it. No matter how I cut it, Isabella had given to our park and her program allowed me to be here. I tried to be thankful, and I just prayed the Ocean wouldn't mind us visiting for a few weeks.

When we arrived at the island, Sergio docked the boat, and we went down a marble-like pathway lined with palm trees. We entered a tidy garden with fruit and orchids bulging from trees, a stone sculpture of an Indigenous woman's head at its center. It was smooth and big, and I saw my own wide nose and heavy eyebrows in her face. I already knew the artist: Cris Garcia. Sergio stopped to share that Garcia and Isabella shared a fascination and interest in pre-Hispanic art. Garcia was not an Indigenous artist, which always made me uncomfortable as he was literally carving our bodies into stone now to be set exactly where Columbus arrived having destroyed and murdered thousands of other Indigenous peoples elsewhere.

"Isabella really wants to respect the original peoples of this nation here. Some people whisper that she had an Indigenous lover, but the love was unrequited." Sergio sounded like much of the country with all their stories about her. "But c'est la vie!"

I rolled my eyes. We continued walking, and Sergio showed us where we'd eat, which was basically a restaurant open to the beach. We walked farther, and I felt my skin get dewy with a gentle mist. A fog rested over the walkway, and then I heard it.

A whimper. Sergio's eyes snapped to the forest behind us. April and Jordan didn't seem to hear it, their attention turned to each other talking. I turned to look behind me. There was no one. I thought of the woman's head in stone. My aunties were right: this was a place to be mourned, and I think those living here could feel it too.

I followed closer behind April, and finally we got to the beach where the boobies nested. And there they were, in all their glory. Plenty to distract me from what I'd thought I heard. The birds were hanging out around the small cliffs, some hopping and flapping around, some resting. I wanted to pull my drawing pad out and start sketching.

"My god, they are better than the photos," Jordan said.

April had a smug smile. "Can't wait to get to know you all," she called. Sergio showed us the research center, which was the only modest building. There was a computer lab, various cameras and underwater binoculars on shelves, and scuba gear hung up.

"You've got weeks ahead to get familiar with what we have here. Let's first get you all settled into your rooms. I know I was late getting you all," Sergio said, eyeing the sky.

We passed a few houses mostly hidden by palms, until we got to where we were staying. A huge A-frame house with glass walls. Marble floors, sleek design. I sent Dad a photo because I knew he'd shake his head at all this. I was trying not to like it, but it was beautiful. I'd never stayed anywhere like this. We entered and were greeted by an open kitchen, stocked with various staples from organic oatmeal to fresh fruit. Stairs went up in a circle for two more flights. We had assigned rooms: I was on the top floor, at the apex, and April was on one side of the second floor, Jordan on the other. We all went up the stairs, I think all of us a little dazzled even if I didn't want to admit it. Sergio told us to take some time to get settled. "Damn," I heard Jordan say as he opened his door. I only passed by briefly, but I saw that he had a window overlooking the forest's edge and the waterfront.

I went up to my huge modern room and looked out my window. My third time seeing her. Her brown shoulders sparkled like sun hitting water, and she was walking away from the shore, sinking into the tide. Her head went under, and her cyan and green hair spread behind her and then dissolved. Sand footsteps erased by the waves. I breathed. The Ocean was here on the island. The waves grew larger as she disappeared.

I didn't want to mess with the Ocean. This felt serious. I had heard her cry and return to the sea. My only hope was that she had heard me when I said that I was trying to visit with honor. But I hadn't known for sure she was coming inland. I set my bag down and lay on the large bed. My people are extremely careful when we come to the water. Some of us have never even put our feet in. This is why. She's unpredictable. Strong. A chaotic combination. I tried to distract myself and grabbed a pineapple juice from the personal mini fridge and pulled out my phone, but it was dead.

I turned to look for an outlet, and I saw a white envelope on the side table with my name on it.

I opened it.

Welcome, Miss Dominguez! I am so pleased that you in particular are here. Would you come to my house in the morning, just you? Sergio will bring you at six.

Great. I had thought I'd get to see the birds in the morning. Apparently not.

★ ★ ★

My alarm woke me up early. I sliced up a mango and waited for Sergio out on the front patio. I was surrounded by excess. I really didn't want to go talk with her. I wondered if she heard the whimpers. If the Ocean had visited her too. Let her get a glimpse like she did for me. I don't know if Isabella would have stayed long if she had.

Sergio arrived at six o'clock. He lifted his hat and didn't say much. Maybe he could tell I'm not really one for small talk. I followed him to the main house. He took me through a garden walk past Isabella's large swimming pool.

She sat in a reclining chair with a magazine. She wore a large hat so I couldn't see her face from the pathway, and it looked like she wore a white wrap dress with her hair down—long black locks, striking against the white fabric and surrounding green flora.

As I got closer, she looked up. Her dark eyes went from lifeless to bright.

"Beautiful! It's so good to meet you." She set her magazine to the side. "You can come sit here with me." With a manicured finger, she pointed to the lounge chair beside her. "We have so much to talk about. Do you want a lemonade?"

"Sure."

"Marvelous. Sergio, can you go grab her something?"

Sergio nodded and headed off. I sat down on the chair but didn't recline.

"Now that we're alone, I just wanted to say again that, goodness, I'm glad you got this internship. I hope it takes you a long way. I am just thrilled you are representing Costa Rica so well. Zoology. Brilliant. I had set up this opportunity just for people like you. And in its second year now! What a gift. Had a feeling we might have someone like you here."

I wasn't sure exactly how to respond. She chatted as if we were old friends or had somehow lived life in similar ways, though

I couldn't imagine how. I crossed my arms as she continued to make me uneasy.

"You know, Lana, I went to Harvard. And after, I did some work in the Peace Corps. In India. Truly beautiful. Did a business internship in China and learned Mandarin. All the boys in college told me I needed to know Mandarin for business. Though, interestingly enough, I noticed that with all its tones it was actually much like the Indigenous languages here. Don't you think?"

She wasn't wrong. Our language has many tones like Mandarin, but I didn't want her to even talk about our language. I hated how she was just talking about groups of people as if they were something to gather.

I shifted. She continued.

"Tell me, what got you interested in zoology?" She smiled at me as if she was prying, but it seemed like she was fully in control of this conversation.

"My father," I said. Her shoulders released for a second like she was relieved to hear me say so.

"Oh, yes, your father." She stopped to look at me, but it seemed like she was in another place. Dreaming. "We used to be good friends. I don't know if he ever told you that."

I froze. How could that be? Sergio walked up and handed me a glass of strawberry lemonade with a pink straw. Isabella glared at him for a second, and he shuffled off quickly. Then she leaned back in. My breathing hadn't fully returned, and the cold glass sweated in my hand. My dad and I didn't keep secrets from each other. We had always talked candidly about my mom and his divorce. It had been clear to me: Mom was his first and last relationship. His love was fulfilled with his people, me, and our relatives. And he really did always seem like he didn't know Isabella when people asked. *Who was she?* Was she about to blackmail me somehow? Please tell me that we weren't caught up in the unrequited Indigenous lover story.

"Can you tell me how he is? I think the last time he and I talked, he had just found out that you were a girl. He was so excited. And I always loved that."

"How did you two know each other?" It was starting to rain. I felt increasingly nervous.

"A story for another day. But say, I'd really love to see your father. Do you think we could convince him to come to the island? I've invited him plenty of times, but he always says he's busy. It's sad that I haven't seen him in ages." I thought of her checks coming to the national park. Was it even to help? What were they really for?

"I don't know if he'd want to. He's not really into—" I gestured at the pool and her house "—all of this sort of thing." It was true. He didn't like extravagance. Something he'd passed down to me. Or at least I thought—

"Will you ask him, though?" she said, getting a little irritated with me. She rubbed her neck, and her original ease and intention morphed into a prick of nervousness. "I do think he might like to see the beaches. Those birds are truly enchanting. Spectacular."

I breathed. Selfishly, I did want Dad to see the birds. I knew he'd wanted to see them for longer than I'd been alive.

I heard a whimper again, and I saw Isabella flinch. She could hear her too. Then the rain came down harder.

"So you'll ask him?" Isabella prompted again. Her eyes shifting to the trees.

I pushed my hair back. I didn't think it was me that the Ocean was trying to mess with. I shrugged. Was I trying to prove something?

"Sure," I say.

"Spectacular." She put her sunglasses on and didn't take the time to wipe the water droplets from the lenses. I walked quickly back to the unit, forgetting my drink. As I shivered in the rain, I wondered if I'd done the wrong thing.

★ ★ ★

In the morning when the rain stopped, Sergio took April, Jordan, and me to the see the birds. I spent the first hours letting myself geek out over their sharp beaks, their clumsy takeoffs but graceful dives. We took tons of video footage. I sat under an umbrella cover and drew a full-grown female. I told her how impressed I was by her resilience, and she made me consider how senseless Isabella was. I tried not to wonder how Dad knew her.

I welcomed a little normalcy and sent Dad the photos and videos of the birds. Then after a few messages back and forth, I asked him to come out. He said he was busy. But I said I really wanted him to come, so he agreed. I left out that I knew he and Isabella were friends. Maybe I didn't really want to know. If any of the stories were right about Isabella—the cartel, the blackmail, the weird power games of the wealthy—I didn't want to know how my dad had ever been caught up in those circles. Was it for the money to the park?

I waited by the dock for Dad in the late afternoon, and Jordan brought me a sandwich. We sat on the water. "After you said that nothing has been able to survive here, I can kind of feel it," he said. "It's almost like being stuck on a golf field during a rainstorm."

"I knew you were a golfer." I took a bite of my turkey sandwich and smiled.

"It's pretty obvious. Look at this sock tan." He pointed to his legs where there was a clear tan line across his ankles.

I swallowed and looked back out at the water and teased him. "Pretty hot."

"You know it. God, my dad would never come out to see some birds." He laughed.

"Well, apparently they are the only way I could get mine to leave the shore," I said. "My dad has dreamed about getting to meet these birds. Guess that's why I'm here too."

"That's really cool." He took a drink from his water bottle. "Not everyone gets to share stuff like that with their parents."

"I guess I don't know if he's always shared everything with me. Apparently, he knows Isabella."

"Oh, wild. It seemed like no one really knew her."

"Yeah. I don't know if there is a good way to know Isabella."

"I feel that. I hear the boat." He got up, and the wind snapped his shirt like a flag. He brushed it down. "Jeez. This weather is not great. Stay safe," he said.

"Don't worry. Unlike most people, I'm supposed to be here," I said, though it sounded a little harsher than I meant. I bit my lip. Sikua, Lana. Sikua. Jordan's response was kind.

"I believe it." He smiled and walked back to the units, looking at the graying sky.

When Dad arrived, I told him that Isabella had invited us for dinner. Maybe it was manipulative. I did want him here with me, yes, for the birds, but maybe more because everything felt uneasy.

He lifted an eyebrow, and I think he was gauging if I knew more.

"Fine," he said, gruff. "I'll do dinner. But I am not going to stay long."

Dad brought nothing but himself. He had on the hiking boots he wore to work and the green national park cap. His thick braid was pulled down his back. I wanted to ask him right there about Isabella, but maybe it was better to loosen him up by going to the research center first.

Seeing my father watch the birds was like watching a grandparent with an infant. He sweet-talked them and hummed to himself. He went to this whole other place of love around the animals. They had his heart. He'd given most of his life to our relatives' care. Their survival. He'd never met the booby, but I had a feeling they knew him because they totally showed off.

Preened their wings, gave their weird little er-er-er noises, and I wondered if they knew all he'd done for their relatives just on the other side of the water.

"So how do you know her?" I finally asked.

"Ah, so she did say something." He nodded like he knew Isabella well enough. "It was a long time ago," he said.

"Come on, Dad. Tell me."

"She was different back then."

"Is that why you tell people you don't know her?" I try to catch his eyes and lean just so in front of him.

"I guess it has always felt partly true." He paused. "She used to come visit our tribe. We sort of grew up together. And when we were teenagers, we were together."

"What? Together, like dating?" I stopped and stared at him.

"Yes. But then one day when she was sixteen, she just stopped coming to visit, went to the capital for schooling, worked at an orphanage to cover her costs, and somehow got herself to the States. She got caught up in a lot of things. And returned, building this. Whatever this is..." He shook his head in the buildings' direction.

I thought of her words. How much she'd cared that I was Indigenous. Like I had some *in*, somehow.

"I have kept my distance. When people turn greedy, they do not do well," Dad said. "You know the stories." I did know the stories. The greedy were cut in half by lethal ropes thrown down by spirits. Kept in baskets by their spouses.

Drowned.

"You see how the Ocean is acting?" he said.

I nodded. "I've seen her a few times."

He hummed. "I'm not surprised at all. She's not happy Isabella is here," he said in a low voice. "I don't know what Isabella is trying to do, but this, whatever this is, is not the way."

"Maybe she'll listen to you."

Dad's face softened for just a moment. But then he shook his head. "I don't know, Lana."

★★★

We all sat at dinner, and she had been extravagant throughout the night talking about parties and who she had hosted. Dad had hardly responded. Finally, when he said he wanted to leave, Isabella's eyes looked as if she was about to lose it.

"Won't you stay longer, Daniel?" And she finally just laid it out. "I have plans. I have so missed you. You know I loved you so much. You could head this internship program and others. I'm looking to have more of your people come here and study. I've built this all to help, and I plan to donate even more. For people like you and your daughter. I made the program—" The rain beat down on the umbrella over our heads.

"I don't believe it, Isabella." My dad put his hat back on and wiped his mouth. The snapper in front of us was huge, and we'd eaten most of it. Dad never wasted food, but it looked like he wanted to get off the island as fast as he could. Isabella had dressed up in an emerald dress and was wearing earrings that I knew someone from our tribe must have made. They were made of fish scales.

"I want to gain back what you all have lost." She scanned me with pleading eyes. "I was doing this all for you. To come here. To stay. Can't you..."

I looked at Dad, unsure what to say. "I think you are afraid," Dad said. "All this is catching up to you. And I cannot help you."

Then we all heard a voice from the waters. It was a low grumble. Isabella was afraid, clearly in love with Dad still. But she was also using us.

"If you really cared, you wouldn't have built a single thing. You've damaged this land, and you're no better than the people five hundred years ago. These are dangerous actions, Isabella. You should know what happens to people who do things like this. Didn't we teach you anything?"

Dad got up and turned. I followed him. There was a bellow of thunder. I closed my eyes and remembered the stories of how the

Ocean would rise to meet Thunder when he'd form himself to lightning. Together they were terrifying. I felt terrible for bringing Dad here. I also felt terrible for Isabella because, like Dad said, I knew this charade of hers would cost her. I was sure of it.

"Sergio, I would love a ride back if you will," Dad asked on our way off the patio.

"Certainly."

I looked back, and Isabella stood, her dress whipping in the wind. Her swimming pool dark and pocked with the drops of rainwater. Was she crying now? I think she was.

I returned to my room in the cottage. I'd been Isabella's pawn. I really didn't want to know how upset Dad would be with me when I returned home, but I deserved it. Jordan stopped by with popcorn, and we talked for a while as the storm intensified. I don't know if he could sense my concern, but he offered to sleep on the couch, and I agreed. "I don't know if being up higher helps, but it just feels like it would, anyway," he said. I thought of our Bribri houses and how we keep them elevated for reasons like flooding and hurricanes.

"You're not wrong," I said.

"What are you up to?" I whispered to the Ocean when Jordan was asleep. I prayed that she wouldn't hurt us. I begged her.

I could hardly sleep as rain beat against our windows, lightning cracking, but I just kept hoping she'd leave us be and finally fell asleep. When I woke up to the sun through my window, I looked out, and there were trees splayed out in different directions on the beach.

"This is bad," Jordan said. We went downstairs and saw that flooding had come through the first floor and across the tiles thick with muck and dirt. April was fine, though she looked like she had hardly slept, either. "I tried calling Sergio, but the service is down," she said.

April, Jordan, and I put on rubber boots that were stocked in the front closet and walked past the wrecked units. Broken timbers and shattered glass. Only ours was relatively untouched. We went to Sergio's cottage, but he must have stayed inland after bringing the staff home when their hours were over. We walked toward the main house.

And that's when we saw her. Isabella splayed facedown in the pool like a flower dropped in water.

"Dear God—" Jordan said, his hand to his mouth. April frantically started to make a call, but I knew it wasn't going to go through.

And right there, perched on the arm of a lawn chair was a brown booby. Her head turned and cocked to the side. A yellow spectacle.

I darkly wondered how many times she'd seen this scene. For a moment, just a moment, a glittering hand reached from the forest and petted her head before disappearing.

★ ★ ★ ★ ★

EVERMORE

a remix of "The Raven"
NoNieqa Ramos

"Deep into that darkness peering, long I stood there wondering, fearing,

Doubting, dreaming dreams no mortal ever dared to dream before."

—Edgar Allan Poe, "The Raven"

From the Curious Volume of Forgotten Lore
Species: Homo sapiens
Locations: Earth, the Solar System, Oort Cloud, Orion Arm, Milky Way galaxy, Virgo Supercluster, Universe, 54.5260° N, 105.2551° W, "North America" (1507–2097)…and 18.2208° N, 66.5901° W, Borinquen
Mindscapes: Iris Colón; future progenitor of Zadie Colón Gilead; Yarelis Narváez; future progenitor of Lenore Narváez Contreras

Earth cut the teeth of three hundred twenty-three million tombstones by the year 2049. So many people died from the Upsilon virus, coffins had to be piled on top of coffins, creating an underground tenement of the dead. In the historic hurricanes of 2051, coffins erupted from the ground swells and infested water sources with infection and displaced ghosts. The next wave of plague brought humanity to its scabbed knees. The Omega virus killed 95 percent of the population of Boston, leaving the Freedom Trail untrodden, turning Harvard University into a makeshift mausoleum, and the city into a cemetery of monuments.

Within months, wildlife—long depleted by human demand—returned to Boston Harbor, which once again brewed with lobsters, striped bass, bluefish. Seals hauled back to Little Brewster, Nixes Mate, and Shag Rocks. The humpback whales followed. The sea birthed a new generation of life not seen since the Paleozoic era.

Death birthed a generation of children born into grief. Left Yarelis Narváez without a father. Iris Gilead without a mother…

From the Curious Volume of Forgotten Lore
Location: 18.2208° N, 66.5901° W, Borinquen
Mindscapes: Iris Colón; future progenitor of Zadie Colón Gilead; Yarelis Narváez; future progenitor of Lenore Narváez Contreras

Iris and Yarelis were among the 5 percent of survivors. In 2056, they would move from Boston to Isabel, Puerto Rico, the land of their ancestors, where the water was not yet contaminated. They met exploring La Cueva del Viento in El Bosque Estatal de Guajataca, on the sacred grounds where their ancestors once gave birth. The site was now being marked by gringo prospectors for Bitcoin drilling. A female hook-clawed sloth (a member of a species thought to have gone extinct) revealed herself and her infant to the girls in desperation. Helping the sloth retreat into the recesses of the cave, the girls became fast friends. Over the next few months, they spent hours exploring the rain forest. They witnessed the critically endangered golden coqui frog repopulate and join their resilient siblings, the common coqui, in jubilant song.

The girls sang with them, although the coquis' newfound life could only mean one thing for the humans on the island. The plague was near.

Nunca más la pregunta…
Could there be an end to grief?
Nunca más feeling unheard. Unseen.

Nunca más feeling that everything hurts.
Alone in the endless universe.
Cursed.

Nunca más wondering:
Was happiness a possibility?
Love a reality?

The song notes composed letters of love on their hearts. They were still humming the lyrics when they explored a new section of La Cueva. Their laughter ruffled the air. They interlaced hands. Iris leaned in as if to tell Yarelis a secret. Instead of telling her a secret, she asked, "¿Puedo besarte?" *Can I kiss you?*

Yarelis nodded *yes.*

The wind whispered warning, but that *yes* was all Yarelis could hear as she kissed her first kiss, and as Iris kissed hers. Yarelis's abuela dragged her home by the hair. The girls were forbidden from meeting again. Both were met with the whip of the switch, crying out their final words.

Yarelis, take this kiss upon your brow!
And, in leaving you now,
this much let me vow—
you are not wrong, who think
that our days have been a dream;
yet if hope has flown away
in a night, or in a day,

in a vision, or in none,
is it literally the less gone?

Querida Iris, all that we see or seem
is but a dream within a dream…

Shortly after the kiss, both girls contracted the virus. They survived but experienced debilitating symptoms for months. Their families called it a scourge from God.

Just when the island of Puerto Rico began to succumb to the virus, as everyone fled indoors and her waters brimmed with manatees and hawksbill turtles once again, a cure for humankind was found in the States within the succulent leaves of *Euterpe edulis*, commonly known as the palmiteiro tree. Over the next decade, the vaccine eradicated the Omega virus and led to cures for other debilitating diseases like fibromyalgia, cerebral palsy, and Epstein-Barr. Dubbed the Lazarus era, the bedridden rose by the millions.

Sufferers who'd spent their lives in chronic pain experienced the pleasure of release. Humans rejoiced, their praise overtaking the whistling crescendo of the nightingale, the harmonies of the coquis, the chi of the spindali. New York Hospital developed rehabilitation clinics for long-haulers, who had suffered long-term effects of Omega. Iris's and Yarelis's families moved them from Puerto Rico to NY for treatment, ten blocks and a world apart. Coughing in their bedrooms, each of them wondered: Had God answered humankind's prayers or the Devil's?

It depended on who was asked. Between the sentient lobster on the celebratory dinner plate and the human holding the cracker, opinions varied. The sloths the girls had saved retreated deep into the secret catacombs of La Cueva del Viento, never to be seen again. The golden coquis once again dropped from the trees and decomposed under tourists' feet, and the common coquis sang funeral songs for them once more.

But once the humans' celebratory singing stopped, the sadness began. There was no cure for collective grief. After an initial resurgence, the economy collapsed again, with a spike in depression. The government instituted a Find/Renew Your Religion initiative. The separation of church and state was suspended. The term *death* was canceled and replaced with *passing to the other dimension.*

Boston no longer belonged to lobsters, striped bass, or bluefish. Seals. Humpbacks. New York no longer belonged to the deer, the elk, the moose. The gray wolf. The Moon no longer belonged to herself. Scientific advances skyrocketed. Water-filtration sources were discovered deep within Montes Apenninus, a rugged mountain range on the northern part of the Moon's near side. In their respective living rooms, Iris and Yarelis watched astronauts mine the Moon. The world moved on. The girls grew up. Their families never mentioned the incident at La Cueva again.

Iris wondered if it had all been a dream.

By the time Iris's and Yarelis's children were born in 2077, NASA had discovered a reliable and renewable energy supply: a mineral named Aiden (named after the Garden of Eden) found in a crater on the Moon. Aiden could be mined to generate power without the use of the sun. Solar panels were designed to help sunlight and heat withstand the long lunar nights and extreme temperatures on the Moon. They provided the atmosphere the Moon lacked and cover from the intense radiation. By 2074, lunar greenhouses successfully grew plants in lunar soil, generating a filtration system for the toxic dust. In the past, astronauts had lost, on average, 1 to 2 percent of their bone mass to…

★ ★ ★

From the Curious Volume of Forgotten Lore
Locations: Reckouwacky (Rockaway Beach), 40.5860° N, 73.8166° W, Usher Preparatory Academy, 42.5947° N, 75.6968° W
Mindscapes: Zadie Colón Gilead; Lenore Narváez Contreras; Zakiya Pallas

By the time Zadie Colón Gilead and Lenore Narváez Contreras were born in 2077, so many diseases had been cured that the world population exploded. Schools on earth were over capacity and campuses had to resort to placing dozens and dozens of so-called educational trailers in their parking lots. The United States' solution to this countrywide problem was to establish experimental colonies on the Moon. But building a top-rated school system and university takes time. By 2090, while facilities were being constructed, talent recruited, and the selection process for top-notch students was fine-tuned, schools on Earth would use a lottery system for the time being.

To enter, families had to fill out a packet of forms and submit a photo ID. Students who were deemed to fit the status quo, be compliant, and have high test scores would receive two entry forms to increase their chances of getting a coveted spot.

Normally students with missing paperwork were automatically disqualified. But because of Lenore's high test scores and athletic acumen, she and her mother were called into the high school's central office to complete the missing paperwork in person. The third survey question was *What is your gender?* The choices were *male*, *female*, and *other*. It was known that indicating *other* disqualified one from attendance. Lenore had emailed her form with this question blank. She had not sent in a scan of her ID.

At the high-school entrance, Lenore and her mother were greeted and seated in a vestibule. Lenore asked to use the restroom. After five minutes, she returned to the office, citing a stomach-ache. Her exasperated mother had already filled in the checkbox for *male* on the survey. The committee, which included English teacher Ms. Zakiya Pallas, watched as Lenore fished in her backpack, unable to find her student ID. In frustration, Lenore's mother threatened to dump the contents of Lenore's backpack out on the floor. Lenore found her ID. Ms. Pallas eyeballed the artwork on the ID, then eyeballed Lenore, snatched the ID, and disappeared into her personal office. She returned, handed the ID back to Lenore, and shook Lenore's hand, holding it for a long time.

She said, "I hope I have you as a student." She didn't say, *I saw how you crossed out your name on your ID. How you drew over the photo and drew your true self in.*

Lenore pretended to sneeze and claimed allergies as she wiped a tear from her eye and rubbed her cheek against her shoulder to hide the streak of mascara. A week later she was crammed in a gymnasium that had been converted into a classroom and found a spot away from the athletes, who would inevitably invite her to join one sports team or another because of her build. In her sketchbook, she drew herself made of glass, invisible and empty to some, a vessel of light to others.

Even in the packed gym, teeming with dozens of students elbowing for room on the bleachers, Zadie saw the shape of light in Lenore.

Lenore wore the required uniform: gray slacks, tucked-in white shirt, black loafers. When Zadie took the only available seat by Lenore, they detected a floral, woodsy, green fragrance. Pretending to dig in their backpack, they noted Lenore's pinky nail, glittering with a sliver of silver polish in the shape of the Moon. But what really caught their attention was the self-portrait on the open sketchbook in Lenore's lap. Lenore had drawn herself in the image of a mermaid returned to the sea. Dare Zadie ask?

Zadie dared. "What are your pronouns?" they scribbled on a note. Zadie witnessed something few humans get to see. The moment when the sun's warm reassurance wakes a seed: Lenore smiled.

At school, they stole glances over
chemistry experiments.
Lenore loved watching Zadie
nerd out over hydrogen bonding
affecting the volatility
of liquids and solids.

Reaching for oil paints
in the art closet,
the two brushed fingertips.
Lenore blushed.
Zadie caught their breath…

Zadie loved to watch Lenore painting
a city by the sea.
Caught sketching their face,
Lenore asked, "Will you pose for me?"

From brief moments together,
they purloined hours of daydreams.

On the bus to and from home,
they talked for hours about everything and nothing.
As winter surrendered to spring,
they planned to go to Rockaway Beach…

Gracias a Diosa,
the crisis,
the danger was past.
The torturous loneliness
was over at last.

★ ★ ★

From the Curious Volume of Forgotten Lore
Locations: Reckouwacky (Rockaway Beach), 40.5860° N, 73.8166° W, Usher Preparatory Academy, 42.5947° N, 75.6968° W, Classroom of Ms. Zakiya Pallas
Mindscape: Lenore Narváez Contreras

In Ms. Pallas's class they talked
about philosophy, which literally meant
love of wisdom,
a study of truth, existence, and reality.
How philosophers had pondered the meaning of life
as far back as the sixth century BCE.
She talked about the connection of philosophy and poetry.
She wanted the class to read Gertrude Stein's poetry and decipher the meaning.

Lenore reflected on Gertrude Stein's famous line
"A Rose is a rose is a rose"
and journaled about what it meant.
Dreamily doodled L.N. is L.N. is L.N.—

Then Lenore is Lenore is Lenore on her lap desk.
Until she snapped out of her fugue and
frantically tried to erase it.

When Ms. Pallas touched her shoulder,
she thought it was over.
She'd be outed. Expelled.
But Ms. Pallas whispered,
"I respect your privacy.
Your truth is not mine to tell."

Ms. Pallas continued her lesson,
teaching the history of poetry and philosophy.

The genius minds who had pondered the meaning of life
for centuries.

But in all the vast world,
in all the centuries of thinking about what it meant to be
a good human being,
Lenore could still not find safety.

From the Curious Volume of Forgotten Lore
Location: Reckouwacky (Rockaway Beach), 40.5860° N, 73.8166° W
Mindscapes: Zadie Colón Gilead; Lenore Narváez Contreras

...Swimming at night on Rockaway Beach?
Zadie knew it was dangerous.
But all they could see
was Lenore's Moon-licked skin.
Her eyes, hazel crescents.

Lenore said, "You are my best friend."

Zadie unburdened their secrets.
Talked about their mother and father
and their recent arguing.
How Mom forgot to pay the water bill.
Almost burned the kitchen down, cooking.

Lenore said, "That's hard. I'm sorry."

Zadie said, "Mil gracias, querida, for just listening.
Por fa, now tell me something happy."

Lenore talked about her invitation to the Star Party.
"Imagine what it would be like if you came with me?"
She looked into Zadie's upturned eyes, asking—
"If we could...hold hands—"

"Without disdain or curiosity."

"Imagine if at the very moment Jupiter aligned with Mars..."

"We could reveal our true hearts."

They talked bucket-list fantasies.
Being accepted by both their families.

Salted with the starlit sea,
They floated without fear or anxiety.
Pulled only by Love's gravity.
Winged with unfurling waves,
Their selfhoods could no longer be contained...

In a high tide of starry promises.
Their lips eclipsed.
They kissed.

From the Curious Volume of Forgotten Lore
Location: "Rockaway"
Mindscapes: Iris Colón Gilead; Zadie Colón Gilead

In a brain affected by Alzheimer's disease, the hippocampus is one of the first areas damaged. The sufferer can no longer make new memories. *First in, last out* is often used to describe an Alzheimer's patient's memory loss. Their first memories, like long-term memories of childhood, are the last to fade.

When Iris Colón Gilead's hippocampus started functioning incorrectly, it directly inhibited her ability to process and retain new and recent information. She could remember her daughter's fifth birthday. The princess-themed party to match her pink princess room decor. Everything was perfect. Everyone was pleased. The tea party was a hit! And the faux wedding. How cute it was to pretend Zadie was marrying that neighbor boy! Iris Colón Gilead told her daughter *she* was a mother's dream come true. But no matter how she tried, Alzheimer's disease burned the bridge between what she saw in front of her and what she remembered.

This was why she could not remember if she had given Zadie permission to come and go at odd hours.

Iris couldn't understand if the friend Zadie brought home was—what was his name—Leo? Or maybe…did Leo have a sister? And Zadie's clothing. How long had she been dressing in this androgynous fashion? When had she cut her hair? Who had allowed it?

When was the last time Zadie had put on makeup?

But distinctly, Zadie remembered
that dreadful birthday in December.
How they had asked for a skating party.
How their mother insisted on a tea party.
Forced them to pretend to marry.

How a crowd of grown-ups
asked them and the neighbor boy to kiss.
How his breath smelled like peanut butter
when he neared their lips.
They remembered the applause.
Thinking, I don't belong.

Zadie remembered when they cried and ran outside.
How their mother followed, mortified.
Said, Don't embarrass me.
Let's not ruin your birthday party!

That day Zadie learned what it meant to be embarrassing.
Crying.
Asserting your own autonomy.

Over the years,
Zadie and Mom had talked over,
through, and at each other—
but they couldn't remember
when they talked to *each other,*
or if they ever had.

From the Curious Volume of Forgotten Lore
Locations: Redacted, residence of the Colón Gilead family; redacted, residence of the Narváez family
Mindscapes: Zadie Colón Gilead; Lenore Narváez Contreras

2093 saw a promising new treatment for Alzheimer's, a progressive disease that destroyed the mind. Transformed your family into impostors. Made a stranger out of one's reflection...

...Zadie thought, *My mother might be cured.* But could she ever be cured of hate?

They met at the beach again and again.
Each day a promise of friendship and love kept.
But their joy, made of glass,
could not last.

Pendulum like a scythe,
the clock cut into bliss.
The hours could not be torn from time.
One day, they were both late for dinnertime.
They each rushed to their house of lies...

Still smelling of the shore,
the rare and radiant Lenore
tiptoed on her parents' porch.

She stressed about her appearance.
How she could hide her sun-kissed skin.

Zadie's violet kiss curling the corners of her lips.

The tan lines that outlined how she wished to be seen.
She couldn't wait until the Star Party.
For the third conjunction where Jupiter and Mars would meet,
For the revelation of their true identities.

She couldn't wait to tell her family her truth.
She knew they believed in God and Jesus and goodness,
so they'd have to believe in her too.

No more scrubbing her face with makeup-remover wipes.
Yes.
Tonight she would hide her bikini
and summer dress for the last time.

But when she opened the door,
She saw her mother crying on the floor.
Her stepfather yelling into the speakerphone,
How long had Ms. Pallas known?

Heard her teacher Ms. Pallas apologize.
Asked how she could support them at this challenging time.

"How could you out me!?" Lenore yelled into the phone.
"I trusted you."
A beat later Ms. Pallas answered, "Because I had to.
I have to out kids to their parents or lose my teaching license.
I'm so sorry, Lenore. You deserve so much better than this."

Ms. Pallas sounded like she was telling the truth,
but what difference did it make?
Who could Lenore trust to keep their word?
Where could she feel safe?

Ms. Pallas cried, "How can I support their transition,
help Lenore?"
Yarelis Narváez answered, "Don't call him that.
Call him Leonard. And don't call here anymore."

The rare and radiant Lenore
would be deadnamed in her household forevermore.

Ms. Pallas refused to call Mrs. Colón Gilead and out Zadie.
So the principal personally called Zadie's home that same evening.
A week later, the school district revoked Ms. Pallas's license and accused her of child abuse
for protecting LGBTQIA+ youth.
Her classroom erased as a safe space at Lenore and Zadie's school forevermore.

Lenore's tears like acid rain,
burned in Ms. Pallas's brain.
"Craven and cold, I forsook Lenore."
In this world, she vowed, "I will teach nevermore."

Before she left, she slipped a brochure under Zadie's and Lenore's front doors.

From the Curious Volume of Forgotten Lore
Location: Greenwich Point Park, 41.0102° N, 73.5696° W
Mindscapes: Zadie Colón Gilead; Lenore Narváez Contreras

Lenore and Zadie met on the beach
in their city of crumbling dreams.
Fell to their knees.
Zadie said, "They can't take you away from me!"
Lenore uttered, "Or you from me..."
Or, Lenore shuddered, me from me.

Lenore retired home.
Found the screen taped with a note.
"Leonard, you chose,"
her mother wrote.
"When you remember who you really are,
You can come back home."

Lenore turned away from the door,
dead to her mother, forevermore.

Her mind filled with fantastic terror.
Were her family ties really severed forever?
The next time Lenore returned, alone,
to Rockaway Beach,
she was in too deep.
In
too
deep.

Said Lenore, "I stand amid the roar
of a surf-tormented shore,
and I hold within my hand
grains of the golden sand—
trod by a love I can never have.

O Goddess! Can I not grasp
them with a tighter clasp?
O Goddess! Can I not save
one from the pitiless wave?
Is all that we see or seem
but a dream within a dream?"

Lenore swallowed pills;
waited to be claimed

by the sea.
Zadie found her by the shore,
barely breathing.
Three months later,
in County Hospital,
Lenore was still in a coma, fast asleep.

Now, scrolling through old messages,
a selfie of Zadie and Lenore
entangled in a violet kiss,
Zadie grabbed the brochure to their chest,
read the note attached from Ms. Pallas
that she had slipped below their door:
"It doesn't have to be like this."

From the Curious Volume of Forgotten Lore
Locations: Redacted, the private residence of the Colón Gilead family; Reckouwacky (Rockaway Beach), 40.5860° N, 73.8166° W
Mindscape: Zadie Colón Gilead

By 2094, surgeons could perform organ transplants without fear of rejection by the recipient's body. Removing a bit of thymus from the donor, which sits just in front of and above the heart, along with the desired organ, warded off the recipient's often deadly autoimmune-system response. The thymus trained the patient's body to recognize its new self and not attack. The principal of Usher Preparatory Academy proudly returned from an organ transplant, crediting a deceased tenant for his new heart.

Zadie witnessed miracle after miracle. But there was no miracle for Zadie.

Rising upon a midnight dark,
Zadie pondered, how to cure a broken heart?
Could music provide relief?
They could hardly breathe.

Softly each song sound tracked a memory,
the cringe teacher blasting the song "Weird Science" in chemistry.
Of Lenore in oversize goggles, giggling and dancing.
Of the moment Zadie knew what it felt like to be happy.

Chest shuddering,
Zadie sought to borrow
from their books surcease of sorrow.
But each dog-eared page
of poetry
now dogged Zadie's deepest beliefs.
In the unconditional love
of family.
In love conquering bigotry.

Now they couldn't even confide in Papi.
Mom caught him on the phone,
with GLSEN—
The Gay, Lesbian & Straight Education Network—
asking for help.
Zadie stayed up all night listening to Mom yell.
Mom accused Papi of "grooming" Zadie.
Said if he didn't stop, she'd call the authorities.

Distinctly. Zadie remembered that day in July,
When they learned everything they understood about family
was a lie.

With Mami's gross and ghastly accusations against Papi,
that he was grooming Zadie,
the state called it child abuse
and took away his parental rights and custody.

Mami's final words
croaked in their consciousness.

She said it with her full chest:
"Now we begin again.
Now everything is perfect."

Zadie tossed the poetry.
Desperately turned to scrolling.

But each scroll unfurled
a bucket list of fantasies,
now dumped.
Emptied.

Was life meaningless?
Their eyes closed with the memory of Lenore,
dress billowing as she whirled on the shore.

Rejected by her parents' version of religion and salvation,
she became the Moon's child.
Cradled by the ocean.
Loved by the Wild.

No.
Every atom in Zadie's being
told them belief and truth weren't always the same thing.

From the Curious Volume of Forgotten Lore
Location: St. John's Episcopal Hospital, 40.5986° N, 73.7527° W
Mindscapes: Zadie Colón Gilead; Lenore Narváez Contreras

Dreaming dreams within dreams,
Lenore hid beloved memories.
Buried her identity.
Then, she thought, the air grew denser,
perfumed from an unseen censer.

She awoke to the stranger at her bedside,
an angel with golden tourmaline eyes.
Whispered, where am I?
Who am I?

Before Zadie could reply,
her beloved's name and identity were reassigned.
Lenore answered when her parents used her deadname,
but clutched the angel's hand as if in pain.
Her mother had the nurse infuse her veins with lidocaine…

The doctor said with time there could be recovery.
But Lenore's family took her home
without rehabilitation or therapy.
Hoping she would never remember her queer identity.

From the Curious Volume of Forgotten Lore
…Reckouwacky
Mindscapes: Zadie Colón Gilead; Lenore Narváez Contreras

By the middle of 2095, the first astronauts and their families were living on the Moon. Select youth were recruited for their talent in chemistry, engineering, academics, creative writing, and art. Puerto Rico established the first colony of biodomes on the Moon.

Several biodomes were designated as social experiments. One such biodome, *Evermore,* was engaged in the most revolutionary human experiment of all, which had failed infinite times on Earth: one in which all people, of all ethnicities, cultures, Indigenous religions, genders, and sexual orientations lived in equality. Recruiters for the experiment had invited seniors from Usher Preparatory Academy to attend their information session.

It seemed many and many a year ago,
in that paradise by the sea,
that a maiden existed whom you may know—
loved by Zadie.
And this maiden lived with no other thought
than to love and be loved by Zadie.

Zadie's eyes fell on the brochure
so long ago slipped by Ms. Pallas under her door.
Of a spaceship called The Raven.
A biodome called Evermore.

An invitation to escape to a queer new world.

With Zadie's proficiency in the sciences and the arts, they were a top candidate. Unbeknownst to Mami, Zadie forged her name on all the necessary paperwork, enrolling Zadie in the space program. When Zadie was at trainings late each weeknight and on weekends, Mami often forgot Zadie was born. In Mami's mindscape, Mami spent nights in La Cueva leading a sloth to safety. Zadie prepared for a life in space for three months. The spaceship, *The Raven*, shaped like a raven, with a 562-foot (171.298-meter) wingspan, would launch into space with chemical propulsion and, once in orbit, would use nuclear thermal propulsion to make the trip to the Moon in a day. But even after their training and acceptance, even at the graduation ceremony, Zadie had not made a final decision.

Could they leave behind their sick and ailing mother
right before she saw the light?
Could they leave behind any hope of reconciliation
with their father and say goodbye?
Would this mean they were surrendering the fight for
LGBTQIA+ rights?

Could Zadie leave their precious Lenore behind?
Her eyes open, but blind?

After decades of refinement, pulses of light were being effectively used to stave and eradicate Alzheimer's disease by enhancing cognition-boosting electrical brain waves. Patients who, like Zadie's mother, were at the latest stages of the disease, could potentially experience an 80- to 90-percent reversal of their symptoms with the help of infrared light treatments.

Heart torn, Zadie cried on the floor,
packing and unpacking clothes
from overturned drawers—

they clutched a purple blouse to their chest,
a temple housing Lenore's scent—
reliving the day that she dazzled in it again and again.

If they left Lenore behind?
Would every memory of her unwind?
Was their love earthbound?
Or could it transcend the clouds?

What if Lenore regained her memory
and found herself completely,
utterly, alone?

Like a gavel, Zadie's conscious rapped.
Even if she escaped the homophobic Earth
and found her freedom,
could they live with that?

Still, what about the idea of found family,
love defying gravity,
being blessed by the galaxy?

Resting their head on a velvet sleeve,
Zadie nodded nearly asleep.
Suddenly there came a distant tapping,
as of someone gently rapping.

From the Curious Volume of Forgotten Lore
Mindscape: Zadie Colón Gilead

Before the big send-off to *Evermore*, graduates would enter an isolation chamber with a parent or guardian for the course of three days. During that period, they would be decontaminated, treated for any illness, and implanted with an internal thermometer, heart, and brain-monitoring device to ensure their vitals were stable. To prevent Spaceflight-Associated Neuro-Ocular Syndrome (SANS), a condition in the eye that can lead to deterioration of vision and swelling and flattening of structures in the eye, specialized ocular lenses would be fitted for each traveler. Then the great sleep.

The sleep wasn't for a great duration—it only took twenty-four hours to get to the Moon—but it would deliver miraculous regeneration. Graduates needed to be in top shape to contribute to *Evermore*. Parents or guardians could tuck their children in and watch nepenthe (the drug that would usher their children to sleep with preprogrammed dreams) be administered. Preprogrammed dreams could stem from fantasies. Zadie had programmed their dream to center around the Star Party.

Now, three days before *The Raven* would launch, Zadie heard that gentle rapping. The floorboards whined outside Zadie's bedroom door.

It's just the house that creaks.
Not Child Protective Services coming for me.
Because the governor made it against the law to be me.
Forced a teacher to choose between losing her job and reporting me.

Not the police because I swore that I'd flee.
Just one more week before I turn eighteen.

Only the wind whispers at my door.
This it is and nothing more.

But the brass doorknob rattled,
the door shook its frame.
It was the wind, the wind,
they heard.
Not wisps of their name.

Yes, the bones of the house were shifting,
the copper pipes whispering—

It isn't Mother screaming that's she's been trapped,
sundowning in the shadow Alzheimer's had cast.
Her accusations falling like a guillotine—
that they were killing her slowly.

No, Mami wasn't crying for help;
raging against the night.
Claiming that "they" imprisoned her,
poisoned her with light.

Presently Zadie's soul grew stronger—
they could not wait a minute longer.
"Yes?" they called out tentatively.
Would their mother answer coherently?

When Iris Colón Gilead could no longer care for herself, Zadie had become her caregiver. As such, they had control of all medical treatments, including the most important, the light box. The doctor said it was a simple treatment. All her mother needed to do was bask in the light of the box for thirty minutes a day to regain her faculties. Within months, Iris Colón Gilead would slowly return to herself, to the period before the onset of Alzheimer's. To the time when Iris had asked Zadie to stop being herself, loving herself, being loved unconditionally.

Though Iris's mind would eventually recover, the deterioration of her body could not be undone. She had fallen and shattered her pelvis. She would always require a wheelchair. Zadie helped her mother use the toilet. Bathe. Comb her hair.

Had circumstances been different, Zadie would have held sacred every moment she cared for Iris. But her devotion now came with conditions her mother could not meet. Still, her sense of responsibility and overwhelming guilt stopped Zadie from abandoning her. To leave, she would need her anger to be fresh.

Zadie experimented with the light box to take them back in time.

They began the scientific method. What would happen if their mother basked in the light for an hour...two hours...instead of thirty minutes? Would this accelerate her progress? Would she somehow accelerate in time and memory to her last weeks of coherence? To the time when she had uttered her ultimatums against Zadie? They formed a hypothesis. More was better. Zadie made an attempt to move forward in time. Their mother's rejection, anger, and rage would make it easier for them to leave. To join Ms. Pallas, board *The Raven*, and never look back.

It turned out accelerating the light treatment only caused her mother migraines and first-degree burns.

Zadie knew if she took away the light, her mother would most certainly deteriorate and die. But what would happen if she adjusted the amount of light and the length of time between doses?

If her mother skipped a week of light treatment, how long until she regressed? Zadie discovered if she doled out the light intermittently, she could keep her mother in stasis, suspended in the amber of a particular memory. A memory that Zadie could not entirely decipher but knew was important. Zadie listened.

"Nunca más unkissed…
Cupid's bow launched with our lips…"

Zadie heard their mother speak of the interrupted kiss,
And the words of her abuela that made her ears ring…

Till the dirges of her Hope that melancholy burden bore:
"You will see, Yarelis, nunca más. Nevermore."

Zadie dropped to their knees.
Could it be?

"Doubtless," they said, based on what my mother has muttered
perhaps what ugliness she to me had uttered
was their only stock and store?
Caught by her family, internalized homophobia
repressing her memory,
a merciless murder of her true "identity?"

Now a being stood knocking on the other side of their bedroom door.
Was it the woman who loved Yarelis, their mother,
or the woman who couldn't love them anymore?

Deep into that darkness peering,
long Zadie stood there wondering, fearing.
Engaged in merciless guessing, but no syllable expressing.

Then once a flicker, twice a flicker in the night.
Mami held the light box to her heart, tight.

"Child," said she, "the moonbeams showed me things.
I've dreamed dreams no mortal ever dared to dream."

Startled at the stillness broken
by a reply so aptly spoken,
Zadie stared at the figure wheeling toward her door,
sitting as stately as a saint of yore.

Her normally crusted lips painted red.
Her disheveled hair tightly braided.
Her pink robe properly buttoned.

Trembling, Zadie answered, "What do you mean?"

"I dreamt," Zadie's mother said, "of a spaceship
sailing to Night's Plutonian shore.
Severing me from love, evermore."

With mien of lord or lady,
she motioned for Zadie to sit beside her.
She gazed at the light box,
kindling the words inside her.
"Nunca más
in my arms…
Nunca más
safe from harm…
Now she's gone!"

"Who's gone?"

"My girl, precious and perfect.
Heaven sent.
She's vanished."

"When you speak of this precious and perfect girl,
do you mean Yarelis?"

"Yarelis?" Mother nodded No.
"What happened between us was many a year ago.
I mean my daughter.
She has disappeared.
But I sense her near."

"I have never left.
Who I was and who I am has always been clear.
It was you who disappeared, Mom.
Or were you ever here?"

As if the light box thawed her hideous heart,
everything Iris thought she'd ever known fell apart.
Zadie will leave me, she thought,
as my Hopes have flown before,
to be seen Nevermore.

"Zadie!" she clutched their hands.
"I can't claim that I understand.
Nothing in my life has gone as planned.
I'm so sorry for causing you pain.
What can I do to make things right again?"

An uncertain rustling flitted in Zadie's brain.
A terrifying marvelous idea began to take shape.
As if a curtain lifted, they formulated a plan
to change their fate.
If they could switch places with Lenore,
their love could be saved.

Iris agreed to talk to Yarelis.
to distract her with memories.

The plan: while Iris spoke of a cave and Love's purest kiss,
Zadie could take Lenore to the safety of the ship.

From the Curious Volume of Forgotten Lore
Mindscape: Lenore Narváez Contreras

Iris and Zadie visited Yarelis unexpectedly.
Zadie asked to use the restroom as they drank lavender tea.

"Who are you?" said Lenore, peeking through her cracked bedroom door.
"I am your friend." Zadie spoke softly. "From before."

"I can't remember much before the accident," Lenore said.
"If we are friends, then we meet again."

With a bow and a smile, they said,
"Then, let me reintroduce myself. I'm Zadie.
I'm here to take you to the Star Party of the century.
Last May you were supposed to go," Zadie blushed,
"with me."

Lenore blinked.
Shut up in a sepulchre by the sea
floated Lenore's memories.
To these, Yarelis had the skeleton key.
Night by night, by glow of lamplight,
Yarelis had told Lenore "childhood stories."

Lenore marveled to hear words spoken so plain,
though their contents little meaning bore;
in truth, Yarelis employed falsehoods to leave that homosexual "persona," Lenore, drowned at the shore.

So that their godly child Le——rd would remain with them forevermore.

From Yarelis's deception, Lenore understood how she was expected to act, think, and dress—
but no matter how animated her parents spoke about the past,
Lenore had questions she knew better than to ask.

Why do I feel like an impostor in my own home?
Why do I feel like I am wearing a costume instead of clothes?

No matter what Lenore's parents said,
they had energy that only fit and flourished in a dress.

Lenore opened the door to Zadie—
to answers and possibility—
to the magic of the Star Party of the century…

From the Curious Volume of Forgotten Lore
Biodome: *Evermore*, Lunar South Pole, 90° S.
Log Captain: Zakiya Pallas

Just minutes before the lunar eclipse,
she thought of that fateful day
when she outed Lenore.
Gutted Lenore and Zadie to their very cores.
When she got the news of Lenore's attempted suicide.
And thought of taking her own life.

When she was contacted by the director of Project Evermore
and asked to join the teaching faculty.
When Zadie enlisted for training.
When Zadie asked her to help Lenore take their place
and change her fate.

Zakiya told her she would do it—
but they had to understand what giving up their spot to Lenore would mean.

Zadie wouldn't be permitted to reenroll in the program
for a decade and a day.
Zadie said they'd do it anyway...

From the Curious Volume of Forgotten Lore
Locations: 28.3922° N, 80.6077° W, Cape Canaveral Air Force Station, 28.6555° N, 80.6318° W, viewpoint for *The Raven*'s launch; Playalinda Beach
Mindscape: Zadie Colón

I watch The Raven *rise.*
My love Lenore, taking my place,
hibernating in a sleep capsule,
a slumbering beauty inside.

Nunca más will you need to hide
your identity.
Nunca más will you have to change who you are
for anybody.

The Raven *disappears.*
But so does fear.

Time and distance cannot
dissever what Lenore and I had together.
Our love is stronger by far than the love
of those who are older than we—
preserved in the amber of memory
we are star-crossed for eternity.

But what of the consequences?
Lenore's parents called the police.
Accused Ms. Pallas of kidnapping.
Demanded that Lenore be remanded to authorities.
The people of Evermore *refused to extradite*
Ms. Pallas to Earth for trial.
And as Ms. Pallas had adopted Lenore,
she could not be arrested for protecting her child.

Iris was accused of being a kidnapping accessory.
Yarelis testified at the indictment hearing:
"She talked some nonsense about a cave and a kiss."
Then she spaced out and stared at the ceiling
and said, "Love wins."

In the end, I testified that Iris
was confused.
A hostage of her disease.
A victim of eroding memory.
The court committed Iris
to a hospital for treatment.
Sentenced to remember everything.

True!—nervous—very, very dreadfully nervous I had been and am;
would you call my actions
vicious?
Repugnant?
Treacherous?

But by that God we both adore—
By the heaven that bends above—
All I am guilty of is love.

Now I await here on this beach.
My papi is coming for me.

Together we will fight for our human rights.
But for now, I watch the stars rise.

And never will the stars rise
without seeing
the bright eyes of my darling Lenore.
An angel reborn on Night's Plutonian shore,
beloved, evermore.

From the Curious Volume of Forgotten Lore
Biodome: *Evermore*, Lunar South Pole, 90° S.
Recruiter Z8's Log
Mindscape: Lenore Pallas

Do you watch the Earth and Moon eclipse?
Do you feel my breath? Feel my kiss?

Where once I found darkness,
in 1,000 lonely lunar nights,
You are my light.

One more year and a day
'Till I see your face evermore.

★ ★ ★ ★ ★

CELIA'S SONG

a remix of "The Little Mermaid"
Jasminne Mendez

"'But if you take my voice,' said the little mermaid, 'what will I have left?'"

—Hans Christian Andersen, "The Little Mermaid"

Far out in the ocean, where the water was as blue as the prettiest larimar stone and as clear as a spring raindrop, sat the island of Quisqueya. The island of Quisqueya was a tropical place, lush with pirouetting palm trees and sugarcane stalks as tall as a church steeple. Bright red flame trees exploded in the sky, and pink and purple bougainvillea dressed the streets in layers of color.

In the center of this island there was a cave known as Los Tres Ojos—The Three Eyes. It was called this because inside the hundred-yard open-air limestone cave there were three lakes: Lago de Azufre, whose bright blue water was as toxic as sulfur; La Nevera, whose water was so cold, cold, cold it was capable of stopping a warm-blooded heart on contact; and El Lago de las Damas, where the water sparkled like diamonds and hummed with song because that was where hundreds of sirenas lived. Outside of the caves there was a fourth lake, Los Zaramagullones.

This was where La Ciguapa lived and where, by order of El Rey, las sirenas were forbidden to go.

La Ciguapa was a sea monster who had backward feet and was covered in long black hair stolen from the severed heads of mermaids. La Ciguapa did not swim in the lake but rather prowled the lake's floor. On full-moon nights, La Ciguapa would rise to the surface and roam the nearby forests in search of a lonely man or a lost mermaid. If she was lucky enough to find either, she would cast a spell and take from them whatever she wanted.

Las sirenas were ruled by El Rey de las Cuevas. El Rey had six daughters, each born one year apart: Celia, Cardi, Ivy, Rita, Gloria, and Amara. Each of his daughters had beautiful locks of different shades and textures. Their hair was their prized possession. Celia, Rita, and Gloria had wonderfully wild auburn curls. They liked to wrap their tresses in red algae and treated their scalps with fish eggs. Cardi and Ivy had red puffer fish kinks and coils. They were low-maintenance and liked to keep their hair in two Afro puff pigtails. Amara, the youngest, had long flowing locks of almost perfectly straight black hair.

Each of El Rey's daughters was unique and special in her own way. But El Rey had always favored his eldest daughter, Celia.

When Celia was born, her chest glowed yellow like flor de mantequilla. When Celia let out her first cry, it smelled and sounded like azucar, if sugar had a sound. When Celia let out her second cry, a ray of light so bright it lit up the sky shot through the dark blue of the ocean, and as her mother held her in her arms she had to look away. Because Celia's voice and songs were filled with desire and danger.

Celia's heart of gold meant she felt things more deeply than other mermaids. When she was sad or angry or elated, her heart warmed and glowed with the power to move the water and shake the earth. Celia's heart was also sensitive to the feelings of others, which could become her own if she was physically near them.

Sometimes this overwhelmed Celia, and she had to spend time away from the ones she loved so she wouldn't absorb too much.

Celia worked to control her emotions because her abilities sometimes frightened her sisters and the other sirenas. Once, when she was just a girl, she became upset because Cardi cut a lock of her hair while she was sleeping. When Celia awoke to find her hair shorn, she screamed and cried. And as her breath quickened, her heart warmed and pushed and pulled the waters all around her until the entire ocean floor became a swirling funnel that spun her sisters round and round in a circle; it eventually became a hurricane on land and in the sea. It took weeks to repair the damage, and several of her sisters suffered from dizzy spells and nausea for days after. Celia was guilt-ridden: she hadn't meant to cause so much destruction. She became fearful of her powers.

After that, El Rey knew he had to protect Celia, his family, and everyone else from the power of her golden heart. El Rey wanted to prevent anyone with bad intentions outside of the sirena kingdom, like the evil Ciguapa, from finding out about it. So El Rey built a cage around Celia's heart. Using his magical spear, which cut her skin so smoothly there was no blood, he carved open Celia's chest and carefully peeled away the skin. Then, one by one, he placed filed-down shark teeth all around her beating heart. He sealed the lock with a hermit crab shell, then placed the key inside a purple seashell and tossed it into the bottom of La Nevera. He knew it would be safe there because any mortal or hot-blooded sea urchin who tried to enter that lake would freeze to death almost instantaneously.

Celia knew her heart was locked in its cage for her protection. But over the years she had searched for the key because she wanted to know what it would feel like to free her heart and feel *everything*, as fully as she wanted to feel it. She yearned to laugh loudly, and cry hard, as she had when she was just a girl. But every time her heart began to expand or beat fast with feeling, it would knock, knock, knock against its cage and cause a deep throbbing pain in her chest she couldn't bear. Celia kept her feelings small for the sake of her sisters and the rest of the world under the sea.

Despite all of this, Celia was close to her five younger sisters. They spent a lot of time swimming back and forth from El Lago de las Damas into the ocean, talking and telling stories.

Every morning, Celia woke up singing. Her song was heard by all las sirenas across the lake and often she was told to keep it down because her song would wake her sisters. One particular morning, her song was even louder and filled with more warmth and vibrato than ever. This special day, she and her sisters would head out to sea to find pearls and precious stones for their fins and for Amara's quinceañera corona: on the next full moon, Amara would turn fifteen. She was the last of the sisters to do so, and on her birthday, as was the custom, she would spend one whole day on land, or the *surface* as las sirenas called it, doing whatever she pleased. Celia was filled with joy as she thought about her youngest sister finally growing up.

Only on their fifteenth birthday, El Rey had the power to turn the quinceañera's fins into feet for twelve precious hours. Their fins would transform once on land, and they could explore the island freely. El Rey would caution them not to go too far inland, however, because once the twelve hours passed, las sirenas would have to make their way back to the sea immediately or risk their legs turning into sea-foam. If this happened, their fins would never return, and they would be stuck between land and sea forever.

That morning, Celia gathered fish and seagrass for their breakfast. She sang and hummed while she cooked, set the table, laid out her sisters' clothes, and woke them for the day. After they got dressed and ate, Celia helped the youngest—Amara, Gloria, and Rita—French-braid their hair. Cardi and Ivy fussed over makeup and jewelry, offering Celia no help at all.

"Ow! You're pulling too hard!" groaned Gloria.

"Why is the left one lopsided?" Rita huffed and rolled her eyes. "And have you seen my pearl pin? I can't find it, and I'm not going *anywhere* without it!"

Celia sighed wearily, closed her eyes, and absorbed Rita's frustration. She was tired of their bickering and wanted to be done with their hair. So she allowed her heart to lean into the feeling and harness just enough power to move the water. Her heart warmed in her chest and glowed so bright it lit up the entire lake. She clutched at her chest because it ached, since she only used her power when absolutely necessary. And she normally wouldn't have used it for something as silly as a hairpin, but today was an important day, and she needed things to run smoothly. So despite the pain it caused her, she called the pin to come forth, and moments later, from beneath the husk of a turtle shell, Rita's pin floated toward Celia.

"Finally!" Rita rushed wistfully away, placing the pin in her hair. Afterward, Celia took a few deep breaths until her heartbeat steadied and the pain in her chest eased, then sat Amara down and braided her hair.

Amara stroked her braid, smiled sweetly at Celia, and said, "I love it. Thank you, hermana." She was the only one who appreciated her eldest sister and told her so as often as she could.

When she was done helping her sisters get ready, Celia handed out their baskets.

"Hermanas, less bickering and bochinche. Let's go fill these baskets with treasures untold!" The sisters swam out from the lake to the sea in silence until Amara spoke.

"On my quinces all I'm going to do is eat, and eat, and eat all the human food I can find. I think it will taste better than the fish we have to eat day after day!"

The other girls giggled and talked about what they did and wished they had done while on the surface. Ivy had reveled in the sunset, Cardi had sung for an adoring audience, Gloria had taken long walks on the beach, and Rita had flirted (of course). All of them except for Celia, who just listened with wonder and awe.

Celia was the only sister who hadn't had a quinceañera. On the eve of her big day, when her mamá went out to find her pearls and stones for her corona, she was bitten by a sea wolf and fell gravely ill. Celia canceled her sweet fifteen and never made it to the surface. Mami had lain sick in bed with aches and pains for the five years since. Celia assumed her responsibilities as eldest daughter and took care of her five younger sisters and her sick mother. Over the years she had begged Papá to let her go to the surface just for a day or even a few hours. But El Rey knew going to the surface was especially dangerous for Celia, and he wasn't going to risk it. Celia had missed her quinces. She had missed her chance.

Despite missing out and having so many responsibilities, Celia enjoyed being in charge of the household and watching after her sisters. It made her feel important and useful. But sometimes she longed for something more. She longed to visit the shore and see the blue sky and feel the fresh air on her skin. Even though she sometimes poked her head out of the water, it was only at night when there was a smaller chance of being seen by humans who might want to hurt her. Celia also longed for applause and joy. She knew she had a beautiful, powerful voice, and she wanted to share it with the bigger world outside El Lago de las Damas.

But she kept her dreams to herself. It was no use to wish for things that would probably never come true. Under the watchful and commanding eye of her papá, Celia knew wishing for the impossible was a waste of time. And she was afraid if she longed too much, her heart would swell and she'd be unable to bear the pain.

Amara was nowhere to be found the morning of her quinces. The sisters scoured the caves and searched every nook and cranny for her.

"Where could she be?" Ivy asked, flipping over a rock with her fin.

"Well, she's not going to be under a rock, stupid!" Cardi said.

"We have to find her. It's her quinces. She can't miss it!" Gloria, the ever-anxious one, swam round and round her sisters.

"Everyone, calm down. I think I know where she might be." Without another word Celia swam away to El Lago de Azufre. When they played hide-and-seek as little girls, it had always been Amara's favorite hiding place.

Celia found her sister sitting on the edge of the lake. She was staring into the deep blue water, crying. Celia draped her long curls around Amara's shoulder and wiped her tears away.

"What's wrong, my little mermaid? Why are you crying?"

"Because I'm scared of the surface. I know I'm supposed to be excited, but what if something happens to me like it did with Mamá? What if I don't come back?"

"Amara, nothing is going to happen to you. All of the others came back just fine. You will too."

"But Mamá didn't. And she wasn't even on the surface for long. Just a few minutes and then..."

Amara began to cry again. It was hard for any of them to talk about Mamá. Celia pulled Amara close and hummed her a lullaby. Her heart of gold pulsed warm and yellow. She absorbed Amara's fear, and Amara sank deep into Celia's arms and relaxed.

"Ay, hermanita, how else can I help you?"

Amara sniffled. "Can you come with me?"

"Me?! No. I can't. Tradition says it's important for you to go alone."

"But it shouldn't matter if I go alone or with someone. Just that I go. Right?"

"Hmm, I guess so. But I don't know if Papá will accept it..."

"Celia, you never had your time on the surface. Don't you want to experience it too?"

"I guess so..." Celia's heart swelled with desire she tried to stifle. She wanted to do what was right by her sister. It was important for Amara's day to be special and all about her. But her fast-beating heart of gold filled with yellow light, and she felt a sudden thrill at the possibility of being able to swim to the surface.

"Of *course* you do!"

"But it's *your* day. You should—"

"Yes, it's *my* day, and I should get what I want. And what I want is for you to come with me."

"Okay, if that's what you want."

A wide smile stretched across Celia's face, and joy trembled in her heart. She pressed her palm to her chest because the pressure was so great. She took a few deep breaths. She might be going with Amara to the surface to see the world she longed to see.

Amara hugged her sister tight, and they rushed to find Papá to ask him permission.

But El Rey was not easily convinced.

"No! Absolutely not. It is not the custom. Only one mermaid on the surface at a time."

"¡Pero Papá!" Amara huffed.

"¡Pero nada!" El Rey's face grew red and hot with anger. He lifted his hand up in the air as if to signal the end of the conversation.

But Celia was not going to give up so easily this time. She knew this might be her one and only chance to get up to the surface, and she wasn't going to let it slip away. She swam up next to her father, placed her head on his shoulder, and began to hum her sweet song. Her chest glowed gold and trembled just enough to absorb her father's anger without causing herself too much discomfort. El Rey closed his eyes and relaxed.

"Papá, I know you are scared for me to go to the surface..."

He opened his eyes abruptly and puffed up his chest. "Hmph. I'm not scared. Who said I was scared? It's just risky for you. You missed your quinces, so I'm not able to turn your fins into feet, and your heart of gold is a target for thieves and con men—

you won't be able to run away from them. And what about La Ciguapa and—"

"And I know you *worry* about our safety. But, Amara es la bebé, and she's more naive than the others. I don't think she should go alone. You raised me to be strong and capable. Let me chaperone Amara. Even without feet, I can use my voice and my heart of gold to protect us if I need to. You trust me with everything else in our home, so please trust me with this. I promise you I will bring her back safe and sound." She leaned in close to her father, held his hands in hers, and warmed her heart a little more. This time it *did* hurt. Celia wasn't truly sure if she could protect her sister from *all* the possible evils of the surface, but just this once she was willing to use her heart of gold and take the risk.

El Rey shook his head and gave a heavy sigh. "Fine. Just this once. But because you missed your own quinces, I will have to cast a shell of protection around you. And you *must* be back in twelve hours, or your whole body will turn to sea-foam. So you both better be back before the sun sets and the moon rises again. ¿Me oyen?"

"Sí, Papá," Celia and Amara said in unison. Then they hugged their papá tight and finished bedazzling their fins and Amara's crown for their trip to the surface.

After much singing, dancing, and eating under the sea, Celia and Amara said goodbye to their sisters and swam out. When they arrived, Amara's fins turned to feet just as expected. Celia's fins did not. Fearing mermaid hunters, Amara, who found it difficult and painful to walk at first, stumbled around the beach looking for something to cover Celia's fins. She found a hammock tied to two palm trees. Underneath it was a purple sarong. The woman in the hammock was sleeping, so Amara whisked the sarong away quietly, and clumsily ran back to her sister. She covered Celia's fins with the wrap before anyone noticed, and they both let out a deep sigh of relief. They lay out on the sand

and watched the sun glisten over the green hills of el campo. Their plan was for Celia to sunbathe and watch the water under the wrap all day while Amara explored the island. Before sunset, Amara would return, and when no one was watching, they would slip back into the ocean unnoticed.

Amara didn't want to leave her sister alone at first, so they both sat on the sand and watched children build sandcastles nearby. As the sky filled with pink and purple strokes of magic just like Ivy had said, a man began frying fish and plantains nearby. The smell of it circled the air and wafted over to the sisters. Amara's mouth watered.

"Celia, I'm so hungry."

"But we just ate!" Celia laughed.

"I know, but whatever that man over there is cooking smells delicious. How do we get some?"

Celia had an idea. She told Amara to go to the vendor and ask him if he would trade food for a song. The vendor happily agreed. Celia and Amara sang for the cook, and he gave them plates of fried fish, rice, beans, and plantains. Their fingertips became slick with salt and grease, and their bellies bloated with food. People came by and asked to take pictures with them. Celia and Amara smiled and obliged.

When Celia tired of eating, she sang some more but asked for nothing in return. As she sang, a crowd of people circled around her to listen.

She sang joyful melodies and haunting ballads. Her songs were so powerful that almost every human in the audience cried. They clapped and cheered. They showered her with gold coins, roses, pearls, and amaryllis flowers. Every time Celia sang a new song, more and more people gathered around to listen. And the more applause she heard, the faster her heart began to beat and the brighter it glowed. The tide began to rise, and waves crashed against the shore. At first her chest throbbed and ached, but soon she was overcome with so much emotion that she felt her heart thump, thump, *thump* against the cage and crack it. Celia had never experienced anything like this. That crack gave her just enough room around her heart to sing and feel elated like she never had before. Her skin filled with goose bumps, and her fin began to flap beneath the sarong. Celia had to focus on holding the lower half of her body still so as not to reveal her fins. She didn't want to get discovered because she didn't want this feeling to end, and she wished there was a way she could stay on land forever.

While Celia sang, Amara decided to explore the island. She pulled fruit off the trees and bit into juicy sweet mangoes. She went to the market and ran her hands across jangly key chains and smooth leather bags. She picked up treasures humans had dropped on the ground, like hairpins, scarves, forks, and even a red high-heeled shoe someone had left underneath a park bench.

All afternoon people came and went, watching and listening to Celia. Some had asked her to get up and dance or walk with them to town so others could hear. But Celia waved them away, saying she should remain where she was so her sister could find her. As the sun began its descent, Amara returned from the market as the crowd around Celia dissipated. Their twelve hours on the surface were quickly coming to an end, and a storm rumbled in the distance. The ground shook when it thundered, and lightning pierced the sky. Rain poured down. The sisters had never felt rain on their skin before, and it startled them. They were enraptured. They let the rain soak them. Amara skipped and danced while Celia stuck her tongue out and tasted its sweetness. When the moon peeked through the gray clouds, Celia shrieked.

"Amara! We must go now!"

They gathered their trinkets and treasures and dove into the water. They began to swim back home. But the sea was dark, and the rain was pounding hard now. It was hard to see, and their arms and hands were so full, full, full the sisters got lost and ended up in Los Zaramagullones, where the water was dark green, almost black, and very warm.

Then, in front of Celia, hovering over a porous rock, and covered in long black hair from her head down to her backward feet stood La Ciguapa. She opened her mouth, and out rang a hissing screech like a balloon slowly deflating. The sound wrapped around Celia's throat and choked her. It put Celia in a trance. La Ciguapa then reached her algae-green arms out for Celia's long flowy hair.

"No! Stop!" yelled Amara. She swam between them and pushed her sister out of the way. La Ciguapa yanked Amara back and grabbed a fistful of Amara's long black locks, using the hair to bind Amara's arms behind her.

"Hmmm. Your hair issss better. Niccccer. Looonger. Sssss-soofter," hissed La Ciguapa as she stroked her face with Amara's hair. Celia could see La Ciguapa's long sharp nails glistening in the water. She lifted her other hand and wrapped it around Amara's throat, digging her nails into the back of her neck. Amara closed her eyes and screamed. La Ciguapa knew what she wanted. And she was willing to kill for it if she had to.

Celia rushed toward La Ciguapa to try to save her sister.

"Sssstand back! Or I'll slice her up and cut off more than just her hair! I'll take her whole head if I have to. It's sssssooo preeeetty." La Ciguapa dug her nails into Amara's neck. Amara flinched and writhed, trying to release herself from La Ciguapa's grip.

"No! Stop. Please stop!" pleaded Celia, "I'll give you anything. Take my hair! And all these pearls, and gold, and hairpins from the surface. Take it all, and please let her go."

La Ciguapa thought for a moment and swam in circles around Celia. She stroked Celia's hair and ran her fingers through it.

"Too coarsssssse for me," she huffed. Then she sniffed Celia's neck and pressed her ear against her chest. "But thissss...this is sssssspecial." She pressed her palm against Celia's fast-beating heart. "You, my dear, have a heart of gold."

Celia knew what La Ciguapa was going to ask for. But she didn't know if giving the creature her heart of gold was even possible.

"Give me your heart, and I'll let your sssssister go."

"No, I can't. I mean, it's locked up. I don't know how to get it out without the key..."

"Well, then, go get the key."

"But I don't know where it is."

"That'ssss not my problem, issss it? Either I get your heart and your sissssster lives, or I don't and you *both* die."

Celia's heart began to beat and shine so brightly it shook the seafloor beneath them and nearly blinded La Ciguapa.

Celia's heart throbbed and pounded. It pushed against its cage, already fractured from her time on the surface, and the shark teeth began to splinter. The seafloor trembled, and funnels began to form in the water.

As her heart beat harder and harder, its cage cracked and split some more. Celia realized that she no longer needed the key to free her heart. She could use her greatest strength, more powerful than any cage: her voice.

Celia began to sing. She sang high notes and low notes. Her voice trilled and bellowed. The more she sang, the more her heart glowed and pounded. Celia's voice shook the earth open. The water around her began to swirl and spin until Celia was in the center of a whirlpool and La Ciguapa crouched near a rock, afraid. Celia felt the cage around her heart shatter into pieces.

She rushed to her sister and hugged her. She was about to untie her when La Ciguapa pushed Celia out of the way.

"Not ssssso fassssst, my singing sssssiren! A deal is a deal. You get your sissssster back when I get your heart."

"I will give it to you, but I want something in return."

"Ha! What do you mean? You get to keep your sissster alive. That'ssss what you get!"

"Yes, but if I give you my heart, I will die. And I do not want to die. Not yet. So…so…"

"Ssssso, I will give you a human heart. You won't live as long as you would have, but you won't die today. Issssss that good enough?" La Ciguapa was growing very impatient with this conversation. But Celia was not satisfied.

"That is not enough. My heart is very powerful and worth more than you can even imagine. It is coveted by many. If you want my heart, I need more from you."

"Ugh! You mermaidsss are exhausssting! What *elsssse* do you want?"

"I want a human heart *and* human legs!"

La Ciguapa laughed.

"Why on earth would you want human legssss?"

"Hermana, what are you doing? Why are you asking for legs? Just take the human heart and let's go! Please!" Amara wiggled and writhed on the rock.

Celia swam to her sister and hugged her close.

"I know you won't understand this, but I'm not going to go back home with you. I need legs if I want to live and survive on the surface."

"What are you saying? I don't understand."

"Amara, all I've done for the last five years is take care of you, our sisters, and our mother. And I love being able to do that. But I have dreams too. And as much as I love you all, I realized while on the surface with you that I also love singing and when other people appreciate it. No one down here cares about my singing anymore because they've heard it for years. All sirenas have beautiful voices, and it feels as if I am not special under the sea. But out there on the surface I can be somebody. Don't you see? Amara, I have spent every day since I turned fifteen making sure everyone else in our family is okay and happy. But singing brings *me* joy. And don't you think it's my turn to be happy?"

Amara nodded and began to cry.

"I understand, hermana. But I will miss you. Mamá and Papá, Gloria, Rita, Ivy, and Cardi…we will all miss you."

"I know. And I will miss you all too."

"Oh. My. God! Mermaidsss are insssufferable!" La Ciguapa groaned. "Can we get on with it? You'll get your human heart and your legsssss. Just give me the gold heart, already!"

Celia hugged her sister one last time. She swam to La Ciguapa and unclasped her seashell bra to expose her chest. Her heart glowed and shook. Celia's chest opened, and her heart shimmered and thump, thump, thumped. La Ciguapa ripped Celia's heart from her chest, and the lake filled with light and warmth. Celia collapsed onto the seafloor.

"Celia!" Amara wiggled and writhed on the rock. She screamed at La Ciguapa, "Give her what she asked for! She's dying! Give her a human heart!"

La Ciguapa rolled her eyes and sighed.

"Calm down, little mermaid. Your sissster will get what she asked for."

Without letting go of the heart of gold, La Ciguapa reached her other hand out and began to emit a high-pitched screeching hum that sent all the fish and sea animals scurrying away. A bright light shot forth from her mouth and covered Celia in a blue glow. A human heart took the place of her heart of gold, and her chest closed back up without a scar or a drop of blood being shed. Her fins dissolved into the sand beneath her, and two feet attached to two legs took their place. After a few moments, Celia jolted awake but struggled to stand on her new feet and legs. She knelt in the dirt gasping for air.

"Celia! You're alive! You're alive!" Amara cried tears of joy.

"Untie my sister now. Let her go!" Celia screamed as she struggled to breathe.

"A deal isss a deal." Still holding the heart of gold, La Ciguapa went to Amara and untied her. The ropes of seaweed fell to the seabed. Amara freed her wrists and, without a second thought, reached up into her hair, pulled out a long silver hairpin with a sharp point, and stabbed the still-beating heart of gold in La Ciguapa's hand. A ciguapa with a heart of gold was a dangerous thing.

"Go, hermana! Go. Swim to the surface! Fulfill your dreams. Go!" Amara screamed as she too began to swim away as quickly as she could.

La Ciguapa held the barely beating heart in her hands and screamed.

"You wretched sssssirena! I will dessstroy you!" She lunged toward Amara. She reached for her and cut off Amara's long flowing locks with one slice of her scissor-sharp fingernails. Amara yanked her head forward quickly enough to escape the creature's full grasp and swam back to El Lago de las Damas. La Ciguapa cried and sank to the bottom of the lake with a clump of hair in one hand and the dead heart in the other.

To this day, it is said that if you get really close to Los Zaramagullones, you can hear La Ciguapa's piercing sobs for the heart of gold she almost got away with.

Amara had escaped. Celia had escaped. But the sisters never saw each other again.

Amara returned to the palace and told everyone that Celia had sacrificed her life to save her. Celia, the legend goes, traveled the world singing and dancing for the people. After giving so much of herself to her family for years, it was finally her chance to do what *she* wanted. She was adored for her unique voice and the joy she brought people with her music. And even though she never returned home, whenever she could she'd walk along the beach and sing songs to the sea in the hopes that her sisters would hear her voice and know that she had not forgotten them.

★ ★ ★ ★ ★

ESMERALDA

a remix of *Sir Gawain and the Green Knight*
Laura Pohl

"Hit seemed as no mon myght
Under his dynttes dryye."

—Sir Frederic Madden (ed.), *Sir Gawain and the Green Knight*

It was Christmas at Fazenda Bosque Verde, and when Gal arrived, the path was sodden with mud. Their cloak was drenched from the rainfall, dragging bodily behind them, boots sinking into the sludge. Such a bedraggled entrance did not befit them, but Gal hardly cared about their appearance after the long journey. It had taken the better part of the day to cross the deep waters of the black river with only one man to guide the boat forward. Gal had reached out to touch the surface, but the old man had halted their hand with a warning. "Full of sucuris twice as big as your arm, child."

Gal kept their hands to themself after that.

The boat delivered Gal to a rickety wooden pier, the tall grass swaying under an invisible breeze. They spotted no animals, but that didn't mean there weren't any. The only sounds were the cicadas, loud and buzzing, and mosquitoes flying near. Gal turned back, but the boatman had already pushed himself away from the pier, wading back into the waters.

Gal squeezed their fingers around the strap of their bag and continued on their path.

The green here was different. Ranches hadn't been established, hadn't crossed into the wetlands this far west. It was only a matter of time, of course, as were all things in this kind of country.

Gal spotted the house first. It was made of white stucco, with a red tiled roof, and the blinds and windowsills were a vivid green. It was taller than it had any right to be, the roof stretching to a great height. And beyond there was the forest, and the green was also different. It wasn't the mantis of the pastures and ranches, or the sap of the marshes that hid snakes and alligators, nor the pine of the dyed fabrics that Gal's mother wore. It was a sickly shade, pulsing and oscillating forward like a wave, like a vine viper waiting to strike.

At the edge of the forest, almost engulfed by the vegetation, the jatobá leaves brushing its roof, was the Green Chapel.

Gal's gaze did not linger, but they could feel the chapel looking back at them. A calling to the promise.

They crossed the stretch of land, aware of their footing. Ants scuttled away from their steps, and the droplets from the rainfall glistened over the blades of grass. In the house, there was a warm yellow light gleaming over the porch, a single lantern to guide travelers to their last stop.

Gal cleaned their boots on a cast-iron scraper in front of the door of the main house, a thick layer of mud dragged from the creases of the leather soles. They pushed their wet hair away from their face and knocked.

Almost at once the door opened, and there stood a young man, not much older than Gal, with dark brown hair. His eyes were covered by a black fabric that was tied behind his head, a black void of nothingness cutting his features.

"Come in," said the young man, a smile stretching on his lips. His robes were black, and there was a single square of white beneath his Adam's apple. "You must be tired from your journey."

"How long are you staying?" the priest asked Gal, after the quiet had stretched for too long. He guided Gal inside the house, which seemed uncannily vast on the inside. The roof was cavernous, the white walls bare, with no paintings or curtains to break the monotony of the featureless square windows. The priest was guiding the way forward with a single flickering candle, through an endless maze of corridors and rooms.

"Until New Year," Gal replied.

The priest nodded. Gal waited for the next question, but it never came.

They continued down the hall, the house engulfing them. The priest did not take off his blindfold but continued with assured steps. The room he showed Gal contained a four-poster bed, with a diaphanous canopy made of netting to keep away mosquitoes, a wooden cabinet covered with an ugly white hand-crocheted towel, a water basin, and a velvet chair in the corner, with an even uglier matching crochet coverlet.

"Please." The priest gestured, and Gal went through. "This will be your room until you are ready."

"Thank you," Gal said, bowing.

The priest bowed in return. "Be free to roam these halls at will, though I imagine you'll want a much-needed rest."

He made the sign of the cross over Gal's brow. His touch was light, ephemeral, and it sent a cold chill to Gal's spine.

"Thank you, Father."

"Sérgio," he corrected. "I haven't been fully ordained yet. Rest well, and may the Bethlehem star that witnessed Christ's birth keep watch over thee."

★ ★ ★

When Gal woke up, they heard the rooster crowing. During the long journey, they had not heard a single sound from domestic animals—entrenched deep within the mosaic landscapes of the pantanal, there was the soft purr of the occasional jaguar, the cawing of the carcará, the howling of a wide range of monkeys. No roosters. No cows.

There was a small window in the room, and getting up from bed, not bothering to dress, they looked out to the garden where, to their surprise, they could see the farm like they had not seen it under the cover of darkness. There was resplendent grass stretching, and what they mistook for a flooded space was in reality a sprawling field of soybeans, the blades rippling under the breeze like the surface of the water, a vast ocean of green.

"You're finally awake," a voice said, and Gal jumped, clutching at the nearest thing they had to cover themself, which was the curtains.

There was a woman sitting in the chair. Her hair was a light brown, braided in two sets that framed her face, and her face was pale like cow's milk. She had big brown eyes, lips plump and rosy. Gal covered themself as best they could, feeling heat prickle up their neck.

"Forgive me," they said. "I hadn't realized I had company."

"No need to apologize," she said, seemingly unfazed. "My guests will do as they please."

Gal noticed the emphasis on the word. "Am I speaking to the lady of the house?"

"Yes. You may call me Izabel."

"Lady Izabel—"

"Izabel," she corrected again, and Gal noticed how young she also was. Not a woman. A girl. Couldn't be older than Gal themself, whose eighteenth birthday loomed on the horizon like the warning of an oncoming storm. There were no markings around her eyes. No red scratches from the sun. "You've slept for the past two days. Your journey must have been harrowing."

Two days. Gal looked out the window again and realized the rooster was not crowing for daybreak. Twilight was already upon them.

Gal turned to her again, but Izabel was no longer there. Shaking their head, Gal looked for their clothes, but their sack was gone. Opening the wardrobe, they found instead a rich assortment of clothing—dresses and breeches with such fine embroidery that Gal dared not touch them. Picking the more modest of tunics, they dressed and left the room.

The house was entombed in silence, and turning a corridor, Gal found themself in a kitchen, where a fire was burning in the woodstove. The smell made their stomach grumble, and they noticed the food laid upon the table in brown clay dishes: peeled oranges, black beans, thinly sliced collard greens, tomatoes soaking in olive oil. In a jug inexplicably shaped like an ananas was cold caju juice. Almost as an afterthought following the admiration of the banquet before them, Gal noticed Sérgio sitting at the head of the table.

"Please," he said, gesturing that Gal should approach the spread. "You must be hungry."

Gal did not need to be asked twice. They sat down, wolfing down the meal, barely feeling the taste it left behind. Sérgio ate in silence, in a more restrained fashion. It seemed as though the priest-to-be was watching Gal, but he still had the blindfold, a black streak crossing his face.

"Are there no other penitents?" Gal asked once they'd finished eating.

Sérgio shook his head. "Not at this time. If you'd like, you could join me in prayer tonight."

"In the chapel?" Gal asked.

Something stilled in Sérgio's posture. "No. Only those whose time has come to fulfill their promises venture there."

"And may I ask what I do here, while I wait?"

"There is only one rule to peaceful conviviality here, and that is God's law," Sérgio said, getting up, the invisible gaze seemingly directed at Gal. "Be fair and just, and speak no lies. Do unto others as you would have them do unto you."

On the first day of their stay, when Gal woke up, Izabel was there. They'd slept clothed this time, but her presence was still jarring. She wore golden rings on her fingers and a long brown dress. "Would you like to see the property?"

Gal nodded, not wanting to cause offense. Together, they headed outside. The soybeans encircled the curves of the river, making it hard to determine where the vegetation ended and the marshes and water started. Rosy-colored spoonbills fished in the margins. There was a small pasture for cows behind the house, a kitchen garden, and an orchard with plantains and mangaba trees. The sunlight was harsh, the heat suffocating.

Izabel took Gal's arm, entwining them both. "Which far corners do you come from?"

"North," Gal replied. "And east. The journey here took almost a month."

"No wonder you slept for so long," she said, throwing one of her braids back. Gal noticed she wore earrings made with blue udu feathers. Gal's mother had a similar pair. It had taken two years to collect the feathers, all from the same bird. Gal had gone with her more than once down to the udu's nest, watching as she carefully picked the discarded feathers, the beads on her bracelets ringing like music. Gal remembered their mother's smile, and the pat on the cheek for keeping her company, and all the walks they had taken together. Their history was written on those feathers, even if not in words.

Izabel had not made her earrings by hand.

"It's always nice to receive visitors," she said. "Some of them even choose to stay."

Gal finally saw, then, the first people other than Izabel and Sérgio—workers with wide-brimmed straw hats, the hems of their pants folded up, working the soil of the farm, carrying basins toward the house, sealing up horses on a wagon.

Gal felt the tension in their bones. "Why did they come here?"

"Same reason as you," she answered. "Your fate could be the same as theirs."

Gal looked at the workers again. Their features seemed to blend together, old and young indistinguishable, heads bent, and all silent. Gal glanced back at the direction of the chapel. Was the fate waiting there so much worse than this one?

"It's a charming place," she continued. "I've never left. My family has owned this land for six generations."

Gal did not scoff at Izabel's proclaimed ownership, even when the declaration seemed childish. A land had no owners, even when people with skin the same color as Izabel's declared it so through a piece of paper. Gal's family had no lands, even before the colonizers came: they merely lived in it, borrowed its resources and its time, and gave back when they could. They took care of the land; the land took care of their own.

"And where are your parents?" Gal asked.

"Away," Izabel replied, tone terse. "It is only you and me."

"And Sérgio," Gal felt the need to add, thinking of the way the future priest had welcomed them into the house, who seemed to be as familiar to those halls as the lady of the house herself.

Izabel shot Gal a peculiar look, but she said nothing.

She guided them in a full tour of the property, almost to the margins of the river bend. She never approached the forest, a wall to the west side of the farm, or acknowledged its existence. Gal could feel its presence, restless, unsettling. Calling to them, as if it somehow knew what Gal was doing there.

Gal felt the weight of the promise, a lump in their throat, a stone thrown into the bottom of a smooth lake. They wondered what their mother would think of this place. If she would feel its presence and see it as a blessing or an ardent wrongness lodged in the midst of the forest. If, upon seeing it, she would have changed her mind, she would have let her child turn their back and return unharmed.

She was not there to judge. Only Gal was. They looked at the edge of the forest, toward the roof of the chapel, heart thumping harder.

Izabel took Gal to see the horses, to see the river, to read in the enormous library of old volumes. Every time Gal looked at her, her eyes were staring, straight into their soul, until Gal almost felt dizzy.

At sundown, Gal finally took their leave. "I've had the most lovely day."

They brushed their lips against the back of Izabel's hand. Instead of stepping away, she approached, and her lips touched Gal's cheek softly. "See you tomorrow, gallant penitent."

Gal remained in the room until there was a knock, caught by the same restless thoughts of uncertainty that had permeated the whole journey there. Surprised, they got up to open the door and found Sérgio standing there, a flickering candle in his hands.

"I hope your day has been pleasant," Sérgio said by way of greeting.

"Pleasant enough," Gal answered, thinking of Izabel's lingering gaze, the way her hand was always heavy guiding them through the house. Then, "Would you like to come inside?"

"I would not trespass on your courtesy."

"It's not trespassing."

Gal opened the door wider, and Sérgio entered the room. All of a sudden, it seemed too stuffed and stagnant. Sérgio stood motionless, and Gal took the time to watch him in detail. The fine brown hair, which curved slightly at the nape of the neck. A wooden cross over his chest. His hands, holding the candle, with thin veins, of the slightest mint coloring, underscoring the tanned skin.

"I trust Fazenda Bosque Verde has been welcoming," Sérgio said, carefully enunciating the words.

"It's a beautiful place," Gal affirmed. "Lady Izabel told me it has been in her family for generations."

"Indeed."

"But she did not mention you," Gal said, watching Sérgio's face, waiting for a reaction.

Sérgio's lips thinned. "My existence is a mere inconvenience to her, I'm afraid."

There was silence again.

"As is the Green Chapel?" Gal asked, probing.

Sérgio stood stiff as a crucifix, shoulders rigid. "There is nothing I can tell you about the chapel that you do not already know."

"You live here. You know what awaits me."

"There is a power beyond man's understanding. It is here, for us to behold and accept. The question is, as always, whether one can."

"You know I have come here because of a promise."

"Yes, and I am sorry," Sérgio said.

Gal noticed how his lips trembled. They were blanched of color, pale and sickly.

Sérgio raised his head, as if looking directly into Gal's eyes. All Gal could see was the blackness and void of that streak. There was an impulse in the moment where they almost reached out to caress his cheeks, hoping to put some color back in them. Kiss him to warm his bones.

"Be careful," Sérgio warned in a whisper. "God watches us all, even in the dark."

"Today we are going to the lake."

Izabel said this not as an invitation but as a demand. Gal followed her tracks, carrying her things as they trailed the path following the winding river, toward a northern part of the farm. There, in a clearing surrounded by flowering ipê trees, whose purple petals fell into the rocks and the surface even when they should have long borne fruit, Izabel started shedding all her clothes. Gal quickly averted their gaze as she stripped, splashing into the water after a moment.

"Won't you join me?" she asked, turning her head so Gal stared at her profile, her tiny button nose, the curve of her neck. "It's been so long since I've had the pleasure of company."

It was dangerous water to tread. Izabel had made a point of letting Gal know she was alone, but that did not mean it wasn't a trap: the temptation was very clear, and Izabel was powerful, while Gal was not. Gal was young but not inexperienced, and it was always best to be careful. "The view suits me from here."

Izabel smiled, raising her head above the surface, her collarbones highlighted. She wore something around her neck. She swam toward the rocks nearest where Gal sat, and much as she tried to appear like an adult, Gal still saw a mirror of their own inadequacies—round cheeks, ungainly limbs, a permanent childlike softness.

"Are you afraid of the piranhas?" Izabel asked. "They've all been hunted down in this lake to make soup. There's nothing in these waters."

"It pays well to be careful."

"Then, you shouldn't have come all the way here."

Gal leveled their eyes to her.

"Do you mean to the chapel?"

"When my great-great-great-grandfather crossed the river, he was carrying his newborn son and his dead wife's body," she said. "When he arrived safely, he built the chapel for São Justo, protector of fair men, antagonist to lies. It was built because he'd made a promise to himself if his son survived the journey here. It was built for all those who asked for favors and needed to prove their worth in receiving them, and the pilgrims all come to face the consequences of their requests. The chapel judges, and the Saint judges impartially."

Gal thought about the willingness of making a deal with God—making a promise in return for attaining something. A promise, an oath, a vow, a bargain: the word itself hardly mattered when the essence was the same. And every promise had to be fulfilled, no matter the consequences.

Gal remembered their mother's warning, while she stirred a hot cauldron of acarajé stuffing for them to eat with the neighbors. "It's bad enough to be in debt to poor people," she said, a certain amusement piercing her voice, an amusement that would later turn into sourness, "but never let yourself get indebted to God."

Gal had thought repeatedly about that sentence on the journey to the chapel, and each time, the sourness seemed to carry weight enough to drag an entire ship down.

"I didn't make any promises," Gal said. "It was my mother's."

Izabel tilted her head. "Then, why you?"

Gal shrugged.

"Do you think your mother would want you to die to keep her word?"

Gal did not say the words out loud, but they knew them well. *If I must.* So they shrugged again.

"Do you think that it's fair that she asked this?"

It wasn't as if Gal hadn't heard the stories. Even before Izabel's ancestors arrived, there was already power in these parts. Tales of creatures with hair of fire and feet put on backward, whose purpose was to confound all those who wandered among its trees. Tales of water damsels whose sweet voices sang men to sleep in the depths of the river, drowning them remorselessly.

And there was always the forest, that verdant space, and its protector, its role as obscure as the nature of its power.

"You have seen it?" Gal asked, curiosity getting the better of them.

At that moment, even the wind seemed to still, the leaves freezing upon their branches, petals undisturbed in the static surface of the lake.

"They say it's the forest personified, the Saint embodied through its growth. They say that its appetite is as big as the ocean," Izabel replied, her gaze fixed once more on Gal, her voice seemingly hoarse. "That it devours souls and eats men's darkest dishonors, and swings its ax upon cowards and liars."

"I asked not the legends," Gal said. "I asked of you."

"This is my home. This is my land. Do you think there is anything that walks here that I have not witnessed?"

The breeze returned, the forest taking a breath. It was a non-answer, but an answer in itself. Izabel was at the center of its mystery, the descendant of the man who had built the chapel for all the others that would come after him. All the others who needed a favor from God and could only promise in return that they pay at the feet of São Justo whatever God thought was equitable.

They asked, "Are you afraid of its power?"

"I was born under the crucifix that embellishes its tower," she replied. "It is a gift."

"And a burden," Gal replied. "You cannot leave."

Izabel's cheeks flushed. Casting them a dark look, she submerged herself. When she returned to the surface, her hair had been undone from its braids and ran sleek past her shoulders, covering her skin, and she started wading out of the lake. Gal turned their eyes.

"You may look," she said, after a moment. She was dressed again in a white shift, which clung to the droplets on her skin. She approached Gal, and before they could act, she fingered the embroidery of their shirt collar, her fingers tracing the delicate skin of their throat.

"Do not go into the chapel," Izabel said. "It will not spare you. It has not spared anyone in all these years."

She tiptoed to reach up, her breath smelling of the river. At the last moment, Gal turned, and Izabel's mouth rested against the corner of theirs. They felt the almost-kiss burning there like a mark. When their eyes met again, her look was hateful.

"No man survives."

"Then it's fortunate I'm no man," Gal replied with ease and a lopsided smile, but again they did not say what they were thinking.

If it had been fair of their mother to ask, then she would not have asked—not that it mattered to Gal. They would do what she asked, because no one kept God waiting, and no one raised a hand against the womb that birthed them. It was a simple tenet to live by, even if they hadn't always seen their mother as the light of the sun, as if life and death did not depend on her say-so.

Their mother had asked them, whether in bad faith or not, and in good faith Gal would do her bidding.

"I will be fine," they said instead.

Once they got to the house, Izabel disappeared again, and Gal was left to their devices. They walked out again into the heat, staring out at the lush greenness of the forest, the unknowable things that protected it. Gal's heritage had taught them to respect nature, to be careful of its fickle essence: it gave, and it destroyed. It was no different than the God they had all accepted when He came to this country, bearing crosses over wooden boats.

The forest roiled, coiled, and rumbled, its sounds like the drawing of a blade, ready for the slaughter.

And once it was dark, and there was no moon in the sky, and the thunder announced a heavy rainfall, a figure seemed to walk from beyond the chapel, in black robes, making their way toward the house. In his hands something trailed, and for a moment, Gal almost mistook the pending crucifix for a weapon. Sérgio walked with certainty on the wet ground, his steps never faltering. He came to a stop when he was close to Gal, head raised in the same direction, as if Sérgio, too, could hear the call of Gal's heart and where it was drawing them.

"Only one more day," Sérgio said, almost to himself.

"One more day," agreed Gal.

They stood side by side. Gal was taller than Sérgio by almost a head. They grew no beard, but their hair was longer than it had been in years, falling straight to their shoulders. Gal thought of home, of their mother, and of the new year.

They thought of their mother's hand in theirs, of the look in her eyes as she asked Gal to make the journey to the Green Chapel and fulfill the promise she'd made.

"May I ask a question?" Gal asked now.

Sérgio considered this. "I assume by your hesitation it is about my blindfold."

"Yes. Why?"

"So I don't raise one penitent above another," he answered. "So that I may look at all lost lambs equally."

"I thought the eyes were the windows of the soul."

"Yes, but the eyes are easily deceived and fall into temptation."

"How will you know you are strong enough to resist it if you do not face it?" Gal asked, and Sérgio's lips parted in surprise.

Gal wanted to reach out and put a thumb over the perfectly formed seam in the middle of the bottom lip. Trace that line to the edge with their tongue.

They were too close now. Under the stars, Gal's lips found the corner of Sérgio's, fluttering like the wings of a colibri. Gal felt their heartbeat in their ears, the sound like a powerful drum. Right at that moment, the rain started falling heavy.

Sérgio bristled, chin trembling. He clutched Gal's collar, hand balled into a fist, trembling like a weed to the wind. Gal noticed the veins in his hand, which seemed even brighter and vivid by green light. Sérgio let go and entered the house without a word, and Gal stood there, facing the thicket sage, the savage emerald.

On the morning before the new year, Gal did not wake alone in the room. Izabel sat by the other side of the bed, watching them, gaze intent. She grabbed their hand, holding their whole body in place with a steel grip.

"I will say one more time," she said, her voice low, a threat in the tense air, "if you go into the chapel tomorrow, you will die. I have seen justice swing its ax. I have seen the Green Saint eat souls much stronger than yours."

Gal listened quietly to this outburst. "Do you think I am the same as the rest of them?"

Izabel's contempt was stamped on her face. "What makes you think you are different?"

Gal didn't believe they were different. They were the same as all desperate folk who made the journey there, the same as all penitents coming to pay the price for what they'd petitioned for, to a God that was mercilessly evenhanded.

"Let me relieve you of your burden," Izabel whispered, leaning closer. "Stay here. You've come this far. Your mother will never know if you never took the last step."

For a moment, Gal blinked, and they saw a different future. A future of staying within the comforts of the house, of swimming in rivers, of remaining in the same place where their name and their history did not matter. A place so isolated from the rest of the world that they could feel entirely weightless and there were no consequences. A place where they could become like all the others on the farm, without having to ever step in the Green Chapel, with no one ever knowing the truth.

There was a power in that future. The power of erasing a history of hurts, a generation of obligations.

Gal entertained it for a moment of glorious beauty, and when they opened their eyes, all they could see was their mother's plea and all that she had ever done for Gal from the moment she carried a tiny child in her womb, every single day of those long seventeen years when all they'd had was each other.

Gal could live, as long as they stayed there. As long as they never faced their mother again. As long as the past was past and there was no future beyond Fazenda Bosque Verde.

Either way, the chapel would be Gal's end.

Izabel saw the choice in their face, plain as daybreak.

"I have seen what happens to all of them," Izabel said, her tone harsher. "I love this place, even though it is a cruel and brutal thing. It will break my heart to watch you go."

She caught Gal's head between her hands, keeping them in place.

"Don't go," Izabel said. "You're too young."

"So are you."

"Yes, but I will live to a hundred if I stay here. You will not. Do not waste your life."

"I cannot go back on my word."

"What is a promise worth?" Izabel demanded. "You have made it this far. You don't have to go inside. Do you want to die for nothing?"

Gal considered this for a long while. They took Izabel's hands, finding comfort there for the first time. The unpredictableness of her nature was gone.

"It's not for nothing," Gal said. "It's for my family."

Izabel pursed her lips, and she did not argue further. There was a silent understanding between them both. She was the heir of Fazenda Bosque Verde.

Gal was the heir to a promise, and honor was the only thing they ever had to give.

From inside the folds of her dress, Izabel took something, raising it above her head. A devotional scapular. Its thread was worn but a vivid green, like the devouring forest outside. On one side was the body of São Justo, on the other, his head. "Wear this, then. No harm will come to you while you wear it."

Gal looked down at the scapular in their intertwined hands.

"Wear it," Izabel repeated. "You'll keep your promise and still come back alive."

Gal took the scapular, putting it over their head, tucking it underneath their shirt.

And then, at last, Izabel pulled Gal close, took their head between her hands, her fingers sinking into their soft hair. She kissed Gal with a ferocity reserved for the wild.

Her touch was light when compared to the stone lodged in Gal's stomach, as they felt the image of São Justo burning against the skin of their chest.

Gal stayed awake the whole night in the room, watching the stars. Izabel had not stayed with them.

Then at last, when the sky started changing color from its deep midnight mantle to tentative rays of celestial, Gal put on their clothes, the scapular hidden underneath the linen. Then they walked in the direction of the call they had not stopped hearing ever since they had gotten off the boat.

They stood there in the dark for a long time, simply staring at the chapel.

It was green, half-engulfed by the foliage, the walls crumpling and the paint chipped. There was a bell in a small campanary above its door. The door pulsed red, ibirapitanga wood. Gal reached their hand for the doorknob, hovering only a centimeter above it, not daring to touch it yet.

There was a rustle of leaves and wind, and Gal turned to see Sérgio standing there, close behind.

"I will not ask you not to go in," Sérgio said, his voice calm. "You have made a promise, and I understand that some things can't be broken."

"It wasn't my promise."

Something glistened in Sérgio's cheek. It fell to the ground, wet, the water disappearing before Gal could take notice.

"Far worse," Sérgio replied. "And far more binding."

Gal almost smiled, but it didn't quite reach their lips. They tried not to fidget, to wonder what it would be like walking inside. Feeling the weight of the scapular beneath the shirt, and the wondering, wondering, always wondering during the journey, and now it would all come to a stop.

Why shouldn't Gal survive? Why should they keep a promise that was not even theirs, and deliver its final prayer where they ought, and walk out unharmed? Gal deserved to live, too.

Then, again, something glistened on Sérgio's cheek. This time, it wasn't lost to them that when it fell into the ground, something blossomed. Gal looked down, carefully watching as the magic of the world unfolded, as everything fell at once into place.

The chapel would judge, and the Saint would judge impartially.

It was only the land, and Gal knew the land. This land had existed long before God had arrived and claimed it as His. There was no great fear of the ineffability of divinity, of the mercilessness of its demand. Right there, when the spring blossomed at Sérgio's feet, the answer was simple. Honor was the only thing that Gal had ever had to give, and it would be freely given, without a shadow of doubt.

In the end, it came down to the three of them—Gal, Sérgio, and Izabel—and the roles they played in this leafy stage. Their mother's face seemed faraway and unreachable, and her promise barely weighed anything at all on their shoulders as they looked at Sérgio, coiled and ready. Gal knew what they were facing inside the chapel at last, and the fear of God did not enter into this equation.

Gal unfurled the scapular from their neck and handed it to Sérgio, folding his hands over it. They would enter the chapel bearing no lies or subterfuge. They would come as themselves. As their mother's child.

Sérgio bowed his head to the thread of green, standing completely still at the weight in his palm.

Gal leaned in to kiss Sérgio. It was a kiss of forgiveness, a kiss of promise of the choice they wanted to make but couldn't yet, a true acceptance of whatever came next. With their hand, Gal untied the blindfold from the back of Sérgio's head. The wind took it, flung it away as the knot came undone while their mouths still were carefully placed against each other.

Finally, after a lifetime, Gal extricated themself from the kiss. The sun was burning orange on the horizon, casting rippling bright shades over the water. Sérgio opened his eyes, and the irises were like flowers, blossoming emerald green.

"I'll see you inside," Gal said, and stepped in to honor their mother's promise.

★ ★ ★ ★ ★

TWENTY THOUSAND LEAGUES AWAY FROM ME

a remix of *Twenty Thousand Leagues Under the Sea*
Eric Smith

"We may brave human laws, but we cannot resist natural ones."
—Jules Verne, *Twenty Thousand Leagues Under the Sea*

I've always been jealous of whales.

If only I could dive deep enough to hide from the damage we've done. From the surface of the ocean, far warmer than it should be, and from the coasts that have been swallowed by an angry, wounded sea.

The hydrofoil on *The Aronnax* thrums, and the massive tourist ship my family and I call home hoists itself off the surface of the water, rising above the rippling waves of the sea. The ship vibrates as it reaches optimum height, the quivering held still with a loud snap. I hold on to the guardrail, bits of water misting my face, listening to the sound of our guests laughing and sighing with relief and amazement. Dad says you used to see hydrofoils on wealthy folks' yachts all the time, the ship riding ski-like blades on the water, boats held aloft like they were on stilts.

Despite the ruined waters below and the looming promise of returning to a shattered shoreline, it seems like everyone's happy. Maybe they're eager to forget or have enough money that they don't even think about it. Probably the second thing.

"We're now at cruising speed," Mom says. I glance over to see her chatting up this trip's guests. She holds court over them, standing at a little raised section in the middle of the ship. Even though none of these people would be bothered with us outside a setting like this, here they're *paying* to be on our ship, our home. I can see it in the way their eyes flit away from me, how they walk by my father like he's not even there—the man who engineered this ship and likely worked on some of their pointlessly huge yachts, reduced to a wallflower. It's never ceased to piss me off.

As far as I know, *The Aronnax* is the last ship of its kind on this side of the country. Sometimes Dad radios other former research vessels in the West, some of whom are doing the same: working as tourist ships for the affluent or just existing as floating homes. If the rich want to see the creatures they've made this planet mostly uninhabitable for, they have to pay people like us. The same people they put out of business and couldn't be bothered to fund when it mattered, setting us on a course to all *this*.

"The specialized foil keeps us above the waves and gives us the ability to travel at greater speeds without hurting any of the ocean life who still call this part of the Atlantic home." Mom gestures out toward the open water. "Research vessels like this were used to study migration patterns of whales and other large ocean life, like sea turtles, giant squid, and manta rays, until those programs were shuttered."

Mom always says this so matter-of-factly, like her parents didn't lose their humanity when people and governments gave up on trying to save the oceans. When funding was cut to make *people* more comfortable, instead of restoring the damage done to the planet and its waters. When talking heads on news networks shrugged and said *What's a few degrees?* even as more and more sea creatures died off.

I love it here with Mom and Dad, but I hate it here with the tourists.

I miss when Grandpa was here.

Every minute of downtime he had, he spent nudging them to explore a little. Regain a bit of what they'd lost. Some adventure. And on days without sun, when rain thundered down on the deck and I hid in my room, he'd tell me stories of the world we lost, that he wished I could explore with him.

I spot Dad fussing with a control panel on the other side of the ship. *The Aronnax* is massive compared to other boats we see out here or docked back along Cape May. There are still a few super yachts floating around, and leisure ships, all with massive solar panels that could power a small town. But the seas aren't friendly anymore. They haven't been since we practically boiled them. Massive storms, huge waves, and angry, desperate, hungry animals…

You're safe if your ship can rise above all that.

But we're not above anything anymore.

Not really.

Ever since I was a kid, my parents have been using Grandpa's research vessel as a tourist trap, for the wealthy who have disposable income. That way, we can continue to maintain it, since it's our home. It's wild how we definitely can't afford a proper vaulted and conditioned home, safe from the rising seas and battering sun, but can work our butts off to live on a ship worth more than its weight in gold.

I try not to think about how disappointed he was, Grandpa, seeing his life's work made into…all this. But what choice was there?

Mom and Dad argue about it all the time. Sell it, get a home, and then…have no income. Stay on it, have income, but waste it away trying to keep our home. A vicious circle, one that I'll have to repeat myself when it's my turn to take over. The ship, it's my birthright…or adoptee right, I guess? I suppose that phrase doesn't totally work for me.

When all the world's homes are underwater, my family will be here, racing the sun.

A shuddering sigh escapes my chest as more ocean mist sprays against my tan skin. The invisible UV shield that protects *The Aronnax* stops me, my family, and any guests onboard from getting sunburned or heat sick, dimming down the sun's rays with a technology I don't understand. It's the same shielding that hums over the inland cities that survived the floods, in a place my parents call *the Midwest.*

I reach out beyond the guardrail, my hand over the water, and breach the veil of the shield.

After just a second or two, the heat is too much, and I pull my hand back in.

"Hey, hey you!"

I startle back, and there's a man standing near me, a glass in his hand. He's glaring down at me, annoyed. His skin is spectacularly clear and taut, like he's never had a blemish or wrinkle in his life. Like he's never been stung by any heat.

"Whiskey." He jiggles his glass around and hands it to me. "Thanks."

He turns on his heel and heads back toward the group, who have moved away from Mom to look out over the bow of the ship. He slips an arm around a woman, who turns and smiles at him.

I glare at the glass in my hand.

"Victor." I look up and there's Dad, walking toward me. It's pretty easy to see the striking difference between a man like my pops and someone like that rich guy. Dad's white. So is Mom for that matter. I'm adopted, whatever remains of my Honduran birth family somewhere beyond the horizon. But Dad bears the marks of someone who has done real work. Burn marks from the sun pock his skin, lined from where he's been nipped by a piece of heated metal or bitten by machinery. He's tan, but not like me. He's brown in the way a piece of leather you leave out in the sun gets tanned. Damaged, but still handsome.

He wipes at his forehead with a cloth, sweating even in the cooled environment, having been working on who knows what, and tucks the rag back into his belt, lined full of tools. Gadgets I'm going to have to learn to master at some point. The inner workings of the UV shielding can't remain a mystery to me forever.

"I know what you're thinking." He grins, grabbing the glass out of my hand. "But the ocean doesn't need more garbage in it."

"How did you know I wanted to throw that man into the sea?" I ask, smirking.

Dad sputters out a laugh and leads me away from the guardrail, toward the bridge. He swings open a bulkhead door like it's nothing, thanks to the small robotic brace supporting his elbow. I've heard about people on land wearing entire exo-suits using that kind of robotic framework, enabling them to lift dead vehicles off roads and build new homes like it's nothing. Sometimes, when I look at his exo-arm a little too long, I still feel a stab of guilt. And when he catches me doing that, he just shakes his head and says the same thing.

I'm stronger now. We both are.

The door shuts behind us with a clang. Dad exhales and leans on the command center. It's cool in here, the artificially chilled air nipping at my skin.

"Tell me this trip is almost over." I sigh, joining him against the console.

"Four more days, kiddo." Dad looks at his smartwatch. "After that, we have to head back to port. I need to pick up some parts."

"Are you ever *not* going to be fixing this thing?" I ask, looking down at the ship's console. A large sonar screen shows the water stretching out far ahead of us, little symbols for other ships and remaining wildlife deep beneath the waves lighting up in the blue. I wonder what's there, swimming under us, and I trail my finger along some blurred blips. Grandpa had this wild ability to just point at blue blobs on the sonar and rattle off what creatures they were. A pod of dolphins. A whale. A giant squid.

"Funny." Dad snorts and then sighs. "That's the joy of owning a ship, kiddo. Always something to repair. But at least we can go wherever we want. Most folks are stuck on land. Here, we're free."

The question *Are we?* sits in my mouth. Dad looks out over the bridge, out the window, and at Mom, who is talking to the guests again. He stares at her like he's the ship and she's the engine that keeps him going. She's over by my grandpop's submersible—a small, two-person research submarine that hangs over the side of the ship.

The Nemo.

It's not hard to pilot. It's all mostly computers in there. Mom and Dad have taken me in it before, and sometimes they'll give rides in it to kids at the port in Cape May, saying how it's important to "instill wonder" in people who don't get to experience much of it these days. Grandpop loved that thing and was still exploring in it until the day before he died, taking me into the depths while Mom and Dad were napping or sleeping in. It was worth every moment that they chewed him out, insisting it wasn't safe, to be able to see what remained on the seafloor and in the still-cooled parts of the ocean. Reefs and coral, crustaceans of impossible sizes. Lobsters half a century old, refusing to die even when each year their carapace threatens to kill them as they age.

"Time doesn't give you much of a choice, when it comes to growing up," Grandpa would say, anytime we found one of those beasts. "It's not always the world that crushes you. Sometimes you do it for them. Don't do that."

I feel like one of those lobsters now. Like… I can't break out of my own skin. Wondering when I'll be able to grow.

"Huh."

I look over at Dad, and he's scowling at the sonar panel now. There's a sizable blur of pixels near our ship, and it doesn't look to be moving away from us. I think about Grandpa, and what he would say regarding that, but...it can't be.

He taps at the screen and continues looking at it, his brow furrowed.

"Must be an error—"

He's still talking when someone screams.

Dad jerks back and looks up through the glass, and I follow his line of sight. The rich people are all on the opposite side of the ship, and Mom is running toward us, her eyes wide.

Oh, no.

I've *seen* that look. Someone's gone overboard. My heart hammers in my chest, and I have to grab the console to stop myself from falling over.

Dad pushes open the door to the bridge, the metal screaming. He bolts out, and I join him, forcing my legs to find and hold the ground again as I push myself toward him, the guests all still milling around the edge of the guardrail.

"Gary," Mom says breathlessly. "Over here...you have to..."

The guests...

They're...

Laughing?

"You're not going to believe this." Mom reaches out and grabs my hand, a smile on her face. She pulls me along. Dad follows, the tools around his waist clinking about. When we reach the guests, I'm immediately overwhelmed not just by their energy but the sharp smell of sunblock and various body sprays.

The man who asked me to refill his whiskey catches sight of me and holds his hands up and out, expectantly. Great. I forgot the empty glass on the bridge. I wince and he scowls at me, before looking back down at what everyone is fussing over.

And I can't believe what I'm seeing, either.

No one fell off the ship.

It's a calf.

A humpback whale calf. Right frickin' there.

It's swimming alongside the hydrofoil blade, somehow keeping up with us. Its tail slaps hard against the water.

"My god," Dad says, his voice an almost reverent whisper. "Your grandfather would have lost his mind over this." His hand clasps my shoulder. He walks up closer to me and scans the water, looking up and down the side of the ship, before leaving and hustling to the opposite side. I watch his eyes scour before turning back to the calf in the water.

It feels silly to say the calf is small, when it's gotta be like… fifteen feet long? An adult can be close to fifty feet long, though, and we really only see them from a distance on the ship, but the baby here is so close to us. I feel like if we lowered the hydrofoil, I could reach down and touch her.

Oh. The hydrofoil.

I lean over the guardrail some more, my heart hammering. Ships from decades ago were notorious for cutting whales and other creatures in the ocean or in saltwater bays, like manatees or dolphins, with foils that raised their ships. I know Grandpop outfitted our home with safer ocean blades, but still…

The ship rumbles, the guests gasp. I grip the guardrail and spot Dad working on a console on the other side of the ship. We start lowering, slowly, and the ship also slows down in the water. Without the quick breeze provided by the speed of the ship, even with the UV shield and cooling system, it starts to feel pretty warm immediately.

"Victor, keep an eye on the calf!" Dad shouts across the ship.

Eventually we're only a few feet above her on the deck. I don't need to be within touching distance to see she's not exactly swimming well despite keeping pace with us earlier: she bumps against the side of the ship a little, rattling us around. Some of the guests laugh joyfully, others yelp in surprise. The guy who has been glaring at me, who asked me to fetch him a drink, seems displeased.

"It's getting warmer," he says, looking at me.

"Yeah, the sun will do that," I mumble.

"Are we gonna get moving soon?" He glances around to the other guests, and two of them move to stand beside him, their arms crossed, glaring at me expectantly. "What's going on?"

"Aren't you here to see wildlife?" I ask.

"Psh," he grumbles. "My wife is here for that." He rattles an empty glass at me. "This is all I'm here for." He looks at me for a beat. "So?"

"I'll look into it," I huff, taking his glass. Where'd he even get another one? The guy turns back to his friends and pulls a flask from out of somewhere, passing it between them.

Great.

I remember the first time I started trying to serve guests on the ship, how annoyed Grandpa was with the whole ordeal. "He should be exploring. He should be learning about the sea," he'd say.

It all exhausted Mom and Dad. They didn't disagree, but exploration and research just wasn't a *thing* anymore.

"How's she looking?" Dad's voice asks, and I turn to see him hurrying my way. He peers over the guardrail, and a smile just blooms across his face. "My god. Have you ever seen something so beautiful? Besides your mom, that is."

"Jesus, Dad." I roll my eyes, and he nudges me with that robot arm of his. He pauses for a beat and then sighs as the whale splashes the side of our ship.

"Dad?" I ask.

He shakes his head, sucks at his teeth.

"Something is wrong with it, isn't it?" I press.

He nods, swallowing. "That baby shouldn't be out here without her mamá. Babies nurse for a good year."

The calf slaps a fin against the ship. The ship rumbles a little. Guests gasp and laugh. Someone applauds.

"Hey!"

It's that guy again. He hustles over and tucks away his flask.

"What's the plan here?" the man asks.

"Sir, we don't permit outside liquor on the ship," Dad says and slowly moves himself around me. "I'm gonna have to ask you to—"

"To what?" the man scoffs. "It's what I have to resort to. I asked—" he looks at me and waves his hand around "—your help here to get me a drink and—"

"That's my *son*," Dad snaps.

The exo-skeleton on his arm whirs loudly.

Dad's making a fist.

It trembles at his side.

"If you want another drink, you can order one using one of the tablets on the ship, like everyone else," Dad continues, his teeth gritted. "We explained the rules when you boarded. And you'll treat everyone on this ship, whether it's crew or *my family*, with respect."

There's a beat between my father and this tourist.

"Fine," the tourist grumbles. "But you better fix this." He points at the calf along the side of the ship, like the whale is an engine or something. "I didn't pay all this money to get burned up in the sun."

He walks away, and Dad's exo-skeleton arm whirs down.

It goes silent.

"Dad, are you okay?" I ask.

"Yeah." Dad clears his throat. "Yeah, I'm fine. I'm more interested in knowing if you are okay."

"I'll be all right." I shrug. But I'm not all right. I'm not sure what good going into all of it would do. Between that man reminding me I don't look like I belong and that...jolt of fear, of intense feelings returning, feelings that are still swirling around, when I thought someone went overboard…

Like it all happened yesterday.

"My boy," Dad says, cupping my cheek. "I'm sorry. Why don't you go relax in your room or something? These goons will be out of here soon enough."

"Shouldn't I get him his refill?" I ask.

Dad snorts out a laugh. "I think he's had enough."

I glance down at the whale and then at my dad.

"I'll take care of her, don't worry," he says.

I turn to the tourists. The whiskey guy is busying himself at a tablet with his pals. Mom is talking to some of the women: a few are taking photos or videos or holos over the guardrail. Whiskey Guy glances up, glares at me and my dad, and turns his attention back to the tablet and his buddies.

To hell with this. I don't need this.

I make my way toward the bridge, pulling open the steel door, and walk down the small flight of stairs to my and my family's rooms. They're separate from the rest of the ship's quarters, a set of three. There's Mom and Dad's bedroom, a living quarters where they've tried their best to create some semblance of normalcy for me with a holo for remote schooling, and my bedroom.

I have vague memories of when they made it a bedroom for me. It used to be an office, where they handled all the paperwork and registration needed for the ship and business. The living quarters used to be Grandpa's room, but they redid it years ago after he passed. They moved their desks and other things into their room when it became clear this was going to be my new home.

When…the accident happened.

The initial shock on the ship's bridge rockets back to my chest. The screams. The looks of horror on people's faces. The helpless hollow that gnawed its way through me.

I try to shake it away, but it stirs at something deep inside, a memory close to the surface but still under the waves. Blurry. Distant. Painful.

I throw myself on my bed and reach for my tablet to load up some comics…

When there's another scream outside.

And another.

And they all sound angry.

I toss my tablet on the bed and hurry back out. I was only downstairs for a moment, but it's already noticeably warmer out here than it had been. A few of the tourists are near the guardrail angrily arguing with Dad, while Mom is on the other side of the ship with a few other people who look wildly concerned.

I walk toward Dad…

And that's when the whiskey guy throws something over the guardrail. A cup? A glass? Something. My Dad shoves him away, there's some more heated words exchanged, and I peer over the edge into the water just in time to see the cup hit the whale calf.

I swear as it flinches.

"What are you people doing?!" Dad shouts. I hear his exo-arm whirring, but again, he's holding back. "Stop it!"

"Get this ship moving!" Whiskey Guy bellows. "Get that thing out of the way."

"Knock it off!" Dad yells as the tourist grabs a chair off the deck. "Stop it. You're going to have to pay for that if—"

"Oh, like I care!" Whiskey Guy laughs and tosses the chair. It hurtles over the guests and hits the guardrail with a loud pang, before tumbling over and colliding with the whale.

The calf cries.

Its song wails through the water and reverberates up into the air.

And it rips at my heart.

"Let's go!" the whiskey guy yells, reaching for another piece of furniture. Dad swats it out of his hand, but this time lets the full force of his arm do the work. It whirs as he swings his arm through the air. The small table splinters, and pieces of plastic fly everywhere.

"Stop it!" Dad shouts again. He glances over at Mom and the other tourists, who are huddled on the other side of the ship. He turns his attention back to the man. "You're embarrassing yourself."

"It's hot!" Whiskey Guy growls. "Push away from that thing."

"You really need to have some empathy here, tough guy." Dad takes a step toward him. "That kid is out here without—" He stops, wincing. "That *calf* is out here without her family. We need to call the coast guard and see what we can—"

"That will take ages!" Whiskey Guy roars.

The sound of their arguing disappears.

My heart. It pounds so hard I can hear the blood thrumming in my ears. Everything gets muffled.

The way Dad said it.

The phrasing.

That kid...

He was feeling pulled back, too.

Their back-and-forth comes back with a roar.

"You can go downstairs into your rooms!" Dad shouts. "We have air-conditioning and—"

"If I wanted to be in air-conditioning I'd have stayed at home!"

"Well, what did you really want, huh?" Dad snaps. "Coming here, onto my ship, onto my home. Drinks and cool air? You probably have that in one of your high-rises."

"I'm trying to..." The man looks over at the woman across the ship, who he had his arm around earlier. She turns away, embarrassment written across her face.

Well. Ruined that romantic trip yourself, tough guy.

"Look, we need to help her find her way home, okay?" Dad

pleads. "Just head downstairs, and we'll provide some refreshments while we call..."

I turn away from them fighting and grip the guardrail to look down at the calf. It wails again, her song echoing across the water. Channeling into the deep. Searching for someone who cares. Who misses her.

For a moment, she flips over onto her side, and I think, this is it. She's going to swim away.

But her eye, huge and impossible and imploring...settles on *me*.

She blinks. The thin membrane of the whale's eyelid...it blinks.

I know in my heart and in my mind that it's just water from the ocean, but for a second it looks like the whale sheds a tear, before rolling back onto her belly, her tiny, almost nonexistent dorsal fin peeking out of the water.

Dad starts ushering the frazzled guests down to the galley, to their rooms, and the tourists with Mom do the same. The woman with Whiskey Guy catches up and smacks him upside his head, yelling a bunch of stuff at him, and soon, I'm alone on the deck of the ship.

The whale cries.

And I look to Grandpop's submersible.

I know what he would do.

This...

This is a bad idea.

I feel myself drawn to it. I walk toward the little submarine, the one Mom and Dad have taken me in so many times, but Grandpa stole away in. The two of us, on tiny adventures, on stolen time. Exploring the ocean floor, picking up lost relics from abandoned ships. Where he taught me about responsibility, about how we have to care for each other, even when we can't see one another. And care for our oceans and world just the same. The console in front of it, where it hovers, latched to the side of the ship, glows at me.

Like an invitation from a ghost.

I press my hand to the screen, and it blips green.

This is a truly bad idea.

I type in a few commands, squinting as I try to remember every movement Mom and Dad have made around this thing. Grandpa would operate it without even looking at the console, talking while his fingers fluttered over screens and buttons, effortless. Inside I know what to do, but getting it into the water... it is taking me a minute. It only takes a moment before *The Nemo* hums to life. The robotic claws that hold the little boat in place rattle and click, shifting and lifting it up. The door opens, and the tiny submarine looks like a large pill that would be impossible for anything to swallow. Maybe a whale, but whales can't actually swallow something this big. *Pinocchio* was a lie.

Am I really going to do this?

A memory flashes across my mind, and I try to shake it off, but it claws at a space inside my chest. Like a crab devouring its way through the skeleton of some sunken creature on the ocean floor, hungry but eager to get out. The storm. The guardrail. The screams. I hold a hand up against the console, steadying myself, breathing deep. All the time it took to adjust to this new ship, this new life, this new family.

The whale cries.

I can do it.

I can save her.

This time I can save her.

I get inside *The Nemo*. It's not exactly comfortable: there are only two proper seats up in the front, a large window like a bubble. A small storage space is behind the seats, perfect for snacks or supplies or a small person (me), despite the Warning: Two Person Occupancy sign right on the side of the ship. I get myself situated in the pilot's seat and press a button to close the door—

"Victor!"

I glance out and see Dad rushing toward *The Nemo.* Mom is right behind him.

"Victor, don't!"

I hit the button to close the door, and it lowers with a loud crack. The muted yells from my parents thunder outside the ship, and there's a thumping on the side. Through the bubble, I can see Dad as he peers over the edge. He shouts again, but *The Nemo* descends along the side of the ship. The whirring of the metal is loud, and suddenly, it's in contact with the water. I watch outside the bubble as the horizon slowly disappears.

So much empty water.

In the nature programs I've watched endless times in my room, for school and just because, a quick descent this far into the ocean would be teeming with life. Small fish, large terrifying ones, whales and dolphins and more.

But there's nothing.

A vast emptiness fills my chest and mirrors the ocean in front of me.

Grandpa always knew where to go to find creatures. Where the currents brought cool water, where the depths stayed at a temperature that kept life thriving. But here, it's vacant. And I'm wondering how I'm going to find some life for that little whale.

I tap a few things on the console, and lights snap on. *The Nemo* disconnects from *The Arronax.* Almost immediately the speakers inside roar to life as well.

"Victor!" Dad's voice pleads. "Victor, I'm not sure what you think you're doing, but you need to turn that submarine around. The coast guard is coming. They can help the calf—"

"No. No, Dad, I have to do this," I say, but I feel my own voice trembling. I don't really know what I'm doing. But I feel like I have to do something.

"Son, you don't. There are professionals coming. And we can help, but from the ship! Where it's safe."

"You don't really know how to work *The Nemo*," Mom stresses. "There's so much to keep track of, *your dad and I* had to run it together. Your grandfather was the one who could do it all."

"I know what I'm doing!" I insist.

I don't.

"Sweetheart, please," Mom says. "Just—"

I turn off the speakers.

And grab the controls.

The Nemo steers through the water smoothly, despite the chop surrounding the ship. I've been in the back seat enough times. I've seen everyone in my family operate this thing. I've watched holos, and I've driven around with Grandpop, preparing for the day it would be my turn.

I can handle it.

The baby humpback whale comes into view quickly. The lights shimmer off its gray skin, and I can see that the ocean has taken its toll on her. Scratches and scars mar her side. I pull the submarine up alongside her, but not too close.

She seems to trust our ship.

But I don't know if she trusts me.

I move the submarine away a little and flash the lights at her. I flip a few switches, finding some whale sounds. Once upon a time, Grandpa used to play them in here for me, so we could catch glimpses of whales in the deep. The music makes the sub vibrate and echoes through the hull and the water. I can see her pupil contract in the one eye facing me before she shuts it...but it works. She moves away from *The Aronnax* and swims toward me, just as another piece of furniture splashes into the water near where she was swimming.

Goddamn Whiskey Guy must be back on the deck.

"It's okay," I say. "Let's just...lead you away from all this."

And that's when I realize I have no real plan.

What am I doing?

Where am I going to take her where she'll be safe?

I look down at the console in the submarine, at the sonar. It's not like I can see a pod of humpback whales on the thing. And I wouldn't, anyway. Humpback whales travel mostly solitarily, the mother with the baby until it's ready to go off on its own. The console shows me the calf, *The Aronnax*, and the emptiness beyond.

I turn on the speakers again.

"Victor. Victor, come in."

"Hi, Dad," I mutter.

The whale stares at me.

He exhales. "Listen, we aren't mad. Just…come back with *The Nemo*, son. This…this isn't a good idea. There's nowhere out there to go."

"I can't let that guy hurt her," I say, feeling my lip tremble. "I have to save her."

"Victor, I…" Dad sounds like he's about to cry.

It's quiet on his end. He must be in the cabin or inside the command center at the console. He has to be away from all the guests, from the troublemaker. But I know that he also understands what I'm saying. That he wants to save her as much as I do.

"I know," Mom chimes in. "But…it's not her."

Ripples in the water. Someone has thrown a table into the ocean. I watch it sink.

My heart pounds. That night flashes, bits of memory. A guardrail. A scream. A storm. Strong arms wrapping around me. Mostly feelings. The hollowness. The devastation.

"Sweetheart…we've done our best with you and what we have," Mom says, her voice shaking. "And we'll do the same with that little one floating in front of you right now. We've called the right people. The best thing you can do is stay put in that submarine until they arrive."

The whale looks at me.

"You can keep her away from the ship and keep her safe. But

this…it won't bring your…m-mother back." Mom stammers it out, like the word is hard for her to say in reference to someone else.

It's been years since my mother took me onboard *The Aronnax* to go whale-watching. I don't remember much. We were poor. There was a lottery, though, for free rides for people in the community down in Cape May. Those of us who weren't these millionaire types, who still wanted to see the natural world left behind.

I'd pleaded to enter. Begged.

And during a wild storm, Mom went overboard.

Strong arms held on to me. I wanted to dive in after her. A six-year-old who didn't even know how to swim, wanting to save the only family I'd ever known.

And I couldn't save her. No one could. Even when the man who would one day adopt me went overboard in his own attempt to rescue her, losing his arm in the process, when the ship jarred in the storm.

Mom and Dad here, on the ship, took me in. Grandpa was thrilled. And anyway, where else could I go? One of the group homes, in the ravaged countryside? Here, on the site of my biggest tragedy, was the only hope I really had.

"Just…come back, son," Dad says. "The coast guard is coming."

"How do you know they'll help her? How do you know it'll all be okay?"

There's a beat. Silence. Nothing is okay anymore. Not after all that humanity has done to our planet, our animals, our ocean. How could anything ever be okay again?

The whale sings, floating near the glass. Her eye looks right at me.

"We don't know it'll be all right." Dad clears his throat. "But *The Aronnax* has all kinds of technology. We can ferry these tourists home with the coast guard and try our best. And if our best isn't good enough, maybe one of those saltwater sanctuaries that are set up along the coast, floating in the currents where the water is cool. There are answers. Just stay, keep a few feet away from the ship, and we'll wait it out together."

The glass is cold under my palm. I press a button, whale songs floating through the water.

"Okay." I sigh, sniffling. "Okay."

Mom and Dad sigh into their microphones.

The calf sings, perhaps a little beat-up, but still alive. Still okay.

And *The Nemo* sets a course back to the ship, the calf trailing close behind.

★★★★★

HEART OF THE SEA

a remix of *Frankenstein*
Zoraida Córdova

"It is true, we shall be monsters, cut off from all the world; but on that account we shall be more attached to one another."

—Mary Shelley, *Frankenstein*

1.

"Swim to me."

The words, clear but distant, pulled her from the deep slumber that precedes creation. She opened her eyes. Consciousness bloomed like a quickened sunrise. Sound. Light. Thoughts. Sights. Touch.

Touch.

There was a gentle hand wrapped around her wrist. *Fingers*, she knew the word. She didn't know how she knew it, but it came to her. Other words rushed in when she blinked. Tail. Metal. Silver. Sky. Blue. Cloud. Man—no, boy.

A boy peered down at her. Tall and skinny with brown hair pulled back. She studied his face, littered with pearly scars along hollow cheekbones. His lips were parted, a ring like the open ceiling above them.

He pressed hard against her pulse. She had a pulse.

"Where am I?" Her voice *hurt* at first, but she wanted to try again.

The boy let her hand fall and gestured to the hole in the ceiling, the dingy white walls, the sharp tools hanging everywhere. A smattering of blue-green patina coated a podium control. He tapped a button on the panel, and a whirring noise filled the room for a moment.

"Home. Well, my lab. That's *laboratory*," he said, emphasizing the word. "I wasn't sure if you'd retain vocabulary."

He grinned as she nodded. She did understand, but it took her a moment to catch up to the speed of his words, and for the ringing to stop. The tumble of light and sound left her dizzy. One question blinking in her thoughts as she took in the gray metal of her tail, twitching to life on the examination table. What. Am. I. What am I?

"*What* am I?"

"You are made." The boy smiled then. "My creation. I made you."

Made.

She was made by another. *Creation.* He said the words himself, so why didn't she feel *made*? She felt as if she had always been and always would be.

She stretched slowly, moving her torso a fraction this way and that, every muscle aching with newness. The soreness stopped at her waist, where the jagged scar marked where her flesh stopped, and her metal tail began. Creation. *Monster.* No, that's not what she was. Another word rushed to mind. *Mermaid.*

"Why?"

The boy frowned. His thin lips almost blue with cold. "Why what?"

"Why did you make me?"

He smiled again. A smile that made the sharp edges of his face soften. Dark eyes cut skyward, then back at her. She followed his stare to her tail fins. Metal, cold, and shimmering under the circle cut out in the ceiling. *Skylight*, she thought.

The boy seemed transfixed, pleased, by what he saw. The ends of her tail fins were bendable, an iridescent series of panes that looked fragile. Commanded by her thoughts, her delicate fins fluidly lifted. She touched the thin material. Wanted to know why she was made, yes, but also what she had been made of. She retraced the taut skin of her upper body. The ashen undertone, the mottled green and purple bruises along the seams of her scars.

"I made you because I need you," the boy finally said. "I made you because the world is gone. *Everyone* is gone. There is just me and the disgusting river and the acid rain." His words got softer. His eyes sadder. He was an open wound, fragile and hungry. "I made you because there is nothing left, and if the world is to end, I do not want to be alone."

"It's all right," she said. Something inside her needed to appease him, even as a worm of discomfort burrowed within her. "Now you won't be alone."

He smiled again.

"Do I have a name?" she asked.

"No. You may call me Vic."

"Vic." She mimicked the way he rubbed his arms, though she was not cold. "I *need* a name, Vic."

He frowned. "You don't need one."

Everything had a name. The names of things rushed at her, almost overwhelming. Tray, scalpel, mermaid, clouds, sun. What could she call herself? Girl? Mermaid? Made? "Then, how will I know when you call for me?"

He seemed to think on that, gnawing on his pink bottom lip. "Fisher."

She said the word in her mind before trying it out on her tongue. "Fisher."

"Get it?" he asked. "Because that's your primary function."

She felt her face tighten. Was she frowning? She supposed it would do. For now.

"Now, let's teach you how to swim."

Teach her to swim? Shouldn't she already know? He made her a mermaid, not a human girl. There was a fuzzy blackness in her mind when she imagined what it was like to swim. To exist, even. She rubbed at the hole in her thoughts, like a stain she could wipe away. Instead, the dark persisted, and she was left unknowing. What was she capable of? Why wouldn't he *make* her know how to swim? How should she swim without water?

She was about to ask him, but he pressed a red button on the podium panel and there was a crushing, grinding sound of warped steel. She pressed her palms against her sensitive ears as a long grate on the floor retracted and opened to reveal gray-green water coated with a slimy film.

The exam table beneath her tipped over, and she plummeted down into unknown, murky waters.

2.

She thrashed her arms in the polluted water. At first, she'd sunk and sunk and sunk. Later, Vic would tell her she was in the Hudson. The murk that had overtaken everything after the great flooding of the country. He'd explain that their laboratory had once been the penthouse of a building, and the sea level had risen to meet it. But in that moment, as Fisher sank, she knew nothing of what had happened to the world.

When she reached the bottom, she found another room, instead of a riverbed. Slick green plant life and fish darted through the dark caverns made of brick and metal. It was down there, blinking against the silt in the water, that she realized she did not need to breathe. Her first instinct upon going under had been to hold her breath tight—like it was the last one she would take.

Fisher gripped at the water helplessly before she realized she could push herself up on her tail. She gripped the nooks and crannies in the rotten walls, the metal beams that curved like a rib cage in the ruins of the building. Rung by rung she pulled herself back to the surface and wept without tears. Her body was not accustomed to this new reality, this new sense of being.

"Good," Vic said as she clung to the lip of the pool. "Good. Now, swim to me."

After a moment, she did because she did not want to sink so fast again, and she needed to stop herself from crying. Her tail was cumbersome and Vic too demanding. But with every stroke, her fins moved softly in the water. Back and forth and back and forth until she stopped. She stilled the urge to inhale and simply floated until Vic threw chunks of brick into the water to get her attention.

"If you can swim," she said, "why don't *you* do it?"

Vic looked up from where he knelt at the opposite edge. His dark hair and eyes had the sheen of an oil slick. When he snapped his fingers, something impatient and mean flitted across his slender features.

"There must be something wrong with your programming." His words were clipped. Then he snapped his fingers again. "Can you pull yourself back up?"

It was her first mistake. Later, she would regret showing him how strong she really was. But she didn't know any better back then, and in that moment, she felt the need to obey him. So she did. She pulled herself up and sat on the lip of the pool.

Pool was not the right word for it. Deep in her mind, she could see the image of pale blue water, a real pool. This was something else: a hole in what once was a floor, a mouth leading to the flooded river. This was *the after* of a world she only remembered in flashes.

Despite his thin frame, he lifted her up in his arms like there was nothing inside her but air and clouds. He carried her a few paces back on the exam table and strapped her in. She remained perfectly still, like a doll getting a broken limb mended.

"What's wrong?" She really wanted to ask, *What's wrong with me?* She could tell he was worried, but he kept his lips pressed so thin, it was like a slash across the bottom half of his face.

Vic placed circular tabs on the insides of her wrists, on her chest. "I'm not sure. Your verbal configuration is advancing at a faster pace than I expected."

"Is it bad?"

Vic peered up at her. It was like he saw her, right through her skin to her insides. "No. It's surprising. Look at what I have made, and there is no one alive here to see it. My mother spent her life in this same lab trying to do this very thing."

"This?" She stopped herself from adding *thing.* This very thing.

"An organic android." He chuckled, his mood brightening as he read the lines on the monitor that beeped a steady rhythm. Her heart, she knew. She had a heartbeat but did not need to breathe underwater. She was a mermaid but didn't yet know how to fully swim. She was a creation, made, a thing, but there was something missing. Something he wasn't telling her.

"Why is everyone gone?" Fisher asked. "No one is alive but us?"

"I'm alive," he corrected her coolly. "You're...liminal, I suppose. It's like turning on an engine, lighting a match. You can be turned off. A fire can be put out."

She frowned. She *felt.* It was a sensation foreign to her, like a punch right at her core. She watched the monitor race as the feeling intensified and her breath came faster and faster. *Hurt. Anger.* He'd made her feel those things with only a few words.

"What do you mean I can be turned off?"

"You'll see momentarily. I'm sorry, but I need to inspect your programming, and it will be a lot easier if you're not asking a million questions."

She heard the flat line of her own heart as she powered down.

3.

"Swim to me."

This time when she blinked awake, she knew exactly where she was. Vic tapped his long, slender fingers against a plastic bottle full of green liquid.

"How can I swim to you?" Her voice was groggy as she sat up. Her tail fins swished where they hung over the edge of the exam table.

Vic frowned. He glanced around the room, then at the closed grate on the floor. "I didn't say anything."

She felt herself mimicking his frown. She didn't want to get powered-down again. She didn't want to be in this place. She didn't want to be *with him.*

The thoughts surprised even her. She, after all, had been made by him. Made for him?

"I must have been dreaming," she said sweetly.

Vic perked up at that. "*Fascinating.* You can dream?"

She could not. At least, not that she knew. But she had heard a voice call to her, just like the first time she'd woken up. Wasn't it Vic calling to her, *telling* her to swim to him? If not Vic, the only person with her in the building, submerged in a watery grave, then who?

Or what?

Perhaps, it was not a dream necessarily but a memory. *Memories* belonging to the human parts she had once been. She saw the world as it was before the great flood: a billion lights, Coney Island, boom-box music, hot sticky summers on a boardwalk, cotton candy melting on her tongue. Sun searing freckles on golden-brown shoulders. Sisters looping their arms with hers like chain links bracing for the impact of a brutal world. That was the last summer before the end.

"I dreamed of a wave," she said, watching his face carefully for a reaction. "Of swimming in a great wide ocean that filled in the world."

Vic shut his eyes, rubbed them hard with the knuckles of his fists. He took a deep breath, his eyes glassy. "Well, there's plenty of ocean. Now, let's continue our swimming lessons. You need training for your first hunt."

4.

Swimming came easier the more she let go. Once, she did a lap around the building's exterior. She floated on the surface and watched the dilapidated tops of scattered surrounding skyscrapers. Empty. Quiet. The kind of quiet that perplexed her because it was still so very loud. She watched the dead, drowned city until her skin was too warm from the hot, white sun. Until she felt lonely enough to miss Vic.

When she was ready, she was sent out into the watery depths with a small metal cage strapped to her back. Vic expected her to bring him food—anything organic that could sustain him. Anything useful that she found. He'd told her to use her judgment.

She swam down through the hollowed wreckage of what had once been a squat building and right back out of a shattered windowpane on the next level. She went lower, hovering just over the drowned Manhattan streets. Thousands of cars were bumper-to-bumper, some doors still open, as if the drivers had rushed out, running for their lives, so scared they didn't bother to shut the doors.

"I wonder if they made it," she said. The first time she'd tried to speak underwater, it had come out in bubbles. Now she was used to it.

She came to a stop, proud of the way she commanded her tail. She used the tips of her fins to steady herself. Most of the rusted cars were full of seaweed and clumps of seagrass. Slimy mosslike nests were home to minnows and other fish, but they were too small to feed Vic. For a boy who was so desperate, he was certainly picky. He'd been very clear that he was down to his last month of nutrient drinks, a sludgy green concoction that fed his body.

She'd had the idea of catching a hundred minnows and frying them like popcorn.

"That's revolting," Vic had said. "Bring me something better."

Now she was just supposed to guess what *better* entailed, like their minds were linked? Like she should anticipate his moods and wants. Minnow popcorn had sounded like a brilliant idea, and *she* didn't even eat. Vic had made her so she was sustained by a compound mixture of oxygen and salt and the battery that powered her entire being.

Deepening her search, she pried open the door of a car. Brittle bones floated out, disturbed by her movement of the water. Giant blue crabs scuttled away from her over the mossy hood. She chuckled at how they moved, walking sideways like they were in a hurry. Hadn't anyone told them? There was nowhere to go because the world was gone.

That's not right, though, she thought. Peering up the streets to the underwater forest that Central Park had adapted to, she realized there was everywhere to go.

She swam fast, pushing with three flicks of her powerful tail, and caught up to the crabs. She snatched up two big ones and secured them in the metal cage. She grabbed a third. Licked her canine. Her teeth were sharp. She bit down on the shell of the crab. She knew she couldn't eat, but an overpowering hunger snatched up her better reasoning. It was a desperate thing, the need to consume. To devour. She crunched through the shell of the crab, felt it twitch and then die as she ground its flesh between her molars.

As she moved on to the next crab, she was flooded with more memories, a winter night. Her mother untangling a string of lights. Her father adding tiny packets of seasoning to the boiling pot of water. Her younger sisters trying to free the bucket of blue crabs they ate for every Nochebuena when everything was warm and magical and hopeful as Christmas approached. They were the only family on their floor that celebrated with a seafood boil and tiny red potatoes dusted in shimmering sea salt. "Just like back home," her dad would say. Every year he said the same thing.

That apartment, that street, this city—it was home. But as she swam in a circle, her chest tightened when she realized she could never find it. Not again. Not from where she floated all alone.

She felt her eyes burn, her stomach squeeze violently. As the memories cleared, she knew something was wrong. Everything was wrong. *She* was wrong, and home—home was gone.

5.

"I told you," Vic said harshly as he shoved a tube down her throat. "You can't process organic food. You don't have a human digestive track or—parts."

Her throat burned. Chunks of crab pumped through her stomach and out of her mouth. She wanted to cry. She felt the ache around her eyes, but she couldn't make tears. Vic hadn't made her so she could cry.

When it was over, he left the lab and didn't return. She watched the sky darken in blues through the skylight for a long time. She felt empty. Strange. Unfinished. She'd been made but not made whole. Vic had given her a tail but had had to teach her to swim. He'd turned her into a creature of myth but gave her guts of wire and data chips. He'd *made* her his—to protect him and feed him and accompany him at the end of the world. But perhaps the world wasn't over. It was just made anew. Made like she'd been made: unwillingly, violently.

She didn't even belong to herself.

She didn't even have a true name.

It was that thought that tipped her over the edge. She sat up on the exam table and dragged herself off the edge, walking on the palms of her hands to the open grated floor. She dove back into the flooded city.

What am I searching for? she wondered, swimming over the top of the wild, underwater Central Park forest. Vic had told her, and later she remembered, that there used to be a place where land ended and the water began. After the meteor, after the Hudson and the Atlantic blanketed the city, there were no more shores, no seven oceans. It was just one sea. Part of her, the squishy human parts, longed for that old world even if she knew this version of herself, this remade mermaid, hadn't lived it.

Hunger came in many forms, and she found a way to feel it. She might not be able to digest, but she could open her mouth and feel the brine of the ocean. She couldn't cry tears, but the salt in the water enveloped her.

She kept swimming, wishing she could fully remember that old life. Even if it hadn't belonged to her, not truly. She felt more in those memories than she did sitting in the cold laboratory with a scared, lonely boy. It felt like a cruel thing to keep her flashes of memories—of parents she could not talk to, of sisters she could not embrace, of love she could not reciprocate. It wasn't fair to have to remember, to hunger for it.

When the ocean felt empty, she realized she was lost. She'd never swum out that far, past the park, past where Manhattan ended and the *true* ocean—no skyscrapers, no abandoned cars with scuttling crabs—began. Beyond the Brooklyn Bridge there was an endless dark. What lay there? She pushed forward, chasing the hunger of exploration.

She made it one, two, three more yards when a sharp current of electricity went through her tail. She couldn't swim. She grabbed at the water. Sank to the cemetery of rusted cars on the bridge. Clung to the metal ropes and waited for mobility to return.

It didn't.

"Swim to me," the voice said.

There, a few yards ahead, was a girl just like her, part human and part metal. Instead of a tail, she had a metal leg and a metal forearm. Her brown, bruised skin was covered in scars like roads on a map that led back to Fisher.

It's you, the mermaid mouthed. She tapped her chest to signal that she didn't have a voice underwater. Still, she pointed at the android girl, then back at herself.

"I'm Reggie. I've been calling to you," she said. "We all have."

One by one, Fisher saw others. A boy with a tail like hers. Another person with limbs and body parts—human and otherwise—grafted and bruised and broken. Created. *Made*.

Vic had made them.

How could she have thought that she was the only one?

No, she was his first *successful* attempt. He'd said something like that to her. His mother had tried, and so had he. The world had ended, but he'd made himself companions instead of learning to survive on his own.

"When you swim too far, you stop working," Reggie explained. "I had to repair myself."

Fisher looked at her motionless tail.

Reggie extended her hand but didn't move forward. Her voice was haunting, like the call of the sea. "Swim to me, and I'll fix it."

Fisher wanted to. Her thoughts felt like silt disturbed in water, clouding her desire to swim. But her programming flared up in warning. When her thoughts settled, she recoiled. Who was this stranger? Who were these creatures? They were no one compared to Vic, her only friend. She and Vic were together in all things, at the end of it all. Without her, how would he keep going?

And so she chose.

She pushed herself back, far enough so that she was within Vic's reach. Her tail rebooted, and she swam back to the lab as hard and fast as her fins would carry her.

6.

Fisher returned with an offering. She'd caught a large, marbled salmon with a split tail and four eyes. She threw it at Vic's feet the moment she broke through the water. The anger scrunching his features was replaced by an expression of deep hunger. He snatched up the fish and vanished, likely to his kitchen. To fill his belly with the food she'd brought him.

She climbed up onto the exam table. It was so cold beneath her wet skin, but she could withstand it. Her long dark hair dried as the day gave way to night. Vic still hadn't come back, and she was doing everything possible to not think about Reggie and the others. To not receive the flashes of memory that came faster and more frequently.

This time, she remembered a feeling of being warm. She rubbed at that memory and saw herself in a lavender dress. It was the last night before the end, and she'd been waiting for someone. She wanted to scratch at that memory, dig her nails into it and pry it open the way she had that blue crab. She wanted. She wanted, and she couldn't want. But there it was, a memory loop. The girl she'd been, twirling in a lavender dress. The door opened. Someone was waiting on the other side. Who waited for her now?

"Look at you," that someone told her. Kissed her cheek. Tied flowers to her wrist. "You are already perfect."

Then came the flood. The water. The world was remade and herself along with it. She blinked and blinked, but tears couldn't come. The cold did bother her then, suddenly.

Vic returned to the lab, his cheeks pink for the first time since she'd seen him. It didn't last. His worry returned. "What is it?"

"Nothing." *Everything*. Everything was wrong, but it wasn't her.

"Did you eat?" he snapped. "Did you eat again?"

"No, I swear it."

He pressed his palm to her forehead, then used a thermometer to take her temperature. "You're not supposed to be this cold."

"Why won't you give me a real name?" Fisher asked. Her empty tear ducts ached. She shouldn't have returned. She should have fought harder against his pull.

Vic huffed and paced around the lab. He yanked open a drawer and rummaged through it. He tore a wrapper open. Grabbed a tiny bottle of clear liquid. Skinny fingers, pink salmon flesh still under his nails, flicked a syringe. She felt the injection into the vein of her arm like a thorn. She cried out. Ice-cold liquid filled her. Made her heart rate slow.

"You're not supposed to feel pain, either," Vic said, more worried for what she *should* be capable of instead of her actual well-being.

"Why won't you give me a name?" she repeated, harder. She blinked to stay awake.

"Please," Vic said, pressing his fingers to his temples. "Shut up. Just let me think."

Was this how he'd treated the others? Reggie and the others way out there in the unknown parts of the ocean? Fisher bared her canines as Vic paced around her. "Think about what? How I'm another one of your failed experiments?"

Vic froze. "What did you say?"

"I know," she said, each word like a sledgehammer against a brick wall. "I *know*. I know about the others."

She knew what he would do. She had, after all, been made to anticipate what he needed. What was best for him. What would comfort him. Fisher swooped to the side. He fell against the exam table, and she landed on her side on the rattling grated floor. Rolling over, she lashed out with her tail as he grabbed for her.

"You don't know anything!" He grabbed hold of her wrist, and she raked her nails across his face. She fought against the sick feeling that filled her at the sight of his pain. What about her pain? Her longing? What about *her*?

"I know you're going to try to fix me."

Vic snatched a hook from his table of metal tools. He danced around her like she was a lion to tame, a shark to reel in. "Your programming needs to be tweaked. That is all. I'll get it right. Please. I'm so close. You're nearly perfect. Why can't you see that?"

He was going to try to unmake her again. To restart. Would he begin all over with someone new? Would her memories be wiped clean and given to someone else? Would he turn her tail into metal legs? Would he take away her ability to swim?

Vic had given her a half-life. He hadn't given her a name, but he had given her a hunger not one of his calculations had anticipated. That, and her canines. He'd given her sharp teeth. She whipped the hook out of his clutches. When he desperately reached for her, she bit down on his fingers. Tasted copper and salt. Felt the crush of bone, the vibration in the way he screamed. She didn't bite them off clean, but when she let go, she could see white bits barely hanging together by squishy, bloody tendons.

Part of her hurt to deny him, to see him hurt. She'd been programmed to return to him, to be his *thing*. Not a friend. Not a companion. And when she'd swum too far, she'd frayed at that connection, that command. Heart racing, she knew she had one chance to flee.

"I am not *nearly perfect*," she told Vic, remembering the words from her memories. "I *am* already perfect."

Every piece of her cobbled together—steel and sinew—was perfect. Her muddled memories and her murky future. She belonged in the remade world, but she did not belong there, in that laboratory sitting on the surface of the drowned city.

She chose herself, and then she chose the sea.

She reached up to the podium and punched the floor grate open. She dove into the waters, letting them wash away the blood on her tongue. This time, when she swam past the park, past the roads, and to the Brooklyn Bridge, she did not see the end of the world that Vic had talked about. It wasn't murk and pollution. Fish cut across the currents, a whale drifted near the surface, millions of lights twinkled from bioluminescent plankton and fish, filling the insides of buildings like it was Christmas in New York.

Sonia. The name popped into her mind, along with a sense of excitement. Her name was Sonia.

When she reached the bridge, she only had to wait for a moment for Reggie and Vic's other creations to appear.

"I hoped you'd come back," Reggie said.

Sonia gave a reflexive flick of her fin to keep herself within Vic's perimeter. She knew she wanted to go, but she was afraid. Beginnings were scary. Endings were scary. Choosing was scary. What if Reggie did not keep her word to fix her tail from Vic's leash? What if she chose wrong?

At the very least, the choice was hers and hers alone to make.

Sofia, part wires and part flesh, swam toward her future—toward a new world and answered the call of the sea.

★ ★ ★ ★ ★

TESORO

a remix of *The Old Man and the Sea*
Sandra Proudman

"Now is no time to think of what you do not have. Think of what you can do with that there is."

—Ernest Hemingway, *The Old Man and the Sea*

Long ago, diamonds were the most valuable of all things. In 2092, diamonds were as worthless as the sand in front of Mimi. Survival mattered more. It was early morning, and Mimi stood at the edge of the desert looking for a new tesoro, her little brother leaning against her torso, his cuerpo small and slender and bony with hunger.

"Mimi, you don't have to go out there," Gus said. "Quedate."

Stay. Instead of venturing into the vast landscape of sand that bled into the horizon. But they were scavengers, and staying where there was nothing to scavenge meant starving.

Mimi turned away from the desert to what remained of the Las Vegas strip. The sand had reclaimed Nevada decades ago. Every year it reclaimed a little more. Luckily, two of the old casino towers housed squatters like Mimi's family. Mamá was in one of those hotels, up there in their suite. Sick with a fever that refused to break, likely dying. And so Mimi was the one who needed to scavenge.

Once, Papá had been here, too, and always made Mimi feel like they'd be okay. He had survived the droughts and the early water wars when Mamá's family hadn't. But Papá had gone to California the day before Gustavo was born. He'd gone to be a groundwater miner, now that water meant wealth, more than it ever had. California had held out for as long as possible, but finally it, too, joined the race to drill deeper into the earth to be the first to capture the buried water. A blessing for those like Papá who needed work. It'd been six years of sending most of his wages home but never having enough to return himself.

Six months back, the money stopped coming. His messages, too. And with time, it was like the sand encroached on her memory of him. Now no matter how hard or quickly Mimi tried to dig his memory out, more sand fell where her hands clawed.

After Papá had disappeared, Mamá found work in the desert. Bringing back technology like old radios and tablets that only worked when plugged into solar-powered battery packs. They sold these to people with money and airplanes that still visited the leftover casinos for a lawless night of excitement. Turistas.

Despite the challenges scavenging brought, Mimi looked out at the desert with hope. Out there was a fortune to be had. Tesoro: long-forgotten treasure of a not-forgotten time.

"Todos los desiertos tienen agua," she whispered to her brother, like Mamá told her every time they went out. Not that they ever found water. Mamá meant that there was always hope, and that's what they held on to. Usually, they found enough to get by.

Gus stared up at Mimi, his brown eyes wide. "Sis, there's no water out there."

It didn't matter, anyway. Mimi wasn't planning to go far. Only a little farther than yesterday. Beyond the boundary that the other scavengers stopped at. People who passed that line usually became another keepsake reclaimed by the desert. She needed to find something that would set them up for a while and allow Mimi to focus on taking care of Mamá instead of relying on Gus to do it.

It had been a week of trips deep into the desert, returning with nothing but wicked sunburns and worn boots full of sand. If that didn't change soon…

"You should let me come with you. Or ask Tiago to go."

Mimi cringed. It was too dangerous to take Gus, but she could ask Tiago to join her. Though she'd been so obviously in love with him since they were Gus's age, she wasn't sure she could survive hours of the awkwardness that had recently grown between them. But more importantly, if something happened to her, she trusted Tiago to help Mamá and Gus.

She needed to do this alone.

Gus motioned to her pack. "Do you have enough food with you? Enough water?"

"I have enough." They both knew she was lying. Mimi left Mamá and Gus with most of the food and water they had in case she didn't make it back.

Gus looked up at her. "Just find something fast, so you won't be long."

Mimi winked. "I'll do that. Now, go back home and take care of Mamá. Regreso pronto." She kissed her brother on the forehead, unable to talk to him about what he should do if she didn't return.

"Te quiero mucho," he said.

"Te quiero mas," she replied, then watched as Gus ran back toward the strip, his hand-me-down huaraches smacking against the ground.

At the very least, she hoped to find him new shoes.

She double-checked what was inside the canvas bag at her feet, which was stout and she hoped would outlast her. Inside was a tiny bit of food, a blue wool blanket, a tinderbox to start a fire, a knife that had a hard time keeping an edge, several yards of rope, and a half-filled sixteen-ounce stainless-steel water bottle.

Mimi reached into the very bottom for a final item. She opened the postcard-sized metal container and took out a small drone shaped like a metallic dragonfly.

"Hola, precioso," Mimi said. "Wake up, Walter." She threw Walter in the air, where his metal wings unfurled as he awoke, and he whizzed like a shooting star against the blue sky. Walter was Mamá's most treasured find. She named it after the famous Puerto Rican astrologer Mimi's abuelita followed religiously, Walter Mercado. Sometimes when they'd look up at the night sky from their suite, Mamá would talk to Mimi about the stars. How people have always used them to navigate the world and sometimes even to foretell their future.

But there was more to Walter than pretty flying. Mimi cleaned the sun goggles that hung around her neck, then set them tightly in place over her eyes. She pressed the On button on the side of the goggles, waiting for a small ding. The familiar sound sung its note. "Connect to Walter," she ordered the goggles. In a whirlwind, the right eye of her goggles turned into a video screen, and she saw the world through Walter's fish-eyed gaze.

The sand was like an ocean of speckled gold beneath him, the sand dunes frozen waves upon an eternal horizon. There was one more thing she needed before starting the day. She reached both hands into the sand next to a small Mexican flag that Mamá used as a marker and pulled out their hidden sand skiff. Mimi had helped Mamá build the skiff out of materials they'd found in the desert: an electric-boat motor powered by a solar capsule, a surfboard, a cross-shaped post made of knotty wood, and hot-air balloon fabric that was yellow and had a black happy face on it. When upright, the skiff stood four feet taller than Mimi. There wasn't much charge in the battery, so Mimi didn't turn it on right away. She would glide down the sand dunes until she found something and bring the item home sin problema once the skiff accumulated enough solar power.

She readied herself and tightly hooked the loose end of the sail up to the top of the post, then used the rope in her bag to create a handle along the horizontal section of the post. She pulled the skiff to the top of the nearest sand dune, using the velocity of the drop to propel her forward.

Walter followed above as Mimi traveled south, drawn to the location of the goggles. She ignored the strain on her muscles from previous days of scavenging, a feeling she was used to but wished she wasn't, considering it meant she was always overworked, and concentrated on what Walter was showing her. She made it to the border at what she hoped was a good hour. The area had once been fenced off. The fence hadn't really fallen. The sand had just overtaken it. The wires on the top of the fence, which peeked out from the sand now, signaled the border between Nevada and California.

If she kept going, would she find her way to California and Papá? She'd thought about trying before.

Mimi went over the line, careful not to scrape the bottom of the sand skiff too much on the wire. She was so alone. She'd heard about caravans. From somewhere farther away than California, kids her age or even younger had once traveled for hundreds of miles to reach a better land. Now, there wasn't much of a better land to get to. You were where you were.

And here she was. Sola but surprisingly not afraid. Determined. Maybe that's what the kids that traveled in the caravans, and their parents, felt as well. *Determined to find una vida mejor,* she thought. A better life.

She was thinking of her familia when, like thunder announcing lightning, she heard the brash sound of an impact. Walter had hit something. A black void blocked the vision in her goggles for a moment. The drone twirled around a few times before leveling off, literally shaking off the collision.

Walter, thankfully, appeared unaffected. The large bird he'd hit wasn't so lucky.

Mimi gaped as it plummeted twenty feet. She sprinted to it,

examined its condition quickly. It had a broken neck, which meant it was dead, but otherwise wasn't in too bad shape to eat. In the city, Mamá had taught her and Gus to keep an eye out for birds that crashed into the tall skyscrapers. This felt like a sign that Mimi was onto something. She cut off a piece of her rope and tied the bird's feet onto the handlebars of the skiff to cook later, when it wasn't as hot out. Then she sent Walter into the sky once more. It wasn't five minutes later that something in the sand glimmered and caught her eye. She pointed the skiff in that direction and, using the momentum from sliding down another large sand dune, arrived at the correct spot.

She brought Walter down and put him into his box. Certain that this was the tesoro she was searching for, Mimi wiped away as much of the sand as she could from the item, eventually revealing metallic red railings, a glass roof still intact, and the top of glass windows and windshield. Mimi was staring at the top of a dune buggy, she was sure of it. She'd seen them in photographs on the covers of old brochures they used to hand out to turistas who visited Vegas.

Mimi gave a grito. Like Mamá when she sang mariachi.

There wasn't an echo in return.

She was out here. Alone. And she had to figure out how to get such a heavy find back to Las Vegas, to Mamá, who would know just how valuable the dune buggy might be.

She had extra rope, at least. She cut off a piece with the knife, set it aside, and began to excavate the small buggy from the sand with her bare hands. By the time she had dug half of it out, her arms felt like rubber, she'd drunk half her water, which meant she had only four ounces left, and the sun was kissing the edge of the horizon. But she couldn't leave the buggy for someone else to snag. This was her find, and she was going to bring it back home, and it would be the biggest trade her family ever made. More importantly, it would keep her, Mamá, and Gus safe and fed. She hoped the skiff had enough charge to pull it out and get her and the vehicle back home.

Mimi turned to the sun, using her fingers to gauge the time the way Mamá had taught her. No one was ever out in the desert past sunset if they could avoid it. Especially not alone. And the day was dwindling. As the sun signaled six o'clock, at this time of the year Mimi had perhaps another hour or two of daylight. If she found high-enough sand dunes, the momentum from the way down might be enough to get her home only a few minutes past sundown. She just wouldn't be able to stop even once.

She tried the dune buggy door. To her surprise, it wasn't locked. But to start it, she needed a key she didn't have. She quickly formed a plan. She got out and fastened a large section of the rope through the top bars, securing it tightly across the windshield. She had no idea if the sand skiff would sustain the weight of the buggy, but she had to try.

She returned to the skiff, tying the loose end of the rope to the frame of its sail. She kicked a red button on the side of the old surfboard, turning its motor on. She ramped it up next with the foot gears, shifting it to max power, the propeller making the smiley face of the balloon fabric inflate. She wasn't sure how long the power would last, so she didn't waste time. As the skiff lunged forward, taking up the slack in the rope, she felt hopeful that her plan would work. That hope abruptly turned into fear as the craft stopped in its tracks as the rope went tight. Mimi saw the sail's frame bow under the strain. The force of the halt had nearly sent her off the skiff, but she managed to grab the sail itself. She wasn't sure what was going to break first: the sail, the rope, or all her dreams. But then the sail began to straighten.

It was moving! Mimi managed to pull the buggy out. With Walter tucked away, and her pack on her back, she headed home. She held her fist up high and called out, "¡Vamos! ¡Adelante!"

The skiff had more power than she thought. Or perhaps the

dune buggy was living up to its name. It was a vehicle that was meant to drive through the desert with ease.

It was a vehicle…that was meant…to drive…through the desert.

Mimi considered what she'd found in a different way.

At first, she'd been thinking only about the money the tesoro might sell for—enough money they wouldn't need to scavenge for a year or more. And in turn, Mamá wouldn't have to work out in the grueling desert. And she could buy Gus new shoes. New everything.

Or she could go to California. Right now, even.

She'd never had a sure way to get there, but here was one if she could figure out how to get it to go. She could go and find Papá and yell at him the way she'd dreamed of doing the past few months. Convince him to come back with her. Or at least find closure before she returned.

She weighed the pros and cons of the idea as the buggy continued onward. But of course, the idea was absurd, like it'd always been.

It wasn't that she didn't want to search for Papá. She wanted to. Badly. Had he died? Was there another reason that they hadn't heard from him? Had he replaced them?

But how could she leave? Mamá and Gus needed her now. She wasn't going to let them down like Papá had.

She wished that she had Gus to talk about this with.

Gus… She moved her thoughts away from Papá, which always made her weary, and instead started making a list of things she could buy her little brother if she chose to sell the buggy when, suddenly, she felt a backward tug.

The skiff jolted and stilled. Then it pulled her in the direction she'd come, leaving Mimi flailing her arms as she tried to keep her balance.

She'd pulled the dune buggy into a sinkhole. The skiff had been light enough and run straight over it. But the buggy was heavier. With one hand, she kept the skiff upright and going forward. With the other, she tried to tug on the rope that held on to the buggy. She could cut the rope before she was pulled into the sinkhole, too. But it meant losing the buggy.

Which meant losing everything.

She wound the rope around her hand three times, though she immediately regretted it. The rope dug into her fragile skin. She let out a cry, but as before, she didn't even get an echo. She was the only one out here. There was no one to help her. Not Gus, or Tiago. Together, the three of them could surely have figured out a way to stop the buggy from sinking. The fact was Mimi alone didn't have the strength to free the vehicle. She also couldn't stand the thought of leaving it. Soon, the sky turned pink, then red, and finally blue before she was in the dark. As if the heat of the desert were powered by a light switch that had been flicked off, it grew cold. She could pull off her backpack and grab the wool blanket she'd brought, but it might lessen her hold on the rope and the buggy would sink. She couldn't start a fire, either. Or eat the bird, the thought of which made her mouth water.

She'd been taught to be afraid of the desert night for so long. But there really wasn't anyone else out here. After hours of fighting it, she succumbed to the cold and to sleep. When she woke up, her whole body was shivering, and it was the middle of the night. Although she didn't feel the pull of the buggy as heavily as before, her right arm had gone numb. The rope was wound too tight around it. She wasn't sure what would happen to the dune buggy if she untethered the rope from her arm, but she didn't have a choice anymore.

On the brink of tears and wheezing from the panic, she hastily took the rope off. She tried to move her hand, her fingers, but the tingling sensation only gave way to pain.

"Shit," she cried, terrified that her arm might never be okay again. Why had she held on to the rope so tightly?

It wasn't until she felt her pinky finger come back to life that she began to relax, despite the pulsing ache that lingered. The dune buggy was half-buried but wasn't sinking anymore. Once again, she wished Tiago was with her. She feared sinking with the buggy but had to try to pull it out. She managed to shift her shaky legs underneath her, just barely at the edge of the sinkhole, and tugged. She tried to reach the skiff, but its position was too skewed for her to both hold the buggy and get onto the skiff. She'd have to free it on her own.

The injuries on her arm burned furiously, yet she stayed on her feet. The dune buggy didn't move at first, but she pushed one side of the railings up with her shoulders, her knees nearly buckling underneath her. As soon as she moved it an inch, though, the sand started to sink again. Taking her with it. She had to hurry. She heaved the buggy, sweat beading at her temples, her whole body tired and drained as she took one step after the other. When she couldn't bear the weight any longer, couldn't take another breath, she glanced back. The sinkhole was far enough behind her to no longer be a threat. She lay back for a moment, gazing at the endless night sky, the buggy beside her. She drank the rest of her water with a shaking hand and thought of how proud Mamá would be of her. Though, Mamá had never not been proud of Mimi. Mamá was always there for her. Had always known what to say when they missed Papá most. How to pull them forward. Now, Mimi was doing what Mamá had always done to make sure that they stayed alive. And it was hard work.

Once more, Mimi thought of the kids who had crossed the desert in search of their own tesoro. Not an object to sell but a place to call home. Safety. Surely there were mamás that walked the hot, sweltering, tiring desert with them.

She also thought once more about keeping the dune buggy. But the choice also wasn't difficult, in the end. Her family needed food.

And for Mamá to be strong again.

If giving up on a way to get to Papá was the way to do it, so be it.

Mimi allowed herself to rest only for a moment. By now, both Gus and Mamá likely believed she was muerta. It was the thought that they would figure her dead that made Mimi force herself up. Though her legs wobbled as she stood, and the pain of her injured arm made her want to pass out, she made it to the sand skiff and picked it up with one hand, testing her luck con un deseo, with a wish.

"Please work," she said. At first it didn't budge. In that moment, she was afraid. Afraid of not making it home to see Mamá and Gus. But she tried the motor again. The engine roared awake, and once more she was off.

She cradled her hurt arm close to her chest, struggling to keep it motionless. Once she got back to the strip, Tiago and Gus would help her mend it.

Mimi stopped minutes later when the hurt in her tummy bothered her more than her arm. She took out the tinderbox and defeathered the bird by holding it in between her knees and using her good hand. She set it to roast the way Mamá had taught her. She only felt a little guilty as she took her first bite of meat. Mamá could have used the food. Gus, too. But Mimi's stomach calmed, and it meant she'd have the energy for the rest of her trip.

When she was done eating, she considered sending Walter up in the sky again. But it would be too dark to navigate using his bird's-eye view. She took a chance on the stars and followed the direction they pointed back home.

A short while later Mimi heard a call in the air over the rush of the skiff. She felt a rumble, emanating from below the skiff that moved up her feet and into her chest. She turned to the west where she found the source: a sandstorm was moving in her direction. From where Papá had gone. Like California was coming to swallow her whole.

She kept going for as long as she could, but the skiff would never outrun the storm, especially with the dune buggy attached. She could cut the rope, return the prize to the desert that so obviously wanted it. But she was tired of losing. Of scavenging. She powered down the skiff, then got into the back seat of the buggy, determined to ride it out from inside.

The winds were a wild fury, and once they started didn't stop. The buggy rocked from one side to the other and front to back. At most, only two tires touched the ground at one time, and at several points she felt the buggy hover as the wind lifted it from the earth.

One gust tore off the rope and sent the sand skiff flying who knows where. Mimi held back tears, thinking of how hard she and Mamá had worked to build it.

It won't matter, Mimi thought, *when I come back with the buggy.*

Then something large struck the vehicle. Mimi screamed as it jerked to the side by the force of the impact. A window cracked. Mimi was sure that if there was another strike, sand would fill the interior, consuming her with it.

Mimi curled up into a ball, placed her hands over her head, her backpack stiff against her front, and wished for it to go away. Every bang she heard made her yelp and her heart plummet further into the void at the pit of her belly. She was shattering along with the dune buggy. She'd been lucky to have found it, but luck was meaningless and the buggy worthless without getting it home in a functional state.

She fell asleep this way, lulled by the sound of a billion grains of sand pinging the rails of the frame, and dreamed of Papá in California. She'd seen it before, in movies and magazine clippings. The rolling green grass on tall hills. The blue ocean lapping against the clean beaches. Papá never made it seem spectacular in his messages. But when Mimi dreamed, she always pictured him happy there, green trees at his back, an ocean breeze hitting his cheeks softly. And sometimes she saw Gus there, too, who'd never met Papá, perched upon his shoulders, as they walked along California coasts, laughing.

The sudden silence woke Mimi up. She startled in the seat. Outside, the stars were fading. It'd be morning soon. Her head swayed with dehydration and tiredness. She pushed the button that would open the door, eager to get home, but it wouldn't give.

She tried it again, her throat tightening. Tried to kick the door open. But nothing happened. It became hard to take in even the slightest breath as panic set in.

Then she heard a rap on the window behind her. She peered out of the tiny slit that hadn't been covered by the sand and was immobilized by what she saw. Papá's face filled the view. The way she remembered him. Dark skin, no wrinkles, earth-brown eyes bright and alert. Right there. But there was no way. His face disappeared, and his knuckles appeared as he rapped on the window once more.

She only had one bad choice to get out of the buggy. She pulled out Walter's box, then turned toward the half-splintered window. She slammed the box against the glass, shattering part of her treasure. But there would be more tesoro, surely, outside.

Mimi wriggled out the window, squirming against the sand that eagerly funneled into the back seat, pulling her backpack along with her.

"Papá!" she shouted, crawling with one arm to the top of the sand dune that had formed next to the buggy. She turned around several times, shouting for him and scanning the horizon.

But he wasn't there.

As she slid back down to the frame, she used the light on the goggles to see how extensive the storm damage was. The rails and paint on its right side had been stripped away, likely making it nonfunctional. Its lights were shattered, a back wheel visible but flattened, and the antennae lost. All that on top of the broken glass.

Mimi fell to her knees, brought her palms to her eyes, and screamed.

"No llores, Mimi!" Papá's voice called out, stilling her. When she scrambled up and looked, he was there, but far ahead in the desert.

She sprang up and toward him but stopped a few seconds into her dash. She couldn't leave what was left of the buggy. She needed to return home with *something*, even if it was junk instead of tesoro. Even if it was only worth another day of food and water. And so once more, with the skiff gone, and only her legs to help her, she dug out the buggy and, with her shoulders, pushed it in the direction Papá was walking. Sweat poured down her face, but she found a rhythm, humming a tune her father used to sing to her.

Arriba en la inmensidad
Un diamante celestial
Estrellita que al brillar
Me pregunto cómo estás…

She could still hear him ahead of her, where dawn kissed the skyline of the strip that appeared out of the desert. Papá had showed her the way home.

At the edge of town, she spotted Gus standing next to Tiago where the Mexican flag stood. Gus ran to her, and she let go of the dune buggy and hurried to him. They fell to the ground and hugged.

"Mimi, are you okay?" he said, crying.

She cradled her arm after Gus hit it by accident, and he cried even harder after he took in the damage done to it: the thick indent left in her skin by the rope as it had cut off her circulation, the red ringlet surrounding the wounded area, and patches of skin that'd been torn off as she'd struggled with the dune buggy's weight. She wasn't sure how long it would take to heal. If it would ever heal. And if it didn't, how would she scavenge? She wasn't okay.

She'd been defeated and hurt by the desert. Failed in her mission. Lost the sand skiff.

"Estoy viva," Mimi replied weakly. Being alive was enough for Gus, who simply nodded. "But where is Papá? Have you seen him yet?"

"What?" Gus shook his head.

"Papá," Mimi said, searching for the familiar face.

"Papá is here?" Gus sounded unsure. Questioning.

Tiago let out a long whistle, staring at the buggy and pulling Mimi's attention to him. "You found that?" Tiago was taller and stronger than her, and he quickly helped her stand. He took her good arm and pulled it over his neck. She let her weight fall into his body. "Te tengo," he said, and she knew it was true. He had her. "We didn't see anyone else appear from the desert, though, only you."

Only her? Mimi was sure she'd seen Papá. "The desert wanted to keep it," she said, referring to the dune buggy. "Papá showed me the way home."

Tiago's eyes widened. In concern? Confusion? Maybe he was just proud of her for making it back.

Other scavengers noticed the buggy. Their chatter sounded like birdsong as they came out from the shadows of the old buildings to check on Mimi and what she'd brought back. There were a few gasps; they pointed at the rare object though dared not touch it, and when they'd had their fill of seeing the beat-up dune buggy—a reminder of the past world—they turned to Mimi in awe that she'd survived the desert.

But Mimi didn't care. She only wanted to get back to Mamá, find Papá, rest.

Tiago and Gus helped her to their casino, into the elevator, to their suite. And when the door opened, Mimi saw Papá standing next to Mamá, who sat on the couch.

But the more Mimi focused on him, the more his body seemed like a shimmer. And Mimi understood that he was a mirage from the desert. He faded, and Mimi focused solely on Mamá. And Mamá, well, she was alert, smiling and stretching out her arms. Mimi ran to her. And in her mother's embrace, it felt like she hadn't failed.

"You're okay?" Mimi asked.

Mamá kissed Mimi's forehead. "Sí, amor. The fever broke. Estoy sana. I was so worried about you."

Gus interrupted, "Mamá, you should see what Mimi found in the desert! It's pretty beat-up, but so cool."

Mimi winced at Gus's words, stiffened as she told Mamá. "It was a dune buggy. But I lost most of it on my way back. And the skiff. Perdóname, Mamá." Just like they'd lost Papá. The thought of having lost the sand skiff that Mamá had worked so hard on made her belly recoil and her throat tighten with the threat of not just tears but heavyhearted sobs. And then the overwhelming feeling of it all was too much. In front of Mamá, Mimi didn't need to be her strongest. She could be fragile. Fragile like the dune buggy had been.

She hugged Mamá, cried into her warm embrace. "I'm so sorry, Mamá. The skiff is gone. I lost it!"

"No llores, amor," Mamá said, holding her tightly and rocking her back and forth. "We'll build another skiff, and soon we'll go look in the same place. Juntas," Mamá said. "Together. And we'll find another dune buggy or something better. I told you, todos los desiertos tienen agua."

Mimi nodded, breathing deep to stop crying. She was at peace for the first time since Mamá got sick. Safe and home, a tesoro in itself.

★ ★ ★ ★ ★

about the editor

Sandra Proudman (she/her/ella) is a Mexican-American author of unabashed Latinx stories and a literary associate living in the heart of California. When not busily immersed in all things publishing, you can find her spending time with her amazing husband and adorable preschooler, catching up on all her shows, and baking five-star pies. She is also a contributor in the YA horror anthology, *The House Where Death Lives*, out spring 2024, and the author of the YA fantasy, *Salvación*, out winter 2025. Connect with her on Twitter, Instagram, and TikTok @SandraProudman and on her website sandraproudman.com.

about the authors

Olivia Abtahi grew up in the DC area, devouring books and hiding in empty classrooms during school to finish them. Her debut novel, *Perfectly Parvin*, was published in 2021 by Penguin Random House Putnam Books for Young Readers, receiving the SCBWI Golden Kite Honor, YALSA Odyssey Honor, and numerous starred reviews. Her sophomore novel, *Azar on Fire*, was published in August 2022 as a School Library Guild Selection. She currently lives in Colorado with her family.

David Bowles is a Mexican American author and translator from South Texas. Among his thirty published books are the multiple-award-winning *They Call Me Güero*, as well as the speculative series *Garza Twins*, *13th Street*, *Clockwork Curandera*, and *The Path*. His work has been published in anthologies such as *Reclaim the Stars*, *Rural Voices*, and *Living beyond Borders*, plus venues like the *New York Times*, *Strange Horizons*, *Apex Magazine*, *School Library Journal*, and *The Journal of Children's Literature*.

Zoraida Córdova is the acclaimed author of more than two dozen novels and short stories, including the Brooklyn Brujas series, *Star Wars: The High Republic: Convergence*, and *The Inheritance of Orquídea Divina*. In addition to writing novels, she serves on the board of We Need Diverse Books and is the coeditor of the bestselling anthology *Vampires Never Get Old*, as well as the cohost of the writing podcast *Deadline City*. She writes romance novels as Zoey Castile. Zoraida was born in Guayaquil, Ecuador, and calls New York City home. When she's not working, she's roaming the world in search of magical stories. For more information, visit her at zoraidacordova.com.

Saraciea J. Fennell is a Black Honduran American writer, founder of The Bronx Is Reading, and creator of Honduran Garifuna Writers. She is also a book publicist who has worked with many award-winning and *New York Times* bestselling authors. Fennell is the board chair of Latinx in Publishing Inc., and she has been profiled in the *New York Times* and included in *Good Morning America*'s inspiration list. Her books include the YA nonfiction anthology *Wild Tongues Can't Be Tamed* and horror anthology *The Black Girl Survives in This One*. She lives in the Bronx, New York, with her family and black poodle, Oreo. Visit her online at saracieafennell.com and follow her on social @sj_fennell.

Raquel Vasquez Gilliland is a Pura Belpré Award–winning Mexican American poet, novelist, and painter. She received her BA in cultural anthropology from the University of West Florida and her MFA in poetry from the University of Alaska Anchorage. Raquel is most inspired by folklore and seeds and the lineages of all things. When not writing, Raquel tells stories to her plants, and they tell her stories back.

Torrey Maldonado was born and raised in Brooklyn's Red Hook projects. He has taught in New York City public schools for over twenty-five years, and his fast-paced, compelling stories are inspired by his and his students' experiences. His popular young readers novels include *What Lane?*, which won many starred reviews and was cited by *Oprah Daily* and the *New York Times* for being essential to discuss racism and allyship; *Tight* won the Christopher Award, was an ALA Notable Book, and an NPR and *Washington Post* Best Book of the Year; and his first novel, *Secret Saturdays*, has stayed in print for over ten years. His newest book, *Hands*, is a Junior Library Guild Gold Standard Selection, won a starred School Library Journal review and amazing reviews from *Horn Book*, *Kirkus*, and *Publishers Weekly*, and is a Best New Book of 2023. Learn more at torreymaldonado.com or connect on social media @torreymaldonado.

Jasminne Mendez is a bestselling Dominican American poet, educator, translator, playwright, and award-winning author of several books for children and adults. She has had poetry and essays published in numerous journals and anthologies, and she is the author of two multigenre collections including *Island of Dreams* (Floricanto Press, 2013), which won an International Latino Book Award. Her debut poetry collection, *City without Altar*, was a finalist for the Noemi Press poetry prize and was released in August 2022 (Noemi Press), and her debut middle-grade novel in verse *Aniana del Mar Jumps In* (Dial) was released in 2023. Her debut picture book, *Josefina's Habichuelas* (Arte Publico Press, 2021), was the Writer's League of Texas Children's Book Discovery Prize Winner, and her second YA memoir, *Islands Apart: Becoming Dominican American*, was released this past fall. She has translated the work of *New York Times* bestselling authors Amanda Gorman, Nikole Hannah-Jones, and Calribel Ortega. She is an MFA graduate of the creative writing program at the Rainier Writing Workshop at Pacific Lutheran University and a University of Houston alumna. She is the program director for the literary arts nonprofit Tintero Projects, and she lives and works in Houston, Texas.

Anna Meriano is the author of the *Love Sugar Magic* series and *This Is How We Fly*. She graduated from Rice University with a degree in English and earned her MFA in writing for children from the New School in New York. She works as a writing teacher and tutor in her hometown of Houston. Anna likes reading, knitting, and playing full-contact Quidditch. Her work can also be found in the anthologies *Up All Night*, *Living Beyond Borders*, and *Game On*.

Amparo Ortiz is the author of the *Blazewrath Games* duology and *Last Sunrise in Eterna*. She was born in San Juan, Puerto Rico, and currently lives on the island's northeastern coast. She's published short story comics in *Marvel's Voices: Comunidades #1* and in the Eisner Award–winning *Puerto Rico Strong*. She's also coeditor of *Our Shadows Have Claws*, a horror anthology featuring myths and monsters from Latin America. When she's not writing, she teaches ESL as a college professor and watches a lot of K-pop videos. Learn more about her projects at amparoortiz.com.

Laura Pohl is a *New York Times* bestselling author of *The Grimrose Girls*. Her debut novel, *The Last 8*, won the International Latino Book Awards. She likes writing messages in caps lock, never using autocorrect, and obsessing about *Star Wars*. When not taking pictures of her dog, she can be found curled up with a fantasy or science-fiction book or replaying *Dragon Age*. Her top three picks for Arthurian knights are Gawain, Percival, and Mordred. A Brazilian at heart and soul, she makes her home in São Paulo.

NoNieqa Ramos wrote *The Disturbed Girl's Dictionary*, which was a 2018 New York Public Library Best Book for Teens, a 2019 YALSA Best Fiction for Young Adults Selection, and a 2019 In the Margins Top Ten pick. Their picture book, *Your Mama*, was a finalist for the Kirkus Prize, a *School Library Journal* Best Picture Book of 2021, a Bank Street Best Book of 2021, *Kirkus* Best Picture Book of 2021, and a National Council of

English Books Notable Poetry Book. They are a proud member of Las Musas and the Soaring '20s PB group. A lifelong fan of Edgar Allan Poe, NoNieqa hopes he would be rather proud of this queer retelling. Check out more works nonieqaramos.com.

Monica Sanz is the author of many fantasy novels, including *Seventh Born* and *Mirror Bound.* When not lost in one of her many made-up worlds, Monica can be found on the sunny beaches of South Florida, where she resides with her husband and their three children, or scouring YouTube for new bands to feed her music addiction.

Eric Smith is a literary agent and author living in Philadelphia. As an agent, he's worked on award-winning and *New York Times* bestselling books. In his author life, his books include the IndieBound best seller *The Geek's Guide to Dating* (Quirk Books), *The Girl and the Grove* (Flux), the YALSA Best Books for Young Readers selection *Don't Read the Comments* (Inkyard Press), *You Can Go Your Own Way* (Inkyard Press), and *With or Without You* (Inkyard Press). He's collaborated and coauthored projects with Lauren Gibaldi (the anthologies *Battle of the Bands* and *First-Year Orientation*) and Alanis Morissette, Diablo Cody, and Glenn Ballard (*Jagged Little Pill: The Novel*). A Honduran/Palestinian transracial adoptee, he explores his complicated identity in a number of his short fiction and nonfiction, including pieces in the anthologies *Color Outside the Lines* by Sangu Mandanna, *Body Talk* by Kelly Jensen, *Allies* by Shakirah Bourne and Dana Alison Levy, *Dear Adoptee* by Nicole Chung and Shannon Gibney, *Bridges and Islands* by Ismee Williams and Rebecca Balcárcel, and more.

Ari Tison is the author and poet of YA novel *Saints of the Household* (FSG/BFYR), which received several starred trade reviews and was selected as a Junior Library Guild Gold Standard Selection and an Amazon Best Book of the Year So Far. Ari was selected as a *Publishers Weekly*'s Flying Start, and she has published a number of poems and short works in various national literary journals including *POETRY*'s first issue for young people. Her short stories for young people have been included in *Our Shadows Have Claws: 15 Latin American Monster Stories* (Algonquin) and *Sing Me A Story: Short Stories in Verse* (Penguin). Her forthcoming YA novel releases in winter 2025 (FSG/BFYR). Ari has her MFA in Writing for Children and Young Adults from Hamline, where she now serves on faculty. Ari belongs to the Bribri people, an Indigenous people group of contemporary Costa Rica.

Alexandra Villasante's debut young adult novel, *The Grief Keeper*, was a Junior Library Guild Gold Standard Selection and the winner of the 2020 Lambda Literary Award for LGBTQ Children's Literature/Young Adult Fiction. Alex is a member of the Las Musas collective of Latinx children's book creators and a cofounder of the Latinx Kidlit Book Festival. Alex's short stories appear in the Young Adult anthologies *All Signs Point to Yes* and *Our Shadows Have Claws*. She is the program manager for the nonprofit Highlights Foundation, which supports children's book writers and illustrators, and lives in the semiwilds of Pennsylvania with her family.